Acknowledgments

As we said in the acknowledgments to our first book in this series, *Gettysburg*, our work is an accomplishment built upon the shoulders and work of so many others.

Special credit, as always, must go to historian Tom LeGore of Carroll County, Maryland. Tom not only guided us through the intricate details of how Gettysburg might have wound up being fought, instead, along the Pipe Creek Line, but has proven to be invaluable in the creation of this work as well.

General Bob Scales, former commandant of the Army War College, came to the fore with his insightful analysis of what Lee, Grant, Sickles, and Lincoln would have been facing the "day after" a Confederate victory at Gettysburg and had a major influence in the shaping of our scenario.

Professor Leonard Fullenkamp of the Army War College has, yet again, shown to us his remarkable grasp of the 1863 campaign and offered invaluable help, along with Professor Dennis Showalter, former president of the Society of Military Historians.

Thanks as well to the brilliant historical artist Don Troiani, not only for his remarkable cover art but for his analysis of our work, and to the historian Steven Sears for his books on Chancellorsville and Gettysburg, which helped to shape our own theories.

So many others were involved as well. Kathy Lubbers, my (Newt's) daughter, who helped keep us organized and on task in what proved to be a highly complex project and, at times, a physically demanding one as well, especially when we were out signing books at Gettysburg in hundred-degree heat. Randy Evans and Rick Tyler of my (Newt's) staff for handling so much of the detail work as well. A tribute as well for Paul Breier and Dr. George Talbot, two dear friends of Bill's, both devotees of history who encouraged him in his work and passed away just as this book was completed.

While out promoting *Gettysburg* last summer, we met new friends and were filled with admiration for those devoted to the study of the Civil War. So many of you offered excellent comments, suggestions, and criticisms that helped us in the shaping of this second volume. In particular we'd like to extend our thanks to the team of Hardtack & Wool, a Civil War educational firm that helped us organize the Gettysburg signing event, and the administration of Montreat College, which provided Bill with a year-long sabbatical, in part to research and work on this series. We must also thank the owners and managers of so many bookstores around the country that warmly greeted us and arranged events.

As always, our fear is that in mentioning some names we fear we might miss others. If we did not mention you here, know that nevertheless we are thankful for your help and support.

Of course, there are three major acknowledgments . . . for our loving wives, Callista, Sharon, and Krys, who allow us time away from home and indulge us in our passion for history.

Finally, as always, for all those young men of a hundred and forty years past, North and South, who fought and, if need be, gave their lives for the causes they believed in. We believe that such strength and mettle are evident today with the men and women serving our nation on so many distant fronts. The bravery of the line infantry of both sides in the Civil War, the nobility of Lee, and the determination of Grant are clearly evident in those of you standing watch overseas. We are profoundly grateful to all of you, past and present, for your dedication and service to our country.

Chapter One

Cairo, Illinois

July 16, 1863

A cold rain swept across the river. To the east, lightning streaked the evening sky, thunder rolling over the white-capped Ohio River.

The storm had hit with a violent intensity and for a few minutes slowed the work along the docks, but already sergeants were barking orders at the drenched enlisted men while rain-soaked stevedores were urged back to their labors. Dozens of boats lined the quays, offloading men, horses, limber wagons, and field pieces.

To the eyes of Gen. Herman Haupt, commander of United States military railroads, the sight of these men was reassuring. They were the veterans of the Army of the Tennessee, the victors of the great campaign that had climaxed ten days ago at Vicksburg, a victory that had come simultaneously with what was now seen as the darkest day of the war, the day Lee defeated the Army of the Potomac at Union Mills.

The soldiers disembarking on the banks of the Ohio were lean and tough, their disciplined, no-nonsense carriage conveying strength and confidence despite their bedraggled, tattered uniforms, faded from rainy marching in the muddy fields of Mississippi, Louisiana, Arkansas, and Tennessee. Headgear was an individual choice. Most wore battered, broad-brimmed hats for protection against hot southern sun and torrential rains. Regulation field packs were gone; most were carrying blanket, poncho, and shelter half in a horseshoe-shaped roll, slung over the left shoulder and tied off at the right hip. Except for the blue of their uniforms, they looked more like their Confederate opponents than the clean, disciplined, orderly ranks Herman Haupt was used to seeing in the East. Few if any would ever have passed inspection with regiments trained by McClellan. These Westerners were rawboned boys from prairie farms in Iowa and Ohio, lumberjacks from Michigan, mechanics from Detroit, and boatmen from the Great Lakes and Midwest rivers. The unending campaigning had marked them as field soldiers. Spit and polish had long ago been left behind at Shiloh and the fever-infested swamps of the bayous along the Mississippi.

They already knew their mission . . . pull the defeated Army of the Potomac out of the fire and put the Confederacy in the grave. They came now with confidence, swaggering off the steamboats, forming into ranks, standing at ease while rolls were checked, impervious to the rain and wind, their calmness, to Haupt's mind, a reflection of the man that he now waited for.

He could see the boat, rounding the cape from the Mississippi River into the Ohio, the light packet moving with speed, cutting a wake, smoke billowing from its twin stacks, sparks snapping heavenward, carried off by the wind following the storm. The flag on the stern mast denoted that an admiral was aboard, but that was not the man Haupt was waiting for.

The diminutive side-wheeler, a courier boat built for speed, aimed straight for the dock where Haupt was standing, the port master waving a signal flag to guide it in.

Haupt looked over at the man accompanying him, Congressman Elihu Washburne, confidant of the president and political mentor of the general on board the boat. Elihu, who had joined Haupt only the hour before, was silent, clutching a copy of the *Chicago Tribune*, out just this morning, its front page reporting the disaster at Union Mills, the advance of Lee's army on Washington, and the riots which had erupted in New York, Philadelphia, and Baltimore.

"I sure as hell am glad I don't have his responsibilities," Elihu sighed as the side-wheeler slowed, paddle wheels shifting into reverse, backing water in a dramatic display by its pilot, who had timed to the second the order to reverse engines.

Its steam whistle shrieking, the boat edged in toward the dock, half a dozen black stevedores racing along the rough-hewn planks, ready to grab lines tossed by the light packet's crew.

Ropes snaked out across the water were caught as the boat edged into the dock, brushing against it with a dull thump that snapped through Haupt's feet, the dock swaying on its pilings.

The stevedores tightened the lines, lashing them down to bollards, and within seconds a gangplank was run over, slamming down on the deck.

There was no ceremony or fanfare, no blaring of trumpets, no honor guard racing down the dock and coming to attention with polished rifles. The door to the main cabin swung open and he came out.

Haupt had never seen this man before but he knew instantly who he was. He was short, grizzled-looking, with an unkempt beard of reddish-brown flecked with gray; his face was deeply sunburned, wrinkled heavily around the eyes, which were deep set and sharp-looking. His dark blue private's four-button coat free of all adornment except for the insignia of rank, which, Haupt quickly noted, was still that of major general in spite of his recent promotion. Slouch hat pulled low against the storm, he came down the gangplank and Haupt came to attention and saluted.

The general nodded, half saluted, looked over at Elihu, and extended his hand.

"Congressman, good to see you."

"General Grant, I'm damn glad to see you," Elihu replied. "This is General Haupt, the man who makes the railroads work."

Grant looked up at Haupt and nodded.

"Heard of you. You do good work, General."

"Thank you, sir, the respect is mutual."

Grant said nothing, gazing at him appraisingly for a moment. Behind Grant two more men came down the gangplank, and again began the ritual of salutes and introductions to Admiral Porter and General Sherman, who towered over Grant, standing as tall as Haupt, returning his salute without comment.

"Let's get out of this rain," Grant said.

Haupt led the way off the dock. As they passed a regiment of troops forming up in the mud in front of a steamer, there was a scattering of cheers, nothing wild and demonstrative, just a respectful acknowledgment, which Grant responded to with a simple half wave, and nothing more.

The wind reversed for a moment, another gust of rain sweeping down, the air thick with the smell of wood and coal smoke. They climbed a slick, mud-covered road, corduroyed with rough-hewn planks, stepping aside for a moment as a gun crew labored up the slippery track, horses straining, pulling a three-inch ordnance rifle.

Haupt studied the crew as they passed. They had obviously seen hard

fighting; the limber chest was scored and pocked by bullets, paint faded and scratched; were the horses were lean like the men.

Reaching the crest to the bluff looking down on the river, Haupt paused for a second, letting the officers behind him catch up.

The view stirred his heart. A dozen steamboats were tied up along the dock; out across the Ohio and around the bend that led to the Mississippi came more, a long line of ships, the view lost in the mists and swirling clouds of rain.

Before him was the rail yard. Before the war, Cairo had already been a thriving port town where the rail line that led into the vast heartland of the Midwest terminated at this connection to the river traffic of two great waterways. The war had transformed it beyond all imagining, the main port of supply supporting the campaigns up the Tennessee and Cumberland Rivers, and down the broad, open Mississippi to Vicksburg and now on to New Orleans and the world.

Dozens of locomotives, marshaled here over the last four days, waited, each hooked to boxcars and flatcars, some of them brought down from as far away as Chicago and Milwaukee.

The authorization the president had given Haupt had been far-reaching, beyond the scope of anything done until now in this war, or in any war. He had federalized half a dozen lines, argued with scores of railroad executives, and made it clear to all of them that they would be compensated, but as of right now he was running their schedules, and resistance would be met with arrest. Haupt reminded more than one of them that Lincoln had suspended the writ of habeas corpus and would not hesitate, if need be, to throw a railroad president in jail if he, Haupt, should request it. Elihu had already shown Haupt the editorial in the *Indianapolis Journal* denouncing him as the "Napoleon of the Railroads."

At the same time orders had streamed out as far away as Maine and northern Minnesota, pulling in reserves of tentage, uniforms, shoes, rations, bandages, field pieces, serge bags for powder, pistol ammunition, horses, mules, oats, chloroform, canned milk, tinware, cooking pots, rifles, packaged cartridges for Springfields, Sharps, and Spencers. Any boxcar to be found on a siding, any wheezy locomotive that could still pull that boxcar was coming in as well, commandeered from across the country to bring forth what was spilling out of the cornucopias made of brick and iron and steam.

The nation was stirring as it had never done before, even as it reeled from the disaster dealt to it by the legions of Robert E. Lee.

The rail yard rumbled with noise, whistles shrieking, cars banging together as they were hooked up. The crews were laboring to load up wood, water, stacking up boxes of rations under open-sided warehouses. Frightened horses cried out and struggled as they were forced into boxcars, men cursing and yelling.

It looked like chaos, but Haupt knew better. He had brought with him more than four hundred of his best men from Alexandria on one of the last trains to get out of Washington before the line was cut just north of Baltimore. They knew their business and, in what appeared to be chaos, there was order. Inbound trains were being shifted to side railings, engines disconnected, run to a turntable, shifted around, greased, oiled, refueled, water tanks filled, then moved up a side track to pick up an outbound load. With the arrival of the first division to come up from Vicksburg, this machinery of a nation at war would surge into motion.

A small rail yard office, which Haupt had selected for the meeting, loomed up through the swirls of smoke and rain, the guards posted out front snapping to attention at the approach of so many stars. A gathering of hangers-on, curious citizens, and a dozen or more reporters stood back at a distance, kept there by a provost guard with direct orders from Haupt, fully supported by Elihu, to arrest anyone who tried to break through.

The reporters shouted their questions, which were all ignored, Sherman looking over at them with a jaundiced eye and muttering a curse under his breath.

"Damn them, now it will be in every paper in the country that we're here," Sherman snapped.

"They knew already," Elihu interjected. "Word of it was coming up the river your entire trip. No use in hiding it; besides, the country needs to hear it."

"Just for once I'd like to move without everyone, especially the rebs, knowing about it first."

Still muttering under his breath, Sherman followed Haupt into the room, the door closing behind them, window shades pulled down.

A fresh pot of coffee rested on a sideboard, bread and slabs of cut ham on tin plates. Sherman and Porter helped themselves, Grant simply taking a cup of coffee and sipping from it as he walked up to the table, upon which was spread a railroad map of the country. He gazed at it for a moment, then went to the wall where Herman had put up a map of northern Virginia, Maryland, and southern Pennsylvania. Red and blue pins, with small foolscap notes under them, marked the latest positions of forces.

Grant turned to Elihu.

"What's the latest?"

Elihu tossed the *Chicago Tribune* on the table, then pulled a notebook out of his pocket and opened it.

"Washington has been cut off from all land communications for the last three days. Stuart's cavalry has cut all telegraph lines and rail lines to the capital. The line into Baltimore was patched yesterday but went down again this morning. Last report from Baltimore was of rioting. Rioting reported as well in Philadelphia, New York, and Cincinnati."

"The hell with the rioting," Sherman said coldly. "What about Lee?"

"He moved from Westminster five days ago, heading toward Washington. He's put up a good screen, no solid reports as to disposition. A courier boat out of Washington docked at Port Deposit on the north bank of the Susquehanna this afternoon with a report that Confederate infantry was reported ten miles to the north of Washington, at Rockville."

"Of course," Grant said quietly. "He has to try it. It's his one chance to win quickly."

"The rain has slowed him down," Haupt interrupted. "Every river is at flood, otherwise Lee could have been into the Washington area three days ago. Old Sam Heintzelman is in command of the garrison in Washington. He sent out some pioneer troops in front of Lee's advance. They've destroyed every bridge and mill dam north of the city and made a real mess of things."

Grant nodded approvingly and sat down at the table, a signal for the rest to join him.

Haupt sat down directly across from him, Elihu at his side.

"Tell me everything, start at the beginning," Grant said quietly, leaning back, rubbing his eyes, then putting down the cup of coffee. Fishing in his breast pocket, he pulled out a cigar, struck a Lucifer, and puffed the cigar to life.

Haupt began his narrative, describing the maneuvers that led to a meeting at Gettysburg, the flanking march of Lee to Westminster, the chaos at the supply head, the debacle at Union Mills, the disintegration of the Army of the Potomac, and the hellish retreat of the survivors to the Susquehanna, finishing with his meeting with Lincoln.

Grant did not interrupt, sitting quietly, wreathed in smoke, stubbing out the end of his cigar and lighting another one, the smoke drifting thick around the coal oil lamp that hung from the ceiling.

While Sherman stood silent, Porter stood up to stretch, walking over to study the map, reaching into his pocket for a flask, which he half emptied into his coffee. He made eye contact with Grant, motioned to the flask. Grant shook his head.

There was a moment of silence and Elihu cleared his throat.

"The political situation, General, to put it bluntly, is on the point of collapse."

"Go on."

"First off, the riots. It's reported that New York is controlled by the mob; scores, perhaps hundreds dead. More than half the city has gone over to the rioters."

"What's being done?"

"General Sickles has been dispatched with a brigade of troops from his corps."

Haupt said nothing. Sickles's move had not been authorized by any real order from above. He had simply announced that as a general from New York he was going there personally to straighten things out and Herman had reluctantly agreed to give him ten trains to move his men from Harrisburg to Jersey City.

"No one had said it openly yet, but the president will most likely face a delegation from Congress, perhaps already has done so, calling upon him to seek a negotiated settlement."

"He won't do it," Grant replied.

"I know he won't. But if Washington should fall, the point might be moot."

"Then we move the capital back to Philadelphia," Sherman said. "During the Revolution we did that. The British burned us out in 1814, and we survived it."

"The capital cannot fall," Elihu replied sharply. "It cannot. If we lose that, I can promise you that the members of Congress from every border state will back off from this war, as will more than one from the Midwest. That is what you must prevent."

Grant shook his head.

"I can't guarantee that we can save Washington. President Lincoln will not want me to throw away an army on a forlorn hope, and if I rush into this fight without preparation, it will be a forlorn hope. To defeat General Lee will take time, sir, and cannot be done with the snap of a finger. If we lose this army now"—and he gestured out the window toward the boats discharging the soldiers of the West—"we will lose this war."

"Congressman Washburne," Grant turned toward his old friend and mentor, "you must convey to the president that I fully understand the political crisis we are in and I will do everything I can, as quickly as possible, in response. The mere fact that we're coming east, even if with but one division to start, will send a message to Lee, and exert pressure on him as well. It will tell him we have not given up, not by a long shot, and will force him to perhaps act rashly.

"However," Grant nodded toward Haupt, "as General Haupt can verify, it will take weeks to move a force of significant size and to assemble the fighting power needed to engage Lee.

"The president should do all he can to protect Washington but be prepared to evacuate down the Potomac and shift the capital to Philadelphia if that becomes unavoidable.

"Personally, I do not believe Lee can take Washington. Sherman and I spent months seizing Vicksburg and it was not nearly as well fortified as Washington.

"I think Lee will presently discover he can bite at our capital but he can't swallow it in the time available before I arrive in the East."

Grant reached into his pocket, pulled out a neatly folded telegram, and opened it up.

"This was from the president," he announced, and put it on the table. "It authorizes me to come east, to take command of all forces, and, as the president himself said, to defeat General Lee's army. That, sir, is my mission."

"And the capital?"

"I hope it holds but I can do nothing for it now or for weeks to come. In fact I hope it barely hangs on."

"Sir?"

"Because it will keep Lee in place," Sherman said with a grin. "It'll be like the snake trying to swallow the hog. It's a meal too good to pass up, but once it is halfway down, he won't be able to swallow any more and he won't be able to disgorge and crawl away. He'll be stuck."

A trace of a smile crossed Grant's features.

"My mission is to destroy Lee, to bring this damned war to an end. That, sir, will take time."

"Can you and Sherman not go to Washington now, sir?" Elihu asked. "Your presence would do much to boost morale."

"It sounds like General Heintzelman is doing a good enough job as is, even though, from what I've heard, he's no great shakes as a field commander. Besides, Haupt, how long would it take to get me there?"

"Four days at least, sir, if I cleared the line all the way to the Port Deposit on the Susquehanna. Then fast packet to the Anacostia Naval Yard."

"It will already be decided by then," Grant replied, gaze fixed on the map. "Let's review the situation in Washington. What forces does Heintzelman have?"

"The garrison in the city is approximately twenty-five thousand. Mostly heavy artillery regiments, several good units. Also some small naval and marine detachments."

"Reinforcements?"

Haupt turned the pages on his own oversized notebook and found the information.

"Three thousand men have been dispatched from Fortress Monroe. They should be there by now. Halleck ordered that operations in front of Charleston be scaled back, half the men there, nearly ten thousand to be transported up as well. If need be, the operation in front of Charleston can be abandoned and the rest of the force brought up as well."

Elihu cleared his throat and looked over at Grant.

"Concerning Halleck."

Sherman walked around behind Grant, who sat unperturbed, silently puffing away.

Everyone knew of the deep tension that ran between Grant and Sherman on one side, and Halleck on the other. The year before, Halleck had worked vigorously to remove Grant from command of the Army of the Tennessee, blaming him for the first day's debacle at Shiloh.

"Go on."

"He has been removed from command, sir. The president will have accepted his resignation as of today; in fact the resignation was effective the moment you arrived here in Cairo."

Sherman grinned and slapped his thigh.

"About damn time, I say."

Elihu reached into his breast pocket and produced an envelope bearing the letterhead of the White House.

"This, sir, is authorization by the president. As stated in the previous telegram, you are in command of all forces of the United States; Halleck's position is now yours, and, sir, you will answer directly to the president of the United States."

"Not through Secretary Stanton?"

Elihu shook his head.

Herman looked over at Elihu with open surprise. Something big, profound must have happened between Lincoln and Stanton for the president to have cut Stanton out of the direct chain of command.

Grant said nothing; it was obvious that Elihu would brief him privately, later.

"Attached as well," Elihu continued, "is a statement from the secretary of the navy. Admiral Farragut will now have overall command of all naval forces, but when it comes to coordination and support of troop movements, he will defer to your orders, sir."

Grant took the envelope but did not open it. Haupt was deeply impressed by the fact that not a flicker of a smile, not the slightest gesture of self-gratification showed. Instead he looked over at Admiral Porter and nodded.

"John, I'm sorry there wasn't something in this for you," Grant said. "God knows you deserve it. We never would have had Vicksburg without you."

John Porter extended his hand.

"That's reward enough, sir, to hear that from you."

There was a long moment of silence, interrupted only by the ticking of a station clock on the wall and the shrieking train whistles out in the yard. Grant gazed at the map of the country and Haupt watched him. This man had just been given the responsibility of running the entire war. All power to do so was now focused in this room. He was not given to flights of fanciful imagination, but he found himself wondering for a second if perhaps someday a painting might be commissioned of this moment, a pensive Grant leaning over the map of the country, thinking upon what blood still needed to be shed, what destruction wrought, to bring it together again, if indeed it could be brought together again.

The second cigar burned down, a third was lit. Haupt got up, poured himself a cup of coffee that was now cold, pulling back the window shade for a moment to look out at the rain lashing down, flashes of lightning illuminating the dark river below.

"I am bringing up three corps from Vicksburg," Grant said, breaking the silence at last.

"McPherson is already coming up." He paused, looking up at Sherman. "Ord's Thirteenth Corps will follow, then Burnside's Ninth Corps along with the men he detached to Kentucky. I also want Banks's Nineteenth Corps from Port Hudson and New Orleans."

"Isn't that stripping the Mississippi down to nothing?" Elihu asked. Even Sherman seemed surprised by the announcement.

"The issue will be decided in front of Washington and Richmond, not on the banks of the Mississippi. Besides, General Sherman here will continue to play havoc with them and I'm also leaving part of your brother Cadwallader's Sixteenth Corps with him."

Elihu smiled.

"I'd like to see my brother again," Elihu replied.

Sherman looked over at Grant with outright dismay.

"Sir, I really think I could better serve going with you," he protested. "Let me loose on Bobbie Lee and we'll show those Easterners how to fight."

Grant shook his head emphatically.

"No, Bill, you're staying in the West. Besides, this is what you wanted, a chance at independent command. You'll have a tough job. You've got to keep what we've taken, then drive what's left of the rebs out of the region with only a third of what we had before."

"Sir," and there was almost a note of pleading in his voice, which surprised Haupt.

A look from Grant silenced him.

"Hear me out, Bill. You're taking command of the Army of the Tennessee."

"What's left of it. I'll have only my own corps, Cadwallader's, and some detached units to cover five hundred miles of river."

"I want someone out west I know I can count on, who can command independently. Ord with the Thirteenth is brand-new to corps command. McPherson is superb as a second in command, but frankly I trust you more in an independent role, and that means command of forces in the West."

He fell silent again, puffing on his cigar, studying the map, and then stirred.

"Where we have failed from the beginning is in concentration. Combined, we outnumber them on all fronts, but we have piddled away our numbers. How many are garrisoning St. Louis right now, Memphis, Louisville, wandering blindly on the coast of Texas, in Florida, even in front of Charleston?"

Haupt smiled and was prepared to go into his notebook, but then realized that the question was a rhetorical one; the hard numbers could be discussed later.

"I want pressure; I want it where it will hurt them the most, at the same time to prevent Lee from being reinforced even as I prepare to meet him. Bill, that's why I'm leaving you out here. Your job will be to keep the pressure on the rebels in the West and never allow them to shift any resources to the eastern theater. We can go over the details later, before I head east."

"What about old Rosecrans and Chattanooga?" Sherman asked pointedly. Grant smiled, knowing what Bill was trying to lead him toward, and shook his head.

"Later. Your mission at first will be to mop up what's left near Vicksburg; then we'll talk about Rosecrans and eastern Tennessee."

Grant looked back at Haupt.

"I want to move the troops coming up from Vicksburg eastward from here. McPherson's First Division is, as you know, disembarking now. That's just a symbolic gesture for the moment. The real effort will start in another week and they already have their orders to move."

Haupt stood and leaned over the table, moving his notebook to where he could read from it.

"To where?" Haupt asked.

Grant pointed at the map.

"Harrisburg," and Haupt smiled. It was where he assumed Grant would want to move, and Haupt had been planning accordingly.

"I assumed, sir, that you would be bringing at least two corps up, and I have developed the following plan."

He quickly flipped through several pages.

"We'll need close on to a hundred trains to move the men and primary equipment for one corps, including artillery, limbers, some ambulances. Horses, except for officers' mounts, will have to be left behind, or moved up later; they take up too much space, and the forage support for the animals makes it difficult, slowing us down. Anyway we can requisition horses in Pennsylvania as needed. Pennsylvanians are angry and will do almost anything to get even with Lee for invading their state.

"I'm planning on convoys of ten trains to move in a block, the line cleared as they go, each convoy spaced three hours apart, to give time for westbound traffic to at least move a stage back up the line. We still have to keep some traffic moving west. Additional equipment is being pre-placed along the line to clear any breakdowns or blockages. The convoys will move from here to Springfield, then to Indianapolis, to Columbus, then Pittsburgh, then to Harrisburg, detouring north through Williamsport, Pennsylvania, since we cannot guarantee safety of the line skirting the Cumberland Valley. We'll have to transfer trains at a couple of points where lines don't join; that will be difficult but I'm setting equipment in place now. I've also factored in an additional locomotive with empty cars for each convoy of ten in case of breakage.

"Men will be issued three days' cold rations, barrels of water set in each car; civilian organizations are being solicited at each depot where trains will be refueled and watered, to try and provide hot food for the men, but there is no guarantee of that. Transit to Harrisburg should take three days."

"Security?" Sherman asked.

"At every major switching and bridge, state militia will be turned out to guard, also at points of transfer. Since the lines are federalized, orders have been posted that any attempts to block or delay trains by civilians will be dealt with as a capital crime."

He hesitated for a few seconds, then continued.

"I can promise completed delivery of your First Corps to Harrisburg in ten days."

"And the rest?"

"Ten days per corps after that. If the Nineteenth goes by sea to Philadelphia, that will make their movement rather easy. The bigger problem of course will be horses, mules, wagons, forage for the animals, but as I said, it's easier to find those in the East than to try and move them all the way from Vicksburg and New Orleans to Harrisburg."

Grant gave a quick nod of agreement.

"Logistical support, supplies?"

"I'm pulling that together even as we speak. Full stockpiles of ammunition, rations, medical and auxiliary equipment are being brought in from across the Union. At the same time, what is left of the Army of the Potomac is being refitted, twenty batteries of artillery, forty thousand rifles, all necessary ammunition."

"What's left of it?" Sherman asked, the slightest hint of disdain in his voice.

Haupt could not help but bristle. The prejudice held by the western armies for the East was well-known. The Army of the Potomac was, however, his army, the one he had supported for nearly two years, and though he would not say it out loud, neither of these men had yet to face up to Bobbie Lee.

"Approximately thirty-five thousand men," Haupt replied, "counting those men that General Sickles took to New York. The bulk of them come from Sickles's Third Corps, Sykes's Fifth, and Howard's Eleventh."

"Point of concentration?" Grant asked.

"Still scattered, sir, from Harrisburg, which Sickles was holding clear down to the Chesapeake; some men are still drifting in. Every bridge over the Susquehanna from Harrisburg to the Chesapeake has been dropped, and the river is in flood; so, scattered or not, once on the north side of the river, they're safe from Lee."

"An army isn't supposed to be safe," Sherman sniffed. "It's supposed to be out there fighting."

"Sir," Haupt said quietly, forcing control, "they put up one hell of a fight. I know, I saw some of it. They lost, to be certain, but they most certainly chewed a hole into Lee as well."

Sherman bristled but Grant extended a calming hand.

"Gentlemen, we are all on the same side. Bill, we got whipped more than once ourselves, so let's not judge yet."

Sherman said nothing, shifting his unlit cigar in his mouth.

Grant looked back at Haupt.

"So you can move my corps to Harrisburg in how long?"

"Thirty days tops, for everything. I can prioritize the infantry, have all of them there within fifteen days, but it will take at least fifteen days, realistically more likely thirty to forty-five additional days, to bring up the necessary support to wage offensive operations."

"I want this done right."

Grant looked back at the map.

"There will be more, Haupt, a lot more."

"Sir, combined with the Army of the Potomac, that should give you the numerical edge."

"I don't just want the numerical edge," Grant replied, and for the first time his voice was sharp, a touch of anger to it.

"Bill, you said it two years ago, that it would take a quarter of a million men, just in the West, to crush this rebellion. That General Haupt is the edge we've always had but have never used, our numbers and our industry. By God, from day one we could have crushed this thing, at a fraction of the cost in blood, if only we had concentrated.

"General Lee is a brilliant tactician, but it seems that we have all become focused on what Lee is doing, and not on what we should be doing."

He placed a sharp emphasis on the word *we*, a note of anger and rebuke. Elihu, who had been sitting quiet while tactics and logistics were discussed, looked up at Grant and smiled.

"I have but one goal before me," Grant continued, "and that is the task set for me by the president of the United States."

He looked back down at the map of the Union.

"To defeat General Lee and to end this war, and with God's help we will get this job done once and for all."

Chapter Two

July 16, 1863

C.S.A Gen. Jeb Stuart pulled off his poncho, water streaming on to the floor. Mud was clinging to his boots as he stomped them on the entryway rug.

"God, what a mess out there," he sighed. Looking up he saw the disapproving glance of his commander at his choice of words.

"Sorry, sir."

Gen. Robert E. Lee motioned for Stuart to come to the table. Gen. James "Pete" Longstreet was by Lee's side, sipping from a cup of coffee; on the other side of Lee stood Gen. John Bell Hood, newly promoted to command of the reorganized Second Corps. The room was dimly lit—half a dozen candles around the table—the small house at the edge of Rockville abandoned at the approach of Confederate forces and now serving as Lee's headquarters. Jed Hotchkiss, chief cartographer for the Army of Northern Virginia, stood behind Lee, his map of the area spread out on the table.

Lee, sighing, rubbed his eyes. He was tired, having been up all day riding slowly, weaving his way through the bogged-down ranks of his exhausted army, which had been slogging for six weary days to make less than sixty miles. His uniform was soaked clean through, change of clothes lost somewhere back on the road, the headquarters wagon stuck in the mud.

Col. Walter Taylor, Lee's aide, offered Stuart a cup of coffee, which

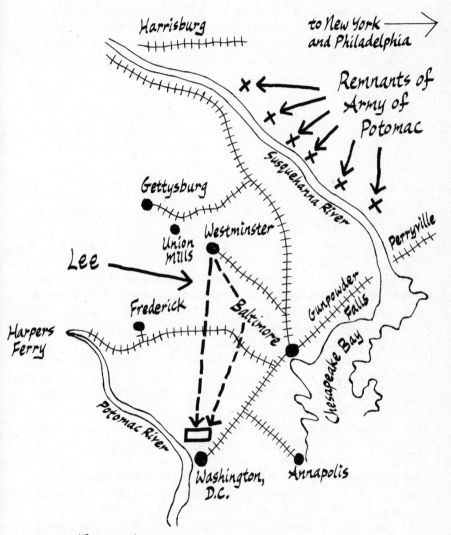

Harrisburg

to New York
and Philadelphia

Remnants of
Army of
Potomac

Susquehanna River

Gettysburg

Westminster

Perryville

Union
Mills

Lee

Frederick

Baltimore

Gunpowder
Falls

Harpers
Ferry

Chesapeake Bay

Potomac River

Washington,
D.C.

Annapolis

From Westminster to Washington

the general took eagerly, blowing on the edge of the tin cup and then sipping.

"Your report, General Stuart," Lee asked, putting his glasses back on to look up at his young cavalier.

"As ordered, sir, I rode a circuit of their outer fortifications and started back here as soon as it got dark. It was a difficult ride, sir. The Yankees have destroyed every bridge, mill dams are blown, one of my men drowned trying to ford a stream. Dozens of horses are crippled—broken legs, mostly—had to destroy them."

"Did you get any prisoners?" Lee asked.

"Yes, sir. Six men. Three from the First Maine Heavy Artillery, two from the First New York, and one officer, a captain, shoulder straps indicate staff, but he's as tight as a clam, won't say a word. The enlisted men were well fed, arrogant, said they hope we attack."

"Their strength?"

"Still not sure, sir. It was impossible to try and develop the situation, to trigger an open skirmish outside their fortifications. No regimental flags were shown."

"Smart on their part," Lee said, "keep us guessing."

"We did pick up a lot of newspapers in a post office at Beltsville, Washington papers mostly, printed this morning, a *Harper's Weekly* reporting on our victory at Union Mills and a *New York Tribune* from four days ago. One of the Washington papers said there's nearly thirty thousand Yankees garrisoning the city."

"Sounds about right," Longstreet said quietly.

"It also said that Lincoln's ordering up reinforcements from as far away as Charleston."

He has to, Lee thought to himself. *He knows I have to come here, and now all other fronts are secondary.*

"The fortifications?" Hotchkiss asked.

Stuart nodded to the army cartographer.

"Your maps are excellent sir. Just as you indicated. They're damn . . . , excuse me, sir, they are massive. Ditching ten feet deep, abatis, earthen walls twenty feet high in places. The fortresses are all within mutual support of each other, and connected by communication trenches. One of the heavy-artillery prisoners said they've got thirty-pounders, even some eight-inch guns, Columbiads, heavy mortars, and hundred-pound rifled Parrott guns in them. It was hard to see through the rain. Fields of fire are well laid out, each fortress covered on flanks by its neighbors. There are no weaknesses anywhere along that line, sir. They most likely have good interior roads as well and can shift to meet any threat."

As he spoke, Stuart traced out on Hotchkiss's map the perimeter of fortifications guarding the landward approach to Washington.

"Well manned?" Lee asked.

"Again, sir, hard to tell in the rain. I pushed skirmishers forward at three points and they were met with brisk firing, no lack of ammunition; they were firing heavy guns at my skirmish line from half a mile out."

Lee nodded. Of course they would. The stockpile of equipment in the capital would be unaffected by what happened to the Army of the Potomac, and their gunners would be eager to get some shots in, their first chance for real shooting since the war started.

"I placed a brigade to cover the Rockville Road, another on the Seventh Street Road, and ordered two more brigades down to cut the Blandenburg Road, the railroad to Baltimore, and anchor our line down to Uniontown. By tomorrow morning the city will be completely cut off."

"Thank you, General Stuart, you've fulfilled your orders handsomely."

"Sir, I must tell you this will be one hard nut to crack. It makes our works around Richmond pale in comparison."

"The difference is," Hood interjected, "it is us doing the attacking, not McClellan. We'll put in the best infantry in the world against third-rate garrison troops."

"Still, sir, when you get a look at those fortifications," Stuart replied, "well, it will be a hard nut, as I said."

"Do you suggest we not attack then?" Hood asked.

Stuart looked at Lee.

Lee took his glasses off again and rubbed his eyes. The hour was late, he was tired. Without asking, Walter put a fresh cup of coffee on the table beside him, and Lee sipped from it meditatively for several minutes.

"Gentlemen, the hour is late," Lee finally said. "We've had another hard day of marching. The rain and mud are exhausting all of us. I think we should get our rest. Tomorrow, General Hood, Major Hotchkiss, and I will go forward to survey the lines ourselves. General Stuart, I would like for you to join us. General Longstreet, I ask that you stay here to oversee the movement of the army."

"One final thing, sir," Stuart said, and, fishing into his breast pocket, he pulled out a soggy, folded up newspaper and spread it out on the table.

"A Washington newspaper, sir, this morning." Stuart pointed to a column on the front page.

Adjusting his glasses, Lee leaned over to read it.

"Halleck has been removed from all command positions and is retiring; Gen. Ulysses Grant is in command and is reported to already be in Cairo, Illinois, with his troops following."

Lee scanned the rest of the front page for a moment. Reports on rioting in northern cities, a rumor that Stanton was to be fired, a report that thirty thousand reinforcements were rushing to the aid of Washington, that four batteries of guns surrounded the Capitol and two more guarded the White House. He sifted through the densely packed columns, some of it hard to read, the ink smeared, and then took his glasses off.

"I don't know this Grant," Lee said, looking around at his staff, "but his reputation is known."

"Sir, I don't think fighting against Pemberton, or even General Johnston, is indicative of his ability against us," Hood interjected.

"Still, I wish I knew more of him."

"It'll be weeks before he can mount anything effective," Longstreet said, leaning over the table to scan the newspaper.

"That is why we must act quickly, decisively, without hesitation," Lee replied.

He drained the rest of his coffee and put the cup down. He did not need to say another word. There was something in his gesture that indicated dismissal, and one by one the three generals bid good night and left, the sound of rain drumming down, echoing in the room as the door swung open. A humid breeze filled the room. As the door closed, the room regained a warm feel as the fireplace drove out the humidity.

Taylor and Hotchkiss hesitated and Lee smiled.

"Walter, I have a comfortable spot right here." Lee nodded to where a blanket had been spread on a sofa. Even though the house had been abandoned by Union sympathizers, he would not take the bed without the express permission of the owner. It bothered him, as well, that outside, most of his army was bedding down in the pouring rain, their dinner cold rations. To sleep in a comfortable bed, under a dry roof, struck him as the wrong example this night, the compromise of a sofa as far as he was willing to go.

Taylor and Hotchkiss saluted, bid Lee good night, and retired to the kitchen, where the rest of his staff were already fast asleep on the floor.

Standing, Lee removed his jacket and unbuttoned his vest. His boots were already off and he stretched, back cracking. He looked down at the map, his gaze following the traces in pencil of the route taken by his army down from Westminster, skirting to the west of Baltimore and now down to here, with Longstreet's men concentrating toward Rockville, and Hood on the road to Claysville and Beltsville.

He looked out the window, a lantern set on the road to mark headquarters barely visible as a sheet of rain lashed down, rattling against the panes.

The miserable weather, which ultimately had played such a crucial role in the entrapment of the Army of the Potomac, now was hampering his own movement. Even the macadamized pikes were becoming difficult to move on, the road surface not designed for the pounding of hundreds of artillery limbers, a thousand supply wagons, over forty thousand men, and ten thousand cavalry. The very rain that had made his decisive victory possible was now making the exploitation of that victory very slow and very exhausting, robbing him of precious time when swift and decisive movement was essential to achieve the final victory.

He let the curtain drop and returned to the table, sitting down, half glancing at the newspaper. Opening it up and spreading the single sheet out since it was uncut, he turned the paper around, pausing for a moment to look at the casualty lists for the Washington, D.C. area posted from Union Mills.

Familiar names, old comrades from Mexico, Texas, and East Coast garrisons, cadets from his days as superintendent of West Point, were there in soggy ink.

Three weeks ago they were still alive. *How much all has changed*, he thought. Dispatches, three days old, had come up this day from Richmond, and there was the *Richmond Enquirer* heralding Gettysburg and Union Mills as the greatest victory in the annals of war, rival to Waterloo, Yorktown, and Saratoga.

Maybe so, but still it continues, the war still continues. One of the dispatches, in a sealed leather pouch, was from President Davis, congratulating him for a victory unparalleled in the history of the Southern republic, and informing him that he would come north to review the victorious army and to offer, as well, a conference with Lincoln to discuss an ending of hostilities.

The implication behind President Davis's letter was clear enough, Lee mused as he picked up the coffeepot and poured half a cup. *The president expects this war to be over within the month, but that means the taking of Washington, the collapse of the Union's will to fight, the draft and antiwar riots in northern cities spreading. Then Lincoln will have no choice but to seek an end to it.*

It was obvious now, however, that the near destruction of the Army of the Potomac had not swerved Lincoln from his path. Lincoln had endured the frustrating repulse of McClellan in front of Richmond, the destruction of Pope at Second Manassas, the bloodbath of Union soldiers in front of Fredericksburg, and now the crushing defeat of the Army of the Potomac along the Pipe Creek line between Westminster and Gettysburg.

Somehow Lincoln had this ability to focus on the positive and to endure no matter what pain was inflicted on the Union forces. Now he was clearly pointing to Vicksburg as proof that the Union could win despite the failures in the East. He was a hard man and forcing him to negotiate was going to take extraordinary effort.

In the last fight, it was the mind and spirit of General Meade and of his generals that I had to probe, to analyze, to defeat. The opponent is different now. Grant? Not for at least two weeks or more, most likely a month before he will become a factor. No, my opponent now is Abraham Lincoln, it is he I must break.

That meant Washington. If the city fell and Lincoln was forced to abandon the city, where would he go? New York? Out of the question, with that city ripped by anarchy. Philadelphia? Yes, most likely there, a symbolic move to the birthplace of the United States. But according to the paper before him, rioting had broken out in the City of Brotherly Love as in its bigger cousin to the north. A president fleeing to a city that would need to be placed under martial law would be a crippling political blow, one he could not recover from.

He looked at the map but by now there was no need to do so. Every detail was memorized, burned into his mind, every approach, every possible avenue of attack thought out, and thought out yet again.

It was indeed, as Stuart put it, "a hard nut to crack." Yet it had to be done and done swiftly. *We must force Lincoln out while the northern cities still burn, while a nation scans its newspapers, reads the tightly packed rows of fine print, recognizes names of the fallen, and asks "Why?"*

He thought of the night of June 28, his epiphany as he realized that the army was not completely under control, under his direct hand, and from that realization, he now knew, had come the victory at Union Mills. He had driven his army beyond the brink of exhaustion, but that driving had taken them to heights undreamed of.

I must do that again, in spite of all, in spite of the weather, in spite of the fortifications and that waiting garrison. This was a test of nerves and the target this time was not the Army of the Potomac, it was the mind of the president of the United States.

He remembered his military history, how after Cannae Hannibal had inexplicably hesitated, giving Rome time to prepare, so that when the Carthaginian army finally did march up to the gates of that city, it could not be taken. Thus the fruits of that great victory were in the end squandered; the war had dragged on for another decade and led to ultimate defeat and finally to the destruction of Carthage.

I must strike now, it must be one solid blow, every available man must be brought forward. The cost will be horrific, a frontal assault straight in, most likely on Fort Stevens. How many will I lose? Five, perhaps ten thousand, upward of a quarter of my men in half a day. One final, terrible price. With luck the garrison will panic once the outer shell breaks and the city itself can be taken then without the grim prospect of a street-by-street fight.

Lincoln? Any dream of capturing him was remote. He would remove himself, take ship, and escape. It would not be the act of a coward. It would be a political necessity, though the abandoning of the capital would spell his doom nevertheless.

He knew that was yet another reason why President Davis was coming north, with the hope of a triumphal march into the White House, there to receive the ambassadors of every European power.

That would be the deciding moment, when word of the fall of Washington was passed on to Europe. Recognition, at least by France and the Hapsburgs, would be certain and, as it was in the winter of 1777 after the British surrender at Saratoga, so it would be in the late summer of 1863. Military victory would lead to diplomatic recognition and support that would then lead to the final victory.

England would not join the others. The antislavery movement in England outweighed any economic or balance-of-power considerations.

He knew that with the perception of victory now so close, any suggestion that the South counter the Emancipation Proclamation with its own announcement of some form of manumission would fall upon deaf ears. But to do so at this moment of victory would strengthen their hand, and perhaps sway England as well. Then it truly would be a final blow.

This is not my arena, he realized. *This is a political, a social question; I must focus on the military*—and he pushed the contemplation aside.

Take Washington, then let Grant come east to that news. With good fortune there would be no fight with him, for the war would already be over.

Lee blew out the candles, left the table, and knelt on the hard, rough plank floor, lowering his head in silent prayer.

"Thy Will be done," he finally whispered and, curling up on the sofa, he drifted into exhausted sleep.

The White House

July 16, 1863

It was nearly midnight. President Lincoln stood alone, gazing out of the second-floor office window. The grounds of the executive mansion were a garrison this night, artillery pieces positioned at the four corners, a second battery positioned and unlim-

bered on Pennsylvania Avenue, along with four companies of regular infantry encamped on the lawn facing Lafayette Square. Stanton had actually wanted the troops to dig in, to build barricades, an indignity to the building and to the position. The president had refused.

Across the street the lights of the Treasury Building were ablaze, couriers riding up with a clatter of hooves, muddy water splashing. Officers came and went, each one with purposeful stride, as if the entire fate of the nation rested upon them this night as indeed it might.

He looked back over his shoulder. John Hay, his twenty-five-year-old secretary, was asleep, curled up on a sofa. The house was quiet. Mary had insisted, earlier in the evening, that at least Tad should be evacuated, and there had been a row. It had dragged on for nearly an hour, her in tears, saying that he didn't care for the well-being of Taddie and was only thinking of what the newspapers would say.

She had finally settled down, calling Taddie in to sleep beside her, and now there was peace.

In part she was right and he knew it, the realization troubling. Every paper would scream a denouncement if he did evacuate his family, ready to point out that while he worried about his own kin, tens of thousands of others had died.

Evacuation was out of the question, and besides, if it ever did come to capture, he knew that Mary and Tad would be treated with the utmost deference by Lee.

An outrageous report had just come to him this morning, that Lee's son, taken prisoner last month, was languishing in a dank cell in Fortress Monroe, nearly dead from his wound. He had sent a sharp reprimand to the commandant, and ordered that the prisoner be slated for immediate exchange as a wounded officer. It was not to curry favor. It was simply the civilized thing to do. He knew Lee would do the same without hesitation.

Strange that the two of us are enemies. I did offer him command of all the Union armies in 1861. A tragedy he turned me down. With his leadership the Union would have been restored quickly and decisively. From the west-facing windows of the White House, he could see Lee's old home, inherited through his wife and now confiscated by the Union, dominating Arlington Heights. Though they were of different backgrounds and social status, he felt an affinity toward the man. He sensed that Lee wished this thing to be ended as well, while across the street there was more than one officer this night who reveled in the power and in the sheer destruction, the opium-like seduction that war could create, the smoke of it seeping into the lungs to control and to poison the mind.

McClellan was like that, so was Hooker; they loved it, the power, the pageantry, the shrill dreams of glory. Perhaps in another age that illusion might have been real, in the time of Henry V, or of Julius Caesar. At least it seemed that way upon the stage and in paintings. But he remembered Antietam, the first battlefield he had ever walked upon, the air thick with the cloying stench of decay wafting up out of shallow graves, soldiers still burning the carcasses of dead horses, the hospital tents overflowing with wounded and hysterical boys struggling before the final fall into oblivion. He had seen it in the eyes of so many women, young girls, vacant-eyed fathers dressed in black. No longer would the gay tunes of a martial band bring a smile to their faces, only the memory of a son, a husband, a boy who had heard that music and marched off . . . never to return.

"God, will this ever end?" he whispered.

"Sir?"

It was Hay, stirring, looking up at him, ready to return to his desk to write down another memo, another order.

Lincoln shook his head and made a soothing gesture with long, bony hands, motioning for his loyal secretary to go back to sleep.

He went back over to his desk and sat down, absently sifting through the pile of papers, documents, and newspapers awaiting his attention. The flow was far heavier than usual, a pile awaiting him every morning, and no matter how fast he attempted to clear it, yet more came in throughout the day and night. He pushed the papers back, tilted his chair, and rested his long legs up on the desk.

The entreaties from members of Congress, those few still in the city and the rest from around the country, would have to be answered, but that could wait. The majority were simply doing the usual posturing for the home press, so they could thump their chests and announce how they had advised the president most carefully on this latest crisis.

The implied threat in more than one letter from Congress was clear. Some were already seeking a way to disenthrall themselves from support of the war, so they could claim all along that they knew the effort to save the Union would be a failure. Others were thundering about who was responsible for the disaster at Union Mills. Several members of the Committee on the Conduct of the War had announced that hearings would be held.

There was even the issue of who was now in command of the Army of the Potomac. Meade was dead; Dan Butterfield had just made it back through the lines this morning, Hancock barely surviving. In his own mind he wondered if that army even still existed or should be quietly disbanded, survivors shifted into other commands. Troops were scattered from Harrisburg to the Chesapeake; the only thing protecting that broken remnant and the cities of the North from Lee was the flooded Susquehanna. Nominally, Couch, who commanded the twenty thousand militia hastily gathered at Harrisburg, controlled the district, but the job was far beyond the capability of a general who had asked to be relieved of field command only two months ago.

Secretary of State Seward was reporting requests from a dozen ambassadors for interviews. Already dispatches were winging to the courts of Europe, with lurid details of the collapse of the Army of the Potomac, and tomorrow more would go out, announcing that the capital was under siege.

How long?

Stanton, puffing and wheezing, had arrived earlier in the evening, announcing that Stuart had been spotted in front of Fort Stevens, and then predicting that rain or not, Lee would strike tomorrow.

He looked back out the window. The steady patter of rain had eased, a damp fog was beginning to roll in from the flooded marshland just below the White House.

If he attacks, will Heintzelman be able to hold?

The general was confident, but then again, nearly all of them showed confidence until the shock of battle hit. Still, the positions were strong, the men within them dry, well fed, rested, ammunition in abundance. Though they were inexperienced compared to the battle-hardened men of the old Army of the Potomac, his sense of them was that they would fight. They had endured two years of jibes and when they came into the city on furlough, even brawls with the men of the field army, who denounced the heavy-artillery units as garrison soldiers afraid of a fight.

Dug in as they were, they'd fight, but there would be precious few reserves, with every fort on a perimeter of thirty miles having to be manned.

He stood and walked back to the window.

He wondered how President Madison had felt, standing here, watching as the couriers came riding in, announcing the disaster at Blandensburg, the fact that the British would be in the city by nightfall.

And yet the republic had survived that. There was never a question of surrender then, nor with George Washington after the fall of Philadelphia, when Congress moved to the frontier outpost of York.

For Washington in 1777 and Madison in 1814 it had been a question of will. It was the same challenge for him this night.

Tonight, he knew that in a fair part of those states still loyal, will was evaporating, burning away under the heat of this war. As the horrific tally from Union Mills was tapped out to distant telegraph stations across the land, the victory at Vicksburg would be washed away in a sea of mourning and recriminations.

He was almost grateful that the city was now cut off. The chattering of most of the voices of condemnation or outright surrender would gratefully be silent in this office.

I could end this tomorrow, he thought. *End it and send those boys home. A month, a year from now they would still be alive, for chances are, if this continues, they will die, if not tomorrow or the day after, they will perish nevertheless in the battles still to be fought.*

He thought again of Antietam, the washed-out graves, rotting corpses half out of the ground. He remembered one in particular, obviously a boy of not more than sixteen, face visible in the clay, wisps of blond hair, decaying lips drawn back in a death grimace, silent, granite-like eyes gazing up at him as he rode past. Somewhere—in Maine, Ohio, or Indiana—there was a family, sitting in a parlor, who read of that boy, the name in small print, the only sound the tick-tock whisper of the clock marking out the passage of their lives, and in their hearts was the question of why did their boy die? And they were asking that again tonight, with more news of defeat. *Why did my boy die for a cause that seems lost?*

Perhaps they hoped that there was some meaning, some cause, a dream beyond that of any individual, that their son had been drawn into that storm and disappeared forever, and yet there would be ultimate purpose, a deeper grief, that in the end would be replaced by a knowledge that through him, others now lived, that from the rich earth of his grave, something now was given back to all . . . forever.

What would they think this night? A logic he had always held in contempt was that the sacrifice to Mars must, at times, be sustained by yet more blood sacrifices to assuage those already dead. To give in was to render meaningless the sacrifice of all those who had already died.

And yet, this night, he did see truth in it. If the war could still be won, then to surrender now would be to render meaningless all the sacrifice gone before, even that sacrifice upon the bloody slopes of Gettysburg and Union Mills.

Can it be won?

He thought of two conversations of the last week, both of them so clear in intent, not the self-serving maneuverings of the political circles about him, rather the simple statements of two soldiers who had been there. Henry Hunt, who had witnessed all of it, and in tears had asked that leaders be chosen that were worthy of the men who served beneath them. He and General Haupt, who so coolly and without emotion had said that if the men could be found, he, Haupt, could marshal the supplies and equipment to support them within a matter of weeks.

That now focused him.

Grant, more than any other, had proven his worth, and he knew without doubt that here was the general he had sought for two long years. A general who understood what he as the president of a free republic expected to be done by the army of that republic. He knew that Grant fully understood the relationship between a civilian government and its general in the field . . . that upon accepting command to scrupulously follow the orders of the president, which were simple, at least in concept . . . relentlessly move forward, unleash the full power of the North and implement a coordinated military plan to bring about a speedy victory.

Ultimately though, that decision—the decision to refocus the industrial might of the nation, to place that might into the hands of those few men still willing to volunteer, and to let the frightful dying continue—now rests with me. Do I have the will to see it through?

He looked down again at the soldiers on the lawn. Several were gathered around a lantern, playing cards, another crowd leaning against a lamppost, trying to read the latest newspaper.

They will die by my orders, if I have the will to give that next order.

If I don't, then all meaning to what has gone before is lost. Our continent will fracture apart—and with a sudden clarity he could see all that would follow. Two nations would quickly break into three, for Texas would go its own way again, followed by four, perhaps five nations, as western states broke away. Then there would be war in Mexico and Cuba, for surely the South would turn that way, and war on the West Coast as those states sought to drive out the British north of them. And at some point war yet again, for vengeance, for control of the Mississippi, or over servile revolt and abolitionists who would not give up their cause.

Yet hundreds of thousands more dead in the century to come. And what of Europe? France would try to stage a return, would goad Spain in as well. The "last best hope of mankind" would become simply like the rest of the world, warring states drenched in centuries of blood, rather than a power that might one day step forward to transform, perhaps even to save, the world.

And it all rests with me tonight.

Though the burden was almost beyond a man's ability to tolerate, especially as he gazed down upon those who, tomorrow perhaps, would pay that price, he knew with a startling clarity what he had to do, what history now charged him with doing. With that clear, there was no longer room for doubt.

"Thy Will be done," he whispered.

Sitting down on the sofa opposite from Hay he slipped off his shoes, wrapped a shawl around his painfully thin, hunched shoulders, and, lying down, drifted off to sleep.

Chapter Three

The ride up from the Jersey City Ferry had been a sobering experience for Gen. Dan Sickles. On the west side of the Hudson River it looked as if all of Lower Manhattan was an inferno. Even from across the river he could hear the rattle of musketry, a sound to be expected on the battlefields of Virginia and Maryland, but here, in his home city?

Coming up West Fourteenth Street he was confronted by chaos, a torrent of refugees, dragging trunks, pushing wheelbarrows, clutching children, pouring down the thoroughfare, trying to get off the island.

Stores lining the street had been looted, bolts of cloth from a millinery were draped over lamp-posts, taverns had been completely cleaned out, shattered glass crunched underfoot as the column advanced, while to either side a dozen or more buildings were burning.

His lead regiment, the Fifty-seventh Pennsylvania, had pushed ahead an hour ago while he waited for the other trains to disembark. He now marched in surrounded by his boys from the Sixty-third Pennsylvania, the other regiments disembarking behind them. Two companies from Berdan's old command of sharpshooters were along, as well as two batteries of artillery. He had originally planned to use his old Excelsior Brigade but then wisely thought better of it; to bring in New York boys to shoot

down their neighbors might cause a backlash. His boys from the old Key-
stone State, having just fought a losing battle on their native soil, would
be in a fierce mood to deal with traitors in their backyard. Also, since there
were few Irish in these regiments, that would not become an issue as well.

As they marched, the Pennsylvania boys, most of them from farms
and small villages, looked around wide-eyed at the towering four- and
five-story buildings that lined the street, block after block. He could

sense they were nervous. It was dark, except for the glare of the fires; panic was in the air, this was not like hunting rebs in the forest or standing on the volley line.

The column finally turned on to old familiar territory for Sickles—Union Square, Delmonico's at one corner. The Fifty-seventh Pennsylvania was already deployed out into company lines, the men standing at ease, looking about in wonder.

From every direction civilians were swarming toward them, frightened, crying, asking for shelter. Beleaguered policemen and a few state militia were trying to keep order, telling people to head for the ferries, to get out of the city.

Up around what he took to be Twentieth Street it sounded like a pitched battle was being fought, flashes of gunfire, buildings burning, a window shattering above him from a bullet.

His regiments continued to file into the square, the heavy tramp of their hobnailed boots echoing from the cobblestones, a reassuring sound to Dan, a sound of order, of discipline, of his army.

He edged across the square, there was still time before his meeting, and besides it was best to keep his "host" waiting for a few more minutes. On the far side of the square a commotion was erupting, and as he drew closer he could see an angry gathering, a bunch of toughs, brandishing sticks, clubs, cobblestones, taunting the troops.

They moved in and out like an undulating wave, pushing halfway across the street, some just drunk and shouting obscenities, others filled with some wild animal rage, shaking clubs, screaming at the soldiers to come on in and fight, then edging back, and some were just consumed by the madness that comes over a wild crowd, some of the participants laughing, dancing, shouting gibberish.

The men of the Fifty-seventh stood nervously, having formed a front of two companies at an angle just inside the park, bayonets fixed and lowered.

The mob started to grow, more pouring in from back alleys. Looking up, Sickles saw some leaning out of windows, looking down; he was not sure if they were rioters or just onlookers.

Dan rode up behind the two companies, a nervous major looking up at him.

"They just started coming in like this, sir," the major said, voice actually shaking. He couldn't remember the man's name but recognized him, a good soldier when the battle was in a field or woods, but this situation was unnerving him. He could sense it in the men as well.

A brick came sailing across the street, a soldier cursing, dropping his rifle, falling back from the line. A cheer went up from the mob.

"Are your men loaded?" Dan asked.

"Sir?"

"Primed and loaded?"

"Yes, sir."

Dan waited. In his years working the wards of New York he knew these people on the other side, perhaps more than one had voted for him for Congress so long ago. He knew their tempers, their moods, their gutter leaders. With luck, one of those leaders would know whom he was facing and call his mob back. But if it was going to start for real, here was as good as any place.

The mob did not disperse, more bricks started to fly, the two companies backed up a dozen paces, and there was a momentary standoff. And then the moment came.

A drunk rioter staggered out, holding a battered American flag aloft, threw it to the ground, unbuttoned, and started to urinate on it, the mob roaring with delight.

An angry cry went up from the Pennsylvania soldiers. Among them, even a captured rebel battle flag would have been treated with far more respect. It was a sacrilege to any who had followed the colors forward into battle. Dan stood in his stirrups.

"Boys, we've shed blood for that flag! Our brothers have died for that flag! Take aim!"

With a resolute will, a hundred rifles were brought to the shoulder and lowered.

The mob hesitated.

"Disperse now, you damn bastards!" Dan shouted.

Some of the mob turned and started to run; he gave them enough time to get off and away, but the rest actually stood there, taunting, some beginning to surge forward again.

"Fire!"

The volley swept the street corner. Dozens dropped.

"Reload!"

There was a sharp, practiced precision to their work as they drew cartridges, reloaded, brought their weapons to the ready.

The street corner was cloaked in smoke, dozens were on the ground in front of them, the mob was gone.

Dan turned to the major.

"If they come back, don't hesitate to shoot. Now get those wounded taken care of, find that flag and have someone clean it."

The major, a bit startled by what had just happened, could only salute.

"Remember, men," Dan shouted. "These are traitors and rebels, the same that we faced in Virginia. The difference is, at least our enemies in Virginia were soldiers like us, who fought with honor."

To his surprise a ragged cheer went up, as if his words had calmed their fears about what they had just seen and done.

He turned and rode back across the square. A bullet hummed by, striking and chipping the brick wall beside him. He looked across the square. It was impossible to see where it had come from.

Hell of a note, he thought, *get shot by some drunk Irishman after surviving so many battles.*

More troops were continuing to pour into the square; another volley thundered from where he had just been, he didn't bother to look back. Reaching Delmonico's, he reined in and dismounted, several staff waiting there anxiously for him.

"The governor and Mr. Tweed are inside," he was informed. "Sir, they say you're an hour late."

Sickles grinned.

"Pass the word to the regimental commanders. I want a cordon around this square, reinforced companies at each intersection deployed and ready to fight. I want some of Berdan's sharpshooters to get into buildings and watch for bushwackers, one almost got me a minute ago, just make sure they don't start shooting each other in the confusion. I'll be out shortly."

Adjusting his sash and saber, Gen. Dan Sickles strode into Delmonico's, one of his favorite haunts since the early days when it had first opened farther downtown. The owner was nowhere in sight, and he chuckled, simply nodding to the maitre d', who even in all this madness was properly decked out in full formal evening wear, though the entire restaurant was deserted except for a small gathering in a darkened corner.

Dan approached, smiling, and "Boss" Tweed stood up, his ever-expanding girth making it difficult for him to get out from behind the table.

Tweed offered a perfunctory handshake as Dan looked around. Governor Seymour with a couple of his staffers half rose, nodded, and then sat back down.

Dan inwardly grinned. He knew Seymour did not want him here. Though the man was terrified, still he would want the credit if the situation was restored.

"The mayor, where is he?" Dan asked.

"How the hell should I know?" Tweed replied. "I guess either trapped down at City Hall, or hiding."

"I sent a telegram to meet me here."

"At three in the morning, Sickles?" Seymour grumbled. "Aren't we getting a little high-and-mighty? And besides, you are the one who is an hour late."

"It took time getting my men across the river and I won't have a spare moment once daylight comes.

"Just be glad that I'm here."

Dan smiled. No sense in getting important patrons upset.

"My apologies, gentlemen, we're all tired, thank you for meeting me."

"Besides, it's a good chance for a free meal."

A waiter brought over a bottle of brandy; Dan nodded. Once the bottle was open, he took it, poured his own glass, and sat down.

"The situation here?"

Tweed shook his head.

"I think we've lost control of the city. Maybe if you boys had won at Gettysburg and Union Mills, it might never of happened, or it wouldn't be so bad. But between that, the casualty lists, and the draft, the city just exploded. Except for some areas around City Hall, the financial district, and where a lot of militia were posted in the wealthier neighborhoods, the city is in anarchy."

Dan drained his glass and poured a second one.

Even within the darkened confines of Delmonico's, the air was heavy with the stench of smoke from the dozens of fires raging out of control across the city. An exhausted fire crew, walking behind their hook-and-ladder wagon, limped past the doorway, several of the men bandaged, one nursing a bloody arm in a sling. One could hear a steady rumble echoing, and it quickened Dan's blood; it was the sound of men shouting, so similar to the sound of a battle from a mile or two away. An explosion thundered, loud enough that many of the men in the square stood up, pointing to the north, and Dan could see a glimpse of a fireball soaring into the early-morning sky.

"I could have won it at Gettysburg and we wouldn't now be dealing with that mess out there," Dan announced. Tweed said nothing, intent on his opening course of smoked oysters, pausing between bites to drain his glass of champagne. The governor, flanked by his two aides who actually had more the look of bodyguards, sat with hands folded across his lap.

"I'm telling you, I had Lee square in my sights that second morning at Gettysburg," Dan continued. "I knew he was beginning to flank us.

Berdan, God rest him, confirmed it just before he died. They were strung out on that road for miles and I'd of cut through them like a whipsaw. Then we could have turned and destroyed each wing of his army.

"But no, damn him! Meade and all the others just stood there like wooden Indians. Damn West Point bastards. Same thing on the march down to Union Mills. I should have been allowed to move to the right flank as I told Meade, rather than march on Union Mills. But again, no! If I had, Fifth Corps would have been reinforced rather than annihilated. And that last bloody charge, my God, what idiocy, it was worse than Burnside at Fredericksburg."

"That's past and the White House and its patronage are still in the future," Tweed grumbled, looking up from his meal. "I'm worried about now," and he gestured toward the open door.

"We let this continue, we lose this city, the blame will come down square on Tammany when it's done. You know damn well the Republicans will blame us for it, say they were knifed in the back by these riots. They will seize any excuse to blame the Irish and the Democrats."

"That's why I'm here," Sickles said. "Somebody's got to restore order and if I do it we get the credit instead of the blame. I will be the man who saved the Union after our defeat at Union Mills."

"One more day and we'll have that rabble under control," Governor Seymour snapped back angrily.

Dan leaned back in his chair, raising a brandy snifter, and smiled.

"If you wish to give the order, Governor, I will withdraw my troops immediately," and he pointed to the square.

Worried looks were exchanged around the table between Seymour and Tweed, the silence of the moment disturbed by the distant echoes of shots, another fire engine racing past, the cries of those fleeing the anarchy out in the street.

"Let's not be hasty, Dan," Seymour replied.

Dan smiled.

"We have to be hasty, Governor, or we'll lose your damn city and with it the war. For or against it at this point, you don't want to be the one blamed."

"You actually think this goddamn war can be won?"

"Think it? I know it," Dan replied coldly.

"And you're the one to do it?"

"You're goddamn right I'm the one to do it."

"Lincoln will never let you take command, didn't you see Greeley's paper today? It's Grant now."

"A drunkard and yet another West Pointer," Dan announced, loud enough that his staff and the infantry guards at the door could hear.

"You honestly think he can do anything?"

"He did take Vicksburg," Tweed offered. "He's got powerful friends, Congressman Washburne for one."

Dan snorted derisively.

"Fighting against rabble out west is one thing. Let him try and tangle with Bobbie Lee. One fight and he'll be like all the others, running with his tail between his legs. . . ." He paused for a moment, looking into his brandy glass, "or dead."

There was no response. Staring at the glass Dan felt a flicker of pain, the memory of that field at Union Mills, watching good men go in by the thousands, only to be cut down in their turn. If only they had listened, it all could have been avoided. The revelation that had just come out, that Lincoln had actually sent a dispatch advising Meade to use discretion, that he was not required to attack, was useful in his own campaign, but at the same time struck hard into that side of him that wished to see Union victory, to see an end to it all.

If only Meade had listened; his own advice had been a reflection of Lincoln's.

"I can end this war," Dan whispered, as if to himself, taking a sip of brandy and setting it back down.

He looked back up at Tweed and the others.

"I've watched the professionals mismanage this for two long years. They don't understand volunteers. I do, for I am one of them."

"But you are not in command," Tweed replied.

"I can be."

"How?"

"I want Meade to be taken care of by the Committee on the Conduct of the War."

"Good God, man, Meade is dead. Leave it rest," Seymour gasped.

"No. His memory still lingers. John Sedgwick is angling for that job, blaming me for his failure. Get your people in Congress to take down Meade before the committee and Sedgwick is hung with the blame as well."

"You forget about Grant," Tweed said. "Remember, he commands the armies."

"He's new, just a day at it. If the word comes from the White House that I now command the Army of the Potomac, he'll accept it. He can't put his own people in yet."

"What Army of the Potomac?" Seymour asked sadly.

"It's still out there," Dan said heatedly. "Most of my corps is still intact. That's going to be the heart of it. I want that appointment confirmed before Grant gets east. I also want sufficient reinforcements assigned to me, the troops coming up from Charleston, Burnside's Ninth Corps; I can bring the number back up to sixty thousand in a fortnight and have the army ready to fight within the month. Then I'll cross the Susquehanna and drive Lee back into Virginia before Grant can even stir. If the rains hold I might even be able to pin Lee against the Potomac and annihilate him."

Seymour and Tweed looked at him with disbelief.

Dan smiled.

"Damn all of you. Think beyond this city for a moment. I take command of the army, defeat Lee, and all opens up. Lincoln and his cronies will be blamed for all that happened before. Even if the war drags into the following year, come next spring I take the Democratic nomination for president, and then, gentlemen, I give you the White House. Think of all that Tammany could do if we moved our headquarters there."

More than one nodded.

"If," Tweed said meditatively. "That's a very big if."

"It starts here, this morning," Dan said sharply. Draining the rest of his brandy he stood up, took the bottle that was on the table, corked it, and then tossed it to one of his staff.

"Gentlemen, I'm putting this riot down and I want your people the hell out of the way."

Dan could see that he had them cornered. It was beyond their control and they knew it.

"What are you going to do?" Tweed asked.

"What should have been done two days ago. I have a brigade forming up right now. I'm deploying them across the width of the island; we will seal every north-south avenue. Then sweep north."

"Why north?" Seymour asked. "The worst is in the southern wards, Five Points."

"Because that's where the money is, you idiot," Tweed interjected. "Save their backsides and we're heroes."

"My men are veterans," Dan continued, "and I'm cutting them loose. They're angry as hell after Union Mills, and I've told them this riot is provoked by rebel agents. At this point they will not stop and they will not be gentle."

No one spoke. The implication was clear.

July 17, 1863
9:00 A.M.

C.S.A. The morning fog was burning off, revealing a slate-gray sky that promised yet more rain.

Taking off his hat, General Lee wiped his brow with a handkerchief. The day was already humid, the air still, warm. Mounted skirmishers rode ahead, fanned out to either side across a front of several hundred yards. A company of cavalry rode behind him, ready to spring forward if there was the slightest indication of trouble. He could see that Jeb was being cautious. During the night there had been several probes by Union cavalry coming out of the city. There was always the chance that a unit could have slipped around the loose cordon of gray-clad troopers.

Cresting a low ridge he could see the forward line, horses tied, men sitting around smoking fires, springing to attention as word leapt ahead of his approach. Orders had been given that there was to be no fanfare, no recognition, but it was hard to contain the troopers that came down to the road, grins lighting their faces, young boys, old men, trim officers snapping to attention at his approach.

"You sleeping in the White House tonight, General, sir?" a wag shouted and a subdued cheer went up. Lee extended a calming hand as he rode past.

"The boys are eager," Jeb offered.

He could see that. Most of them had fresh mounts taken in Pennsylvania; they'd been living off good rations for over a month. They had seen victory and in spite of the painful marching in the rainy fields, they were in high spirits, ready for anything. He knew that if he but whispered a few words, ordering them to form up and charge the fortifications, they would do so without hesitation.

Pressing on, he rode down into a tree-clad hollow, the muddy stream, which for most of the year was most likely nothing more than a brook that a boy could leap, now swollen, dark, coming nearly to Traveler's chest as they plunged across.

Several dozen troopers were at work, fashioning a rough-hewn bridge across the stream out of two logs and heavy planks torn from the side of a nearby barn. An ambulance lay on its side downstream, obviously flipped over when its driver had attempted to ford the torrent.

Traveler, slipping, gained the opposite side of the stream and with a

quick jump took the muddy slope. The skirmishers, moving ahead, had slowed and Jeb nodded.

"We're there," he announced.

Lee nodded and without comment pressed on. Walter fell in by his side, as did Hood and Hotchkiss, the rest of the staff staying back under the canopy of trees.

"We're inside the District of Columbia now," Hotchkiss announced with a hint of ceremony in his voice.

That close, Lee thought and there was a memory of his home, of Arlington. *Not ten miles away now, ten long miles and then it is over. How many hundreds of miles have we marched from Richmond, to Manassas, to Sharpsburg, Fredericksburg, Chancellorsville, Gettysburg, and Union Mills, and now to here?*

All of that, to gain this moment, at this place. One final lunge and it ends it. This one final lunge.

A couple of the scouts ahead stopped, turned, and came cantering back, the rest of the line slowing to a walk then reining in.

A messenger came up, saluting.

"It's ahead, sir, you'll see their line in a minute. Sir, it's rather close."

Lee smiled at the boy's caution. The message was clear, he'd prefer it if the general would stop now.

"I need to see," Lee said softly. "Lead the way, Captain."

The captain saluted and turned his mount, Lee following, with Taylor, Hotchkiss, and Hood following behind.

He could already see the vague outlines of the fortifications, an unnatural straight line, horizontal, cut like a razor's edge a quarter mile away. Gradually it came into clearer view as he reached the forward skirmish line. Most of the men were dismounted, carbines raised, the troopers looking anxiously toward Lee at his approach.

"Sir, would you please dismount?" the captain asked. "They've got plenty of ammunition over there and they like using it."

As if to lend weight to the argument, there was a flash of light from a gun emplacement, followed a couple of seconds later by the whoosh of a shell passing overhead, to detonate a hundred yards behind them.

Lee nodded but did not get off Traveler, who barely flinched as another shell streaked past.

The young captain positioned his mount between Lee and the fort.

Lee smiled.

"Captain, you are blocking my view."

The captain looked to Stuart, who nodded, and the captain moved.

"Sir, if they realize who we are, it means they'll shift troops here," Stuart said.

Lee said nothing, but he knew Stuart was right and, dismounting, he moved down into a shallow ravine, walked up a few dozen paces, and uncased his field glasses.

Stuart and Hood were quickly by his side.

He scanned the fort. It was a significant work, a dozen gun embrasures, what looked to be thirty-pounders, perhaps heavier. He caught glimpses of troops along the parapet, Union soldiers curious, looking over the earthen wall in his direction.

A dull thump echoed and he saw the sparks of a mortar shell lazily rising up, trailing smoke, fuse sputtering. It climbed, seemed to hover nearly overhead, then came plummeting down, striking a hundred yards behind him in a splash of mud, the fuse smothered and going out.

Hotchkiss knelt down by his side.

"Fort Stevens. It always has at least one battery of heavy guns, we're told thirty-pounders, rifled. Also a battery of eight-inch mortars as you can see. Garrisoned also with a regiment of infantry. You can't see them in this mist, but the forts to either flank are within easy gunnery range, enfilading the approaches with at least one hundred-pound Parrott gun in each. Anyone attempting to cross this field will be hit by guns from at least three fortifications."

Lee nodded, stood up looking to the flanks, but the mist concealed the positions.

"The military road just behind the fortifications links all positions and is well maintained, macadamized in parts or corduroyed. They can easily shift significant reinforcements in and move them back and forth to counter any move. I would assume they are doing so now and will bring up additional troops from the center of the city."

Lee focused his field glasses back on Stevens, ignoring another mortar round as it struck fifty yards to the front, this one detonating with a flash just before striking the ground.

"Good gunners," Hood muttered, "cut the fuse right."

"Might I suggest we move," Jeb said, "they've bracketed you, sir."

That caught him. It wasn't "us," it was "you."

He nodded without comment, cased his field glasses, and walked into the hollow. Seconds later a third round whistled in, striking and detonating within yards of where they had been standing.

He looked over at Jeb and smiled.

"Excellent recommendation, General," Lee said.

"They've been firing away since last night, sir. They're garrison troops but well practiced, at least in gunnery." After mounting up they rode a few hundred yards farther on and, crossing the main road, the group reined in again. Lee raised his field glasses once more, scanning the fort, which was half-concealed in the fog.

Ramparts stood at least ten to fifteen feet high, a dry moat, most likely a muddy swamp now with all this rain, six lines of abatis, sharpened stakes ringing the position like a deadly necklace, earthworks running outward, connecting the position to the next fort to the east, a low blockhouse of logs and rough-hewn barriers blocking the road. It was formidable!

A rifle ball hummed dangerously close and then another. One of his escorts cursed and clutched his arm.

"They might have some sharpshooters over there armed with Whitworth rifles," Hotchkiss said. "Sir, I think we should pull back to safety."

Lee reluctantly agreed, and turning Traveler he regained the road and cantered back into the mists. A parting shot from one of the thirty-pounders shrieked overhead.

Near the stream where troopers still labored to build a bridge over the swollen creek, he stopped, Jeb pointing the way to a tarpaulin spread taut in a stand of chestnut trees, a table and chairs beneath.

Dismounting, the group gathered around the table. Hotchkiss reached into his oversized haversack and pulled out a map on rough sketch paper, folding it out on the table.

"I drew this up last night," Hotchkiss said, "after talking to some of Stuart's men and interviewing some locals who claim to be on our side."

"This is Fort Stevens, which you just saw," he said as he traced out the necklace of fortifications that were like beads on a chain embracing the city.

"Are there any weak points at all?" Lee asked.

Even as he spoke and looked at the map, the moment struck him as strange, tragic. This was once his home. He remembered a Washington without fortifications, lush meadows and fields surrounding the city, blistering in the summer but delightful in autumn and early spring.

Hotchkiss shook his head.

"They've covered every approach. Trees and brush cut back in places for nearly two miles to give clear fields of fire and deny concealment. The Virginia side is even worse."

Lee said nothing. He knew Arlington had been turned into a fortified camp. The approach to Alexandria, where the main military railroad yard was located, was an impossible position to storm.

"It has to be here," Lee said softly. "We must stay in Maryland; to cross back over the river and attempt it from the Virginia side is impossible, if for no other reason than the Potomac cannot be forded."

"It will be the same here or over toward Blandensburg or down along the river. The fortifications will be the same."

He looked over at Hood, who was silent, staring at the map.

"General Hood, do you think you can take that fort?"

Hood looked up at him.

"When, sir?"

"By tomorrow."

There was a moment of silence.

"Sir, I'm strung out along twenty miles of road, my men are exhausted. Pettigrew is in the lead, I could have him up by late in the day, but it won't be until midday tomorrow that I can have all my divisions ready. If it should rain again today, sir, I can't even promise that. You saw the roads."

Lee had sympathy for Hood on this. He had indeed seen the roads, the thorough job that the Union forces had done destroying bridges and mill dams from here halfway back to Westminster.

He thought back to just before Gettysburg, the sense of hesitation in his army in spite of their high spirits, the sense that he was not fully in control. Was that setting in again now that the euphoria of victory was wearing thin because of exhaustion and the unrelenting rains? *Am I pushing too hard now, should I wait?*

He stood gazing at the map of the fortifications.

This is the only chance we will ever have, he realized. *We must take it now. I must push the army yet again.*

"It has to be here," Lee said. "To try and maneuver now would be fruitless. They have the interior lines and maintained roads; wherever we shift, they will be in front of us. That and every hour of delay will play to their advantage."

He looked over at Stuart, who nodded.

"We've had half a dozen civilians get through the lines during the night," Stuart announced. "Reinforcements are starting to arrive in Washington from as far away as Charleston. Their newspapers are reporting that as well. The garrison is most likely at twenty-five thousand now; before the week is out, it could be forty thousand or more."

"Then we have to do it now," Lee replied. "Every hour of delay only strengthens them."

"I can't hope to have any artillery support for at least two days," Hood said, his voice pitched low. "They're stuck in the mud from here clear back to Westminster."

"General Hood, the artillery we have will do little if anything against those fortifications."

"So we are to go in without artillery support, sir?"

"Yes, General, without artillery."

"Sir. Respectfully, sir, you know I'm not one to shy away from a fight," and he fell silent, head half-lowered.

Lee looked at him. *I need dissent, I need to listen.* It was listening to Longstreet, the first night at Gettysburg, that had set victory in motion.

"Go on, General Hood, please speak freely, sir."

"Thank you, General. Sir, I have a bad feeling about this one."

Hood looked over to Stuart as if seeking support. Lee followed his gaze and could see Stuart lower his eyes. He was troubled as well.

"Why this bad feeling, General Hood?" Lee asked, his voice pitched softly, almost deferential.

"Sir, we won the most glorious victory of the war little more than two weeks ago, but it came at a terrible price. Pettigrew, who will lead off the assault here, took nearly fifty percent casualties. My other divisions, on average, still are down by twenty percent or more."

"Reinforcements are promised," Lee offered and instantly regretted the statement. It sounded like an attempt at justification. Hood was talking about tomorrow, not what Davis had promised and what most likely would not arrive for weeks.

"Go on, General," Lee said.

"Though well fed these last six weeks, the men are exhausted; many are ill from the weather and the heat. If I go in tomorrow, sir, at best I can muster twenty thousand rifles."

"I am aware of that, sir. The question is, with those twenty thousand, can you take those works?" He pointed back toward the city.

Hood looked around at those gathered, the staff standing deferentially in the background. No general ever wanted to admit that he could not do the task assigned. He took a deep breath.

"I can take the works, sir."

"Good. I will leave the details to you, General. Fort Stevens will be the center of the attack; I need this road to move up our following units. General Longstreet's men will push into the city once you have cleared the way."

The look in Hood's eyes made him pause. Yet again it was rivalry, the sensitivity of who would claim what. He offered a smile.

"General, when we take the White House, you will be at my side."

"It's not that, sir."

"What then?"

"Sir, I will have no command left to march into Washington."

"Sir?"

"Just that, General Lee. I have twenty thousand infantry fit for duty in my divisions. I will lose half of them taking that fort and clearing the way for General Longstreet. The men will be charging straight into thirty-pounders loaded with canister; they throw nearly the same weight as all the guns we faced atop Cemetery Hill two weeks ago. There are some hundred-pounders on that line; a single load of canister from one of those guns can drop half a regiment."

Lee lowered his head, the memory of that debacle still haunting him.

"General Longstreet, sir, has barely twenty thousand under arms as well and, sir, once the outer ring cracks, we might have to fight Washington street by street, clear down to the Naval Yard. I must ask, sir, after that, then what?"

All were silent. Lee looked from one to the other and knew that Gen-

eral Hood had asked the most fundamental question of all. The answer had seemed easy enough two weeks ago; the objective was to destroy the Army of the Potomac, to take it off the field. They had achieved that . . . but still the war continued.

If we take Washington, then what? For over a year he had fought under the assumption that if indeed Washington fell, the war was over, but now he wondered. The thought of capturing Lincoln, of having Lincoln and Davis then meet, like Napoleon and the czar at Tilsit, to talk and to sign a peace, was that realistic?

He rubbed his eyes, picked up a tin cup of coffee someone had set by his side, and sipped from it, gazing at the map, but his mind was elsewhere.

I must keep this army intact. That is what Hood is driving at. If we take Washington but bleed ourselves out, if we have only twenty thousand infantry left, the victory will be a Pyrrhic one. We would be driven from the city and lose Maryland within the month. I must now spend this army wisely. It is all that we have and we cannot form another the way the Union is most likely creating a new one at this very moment.

"General Hood, you were right to ask that, to remind me," Lee said softly, setting down the cup of coffee.

"Our objective is to win this war before autumn. We cannot sustain ourselves at this pace much longer. We must try, however, for Washington. This is the best chance we will ever have to take it."

Hood sighed, then slowly nodded in agreement.

"President Davis will be here within the week. If we can take Washington and present it to him, it will be the fulfillment of the campaign we started a year ago before the gates of Richmond. It will demonstrate to our people, to the North, and to the world that we are a viable nation."

He was silent for a brief moment, then continued.

"But we cannot bleed ourselves to death while doing it."

"Then we attack and pay the price?" Hood asked.

Lee stepped away from the table and walked out from under the awning and back toward the road. The men laboring on the makeshift bridge were still hard at work, struggling to drag the second tree trunk into place. He walked slowly up the slope. The fog was breaking up, swirling coils burning away in the morning heat. The dim outline of Fort Stevens was visible as he reached the top of the low rise.

The ground ahead was clear cut, trees removed; the fields that had once been orderly, planted with corn or wheat, were now weed choked, barren, offering no cover. He could imagine his lines going forward across those fields, the guns of the forts tearing gaping holes into the ranks, the charge hitting the abatis, men tangled up, stopping to cut their way through, stumbling into the moat thick with mud and slime. Even the greenest of troops behind those fortifications would turn it into nothing more than murder, the finest infantry in the world mowed down in a stinking moat by garrison soldiers in spotless uniforms.

He shook his head. Hood was right. His men were too precious for this. Yet he had to do it. If he did not, that in itself would be a victory for the North. Davis would not understand, though that was not his concern at this instant. He had to conceive a victory here, a victory that justified the blood shed at Gettysburg and Union Mills.

He studied the field intently, the open ground free of obstacles, the unfinished dome of the Capitol most likely visible once the fog lifted. It would be lit up with gaslight at night, a beacon, a dream so tantalizingly close, and just beyond that, Arlington and home. *How many nights did I sit on the porch, the boys playing in the front yard—not yet soldiers, one of them a prisoner—the lights of the White House just across the river.*

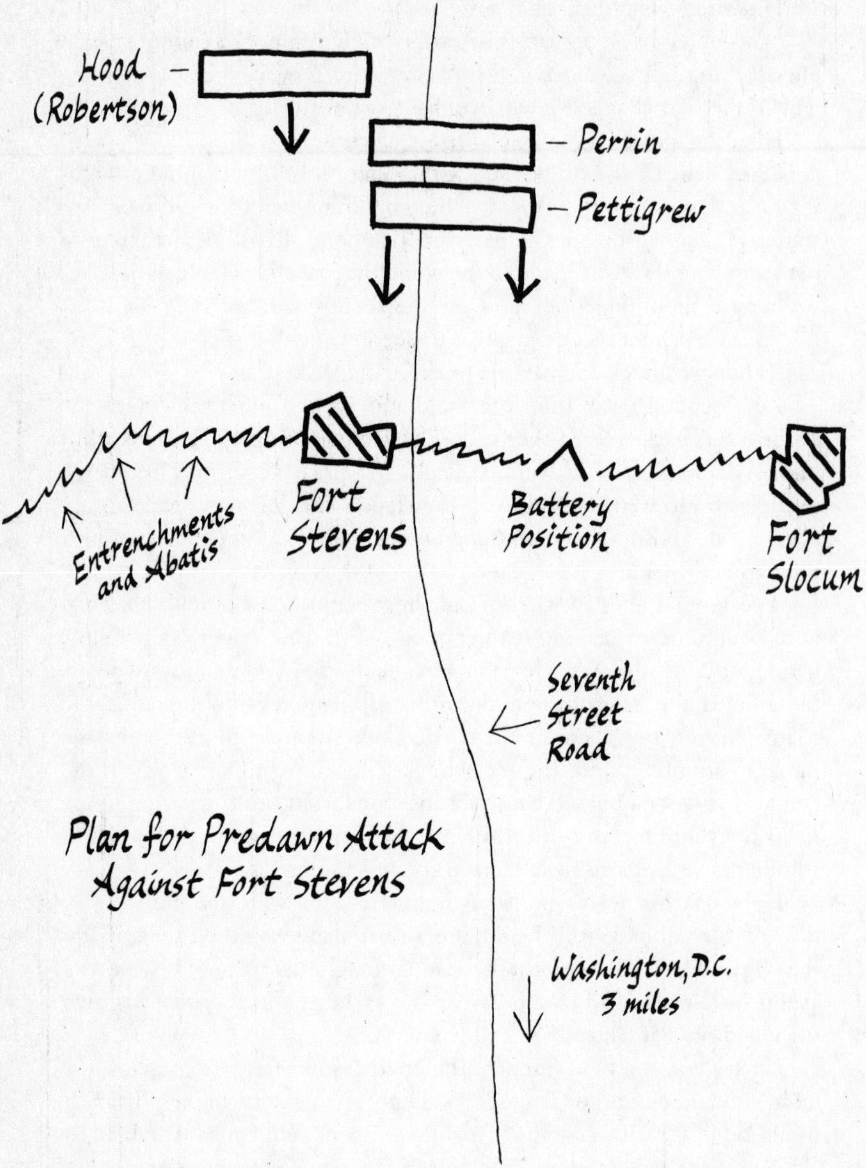

Hood — (Robertson)

— Perrin

— Pettigrew

Entrenchments and Abatis

Fort Stevens

Battery Position

Fort Slocum

Seventh Street Road

Plan for Predawn Attack Against Fort Stevens

Washington, D.C. 3 miles

He stood there and the plan formed at last.

Looking back over his shoulder he saw Hood and Stuart waiting expectantly, the others standing behind them.

He forced a smile.

"We go in at night, gentlemen. That is how we will take it. At night." He smiled as he gave the order.

"At night, with surprise, we'll be into their works before they know it."

Hood and Stuart smiled and, turning, they left him, already giving orders, leaving him alone with his thoughts and dreams.

Chapter Four

July 17, 1863
7:30 P.M.

Gazing out the window of the train as it raced across the broad, open countryside of Ohio, Gen. Ulysses S. Grant found his attention wandering for a moment. He tried to ignore the pounding intensity of the migraine headache that had bedeviled him since last night. But of course nothing would work except for that oblivion from a bottle, which he most definitely could not indulge.

As the train took a gentle curve, heading southeast, long shadows of the cars, cast by the setting sun, reached out across the open fields. The land was rich, the last of the winter wheat being harvested, fields of corn more than waist-high, weeds and honeysuckle engulfing the split-rail fences that bordered the railroad. The train raced past a barn; a farmer and his two boys driving cows in for the evening milking paused, looked up, took off their hats, and waved.

Thoughts drifted back to his own boyhood as he absently rubbed his temples, to the hardscrabble farm not far from here, and his desire to escape its labors, a desire that had taken him to West Point, an institution that glorified a business that would sicken many a butcher. The army had been, at first, an escape, then a burden so intense he had left it. Only this war had brought him back into uniform. And now he was in command.

For a moment his mind wandered across the empty years, the war in

Mexico, the bitter loneliness of California. He impatiently pushed those thoughts aside. A danger to think of that now; self-pity compounded by the headaches was an almost certain first step back to the bottle, and now was not the time, though the temptation was always there.

"What are you thinking, Sam?"

Grant turned and offered a faint smile.

"Nothing much, Elihu, just drifting."

Congressman Elihu Washburne smiled and said nothing.

He was a good friend. Grant knew that. It was through Elihu that he had received his first commission in this war, from a man who was one of the mentors behind the president's rise to power.

Like him, Elihu had come from a farm, up in the bitter cold of Maine. But unlike the Grants, the Washburnes seemed destined from the start for greatness. Five brothers, all of them now in positions of power and influence. One was a general commanding a corps under Sherman, another a captain in the navy, another the governor of Maine.

He envied Elihu for his relaxed, easy air, his nonchalant movement through the halls of power, his urbane manner. He was dressed casually—jacket off, wine-colored vest unbuttoned, linen shirt spotless. Elihu was the type that no matter what the situation would always look and smell clean. And yet he was not a dandy. He had visited Grant during the exhausting winter campaign of the previous year and exclaimed more than once that the rigors of the field were a tonic. He could sit up to dawn with the staff, mount, then spend an entire day visiting units, shaking hands, and like any politician, when he came across constituents, make the most of it, passing out cigars and canvassing for votes with vigor.

As Grant looked over at him he realized yet again that he had a true friend in Elihu, an absolute rarity in the game of politics, where too many congressmen would blow with the wind of newspaper coverage and abandon friendship if doing so got them more votes. Elihu had been the one to back him when there was the falling out with Halleck the year before and Halleck's people had openly spread stories about his drinking. The fact that Elihu was one of the men behind Lincoln was a help, not something he had ever deliberately calculated on . . . but it was a help.

He knew the reasons Elihu was here, riding with him on a train headed east. Elihu was an observer from the White House, sent to evaluate him. That didn't bother him. He was also here as a shepherd, to keep an eye on him and the bottle. The last thing the republic needed now was for their new commander to break down. That didn't bother him either. And finally Elihu was just here as a friend, and that was a pleasure. Once he was fully in command, Grant's nature was such that he would take counsel from no man but the president. But it was good to have Elihu here now.

Though the president had directed that the war would continue no matter what the cost, it was now his job to bring an end to it in the field. Every death, whether it was a death that accomplished something or a death wasted, as so many now were, would be upon his shoulders, and his alone.

As he contemplated this, he reached into his breast pocket, pulled out a battered cigar case, and drew out a Havana. Elihu struck a match on the side of the table that separated them and, nodding a thanks, Grant leaned over and puffed his twelfth cigar of the day to life.

The open window of the car drew out the swirling smoke and flickering bits of flaming ash.

Grant looked around his staff car, actually a railroad president's car that Haupt had "borrowed" for the "emergency." The appointments were rich: red-silk wallpaper, heavy, ornate tables, stuffed leather chairs, and a plush burgundy sofa upon which Ely Parker, a full-blooded Seneca whom he had just "drafted" on to his staff, was fast asleep. He had known Parker casually before the war in Galena. In his mid-thirties, Parker was well educated, a lawyer by training, articulate and a paragon of organization, capable of keeping the vast mountains of paperwork moving smoothly. Behind his back, some of the men ribbed Parker about his Indian blood, claiming he kept Confederate scalps hidden in his haversack. Parker took it good-naturedly, to a point, then his cold gaze shut them down, something Grant admired.

Since leaving Cairo the day before, Parker had not known a moment's rest until Grant finally ordered him to take a break. Within minutes Parker was out, his snoring almost as loud as the rattling of the train as they raced east.

Ornate, cut-glass, coal oil lamps with what looked to be real gold gilding lined the walls of the car; the carpet underneath his feet, also burgundy, had been thick and clean, though tracked dirty now with the constant coming and goings of staff from the other cars.

Elihu had laughed when they first boarded, claiming that the car had a certain look to it. Naively Grant had asked what it looked like, and smiling, Elihu said it reminded him of a bordello in Chicago. That had actually embarrassed Grant. He had never stepped foot in such a place, even during the agonizing loneliness out in California, and though Elihu tried to act sophisticated, Grant knew him well enough to believe that while the man might have been in the lobby of such an establishment, Elihu never went "upstairs."

There was even a private compartment in the front, with a real bed.

He was tempted to try and find a few minuts' solitude there but knew it would be useless, his head throbbing to every beat of the iron wheels. Besides, like many a man who has been in the field for months, he found a soft bed with clean cotton sheets to be uncomfortable, and a reminder as well of other times, when such a bed would be shared.

There had only been a brief moment to spare with Julia before heading east to take up command. She would come along later, and as always the separations from her were an agony. If nothing else, he missed her soothing touch when the headaches came, how she would hold his head in her lap, whisper softly, hour after hour rubbing his brow with a cool, wet cloth until he drifted to sleep.

The door to the privy at the back of the car opened and Herman Haupt stepped out, looking a bit pale.

Elihu chuckled softly.

"Still got it?" the congressman asked.

Haupt nodded grimly as he slipped his jacket back on, not bothering to button it.

"General, if you don't mind, I think our railroad man needs a little Madeira; it's good for his stomach complaint."

Grant nodded, saying nothing. Around his headquarters the custom of asking if a drink was all right had evolved. It was a subtle reminder, as well, that he should think twice before indulging himself.

Haupt at first hesitated as Elihu opened an ornate, inlaid cabinet set against the other wall and pulled out a decanter and two thick crystal goblets. Elihu poured the drinks himself, handing one to Haupt, who sat down by his side, across from Grant.

"Feeling all right, Haupt?" Grant asked.

"It'll pass, sir. I've had worse."

Grant actually smiled, remembering the agony of the army in Mexico, when nearly all the men were down with either dysentery or the flux. More than one man had been reduced to cutting the bottom out of his trousers, so frequent and violent were the attacks, and many a man had died, more than from Mexican bullets. He motioned for Haupt to go ahead and indulge himself with the drink.

Haupt settled back in the leather chair, nodded his thanks to Elihu, and downed half the glass of Madeira. He looked over at Grant.

"How is the headache, sir?"

Most of his staff had learned long ago to never inquire on that subject. His pale features and the cold sweat should be indication enough and it always set his temper on edge. But he indulged Haupt, who was new to working with him and obviously not feeling too well himself.

"It should run its course by tomorrow," Grant said quietly, trying to force a smile.

Grant looked down at the reams of paper piled up on the table between them, accounts from nearly every railroad in the North reporting on available rolling stock, supplies, particularly armaments waiting at factories for pickup, locations of nearly every garrison, training depot, and recruiting station from Kansas City to Bangor.

They'd gone over it for hours, and the sheer waste was appalling. Well over a hundred thousand troops were scattered in remote posts and garrisons up north, or wasted on meaningless fronts. Many of these would not be ready for combat, having lived a soft life for too long, but they could still serve a better function than the one they now occupied, and they'd learn combat soon enough.

Elihu had pointed out to him how damn near every governor would howl when their pet units were pulled into federal service, men occupying forts in Boston Harbor, watching supplies in Cleveland, guarding river crossings in Iowa. The men who had these assignments usually had some friends in politics who had arranged a safe berth for them to sit out the war in comfort.

When Parker awoke, he'd pick up the writing of those letters that would set governors howling throughout the North.

Lincoln had tasked him to end the war and now, after two futile years of watching the stupidity, waste, and outright corruption, he would change anything that kept the Union from winning the war.

For the first couple of days after receiving notice from Lincoln, he had been overwhelmed by the responsibility of it all. For two years the republic had waged war to heal itself, to re-create a single nation, but had done so at cross-purposes with itself, and often to its own detriment.

McClellan had been given the best chance to do so the previous year, marshaling close to two hundred thousand men in Virginia and Washington, then had wasted his supreme effort, with only a fraction of those men ever effectively engaged before Richmond.

The president had not helped, hobbling McClellan with orders to keep an entire army stationed near Washington. Yet it had gone far beyond that. Officers had plotted against each other, jockeying for power. Congress had played its usual games of maneuvering and deal-making, even while men died in the swamps below Richmond. Never had there been a single unifying purpose, a single will shaping the republic to this war. A war that had to be fought with brutal, direct efficiency.

He had sensed from the very beginning that this war would be profoundly different from any other in history. After the bloody battle at

Shiloh he had often talked about it with Sherman, late at night . . . that
Sherman who had been called mad when he declared that in the West
alone a quarter of a million men would be needed. A poet named Whit-
man, whom Julia would often read aloud and whom he hoped someday to
meet, had sung of it, of a sprawling, muscular, urban nation of factories,
and riches undreamed of. In some ways, like the poet's, his own vision
was of a republic stirring, rising, waging a war not of glory, for he loathed
that concept, but doing it grimly and efficiently and relentlessly until the
job was done.

Here was the new strength, the new kind of war of men and machines
to be forged and then used. He had seen it clearly the night Porter ran his
fleet down below Vicksburg. Dozens of ships, sparks snapping from boilers, heavy guns firing, shot bouncing off armor, the sky afire, passing un-
harmed below the Confederate fortifications powerless to stop them.
This was the final extension of power created in the smoke-filled factories
of Albany, Cleveland, Boston, and New York, directed by men who but a
year before were civilians, drawn from factories, fields, countinghouses,
and forests to see it through.

He sat back, rubbing his forehead, looking down at the reports, and
then shifted his gaze back out the window, puffing meditatively on his cigar, a shower of ashes cascading down the front of his jacket.

The troops stationed in major cities, however, would have to wait.
The dispatches picked up early in the afternoon as they stopped for wood
and water at Dayton were grim. All telegraph lines out of New York City
had been cut, but indications were that the entire city was in anarchy. A
New Jersey newspaper had claimed that the entire lower part of Manhattan was engulfed in flames, and ferryboats, packed with panic-stricken
civilians, were docking in Jersey City reporting that insurgent rioters had
taken the city.

Riots were reported in Philadelphia and Cincinnati as well, and troops
in every other city across the North were on alert. The troops deployed to
suppress or prevent rioting would have to be held in place for now, and
that thought filled him with frustration.

The train slowed as it approached a sharp curve, and dropped down
into a narrow valley to rattle across a trestle bridge. There was a glimpse,
for a couple of seconds, of half a dozen tents, troops gathered in formation
as if waiting for review, the men saluting as the train raced over the
bridge.

Here was yet more waste, but until the movement of troops and
equipment from Cairo to Harrisburg was completed, every bridge on this
vital line had to be guarded, especially here in Ohio and Indiana, where

rumors abounded of Copperhead conspiracies and even of Confederate raiders coming up from Kentucky.

This was the core of the problem. Where could he pull troops out, and yet at the same time maintain some level of safety? The motley-looking garrison on the bridge could do precious little if a real force of raiders showed up, but they were still a deterrent against the lone bridge burner or a drunken mob. It was the problem that had bedeviled the Union cause since the first days of the war, exasperated by panicky governors or, worse, selfish governors concerned only with their own state even if it hurt the Union. The thirty men on that bridge, multiplied a thousand times, could be yet another corps facing Lee.

His frustration was compounded by the entire system of mobilization, of state governors responsible for recruiting troops and only then transferring them over to the federal government. The regiments recruited for three years were obviously destined for the front, but for each of them created, there would usually be a three-month regiment that never left their state capital, and nine-month regiments that barely had time to learn their jobs before being demobilized.

Everyone knew the three-month regiments were a farce, a dodge for those who had political connections to avoid service yet wanted to be able to thump their chests and claim they had served. The hundreds of thousands of men who so briefly wore the blue uniform were worse than useless—in fact, a drain on the entire system, taking uniforms, rifles, rations, and pay, while lounging about in garrisons as far north as the Canadian border.

He smiled grimly at the thought of the reaction that would come when those men were indeed called upon to serve.

Though he had never put much stock in the idea when it was first proposed, he found that now, in this crisis, colored troops might very well have a role to play, and he looked back at the pile of papers spilling off the desk, remembering the report stating that enough colored men for an entire division would soon be mobilized out of the northeast and Ohio. He looked back over at Parker, still asleep. Once he was awake, a message would have to be sent to the training center in Philadelphia. A division was a division and to hell with its color, as long as it would fight.

And thus he thought and plotted, a vision of the vast change that an industrial age was creating, a new concept of war, wherein the application of mass upon a single point would transcend the old vision of the past, of lone armies led by an inspired genius fighting but for an afternoon on sunlit fields to decide the fate of nations. He knew that many would claim that this was unfair, but he had nothing but contempt for those who thought thus and had never seen a battlefield the day after the guns fell silent. The job of war was to achieve victory, and in so doing end the slaughter as quickly as possible. How it was achieved, still within the parameters of some basic humanity, was secondary to the final act, the creation of that victory no matter what the cost or how long it took.

Haupt drained the rest of his Madeira and looked out the window. The shadows were gone now, replaced by a deepening twilight. Already the air drifting in through the open window was cooler, a welcomed relief from the hot, blistering day spent crossing the open farmlands of Indiana and Ohio.

"We should be passing through the station in Columbus in about ten minutes," Haupt announced.

Grant said nothing.

Elihu motioned for Haupt to have another glass, and the general, at first reluctant, surrendered and accepted the offer. Reaching into his own breast pocket, he produced a slightly bent cigar and looked at it.

"Have one of mine," Grant offered and Haupt smiled and thanked him.

They were passing the outer edge of the city, transitioning from open farmland to smaller fields of vegetables, a cluster of homes around a church, a blacksmith shop with sparks swirling up into the evening air, several boys, riding bareback astride a heavy plow horse, waving at the train as it passed.

No sign of war here, no burned-out villages, no rotting abandoned farms with bloated bodies lying in the fields—all was neat, orderly, filled with prosperity.

More homes now, streetlights, a large warehouse, a siding packed with cars loaded down with the freshly harvested wheat, civilians out for an evening stroll, the distant sound of a band, growing louder as a shudder from the brakes ran through the train, its bell ringing, whistle sounding.

Elihu leaned out the window for a second to look and ducked back in, grinning.

"Welcoming committee," he announced.

Grant shook his head and said nothing, looking over at Haupt.

"We're scheduled to keep right on rolling," Haupt said, "just slow to pick up dispatches."

Grant offered a smile of thanks. The last thing he wanted now was a waste of time shaking hands, offering some poor excuse for a speech, and then listening to the endless replies, with every city councilman ready to tell him how to win the war. Other generals, he knew, basked in this.

"Too much speechifying and not enough fighting," Sherman had grumbled to him once when they were caught at such an affair, and the memory of it made him grin, forgetting the headache for a moment.

Sherman was furious at being left behind, swearing up a storm right till the moment he had left. But Sherman knew better than anyone that the decision was the right one, and would throw himself into the task of Commander of the western theater with a mad passion to see it through and not let his friend down. It would have been fine to see Sherman by his side, commanding a corps, but far better to have him out west, commanding an army, cleaning up what was left of resistance along the Mississippi and then, when the time was right, heading east into Tennessee and Georgia.

Three- and four-story buildings now crowded in to either side of the tracks, a rail yard opening out to the right, filled with dozens of lattice-like boxcars. Half a dozen locomotives ready to pull trains were in the yard, several of them wreathed in smoke. Haupt pointed them out, mentioning quietly that they were most likely ladened with rations, pork, cattle, freshly made hardtack, ready to be shipped east. In a nearby stockyard several hundred horses were waiting to be loaded.

What Lee would give for this one depot, he thought. *Just for those half dozen locomotives, the supplies, and an open track to move them on.*

A mix of smells wafted in, of the barnyard and steam, oil, wood, and coal smoke.

The whistle of their train sounded again, louder, the engineer playing it, easing it in and out so that it almost seemed to carry a tune, counterpointing the swelling noise of the band.

Haupt stood up, buttoning his uniform jacket, went to the rear of the car, paused, and looked back at Grant.

"Sir, I suspect there's a crowd of well-wishers out there. Do you want to greet them?"

Grant looked at Elihu and shook his head.

"In spite of the press reports that give my location by the minute, this move is supposed to be secret," he announced.

Elihu grinned and said nothing, pouring another glass of Madeira for himself. He hesitated, then poured half a glass for Grant.

"It'll help with the headache, General."

Grant took the glass and downed it in two gulps. It was sticky, far too sweet, but he welcomed it and nodded his thanks.

The train drifted into the station, its platform and the grounds around it packed with a band, dignitaries—several wearing ridiculous red, white, and blue sashes—a line of troops at attention, and, spilling to either side, a crowd of several hundred or more.

He looked back and saw Haupt leaning off the side of the back platform, reaching out to grab a satchel handed up by the stationmaster, and then waving.

The engineer of their train, seeing Haupt's signal, blasted his whistle again; there was a lurch as he poured in steam, and the train edged forward, rapidly picking up speed.

Grant, sitting in the shadows of the car, did not even give an acknowledgment as they sped up, pulling out of the station, the sound of the band receding, the music falling apart as musicians lost their beat in the confusion. Several of the well-wishers ran alongside the train, waving valiantly. Catching sight of several boys racing to keep up, Grant finally waved back. The boys shouted exuberantly.

Rattling and swaying, the car passed over a switch, more stockyards in the shadows, sidings packed with westbound trains waiting for the express to pass. Turning into a curve, the station was lost to view.

It never ceased to amaze him how so many, even now, thought war was a celebration, a party, a time for speeches and bands. They should have been at Chapultepec, Shiloh, or in the stinking trenches before Vicksburg. That would have disabused them soon enough.

Haupt sat down again at the table and pulled open the small canvas bag snatched from the stationmaster. Twenty or more telegrams, simply marked "Grant" on the envelopes, spilled out.

Grant sighed as he looked at the stack of papers and gazed over at Parker, who had slept through the entire commotion. It was just about time to wake him up.

There was also a copy of the Columbus *Gazette* and Haupt opened it up.

"Sir, look at this," Haupt said. Grant looked down at the paper but the car was dark. Elihu struck another match, stood up, and lit a coal oil lamp, which flared to life, golden shadows bobbing and weaving as the train raced on.

"Lee Sighted at Washington," a headline in the upper-left corner announced.

"Panic in Capital," a second headline declared in the center of the paper.

Grant picked the paper up and scanned it. The report was from Port Deposit, a ferry crossing on the north bank of the Susquehanna in Maryland, dated five in the afternoon. It was the nearest telegraph station to Washington in operation. Most likely the dispatch had been run up from Washington by a fast courier boat.

"It states that General Lee, escorted by Jeb Stuart and numerous staff, was sighted in front of Fort Stevens this morning," Grant said, looking back up at Elihu as he put the paper down.

"So he's there," Elihu replied after a moment's pause.

"Of course he's there. That's what he has to do."

He looked away for a moment.

"That's what I would do."

He continued to look out the window, headache forgotten for the moment.

"The president said he'd stay in the city no matter what," Elihu said.

"He has no other choice now. I just wish I had someone in command there other than Heintzelman."

Neither Haupt nor Elihu replied.

The headache did seem to be fading. Whether it was the glass of Madeira or the newspaper, he wasn't sure.

"It's right where I want him now," Grant said softly.

"Who, sir?" Haupt asked.

"Why, Lee, of course."

In Front of Fort Stevens, D.C.

July 17, 1863
10:00 P.M.

C.S.A. "Sergeant, the regiment will form over here in column by companies."

Sgt. Maj. George Hazner, of the Fourteenth South Carolina, Scales's brigade, Pender's, now Perrin's division, saw the bobbing circle of lantern light and pushed his way through the confusion, shouting for his men to follow his lead. Colonel Brown pointed the way and Hazner saluted without comment.

"Remember, Sergeant, keep the men quiet; I'm going over to get some information and will call you when I'm back. Let the men fall out, in position. No fires and stay in place."

Passing along the colonel's orders, Hazner watched with a critical eye as the small regiment staggered off the road and out into the cornfield.

Decimated at Gettysburg and again at Union Mills, the Fourteenth was a shadow of its former self, barely three hundred men under arms. After Union Mills the colonel had promoted him to sergeant major of the regiment, to fill one of the many gaps, a position he didn't really want since it kept him with the color company in battle, a decidedly unhealthy place to be. As for the increase in pay, it didn't really matter, it was in Confederate money anyhow and that kept buying less and less.

Hazner shifted the wad of tobacco in his mouth, nodded, and watched as Brown disappeared into the mist that was beginning to rise up from the damp ground.

The day had been hot, humid, fortunately without rain. The march, a nightmare. The road was a mad confusion of troops, all funneling down this one pike, which had been chewed apart by the passage of the army, so that the macadamized surface was all broken up, turning into a gummy, white soup.

Every bridge was down, replaced in some cases with roughshod affairs of beams and planking torn off barns, but in several cases the men simply forded through the torrent. At the last fording, just at twilight, a drummer boy had been swept away, and then tangled under a log, where he had drowned before his comrades could pull him out.

Hell of an irony, to survive Gettysburg and Union Mills, and then die in some no-name creek by pure bad luck.

He had no idea where the hell they were, where they were going, or what was coming, though he did have some strong suspicions.

The regiment was drawing itself up in a trampled-down field of corn, the rest of the brigade falling in around them, deploying out into line of regiments in company front. All around him he could hear murmuring, swearing, the muddy, slippery sound of shoes getting half sucked off in the gluey ground, stalks of chest-high corn getting knocked down.

Some stars were out, and by their dim glow he could barely catch the silhouette of their regimental flag being held aloft, marking the front of the column.

"Where's H Company?"

It was a lieutenant. He recognized the voice, Maury Hurt from H Company, wounded at Gettysburg but still in the ranks, arm in a sling.

"Back of the column, sir."

"Hazner, that you?"

"Yes, sir, Lieutenant."

Hurt drew closer, a match was struck, and Hurt puffed a half-smoked cigar to light, his drawn face briefly illuminated in the glow.

"I think your company is forming up behind us, sir."

"Thanks, Hazner."

He hesitated for a second. "Sergeant, do you know what the hell is going on?"

"Damned if I know, sir, but from the looks of it, I'd say we're forming up for an attack."

"Sure looks that way."

"But on what?"

Hazner looked around at the confusion, the dim outline of a column continuing forward on the road they had just filed off.

"I think it must be Washington, sir. Heard a cavalry trooper pass by a while ago, claiming he'd seen the dome of the Capitol up ahead."

He didn't need to add that since late in the afternoon everyone had been hearing artillery fire as well, some experts proclaiming that it had a deeper thump to it, meaning heavy guns.

The cigar tip glowed and Hazner looked at it longingly. One thing the Army of Northern Virginia had been well supplied with was tobacco, but they had long ago disconnected from their supply lines back to Virginia and the coveted weed was now in high demand. The plug he had been chewing on was his last and he had been working it all day.

As if sensing his desire, Hurt took the cigar out of his mouth and offered a puff. The end was chewed, soggy, but Hazner gladly accepted and took a long, deep drag, inhaling the smoke so that his head swam for a moment.

He offered it back.

"Too bad about Major Williamson. I knew he was your friend."

"Thanks," was all that Hazner could say.

The memory was still strong, the final moments of the battle before Union Mills, that last look at Williamson and then the ghastly impact of a minié ball shattering his skull. He had died wordlessly, not a sound, just slumping backward into the trench.

He didn't even know where John was buried. They had advanced, leaving their dead and wounded behind. Before moving out, he'd gone through John's pockets and found his diary. It was in his haversack now. He had been debating ever since whether to send it home or just simply burn it. The revelations about his comrade's fears, his failing of belief in the cause, even his desire for his fiancée—Hazner just didn't know how to react to it all.

Writing was something special. His friend had the gift for it. After all, he was the son of a judge, educated, had even gone to college. Words, written words came easy to him. Writing—for Hazner that was a hard task, to be used simply to tell the folks back home you were all right, maybe say how much you love them, but that should be it. To go on for pages about being afraid, confused, somehow it just didn't seem right.

Even as he thought about it, his hand drifted to his haversack and the bulk of the diary inside, its cover stained with dry blood that had spilled onto it from Williamson's gaping wound.

"You write to his folks yet?" Hurt asked and the question startled him, as if the lieutenant were reading his mind.

George shook his head.

"I ain't got the hand for it."

"I'll help you if you want. The judge needs to hear his son died valiantly, facing the enemy."

"Yes, something like that."

Hurt shifted comfortably, looking about.

"Think we go in tonight?"

"Sure looks like it. Column by companies usually don't mean we're settling down for the night."

The cigar tip glowed again.

"By God, if this is Washington, tomorrow night we'll be eating oysters, drinking wine, smoking some damn good cigars, and the war will be over. Should be back home in time for harvest."

"If we break through. Word is they've got fortifications all around the city like none we've ever seen."

"They're beat, Hazner. Beat, I tell you. You saw them run at Union Mills."

"Yes, sir. I seen them run."

He said the words quietly, not reveling in it the way Hurt did. And for an instant he wondered if the jitters Williamson had were in some way transferred now to him through the diary he was carrying.

"Hazner, company officers' call. Pass the word."

George turned to see Colonel Brown running back. He offered a hurried salute to the lieutenant and then passed through the ranks, men looking at him as he pushed through the formed lines, some asking what he knew, for Hazner was always one who knew what was going on.

He ignored them, quickly going back through the lines, letting the few company captains know the colonel wanted them. Most of the companies were commanded by young lieutenants, boys filled with ardent dreams of glory. They usually didn't last long.

He followed the officers back up to the front of the column where the colonel stood, holding a lantern but keeping it hooded with his cloak, the regimental color-bearer standing next to him, the flag marking the commander.

The men gathered around. As regimental sergeant major, Hazner knew he was now part of the group, so he edged his way in.

Brown took off his hat and wiped his brow on the back of a sleeve.

"We're in front of Washington," he began. "The outer line of fortifications is less than two miles ahead on this road."

"I knew it," one of the men said, a touch of glee in his voice.

"We go in two hours before dawn."

The group fell silent.

"We're the second wave. Pettigrew's division is in the lead, they're already filing into position ahead of us. At one in the morning," he hesitated, opening his watch and holding the lantern up to check, "three hours from now, we move to the forward position in a streambed, six hundred yards short of the enemy lines."

"A night attack, sir?" someone whispered, the surprise in his voice evident.

"General Scales said that General Lee decided it this morning. He wishes to spare us unnecessary losses."

"We don't know this ground at all, sir," the questioner replied.

"Damn it, Jones, I know that. Now shut the hell up and listen to orders."

No one spoke.

"Each regiment will have a guide from the cavalry. They've been occupying this ground since yesterday and know their way around. The men are to move in absolute silence. I want every man checked to make sure his musket is not capped. Canteens to be kept full and secured with straps under the belt. Tin cups and anything else that might rattle to be left behind. Again, we must have absolute silence."

He looked around and the men nodded.

"If some damn fool drops a musket and it goes off, I'll run him through and come looking for you later. General Scales made that clear to me. No talking, not even a whisper. Absolute silence.

"As I said, Pettigrew will be in the lead. They will move out at exactly three and storm the enemy line. We are to be in reserve to follow up, or lend support. Once the line is broken, Hood's division will follow through and expand the break. Longstreet's entire corps is behind us and will be up by early morning. They will exploit the break and then move into the city."

He hesitated.

"Pettigrew's division will face an open field of nearly six hundred yards. There are several rows of abatis, then a moat, which is believed to be at least twenty feet wide and ten feet deep. The fort dominating the position has earth walls ten to fifteen feet high above the moat and is believed to hold a battery of heavy thirty-pounders, mortars, a regiment of at least a thousand infantry, and most likely additional artillery support. It covers an acre of ground. Enfilading fire will hit from forts of similar dimensions to either flank.

"Beyond the fort is a well-paved road from the city and a military road that runs inside the enemy lines. We must assume the line will be heavily manned. The attack will go in silently, without any bombardment. All is dependent on stealth and gaining the wall of the fort before the enemy is alerted."

There was a long silence. Hazner looked around. By the glow of the single lantern he saw that some men, especially the younger officers, were eager, whispering among themselves, but the older men were silent.

"Gentlemen, I will tell you my honest opinion. Darkness or not, Pettigrew's boys will get torn apart. It will be our job then to follow through, take the fort, and open the road up to the city.

"I know we've never done a night attack before, gentlemen. It's unheard of. Let's trust in General Lee's leadership as we always have and all will be well. Gentlemen, I promise you that by the end of tomorrow the war will be over. We will march down Pennsylvania Avenue to the White House and throw that slave-loving bastard out and hang him from the nearest tree."

The men knew better than to give a cheer but there was a bit of bracing, a few backslaps and nods.

"Now go back to your men. Brief them on what's coming, then get them to settle down and try to get a little sleep. That's all."

The group broke up and headed back to their companies. Brown turned away, setting the lantern on the ground. It was a praying army and Hazner was not surprised when Brown went down on his knees and lowered his head.

He stepped back respectfully and looked at the color-bearer, who had returned to his comrades, the men gathering around him to hear the news.

All was shadows and rising mist, lending a ghostlike quality to the world around him. He heard muffled talk, some laughter, but not much. These men, even at eighteen, were no longer boys. They had charged at Gettysburg little more than two weeks ago, and held the line through the long, bitter day at Union Mills. They were tired, they had seen far too much, and now they would see more. They knew that they were being called upon once more, for but one more effort, a supreme effort.

One more effort. But one more and it is over. The Yankee capital just one battle away and then the war would be over.

Reaching into his haversack, Sergeant Hazner touched the journal of his old friend, dead at Union Mills. He sat down on the damp, muddy ground, leaned back, and tried to get a few minutes' sleep . . . but sleep came hard that night.

Chapter Five

The White House

July 18, 1863
2:00 A.M.

"Mr. President, General Heintzelman is here."

From his desk piled high with papers, Lincoln looked up to his secretary, Hay, who stood in the doorway. The exhaustion on Hay's face was obvious; in the glare of gaslight he looked more like a ghost than a young man, his tie and collar off, a clear sign that he was about ready to collapse.

"Thank you, Mr. Hay. Now listen to your president, go in the next room and get some sleep."

Hay, who normally would have protested, actually nodded in agreement and closed the door behind the general.

Heintzelman, who was older than the president, stood to attention. His hat was off, under his arm, wisps of gray hair plastered to his skull with sweat. His eyes were dark, almost hollow; the man was breathing heavy and, like everyone else, obviously exhausted as well.

Lincoln stood up and motioned the general to take a seat, and Heintzelman gladly complied, letting out an audible sigh as he settled into the high-backed leather chair.

"Your report, sir," Lincoln prompted, and Heintzelman fumbled to his breast pocket for his spectacles and then started to open a sheaf of papers.

"In your own words, General," Lincoln said patiently.

Heintzelman cleared his throat nervously and, though he wasn't reading, adjusted his spectacles yet again.

"Will they attack?" Lincoln finally prompted, his own tiredness causing his patience to wear thin with Heintzelman's fumbling nature.

"Oh, most assuredly, sir," Heintzelman replied. "There is no doubt of that now. We have enough reports of Lee's army coming straight at us. It is confirmed without a doubt that Lee was indeed scouting our lines personally this morning. A prisoner and a deserter corroborated that information. We know that there are at least four brigades of rebel cavalry encircling our northern front, and we had sure sightings of infantry as well. A civilian of good quality, a Union man who was vouched for by his congressman, managed to get through to our lines and reported that the roads coming down from the north are simply packed with infantry. He reported crossing through a column of Hood's corps on the Seventh Street Road, about five miles outside the District of Columbia. They should be forming up to attack shortly after dawn."

"How did he get through?"

"He acted feebleminded."

Lincoln actually smiled at that one. *So we are dependent on reports from civilians acting feebleminded. What next?*

"The question confronting us then is when and where? Can you answer that for me? Did our feebleminded friend find that out, too?"

Heintzelman cleared his throat.

"I would judge it to be Fort Stevens, sometime later today."

"You're certain?"

"Mr. President, one versed in the military arts can make certain, how shall we say, projections, but never an assumption that is foolproof."

The president turned to look at the general in command of the Washington garrison. He felt nothing but exasperation at this moment. He had dealt with Heintzelman for months, ever since he was, for all practical purposes, relieved of field command and sent back to the safety of the capital's defenses. A crony of McClellan, he had been proven incompetent as a field commander, and thus the reward of this posting. Now the man was clearly rattled.

Lincoln had to admit though that Heintzelman had a good engineer's eye and had thrown himself with vigor into the task of enhancing the already formidable defenses of the city. The military road had been improved, turned into a virtual highway. Additional lines of entrenchments were dug, moats deepened, fields of fire cleared, rows of abatis set in place, and ammunition stockpiled. In that respect Heintzelman had done his work well. Heintzelman had often boasted to the newspapers and anyone else who would listen that he wished Lee and his army would show up for a fight, for surely they would dash themselves to pieces on his fortifications.

His wish had been answered, and like many a boaster, when confronted with reality, he was now having serious second thoughts.

"Fort Stevens then, later today?" Lincoln pressed.

Heintzelman paused and then finally nodded in agreement.

"And your preparations?"

"I've placed one of my better units, the First Maine Heavy Artillery, in that fort, supported by the First New York Heavy Artillery. Well over two thousand men. Two additional regiments are into the entrenchments to either flank, and garrisons are manned in the neighboring forts."

"Garrison troops though."

"All the men with fighting experience were sent out of here long ago, Mr. President."

He had looked over the regimental reports yet again, only this evening. Though the information was not public, most of the regiments in Washington had taken far more casualties from "Cupid's disease" than from any enemy bullets. Most had never even heard a shot fired, except on the practice range. They were well drilled, and looked smart, as garrison troops of the capital were expected to look. But the question was, Could they stand up to Lee's veterans? He knew that no matter how much he pressed on this question, neither Heintzelman, nor, for that matter, anyone else truly knew the answer. But they were about to find out.

Lincoln nodded.

"Reserves?"

Heintzelman shook his head wearily.

"Not many, sir. A brigade deployed just north of the Capitol, which I'll move up once Lee's intentions are clear. We have to maintain the entire line. Their cavalry have been probing all along the front since yesterday. I can't strip any more men out to place in reserve."

"But if they break through, General, the rest of the line will be meaningless."

"If I strip too many men out and the attack on Fort Stevens proves to be nothing but a feint, while Lee is in fact shifting to one flank or the other, we will be broken anyhow."

Lincoln turned to look out the window. The guard around the White House had been increased; the grounds of the executive mansion were carpeted with tents, most of the men asleep but many standing uneasily in the mist, gathered around open fires. Out on Pennsylvania Avenue two batteries of light guns were drawn up, horses hitched to limbers, ready to move.

Always it was about what Lee would do. Though Heintzelman had declared that the attack would strike at Fort Stevens, well over eighty percent of their strength still manned lines along thirty miles of front. The city could fall and most of them would likely never fire a shot.

And yet the general was right. To abandon parts of the position would leave them open, the city being then taken without a fight. It was, he realized, the classic problem of defense, to have to man all positions while the attacker could choose the time and place to strike.

"Any word on reinforcements, sir?" Heintzelman asked.

"Two transports moving up from the Carolinas came into Chesapeake Bay yesterday before dark. No word on how many men they are carrying."

It was beyond hope to think that the vanguard of the force could already be arriving. Several thousand had come in via transport from Wilmington and Philadelphia, all of them ninety-day militia. Maybe they would fight, maybe not. It was the troops from South Carolina, men with hardened battle experience, that he wanted.

So it will be today, he thought, still looking out the window, *and the reinforcements are still not in.*

Of course it had to be. Lee had only this one chance to take the city. Reinforcements were indeed racing in from Charleston, Philadelphia, even Boston. Grant was coming east with his army and additional troops were being called in from as far as New Orleans.

It was a race for time for both sides. It was hard to envision that today the city might fall, but he had to brace himself for that very prospect. Gideon Welles had been in earlier in the evening, yet again urging him to prepare to evacuate to an ironclad tied up at the Anacostia Naval Yard, or at least to send his wife and son there. Welles had reported, in confidence, that a number of senators and two members of the Cabinet had already been down to the yard to demand passage out the moment the attack started.

He had not bothered to ask who they were and he wondered if Seward or Chase had been one of the two. Most likely. After all, to be a senator or Cabinet member usually meant to be a survivor. He had already sent Vice President Blaine out of the city, on the pretext of attending a recruiting rally in his home state of Maine. It would be like Seward though, who still dreamed of higher office, to get out and then somehow try to declare himself in charge if Washington fell and the president was taken or killed.

If they did bolt when the first gun was fired, it would trigger a panic. He thought about rats abandoning a sinking ship, almost uttered the sentiment in front of Welles, but thought it too cruel. It was Welles who then said the same words with a grin.

"So should I abandon my own ship?" he had then replied and Welles, ashamed, lowered his head.

That had ended the conversation.

And now it was Heintzelman who bore the responsibility, and looking at him, he realized that like so many of his generals, the task exceeded the man. Heintzelman should have been out, throughout the day, boosting morale, projecting confidence, being seen by his men and by the populace, rather than holed up in the war office and then coming here at two in the morning, expressing doubts.

It was too late now to change this command. He had to ride this horse to the end of the race.

"General, get some sleep. It will be a long day," Lincoln said, the dismissal in his voice obvious.

Heintzelman stood up and bowed slightly.

"Yes, sir."

"And, General."

"Sir?"

"This city will not fall. I am depending on you for that. We will fight for it street by street if need be. If we lose Fort Stevens, every man is to fall back into the city, barricade the streets, take to the houses, and then fight. I will not run from them. Do you understand that? I will stay here to the end. I would rather see the Capitol and this house burned in smoking ruins and ashes than that they should be tamely and abjectly captured."

Heintzelman looked at him wide-eyed.

"Sir, I understand the secretary of the navy has suggested that you remove yourself and your family to the naval yard."

"I will not do that, sir," Lincoln snapped, and the tone of his voice rose to a high tenor, nearly breaking.

"That would be," he hesitated and then said it, "that would be one hell of a statement to our men out there. To ask them to fight while I hide. I will not withdraw, I will not leave. At the end of the day, sir, either you or General Lee will find me in this building. Do I make myself clear to you, sir?"

"Yes, Mr. President."

"Fine, now get some sleep and then see to your duties."

Heintzelman bowed again, put his hat on, and left the room, closing the door behind him. Lincoln watched him go, and then waited. After a minute the door did not open. Hay was asleep, and there were no more callers. He sighed with relief.

He went back to the window and gazed out. Then on impulse he left the room and walked down the darkened stairs. The White House was quiet, all were asleep except for a black man who looked up expectantly at his approach. It was Jim, one of the White House servants.

"Good morning, Mr. President."

"Morning, Jim."

"A cup of coffee, sir? I have a fresh pot brewing in the kitchen. Maybe a scrambled egg and some fresh ham?"

"No, thank you, Jim. Just want to go outside for a walk."

He stepped past Jim.

"Ah, Mr. President?"

Surprised, he turned back. Jim was standing there, nervous, waiting, a look almost of mortification on his face over this breach of White House protocol.

"Go on, Jim. What is it?"

"Sir. Well, me—I mean the others here and me—we were wondering."

"About what, Jim?"

"If the rebs take the city, sir. What should we do?"

"They won't, Jim."

"I know that, sir. But we've been hearing that the rebs are rounding up colored folk, sending them down south to be sold back to slavery."

He had heard the reports as well, there was no sense in lying about it.

"Yes, Jim, I have heard the same thing."

Jim looked at him expectantly and for an instant he felt an infinite weariness. Here was yet someone else looking for reassurance and he felt as if the well was empty. He looked down at the floor.

"Sir. We here, the colored men who work here that is. We want to fight."

Lincoln looked back up and into the man's eyes.

"What do you mean, Jim?"

"Just that, sir. Myself, Williams, Old Bob, the other men. We plan to fight if they come."

"Jim, how old are you?"

"Nearly sixty, as near as I can reckon. No one ever told me for sure when I was born. My mother said she worked for Mr. Jefferson when I was born. I started working here the year the British burned it down. Helped to plaster the new walls, covering over the scorched ones."

Lincoln could not help but smile, awed at this bit of history living with him. He had never taken notice of Jim, who had quietly served him for two years and never once had he taken the time to talk to him, to find out more of who he was, and all that he had seen. The realization made him uncomfortable and he wondered, if Jim were white, would that conversation have come, the way it usually did, for he loved talking with working people, finding out their stories, driven in part by the instinct of a politician who through such conversations won the votes, one at a time, but also out of his genuine love for and curiosity about common men.

Jim was well-spoken, articulate, his English perhaps even better than his own, which was still mocked by effete Easterners.

"So you've worked here for nearly fifty years?"

"Yes, sir. Every president since Mr. Madison. When my eldest boy, Washington Madison Quincy Bartlett, was born, President John Quincy Adams even gave him an engraved silver cup for his baptism. We still have that."

"Where is your oldest?"

"Up north. He went to join a colored regiment forming up in Pennsylvania. He's the sergeant major. His son, my grandson, joined up as well."

He said the words proudly.

"Any other children?"

"No, sir," and he shook his head sadly. "My second eldest died of the cholera. My two girls both died as well, one of the typhoid, the other, well the other, my youngest, just died."

He fell silent. Lincoln sensed there was an even more tragic story about the youngest but he did not press it.

"I'm sorry."

"You know that burden, sir. I'll never forget the night your youngest died. We wept with you, sir, and Missus Lincoln. We loved that little boy, too."

"Thank you, Jim."

He lowered his head to hide his own emotions, and the dark memories of Mary wandering the White House, night after night, shrieking as he sat alone, horrified at the thought of his baby being placed in the cold ground, unable to comfort her, to stop her wild hysterias, so paralyzed was he by his own grief, came flooding back.

"Our children are together now with the Lord," Jim said softly.

A bit surprised, Lincoln looked back up and saw tears in the man's eyes. The comment struck him hard and he was filled with a profound question. Did white and black children play together in Heaven? Did they mingle freely, no longer servant and master? Inferior and superior? What would Christ say of that question?

"Thank you, Jim, I'll take comfort in that tonight."

"I will, too, Mr. President. In fact I think it and pray about it most every night."

Lincoln was silent, uncomfortable, not sure what to say next.

"About us fighting, sir," Jim said, pressing back to the original issue.

"Yes?"

"Do we have your permission, sir? Some of the soldiers out front said they'd loan us guns if it came to that."

"Jim, if you are caught with a weapon and not in uniform, you'll be hung on the spot."

Jim shook his head.

"Sir, we'd all rather be killed here, or hung here, than be sold into slavery."

And then he smiled and looked straight into Lincoln's eyes.

"Besides, sir. It'd make a great illustration in the papers, a dozen dead colored hanging from the balconies of the White House. It'd show the world what this war is really about."

Startled, Lincoln could not reply. Grim as the thought was, he knew that Jim was right.

"Let us pray it does not come to that," was all he could offer.

"With you here, sir, I don't think it will. But if it does, sir, we want to fight."

He looked at the man carefully, wondering for an instant if it was the old flattery coming through now. But he could see it wasn't, it was genuine.

"We here, sir, we all know you'll hold the course to the end, no matter what. If it comes to it, sir, we want you to leave and continue the fight elsewhere. My son would want that and I do, too."

The president reached out and put his hand on Jim's shoulder. Unlike so many of the colored, Jim did not lower his eyes, or involuntarily shrink from his touch. He continued to look straight at him.

He wanted to say that he would stand and fight beside him and have his gaunt figure added to the illustration, but did not. That was melodrama, posturing, as far too many did. What this man said had come straight from his heart, without artful reflection and seeking of some heroic end as if he were on the stage. It came as a tonic, a deep and profound reminder not just of his responsibilities, but of how he must continue to face those responsibilities to the end. That was his duty now, to not flinch, to not give back a single inch until it was done.

"You have my permission, Jim. I am honored to give it to you, and God be with you this day."

He squeezed the man's shoulder, nodded, and then turned to walk out. Jim, again the servant, followed him, offering his top hat and shawl from the coat rack by the door, which Lincoln took without comment. Jim opened the door and the two guards outside, who had been wearily leaning on their rifles, snapped to attention.

He looked around. A scattering of men were milling about, ghostlike

in the mist and in the hissing glare of gas lamps that cast dull, golden circles around the porch of the White House and out onto the street. A captain started to come toward him and he gestured with his hand for the officer to remain at ease.

He started to turn away from the door, to walk around the grounds, the captain softly hissing a command, calling on a detail to "escort the president," and then he heard it, a dull thump, like someone was beating on a carpet away off in the mists.

The captain froze in place, turning, cocking his head. Another thump, then another and another, until it merged into a steady, continual rumble.

Men who had been sitting on the lawn were up on their feet, looking about. A murmur of voices arouse, tent flaps opened, men sticking their heads out.

The rumble continued, growing, echoing.

He stood silent, hat in hand, shawl draped over his shoulders.

It had begun.

In Front of Fort Stevens

July 18, 1863
4:45 A.M.

In the predawn light Sergeant Major Hazner saw them coming back. One or two at first, then dozens, and now hundreds. Most were wounded, cradling shattered arms, dragging a broken leg, or staggering, bent over, clutching a stomach wound, which all knew was inevitably the beginning of the end.

Moving up to the starting position occupied by Pettigrew's division before they went in, the men of the Fourteenth South Carolina, along with the other regiments of Scales's brigade, had deployed into a shallow defile, cut at the bottom by a flooded stream, and there they had waited for more than an hour. All was confusion, the last mile of the advance through brush, an orchard, a farmer's woodlot. At least a third of the men in the regiment had disappeared in the advance, to be replaced by men from several other regiments. He had simply pushed them into formation with his own companies. They could fight now and sort it out later; he promised them that the colonel would give them affidavits confirming that they had not deserted or dodged the battle. Some of the men were strays from Pettigrew, and as they saw their comrades coming back, more than one expressed outright relief that they had become lost during the advance to the final line before going in.

The roar of battle ahead was continuous. When the first shots had been fired, a wild, hysterical cry went up, the rebel yell, but gradually that had been replaced by the more disciplined, almost mechanical "huzzah" of the Union troops.

Colonel Brown was gone, called forward to an officers' meeting, and, now alone, Hazner paced the line, moving from company to company, offering reassurance to the men, who looked up anxiously, faces pale, as they heard the inferno roaring just ahead.

A panicked lieutenant came staggering back through the lines, blood from a head wound covering the front of his jacket.

"Gone, all gone. My God, my men! My men!"

He staggered through the ranks, spreading dismay, no one touching him or offering help, for they were forbidden to do so.

Hazner watched him disappear into the mist and smoke. Young Lieutenant Hurt came up to join him, obviously nervous.

"It looks bad."

"It always does, Lieutenant. Watch a battle from the rear, it always looks like defeat."

"Pettigrew should have broken through by now."

"Most likely he has."

Hazner knew it was a lie. Someone would have come back down the road by now, proclaiming victory, the rebel yell echoing through the fog from the battle line. All that could be heard was the continual staccato of musketry, cannon fire, and the whirl of spent canister cracking through the trees overhead, clipped branches raining down.

Mortar shells were coming down at random, detonating in the tree tops, some crashing down into the assembled ranks of the division, screams following each explosion. It was obvious that their gunners knew of this defile, assumed it was packed with troops, and knew the range to hit it. Though sporadic, the shelling was unnerving.

"Fourteenth South Carolina!"

He looked back to the front ranks and saw the color company standing up, the regimental flag bearer shaking out his colors, holding them aloft. Without comment to Hurt, Hazner pushed his way back through the ranks of men still lying on the ground.

Colonel Brown was back, sword drawn. Hazner came up and saluted.

"We're going in, Hazner."

"What's the news, sir?"

Brown looked at him appraisingly and then wiped his face. In spite of the morning chill, he was sweating.

"Bad. Pettigrew was repulsed all along the line. Some of the men broke through into the fort, we were almost sent in to expand it, but they were thrown back. Pettigrew is down, they say he's dead. A bad day for North Carolina."

He hesitated.

"Now it's our turn. We'll set it right."

Brown stepped past Hazner and held his sword aloft.

"South Carolina! Men of the Fourteenth! Up men, up!"

The regiment came to its feet, officers and sergeants moving through the packed ranks, which were deployed in a solid square, the men of A Company in two ranks forward, followed by B Company, and so on, back to the last line, three hundred men in a small phalanx, fifteen men wide and twenty deep. To either flank were their comrades of the other regiments of Scales's brigade . . . men who had taken every field of battle they had ever advanced across.

"Fourteenth South Carolina! Now is our time! We will advance in column and take that damn Yankee fort. Once we are into it, Washington will be ours and on this day this war will be won. Do you wish history to remember that it was South Carolina that won this day?"

A shout went up from the ranks. Hazner looked around and saw that the hours of silence, of watching, of fear, were swept away. The battle lust was upon them again.

"Parson. Say some words!"

A graying captain, unofficial minister of the regiment, stepped through the ranks and took off his hat, the men following, all lowering their heads, even Hazner.

"Hearken to the word of our Lord. 'Thou shalt not be afraid for the terror by night; nor for the arrow that flieth by day . . .'"

As the preacher continued to recite from the Ninety-first Psalm, Hazner looked up. Most of the men stood with heads bowed, eyes squeezed shut. Many had their Bibles out, clutching them fervently. More than one was shaking. A young boy, ashen-faced in the dawning light, suddenly bent double and vomited; a comrade, his older brother, reaching out and gently rubbing his shoulders. A few of the men, those without faith, stood in respectful silence, one meditatively chewing on a wad, waiting to spit, a couple of others silently passing a nearly empty bottle back and forth. A sharp look from Hazner caused the one holding the bottle to shrug, take the last sip, and then without fanfare quietly lay it down on the ground.

"Have faith in our Lord this day and remember that they who do not camp with us this evening will sup instead in Heaven."

"I'll skip that meal if I can," one of the drinkers whispered, and a few of the men around him chuckled, even as they continued to keep their heads lowered.

In the regiment beside the Fourteenth, a group of Catholics, men from Ireland, were on their knees, reciting a prayer: ". . . Holy Mary, Mother of God, pray for us sinners, now and at the hour of our death, amen." They made their sign of the cross and stood up, many of them taking their rosaries and hanging them around their necks.

Hazner found he could not say anything, he could not pray, he could not beg for intervention now. If the preacher said that a thousand shall fall by one's side, then surely someone who prayed here would be among those fallen. How could one beg God now to change that? To save his miserable hide while one of the devout stood praying, Bible in hand. Williamson had spent many an hour contemplating that and what did it get him in the end? . . . a bullet in the head and now he was gone.

He wanted to have faith, but found that now, standing here, waiting to go in, he did not. He wished with all his heart that he could have the simple faith and the calm assurance of the preacher, who, as he went back through the ranks, took the hands of many a man, smiling, as if what was to come was no longer a concern, for all had already been decided.

A muffled shout went up. It was General Scales, riding across the front of the column, sword out, held aloft, pointing toward the fight. He swung down off his mount, slapped its rump, and sent it running.

"Follow me, boys! Guide on your colors!"

"The Fourteenth!" Brown roared. "Remember, don't cap your muskets till ordered. Keep your ranks closed and guide on the flag of South Carolina!"

A shout went up as the column stepped forward, the line lurching at first, men in the forward ranks taking half a dozen steps before the men at the back finally began to move, double-timing until they caught up. The regiment to their left stepped off a bit late and then raced to form a solid front. Hazner ran to come up to the front of the column and fell in just behind Brown, who was walking backward, sword aloft.

"Hazner. To the rear of the column," Brown announced. "I want you back there, keep the men moving, no matter what!"

Hazner breathed a sigh of relief, for he knew what would happen to the first rank once they were within canister range. And yet, as he looked at Brown, he felt regret. The man was caught up in the moment. He was at the center of the charge, out in front, and Washington was before them. If he survived this day, if they took the fort, it would be remembered forever.

Impulse seized him, and before moving back he ran up to Brown and extended his hand.

Grinning, Brown took it.

"I'll see you in the fort, Sergeant!"

"Yes, sir."

Hazner ran to one side, to the gap between his regiment and the one on their left flank, and stood awestruck as the column passed. They were wide-eyed, rifles at the shoulder, already hunching forward slightly as if going into a storm, but they came on relentlessly, some of the men shouting, others cursing; even the ones trembling with fear staggered forward, for none would dare to turn back now. The column passed. He ran to fall in at the center rear, where two drummer boys were beginning to tap out a beat. He shouted for them to stop and go to the rear, but both looked at him defiantly and pressed on. He could not stop them, they were fey.

They swept up past an open grove of trees where a tarpaulin was spread, glistening with the heavy dew of morning. Coming out from under the tarpaulin was a knot of officers, and all immediately recognized who was in the center of the group. In spite of orders a shout went up. . . .

"Lee . . . Lee . . . Lee!"

The column swept along the edge of the grove and there he stood, hat off, hand raised in salute.

Hazner saluted as they marched by, and for an instant he thought the general was looking straight at him. He had a foolish thought that perhaps Lee would remember him, the meeting on the road, the first day at Gettysburg when he and Williamson had brought the word about the enemy guns on the Cemetery Hill. He knew that Lee most likely did not even see him, but nevertheless he felt a renewed strength. If Bobbie Lee was ordering them in, then surely victory was ahead . . . for when had they ever failed?

The first casualties dropped, a mortar shell, most likely fired at random, exploding in the air above the middle of the column, men collapsing. The ranks behind them opening, pushing to get around the bodies, then closing back up. He watched carefully. Nearly a dozen men were down, but once the advance had cleared the fallen, six stood up and started to run. The usual cowards, taking advantage of the first shots to try and get out.

He let them go. To try and kick them back into the ranks was a waste of effort. They'd bolt again once the real fighting started. But he recognized several and would be certain to remember their names, along with the name of one of the men lying there dead, Tom McMurtry—he had once fished with him in summer and hunted in the fall, years ago—the top of his head smashed in by the exploding shell.

The gradual slope began to shallow out into level ground. All ahead was smoke, fog, shadows. To the east the horizon was a dull gray, a bit brighter than the rest of the heavens, the ground fog having risen during the night, obscuring the stars.

The grass beneath his feet was trampled down, soaked with dew. Bits of equipment littered the ground, a blanket roll, a discarded musket, and now the first casualties, men crawling back, the column opening then closing to step around them. One of the wounded held up an imploring hand, only one, for his left arm was torn off at the shoulder, the man begging for water. All ignored him, pressing on.

Bullets snicked the air overhead, fluttering by like angry bees, random shots from the fight up ahead; a shell fluttered over, fuse visible, sputtering and trailing sparks.

More men on the ground, dead, twisted up, torn apart, blood streaking the grass. A lone artillery piece, how it got there was a mystery, abandoned, its team of six horses dead, the column having to slow for a moment as it moved around the wreckage, then double-timing to move back up to the fore.

"Double time!"

The cry echoed up and down the swaying columns. The drummer boys picked up the tempo of their beat. Up at the head of the column the flag bearer was holding his banner high, waving it back and forth. A man at the rear went down, the smack of the bullet hitting him in the forehead clearly audible. He flipped over backward, nearly knocking Hazner over. Hazner staggered, then ran to catch up.

Still nothing in the mist. He wondered how Scales knew which way to go. How long had they been moving? Five minutes now, seven, ten? They should be almost there. There was nothing but mist, smoke, scattered bodies. Where were they going?

The tension seemed unbearable again. For a few minutes, in the initial excitement, he—for that matter, all—had forgotten what was coming. Now, as they moved at the double, some of the men beginning to pant for breath, staggering, the fear was returning, the dread of the moment of impact.

And still nothing but mist.

As if in answer to a desperate, terrible prayer, the mist seemed to part. The head of the column actually slowed, men in the rear ranks pressing in, some cursing, shouting. Hazner moved from the center over to the side of the column, looking up through the twenty-yard gap between his regiment and the one to their left.

A dark line seemed to be traced across the low horizon ahead. He caught glimpses of men moving along the top of it. The ground before them was nothing but a mad tangle of bodies, men writhing in agony, others lying prone, hunkered down, curled up, hands and arms covering their heads, a few with poised rifles raised, continuing to fight. The ground was a shambles of torn-up grass, mud, blood, thousands upon thousands of torn cartridge papers, twisted rifles, dead horses, an officer lying against the stomach of a dead mount, head bowed, weeping hysterically.

"Charge, boys! Charge!"

A wild shout erupted from the column; the drummer boys, all sense of tempo gone, began to beat furiously. Men surged forward, the spine-tingling rebel yell rising up in a wild shriek, Hazner picking up the cry, which sounded like wolves baying at the scent of blood.

A flash erupted from atop the parapet, then another and another. The first spray of canister, two hundred iron balls fired from a thirty-pound rifled gun, tore into the flanking regiment, cutting a murderous swath across the front of the line. A second later the next blast struck the Fourteenth. Something slapped into Hazner's face. Warm, sticky, and he was momentarily blinded. Horrified, he wiped his eyes clean, feeling bits of flesh between his fingers, the taste of blood salty in his mouth. He fought down the reflective desire to gag, to vomit, as the realization dawned that it was the entrails of a man he was wiping away.

"Come on!"

Amazingly he could hear Colonel Brown screaming. He was still alive.

"Come on!" Hazner picked up the cry, now edging in, pushing the man in front of him as the column regained momentum, pressing up and over the torn remains of a score of comrades cut down by that first blast.

He caught a glimpse of the preacher, gasping, sitting up, blood gushing from his chest, the man feebly holding his Bible and pressing it to the wound.

In the smoke just ahead Hazner saw the first lines of the abatis. In many places the sharpened stakes had been torn out or pushed down. There were six rows of them, the outer rows broken or knocked down, but the inner rows still intact in many places, here and there with narrow lanes cut through them. More than one dead man was impaled on the stakes. To his horror he saw a wounded man pierced through the stomach, but still alive, screaming.

The column slammed into the first line of stakes. He had heard that some of Pettigrew's men had gone in armed with axes, but they had not fully cleared the way, and he caught glimpses of them, dead, some with axes still in their hands. He was tempted to toss aside his musket and pick one up, but decided against it. He needed to stay with the men, not get diverted.

By sheer brute strength the column was forcing its way through, men slamming at the stakes with the butts of their muskets to knock the barriers aside, squeezing through the openings. The column stalled; men from the rear ranks began to spill around to the flanks of the column pushing up against the stakes.

Rifle fire now erupted from the wall of the fort with deadly effect, men dropping to either side of Hazner as he ran along the flank of his regiment, pushed through the remnants of the first two lines of abatis, and pressed his way into the third.

More cannon fire. He heard a strange, hollow rattling and looked back. One of the drummer boys was standing there, gazing down. His drum had been blown in half but he was still alive.

"Get down, boy! Get down!"

The boy looked up at him, then, without a sound, collapsed. The shot that had destroyed the drum had all but torn off his leg at the knee.

Turning, he began to batter at the stakes, screaming with rage, pushing his way through. A stake directly in front of him was all but split in half by a rifle ball that would have hit him in the stomach. He pushed it aside.

"Come on!"

A mortar shell, fired with only a few ounces of powder, came down silently, striking the ground in front of him, the fuse going out in the muck.

"Come on!"

He looked to either side. The regiments were swarming together, any semblance of formation gone, officers screaming, waving swords, men cursing, heaving, pushing, many—far too many—falling, shrieking, clutching at arms, heads, chests, stomachs.

They surged through the last barrier line. The moat was before him. It was a sight of horror. The filthy, muddy water was pink, the color clearly visible even in the dim light . . . filled with the dead, wounded, and dying. The wounded looked up imploringly, some shrieking for them to go back, those still game urging their comrades forward, a few still unhit rising up, struggling to claw their way back up the muddy wall of the fort.

He saw the flag bearer of the Fourteenth go down. Before the colors had even begun to fold up and drop, someone else held them aloft, screaming for the men to follow, Colonel Brown at his side. The colonel and the flag bearer jumped, skidding down the outer slope of the moat, the regiment surging after them.

Hazner was knocked off his feet by a man behind him jumping. He skidded face-forward down the slope, hitting a body on the way, turning to slide feet-first into the slime.

"Keep your cartridge boxes up!" he screamed, even as he clawed at his own and dropped waist-deep into the moat. Some of the men were already doing that, but far too many, caught up in the madness, simply waded in. With the first two steps he lost his shoes, sucked off in the mud.

He felt as if he was running in a nightmare, each slow step an eternity, water geysering around him. He stepped on a body pressed down into the mud, his bare feet sensing the back, the man's head, and he was glad the body was there, giving him enough footing to leap the last few feet on to the inner wall of the moat.

The nightmare sensation was still there. He tried to stand, to run up, but the ground had been churned into a morass by Pettigrew's men, whose bodies littered the slope.

He looked up and saw the barrel of a thirty-pounder being run back out, barrel fully depressed. He flung himself down, the roar of the gun stunning him, the deadly impact striking the far slope of the moat, cutting down dozens.

He stood up.

"Now! Now!"

He repeated the cry over and over as he staggered up the slope, losing four steps for every one gained. Stepping atop a legless body he gained enough footing to fling himself up nearly to the crest. He paused, looked back, saw that Brown was still up, sword still held high. The flag bearer was up as well, pressing forward; then he dropped. Another man picked up the flag, following Brown, a wedge of men, like an inverted V, pushing behind them.

The crush of men pressed up beside him and Hazner fell in with them. They were almost at the embrasure. He pushed up the last few feet to one side of the gun opening, clawing his way to the top. He caught a glimpse of heads, some wearing blue kepis, most of them hatless, the rammer for the gun withdrawing the staff, screaming for the crew to run the piece back out.

He stood up, aimed at the man less than five feet away, and squeezed. Nothing happened; his rifle was still uncapped.

A gunner, shouting, raised a revolver, and he dropped down atop the crest of the wall, the pistol round cutting a neat hole into the brim of Hazner's hat.

He lunged forward, tumbling over the wall and into the fort. All was madness, confusion. Landing on the firing step, a Yankee, standing above him, screamed, using his musket like a club, swung down, trying to crush his skull. Hazner rolled, avoiding the blow. Kicking with his bare feet, he caught the man on the knee; the Yankee, cursing, staggered back. He tried to stand up, but then was knocked down as another man landed on top of him. He caught a glimpse of the inside of the fort, bodies sprawled everywhere, many of them in gray or tattered butternut. A line of infantry, bayonets poised, were in the center compound, light field pieces deployed across the small parade ground, aimed straight at the wall.

The man atop him grunted, cried out, then rolled off. He came to his feet, saw the man that had been atop him thrashing, screaming, a bayonet stuck in his back, the Yankee who had caught him fighting to pull the bayonet back out.

Holding his musket at the butt, Hazner swung it like a club and brained the man, who collapsed, falling off the firing step into the compound below.

It was now a murder match, men fighting like primal animals, no quarter given or asked. Fumbling, he pulled out a percussion cap, thumbed it on to the nipple, cocked his gun, and swung it around, firing from the waist into the stomach of a man lunging at him.

More men were swarming over the top of the parapet; the few Yankees atop the firing step began to jump off, running. He was about to jump down after them and then saw, to his right, that the crew of the thirty-pounder were still at their position, a sergeant slapping a friction primer into the breech, pulling the lanyard taut, screaming for the crew to jump back.

Colonel Brown was up into the embrasure, turning, looking back, shouting incoherently. He was so close that Hazner could almost touch him. Lunging out he grabbed Brown by the arm, which was covered with blood, and then fell backwards, dragging the colonel with him. Behind

Brown the flag bearer was coming through the embrasure, colors still held high.

The gun went off with an earsplitting thunder crack, the flag bearer disappearing, screams echoing up from beyond the wall.

Dropping his grip on Brown, Hazner crouched, animal-like, looking around, taking it all in, his senses suddenly sharp, clear, the world momentarily focused.

The infantry in the center of the fort's parade ground were firing away, independent fire, picking their targets as they came up over the wall. One of the field pieces erupted with a sharp kick, leaping backward, canister sweeping the top of the fort to Hazner's left, sweeping down a dozen or more men, some of them Union, on the open parapet.

Yankees deployed along the far side of the wall, facing in toward Washington, were turned, crouching down, firing as well; a light field piece over there was turned, pointing straight at them, ready to sweep any charge that came into the parade ground.

He stood up for a brief instant, looking back over the parapet, back across the ground they had just stormed. It was carpeted with the dead and wounded of two divisions. Scattered groups of men were still pushing forward; down in the moat, hundreds, perhaps a thousand or more, floundered about. Any semblance of command was lost in this nightmare.

Where was the next wave? The mist revealed nothing.

"We're getting out!" Hazner shouted. He stood up, pushing his dazed colonel up on the wall. The gunners, not ten feet away, were furiously reloading their piece. For an instant he thought of taking them, but knew it was useless. Bullets were smacking into the earthen wall to either side, fired from the troops assembled below.

He violently pushed Brown, who was still dazed.

"No!" Brown cried, but Hazner ignored him, leaning down, lifting him up with his blacksmith's strength, slamming him over the parapet.

He leapt up, grabbed Brown, and rolled off the top, skidding halfway down the slope. Brown tried to stand back up.

"Goddamn it, Colonel. Lay down!"

"We can still take it!"

"Not yet, damn it. Wait for the next wave!"

"We can still take it!"

Brown tried to stand up, blood pouring from his wounded arm. Exasperated, Hazner reared back, punched him with a numbing blow on the side of the head, and Brown fell, tumbled into the mud, and was still.

Fumbling into his cartridge box while lying on his back, Hazner reloaded, awkwardly pulling out the ramrod, pushing the charge down while his musket lay on his stomach, then rolled over, capped the nipple, and poised his weapon.

Pressed flat against the slope, he knew that for the moment he was safe, though those on the far side of the moat were trapped in hell. Hundreds of men, thinking as he did, had pressed themselves down into the forward slope of the fort, the ground defilade that could not be hit. The thirty-pounder, only feet away, could sweep the far slope and the fields beyond, but it could not touch him, though the roar of it would leave him deafened. Any infantry that tried to pick him off would have to stand atop the parapet, and several did try in the next few minutes, only to be riddled, as a hundred or more fired on them, offering back some small measure of revenge for the carnage.

It was a stalemate.

Hazner looked around, recognizing some faces from his regiment.

"We stay here!" he shouted. "Stay here, don't fall back, or you'll be slaughtered. Stay here till the next wave comes, then we go back in!"

He reached down to his canteen. Uncorking it, Hazner lifted it up. It was light, empty. A bullet had cut it nearly in half.

Cursing, he flung it aside, and then hunkered down to wait for what would come next.

He looked back to the east. The sun was breaking the horizon, dull red as it shone through the smoke and the fog, which would soon burn away. It was going to be a hot day. It was going to be a very long day.

Chapter Six

New York City

July 18, 1863

6:30 A.M.

The smoke of battle was drifting down Fifth Avenue. A gutted mansion to his right burned fitfully, its brownstone walls scorched black, glass from the broken windows lying scattered along the sidewalk, smoke pulsing out of the empty window frames soaring up in coiling plumes. Two bodies dangled from a lamppost in front of the mansion, hand-lettered signs tied to their feet . . . REBEL ARSONISTS, the signs twirling slowly as smoke drifted around them.

The artillery fire had stopped just after dawn, only the occasional rifle shot echoing now in the gloom. The haze of smoke hung low on the street, a fitful rain splashing down, the rain thick with soot, ash, the smell of wet wood smoke.

Maj. Gen. Dan Sickles walked purposefully down the middle of the street, his escort, a company of green-clad Berdan's sharpshooters, fanned out around him in a circle, moving like the veterans they were. Instead of stalking through woods and fields they now moved from doorway to doorway, rifles poised, scanning rooftops, open windows, abandoned barricades, racing forward, going down on one knee, then up again. Disdaining such caution, he walked upright, unafraid, setting the example he knew had to be set. Twice assassins almost got him, one of the shots nicking his hat. Of course he made sure that an illustrator from *Harper's Weekly* knew about that event; with luck it might be on the cover next week, with him standing as a hero in the middle of the street, the skulking coward leaning over from a rooftop. He had made a point of drawing his revolver and firing several shots back—missing, of course, but still it set the right pose. *The country needs a hero in a time of crisis*, he thought, *and I am going to give them one.*

A scattering of cheers and applause greeted him as he strode down the avenue, frightened civilians peeking out of windows, then coming outside to greet him. A beautiful young girl in a soot-darkened silk dress of bottle green came out from a doorway, carrying a flower. Shyly she curtsied and handed him the blossom.

Smiling, he bowed gallantly, took the flower with one hand, and then, taking the girl's hand, he bent over and kissed it gently.

"Thank you, my dear."

"The honor is mine, General."

She scurried back into her house, several of the veterans accompanying him looking at her, grinning slyly. He turned, handed the flower to one of his adjutants, and smiled at the knot of reporters walking behind him.

"You're a popular man this morning, General," a reporter from the *Tribune* shouted.

He smiled, thinking the nation needed a modest hero.

"It's the men, my men who deserve the credit," he replied diplomatically, saying it loud enough so his escort could hear it.

They crossed Thirty-fourth Street, heading south. The four corners of the intersection were piled high with barricades, torn-up cobblestones, upended wagons, dead horses, a streetcar pushed over on its side . . . and dozens of bodies, many of them hideously riddled from the blasts of canister and solid shot, which the evening before he had directed into this rebel stronghold.

He paused at the middle of the intersection to watch as a company of infantry, New York State Militia, and several dozen firemen and policemen emerged out of the smoke and passed by, heading west. The lieutenant leading the group saw Sickles, slowed, and saluted.

"Where are you coming from, Lieutenant?" Dan asked.

"Over on the East Side, sir, down by the docks. Hard fighting, I lost half a dozen men, but we routed them into the river."

"Good work, son."

"We've been ordered over to the West Side now."

Dan nodded. There were still a few pockets of resistance down toward the Hudson, and apparently some of the rioters were trying to seize boats to get out of the city now that the insurrection was collapsing.

The lieutenant motioned to the back of his column. Four bedraggled civilians, hands tied, were being prodded along at bayonet point.

"We captured these men, sir, in a burning warehouse. They claim they're innocent. I'm not sure, sir, what to do with them."

Dan looked over appraisingly at the four. One was fairly well dressed, broadcloth jacket, velvet vest, looked like a clerk or young merchant, in his early twenties.

Dan walked up to him, ignoring the other three, who were obviously ruffians, Irish street-sweepings.

"What's your story?"

"I got trapped in the mob, sir," the young man said nervously. "I don't know how I wound up in that warehouse; I was trying to get out but couldn't."

"Why aren't you in the army?" Dan asked pointedly. "Men your age should be up at the front, serving their country."

As he spoke, his gaze shifted to his escorts. They were looking at the young man with cold eyes. It had not been difficult at all to unleash his men, survivors of the Union Mills disaster, on this mob. The resentment that had been building for two years against stay-at-home slackers was already at the boiling point before the riots had even started.

The young man said nothing, eyes a bit unfocused, obviously still drunk.

Dan turned away and looked at the lieutenant.

"If he were an honorable soldier of the South, like those my comrades and I faced openly on the battlefield, I would risk my own life if need be to save him if he were wounded."

He looked at the men of his escort, who were now watching the drama.

"You there, Sergeant," he nodded toward a veteran, beard flecked with gray, an ugly crease across one cheek from a bullet that had almost killed him the night before.

"Should this man be treated the way we treated prisoners after Antietam or the other battles we were in, where we shared our canteens with wounded rebs?"

The sergeant glared at the captured man, chewing meditatively on a wad of tobacco.

The dazed man looked at him hopefully.

"Hang the son of a bitch," the sergeant growled and spat, the juice striking the man's boots.

Sickles turned away with a dramatic flourish.

"Hang them all."

"Sir?"

"You heard me, Lieutenant. They are insurrectionists not in uniform. The rules of war are that they are to be hung."

Without waiting for a reply Dan started to walk away, ignoring the young man who, stirring out of drunken stupor, began to hysterically scream for mercy.

He did not even bother to look back and, scrambling over the barricade, pressed on south. The *Tribune* reporter came up to his side.

"Isn't that rather harsh, sir? Resistance is collapsing."

Dan pulled a cigar out of his pocket and offered it to the reporter, who refused. Dan then bit off the end and paused to strike a match against a lamppost.

"Harsh?"

"The rioting is all but finished, sir. Isn't it time now for some mercy?"

"Riot? Sir, this was not a riot, it was an insurrection in support of the Confederacy. I wish you reporters would get it right. The size of it, the sheer destructiveness—no unorganized mob could do what was done here to our city, three hundred miles away from the front lines. You see around you the hand of the Confederate government and their secret agents. New York has become just as much a battlefield as Union Mills or Washington."

The reporter did not reply.

"Write that down if you please, son."

The reporter complied.

The screaming of the young man was suddenly cut short, and they looked back up Fifth Avenue. At the corner of Thirty-fourth Street, a body seemed to leap into the air, half a dozen men pulling on the rope, the young man kicking and thrashing. A rifle shot exploded, one of the other three trying to escape, scrambling up over the barricade, collapsing, then half a dozen more shots, the soldiers deciding to dispatch the rest without the ceremony of a hanging.

Dan turned away and continued to walk.

"It doesn't seem to bother you," the reporter said, his features now pale.

Dan took off his hat, which was rain-soaked and covered with greasy soot. He looked up at the morning sky, breathing deeply. It did smell like a battlefield; the smoke, the faint whiff of rotten eggs from the volley just fired, a distant thump of a cannon counterpointed by more musketry.

"You ever seen a battle, son?"

"No, sir."

"You should. Young man your age."

"Are you going to hang me, sir, because I didn't join the army?"

Dan looked over at him and laughed.

"You think that's it? Why I hanged that scoundrel back there?"

"I think it contributed to it."

"At Union Mills I saw the ground carpeted with our dead, and we lost. I saw the same at Chancellorsville, Fredericksburg, where the bodies froze into the ground. Dead, wasted dead, and still the war continues."

He fell silent, the memories sharp, crystal clear. The stench of the field at Chancellorsville, bodies bloating in the heat. Waste, all of it waste. Back here it was just numbers, names in fine print filling page after page of the papers. He had seen it and felt the anguish as men, *his men*, died. They were his men being wasted, and if ever there was a chance to change all that, it was now. By God, the republic had to be saved, and the saving of it would start right here, in the streets of New York. Set the example here that traitors stabbing the army in the back will not be tolerated. And then let his men who fought here return back to the Army of the Potomac and spread the story of what he accomplished. That will affect the morale of all his men for the better.

"If I had but one day in command," he whispered, "and fifty thousand more men, men even like that slacker back there, who I could have turned into an honorable soldier, the war would be over."

He puffed on his cigar for a moment, still looking at the dark-gray sky.

"These are hard times, son. Hard times. We've lost two hundred thousand men in this war and still it goes on. I want what happened here to be a message to our nation. The times have changed forever; the traitors down South forced that on us, and now I shall finish it."

"You, sir?"

He looked back over at the reporter and smiled.

"After today? I saved this city, son. Saved it from becoming a wasteland."

As he spoke, he gestured up and down Fifth Avenue. The refuse of the riot was everywhere—broken storefronts, gutted buildings, bolts of cloth trampled into the filth, smashed-in barrels, broken bottles, torn-up pavement, dead horses, and, from a lamppost at the corner of Thirty-third Street, two more bodies dangling, one with trousers burned off to the knees, the skin blackened.

"If we had lost New York we would have lost the war."

"Isn't it lost already? There's reports that Lee will take Washington today."

Sickles took the cigar out of his mouth and blew a ring in the still air.

"I don't like that kind of talk, son."

"Sir?"

"Just what you said. 'Reports,' you say? Who filed these reports? The government, or some newspaper?"

The reporter was silent.

Not wanting to antagonize this important mouthpiece to the public, he smiled.

"Son. When we see an official dispatch from the government declaring that the capital has fallen, then print it, but not before. Such talk might only lend encouragement to the rebels here in this city. That girl who gave me a flower back there. Do you want her to fall into their hands?"

"Of course not."

"Fear is the enemy here this morning. We've got it under control; let's leave Washington out of it for now and wait until there is official word."

The reporter said nothing.

"And if by chance, if by remote chance the capital does fall, I will lead the Army of the Potomac, in its fury, across Maryland and teach Bobbie Lee a lesson he will never forget."

"Sir, what Army of the Potomac?" another reporter interjected, coming up to join the two.

Sickles smiled dismissively.

"That, young man, is a military secret. Believe me, the Army still exists, I know, for even while here, I am working to rebuild it. You will see it crowned with the laurels of victory before all is done."

Before another question could be asked, he walked away, continuing his inspection tour. Inside he was seething. If Lincoln did allow the capital to fall, there was more than a good chance that peace would be the end result, and then his own aspirations would be dashed. The capital had to hold out so that ultimately he could march into it as its liberator. Of course he had to be the one that was in command.

At first there had been rumors that the Army of the Potomac would be folded into Grant's new Army of the Susquehanna. Congressional pressure was putting a stop to that. Grant was bringing Westerners in to fill up his new army. Eastern congressmen and senators weren't about to have the East's contribution to the Union cause submerged in a western command.

Lincoln was being forced to accept that. There would have to be a reconstituted Army of the Potomac which, yes, would serve under Grant, but which must have its own commander. Now Lincoln was considering whom to appoint to that position.

That hash would be settled before the week was out, of that he was certain. In the end Lincoln would have to turn to him to command the Army of the Potomac. Lincoln needed the War Democrats more than ever, and Dan was their candidate to command the Army of the Potomac. *Yes*, he thought to himself with satisfaction, *in the end it will come out just fine and I will command the army.*

Once he was in command and the army reconstituted, the stage would be set for him to whip Bobbie Lee . . . that would end the war as it should be ended.

Reaching Twenty-third Street and the intersection of Fifth Avenue and Broadway, he saw a knot of men, infantry, a section of guns, two bronze Napoleons, a troop of cavalry, and an ornate, black-lacquered, four-horse carriage, curtains drawn, a militia colonel leaning against the side of it, talking with someone inside. At his approach the colonel stiffened, saluted, and whispered a comment.

The door to the carriage popped open and Dan stepped in, the carriage swaying slightly as he settled in across from Tweed. The carriage was filled with cigar smoke and the scent of whiskey.

"Have you seen the reports?" Tweed snapped angrily, waving a sheaf of papers.

"Which reports?"

"My God, Dan, it states here that over two thousand bodies have been picked up for burial. They're getting hauled over to Brooklyn, even loaded into barges to get dumped at sea."

"Fine. Two thousand less ruffians terrorizing the streets."

"This will cost us a hundred thousand votes, Sickles. They'll blame us!"

"Not when I'm done," Sickles replied calmly.

"The war was a Republican war. We could always hang that on them. But now?"

"We can still do that. I was acting under orders, Tweed. Did my military duty."

"But two thousand dead. The entire Five Points burned to the ground. And what's this about military executions?"

"I wouldn't call it that. Military executions are for soldiers. These were secret agents, insurgents hiding in civilian garb."

"Two thousand of them?"

"Goddamn it, Tweed, what the hell would you have me do? Slap them on the wrist? Give them a nursery bottle filled with brandy and send them home to their mommas? This is a war, damn it. A war."

He shouted the last words, and Tweed, slightly intimidated, fell back into his seat.

"You don't see the broader picture. Back up on Fifth Avenue a girl gave me a flower."

"Charming sentiment, did you get her name?"

"You don't see it. To those Uptown I'm the savior this morning. Not a Republican, just a general doing his duty. Besides, we broke the back of the gangs that have terrorized this city for too long. They're on the run now and I plan to drive them straight into the East River and the Hudson. The average citizen of this town will turn out a week from now and offer us a victory parade. The times are changing, Tweed; this is a new age, an age of power, of industry, of the men who drive them. We saved their hides and they will remember that; I will be certain to remind them when the time comes."

Tweed said nothing.

"We can still play the lower classes, and the best way to do that is to bring this war to its conclusion without the draft. Hang that on the Republicans, that they let it drag on too long, they created the draft while lining their pockets from it and all the wartime graft. We will end the war and then see who is in the White House after the next election."

Tweed puffed on his cigar.

"You heard about Washington?"

"That Lee is attacking."

"That's the word."

"Just rumor for now, but he does have to strike and do it now."

"And if it falls?"

"Heintzelman is no genius, but he's no fool. Put twenty-five thousand into those fortifications and even he can hold it, as long as he doesn't panic."

"But Lee."

"Goddamn it. Everyone always talks about Lee. He can't fly over the fortifications, he has to go through them and it will cost him. All I am worried about now is getting confirmed as the new commander of the Army of the Potomac."

"It's a wreck, Sickles."

"It's all we got now here in the East. Do you think Grant will give me a command? I doubt it. In three months' time those damn Westerners will be dominating this entire region. I need that army command now. I need to act now, to achieve what we should have achieved in front of Gettysburg, or even, before it was thrown away completely, at Union Mills. I need that army, Tweed, and you will put the best face on what happened here in New York and make sure it happens."

"The governor is furious over the destruction and the losses. Said you were like Napoleon in Moscow."

"Well, maybe this country needs a Napoleon right now," Sickles snapped.

He hesitated, pulling back the curtain to look outside, suddenly fearful that one of the reporters might have heard. They were milling about, talking with the militia colonel, no one looking this way.

He looked back at Tweed and smiled.

"Just tell the governor that in a month this will be forgotten, especially after I've personally defeated Lee and put an end to this war. And when I am in the White House, his state and our city are going to be taken care of, really taken care of."

He smiled and patted Tweed's arm.

In Front of Fort Stevens

July 18, 1863
6:45 A.M.

C.S.A. "General Hood, is your old division finally ready to go in?"

Lee looked at his corps commander with unveiled exasperation. The attack was supposed to have been launched with three full divisions in place, instead only two had been ready to go before dawn, and even then, Perrin's division had taken a full hour longer than expected to attack. The third division, Hood's old command, was only now completing its deployment off the road.

"General, the road is a nightmare; I still don't have Law's brigade in place."

"Send everything you have in now or we shall lose our chance!" Lee snapped.

Hood looked over at Colonel Taylor, Lee's most trusted adjutant. Taylor gazed back with unfocused eyes, as if he wasn't there.

"General Lee, the attack is failing. I ask that we hold my division back."

"No, sir. You will commit immediately."

Hood hesitated.

"Now, General! Now! We've lost two divisions trying to breech their line. Are you telling me that the sacrifice is to be wasted? One more push and we break through."

Hood said nothing. Looking past Lee he saw General Longstreet approach, without fanfare, mount covered in sweat, and dismount.

"Have we taken it?" Longstreet asked.

"No, we have not taken it," Lee replied sharply, "yet."

Longstreet nodded sagely, saying nothing, looking over at Hood.

"It was not coordinated as well as we could have wished," Hood said softly. "Night attacks on this scale are simply impossible to coordinate well in the dark and the mud."

Lee looked at him sharply and the commander of the Second Corps fell silent.

"You have my orders, General Hood, now execute them."

Hood saluted and without further argument left the grove, his staff running before him, the deployed troops coming to their feet. There was no cheering now, but the men were game, ready for what was ahead.

Lee turned to Taylor.

"Remind General Hood in no uncertain terms that he is not to go in with the assault. I need my generals, we've already lost Pettigrew this day. Keep an eye on him till the attack goes forward."

Taylor saluted and ran after Hood.

"How goes it, sir?" Longstreet asked.

Lee wearily shook his head.

"It was not properly coordinated, General. Pettigrew went in nearly an hour late. It appears the Yankee pickets had advance warning, at least enough so that their artillery opened before the attack had even hit the abatis. Perrin's men got tangled up moving up to the start position. Now Hood's old division is starting late as well; he claims the road was all but impassable."

"It is, sir."

Lee looked over at him coldly.

"Your lead division, is it ready to exploit the breakthrough?"

"Sir, it will be an hour or more before McLaws is in position; they're filing off the road even now on the other side of the creek."

"An hour? I ordered you to have McLaws up by dawn."

"Sir, we are trying to move our entire army down a single road, at night, through an ocean of mud."

"We won't win with excuses, General Longstreet."

The rebuke in his voice was obvious to everyone within hearing distance.

"We have fought two major battles in little more than a fortnight. We have destroyed one of their armies, and the capital is within our reach. We cannot lose our nerve this day, General. We must hold our nerve if we are to win. I propose to win this war today, sir, because never again will we have such a chance."

A cheer went up . . . the rebel yell. . . . Hood's division was going in.

The Moat in Front of Fort Stevens

CSA Here they come!"

Sergeant Hazner cautiously raised his head to look back to the north. A corporal who had gone up on his elbows to look, only a minute before, was now sprawled in the bottom of the moat, the top of his head gone.

He could hear them, but the smoke was still too thick to see anything. The muzzle of the thirty-pounder ran out again, this time elevated higher, to sweep the field.

"Lower, you bastards," Hazner shouted. "You're aiming too high."

"We'll get you soon enough, reb," the taunt came back from the other side, "once we kill off what's coming."

He lay back down, rolling on his back, looking down at the edge of the moat. Hundreds of men were still alive, pinned along the slope of the fort and down on the inner side of the moat. He held his hand up, risking that it would get shot off, and waved it in a tight circle to draw attention. Some of the men looked his way.

He pointed across the field, to the top of the fort, and then to himself. Some of the men nodded, pulled caps down tighter, clawed at bodies that they had piled up as barricades, fumbling through cartridge boxes to find a dry round and reload.

Colonel Brown, lying beside him, groaned weakly. After knocking him cold, Hazner had feared for a while the blow had been too hard, perhaps he had broken his skull, but the colonel had finally stirred. Brown had tried to get up on to his knees to vomit and he had knocked him back down, and for his troubles the vomit had splattered all over him.

"Hazner?"

"Just lie still, sir. The next wave is coming, then we'll get you back."

"No, I'm going in."

"Just lie still, sir."

Hazner looked up at the sky; the sun was far higher, red through the smoke, but already hot. He hoped that one of the men coming up would have a full canteen.

He could see them now, battle flags emerging out of the smoke and mist, again the formation in columns of regiment in company front.

"Fire!"

The heavy guns inside the fort recoiled back, Hazner hugging the ground, arm over his colonel, the shock wave knocking his breath out.

Screams greeted the salvo; he looked back and saw the entire front ranks collapsing, officers, one on horseback, going down, flags dropping, one with a broken staff tumbling through the air, a hundred or more men falling.

God, that was like us, he realized, *that was just like us.*

The charge wavered then pressed forward, men scrambling over the fallen ranks, color guards picking up fallen flags.

"Volley fire on my command!" The cry echoed from within the fort.

Hazner held his arm up, waving it again, and he prayed that someone down below saw him.

"Fire!"

The volley rippled from the top of the parapet, more men dropping across the field less than fifty yards away.

"Now!" Hazner roared. "Charge, Carolina, charge!"

He stood up, cursing himself even as he did so. His own heroics surprised him; it was an act of wild stupidity. And yet something compelled him, forced him beyond all reason or sanity to do so.

For a few seconds he stood there, naked, exposed, and no one seemed to move.

One man, then another stood up. By his side Colonel Brown tried to come to his feet, sword held feebly up. And then a wild roar erupted from the men of Perrin's and Pettigrew's divisions, who had endured hell in front of Fort Stevens. Officers were up, waving swords. A wild rage was released and a wall of gray and butternut began to surge forward yet again, crawling, kicking, climbing their way up the blood-soaked muddy slope.

"Come on!"

It was only a few dozen feet to the top, the longest yards he had ever attempted or endured. He came up eye-level with the top of the parapet; a rifle slapped down on the top, aimed straight at his face. He grabbed it by the end of the barrel and jerked it hard, pulling it toward him. He heard a curse; the gun did not go off. He pulled harder, using it as a handhold; the owner of the gun released his grip as Hazner came over the top of the parapet. With one hand he hurled the weapon at the gun crew of the thirty-pounder and then used his own weapon to parry a bayonet thrust.

Suddenly more men were up around him, the first few jumping atop the parapet, gunned down even as they leapt up. More came and yet more. He swung his own musket around, aimed at the battery sergeant, and fired, knocking the man backward.

Yet again he rolled off the top of the wall and into the fort. The Yankees lining the firing step were stunned by the sudden onslaught; most were still fumbling to reload. Several turned and jumped off the firing step and ran across the open parade ground to join the companies still deployed in the middle of the field. This time Hazner did not hesitate. He leapt down, knowing that his only protection was to charge right on their coattails.

He looked to either side; several dozen men were with him, all driven by the same realization.

The shock of hand-to-hand battle exploded in the middle of the fort as the feeble charge slammed into the enemy formation.

He heard cannon fire behind him but did not look back as he waded in, dodging, parrying, slashing, kicking, screaming, the madness of battle upon his soul.

A boy charged straight at him, bayonet lowered. He blocked the blow, driving his own bayonet into the boy's chest. The young soldier gasped, staggered backward, and Hazner lost the grip on his rifle, letting go.

He caught a glimpse of a clubbed musket and dropped to the ground, the blow missing. All was confusion, feet—some barefoot, others in shoes with sky-blue trousers—and he feigned that he was down and out of the fight. More feet, all with sky-blue trousers, stormed around him. He curled up, as if hit in the stomach.

Looking back he saw scores of men gaining the top of the parapet.

"On the wall, volley fire on the wall!"

The feet around him stopped; a ramrod came down, stuck into the ground beside him. The men atop the wall paused, rifles dropping down to the firing position. A scathing volley erupted, the man standing within inches of Hazner's face shrieking, falling backward.

Again the rebel yell, this time louder, confident as the men atop the parapet slid down to the firing step, jumped off, and charged across the courtyard.

Another melee, the harsh sound of wood striking wood and wood striking flesh and bone. Screams, men falling, staggering past, cursing, huzzahs, rebel yells, all commingled together into a terrifying roar that seemed to be trapped within the confines of the fort.

A flash of butternut-clad feet, this one wearing only one shoe. More swarms of men were coming over the fortress wall, shouting, screaming. A field piece in the middle of the parade ground erupted, canister cutting down dozens. Still the charge pressed in, survivors climbing over bodies.

The carnage that ensued was beyond Hazner's worst nightmares. Driven to madness by the slaughter, the men of three divisions, who had endured hell since before dawn, exploded in rage. The sally port at the rear of the fort was clogged with Union soldiers trying to escape. In the close confines of the fight no one had time to ask or give quarter, nor was anyone capable of it anymore. Hazner stood up, in shock, watching as the garrison was slaughtered, many of the men of the First Maine and First New York Heavy Artillery fighting to the end, many bayoneted in the back, more than a few bayoneted or clubbed even as they tried to surrender.

Sickened, exhausted, Hazner collapsed back to the ground and sat unable to move or speak.

A flag bearer came up to his side and stopped.

"First Texas, rally to me! Rally to me!"

Hazner looked up at the man and caught his eye.

"You got water?" Hazner croaked.

The flag bearer nodded, unslung his canteen, and tossed it down.

He uncorked it, leaned his head back, half the water cascading down his jacket as he greedily gulped it. There was a bit of a taste to the water, whiskey, just what he needed. He emptied half of it, and then fought down the sudden urge to vomit.

He passed it back up.

"Thanks."

The First Texan grinned.

"I saw you. By God, I saw you go over the wall, the men following you! Hell of a thing, took the fire off of us. Got us in here."

Hazner couldn't speak.

"You hurt?"

Hazner looked up at him dumbly, and then at the tangle of bodies, many of them writhing in agony, which completely carpeted the parade ground of the fort.

He shook his head. *No, compared to them I'm not hurt*, he thought.

The sergeant from the Texan regiment took his canteen and slung it over his shoulder even as he continued to scream for his regiment to rally on the colors.

The Texan suddenly extended his hand.

"Lee Robinson, First Texas. Look me up after this is over, I'll give you a drink in the White House."

"Sergeant Major Hazner, Fourteenth South Carolina, and thank you."

A knot of men were gathering around the Texan, and with a wild cry he urged them forward, to continue the fight.

Hazner stood up, watching as the Texans reformed, groups of a few dozen here and there, and then pressed forward, little organization left but still game.

He turned and walked back to the parapet that they had just stormed, the tangle of bodies so thick he could barely find ground to step on.

"Sergeant Hazner!"

It was Brown, walking like a drunk, coming toward him.

"Sir."

"Re-form the regiment, we're going in."

Hazner looked at the parade ground, at the gun emplacement for the thirty-pounder, the crew dead. He actually felt regret at the sight of that. The gunner who had been taunting him, he'd have liked to find him and offer a drink, but they were all dead.

"Re-form?"

"Yes, Hazner, we can't let the glory of the taking of Washington slip past us. We can't let Texas have this moment. Now re-form the regiment."

"Sir, what regiment?" Hazner asked woodenly.

In Front of Fort Stevens
8:30 A.M.

CSA "That's it," Lee cried. "Go, Texas, go!"

He had come forward from the grove, standing where he had first seen the fort the day before.

It was as if a vision was unfolding, a recurring dream that one forgets upon awakening, that yet hovers at the edge of memory throughout the day, only to return again in sleep. For two years he had dreamt of this moment, the final door unlocked, the end now within sight. Washington was there for the taking; it was the end.

"General Longstreet. Now, bring your men up now!"

Longstreet was silent and there were tears in his eyes.

"General Longstreet?"

"Sir, it will be another half hour before I can even hope to commit McLaws."

"Then send in what you have!"

"A brigade, maybe two, sir."

"Then send them in!"

"Yes, sir."

He turned and rode back and Lee watched him leave. His gaze shifted to the east, to the sun.

"Oh, God, freeze it in the heavens as You did for Joshua before Jericho. I beg You please let it freeze, for time to stop, to give me but one more precious hour."

The smoke swirled, obscuring the sun for a moment, and then it came clear again . . . and to the southeast, he could see the dome of the Capitol.

To the Rear of Fort Stevens
9:15 A.M.

"I can't let you go any farther, sir!"

The captain of his cavalry escort reined around, blocking the middle of the road.

Lincoln said nothing for a moment. He had always felt uncomfortable on horseback, and this mount was no exception . . . a mare, far too small for his long, bony frame, stirrups pulled up too high, so that he was crouching in the saddle rather than sitting.

He had left the White House shortly after dawn in a carriage, but the tangle of troops heading into battle, and the civilians fleeing it, clogged all the roads, making passage impossible. After a difficult argument with the commander of his escort, a trooper had offered a horse, but there had been no time to adjust the stirrups before setting out again.

They were north of the city, close enough to the battle now that the air overhead hummed with shot and spent bullets. A trooper riding at the front of the column had been knocked unconscious by a spent bullet, which had struck him in the forehead. After that the cavalry escort had ringed him in even tighter, using their bodies as shields. The gesture had both touched and annoyed him.

Battered soldiers were coming back, many wounded, all of them panicked, spreading the word that Fort Stevens had fallen.

He could hear the roar of battle just ahead, the sound shocking, a continual thunder, so close now that the rebel yell was clearly heard.

"Sir, we must go back!" the captain shouted.

"No, Captain, we stay here for the moment."

"Mr. President. I am responsible for your safety. I urge you, sir, let's retire to the naval yard; I will send a courier to fetch your family."

He thought of the servant Jim, at this moment most likely rounding up the other servants, telling them to get guns and prepare.

Lincoln looked over at the captain.

"My family will not be fetched," Lincoln said coldly.

"Sorry, sir. I didn't mean it as an insult. They will be escorted with all dignity."

"No, Captain. They will not be escorted, nor will I. They stay where they are, as I plan to stay right here."

The captain started to open his mouth. Lincoln forced a smile, leaned over, and touched the captain on the sleeve, the young officer startled, looking at him wide-eyed.

"Son, if I run now, what will my soldiers say?"

The captain looked at him, unable to reply.

"I'm the commander of this army, am I not?"

"Ah, yes, sir."

"Fine then, son. Let's just calm down, stay here, and do our duty. At the moment my duty is to be calm, as is yours. We can't go running about like headless chickens, can we?"

The captain actually forced a smile.

"No, sir," he responded with an emphasis on the "sir."

Lincoln patted him on the arm.

"Fine, son. Let's just stay here for the moment and see what we can do to make sure this wrestling match turns out a victory for the Union."

He smiled again and the captain nodded, turning away, but ordering his men to form a barrier in front of the president, the captain himself taking position directly in front of him.

Lincoln had to admit that inwardly he was terrified. He had only heard battle from a distance before, the two fights at Manassas, the distant thunder from Union Mills. He never imagined it could be so loud, so all-consuming, and so frightening.

His mount, however, did not even flinch as a shell fluttered overhead and detonated with a thunderclap, the captain looking back anxiously to see that he was not harmed.

He smiled yet again.

"Sir, at least take that hat off." And the captain hesitated.

"What?"

"Your hat. You're tall, sir, that hat marks you. A rebel sharpshooter might see it."

He realized the captain was right. He had somehow retained his stovepipe hat on the ride out. No, if it marked him, others would see it as well; his boys would see it and that was what he wanted.

He shook his head. Exasperated, the captain turned to face front.

A cluster of officers came down the road, riding back from the fight, one of the men swaying in his saddle, blood covering the front of his jacket. In the lead was Heintzelman. The general reined in and saluted.

"Mr. President, just what are you doing here?" Heintzelman shouted.

"Watching the battle, General."

"Sir, battle is not a spectator's sport. The rebs are not a quarter of a mile off and coming on fast."

"What is the situation, General?"

"They've taken Fort Stevens; they have a breakthrough across a front of more than a quarter mile."

"The flanking forts?"

"Still holding for the moment, sir, but it's getting shaky."

"And you propose?"

Heintzelman did not reply, looking back to the north.

"Your plans, General?"

"Sir, we should abandon the line and pull back into the city."

"What has General Lee put in?"

"Sir, it's hard to say. Looks like three divisions, but more will be coming."

Lincoln nodded.

"Like trying to pour a hundred gallons of buttermilk through a funnel. It'll take him time, General."

"Sir, I know that, but the men are running, sir," and even as he spoke he gestured to the open fields, the battered remnants of defenders heading back into the city.

"Calm, General. Let us be calm."

Heintzelman looked at him wide-eyed, as if about ready to explode.

"Calm, General. If we lead we can rally those men. They will invest their fears in our courage. But they must see our courage and rally to it."

Heintzelman lowered his head, nodded, wiping his eyes, and Lincoln was startled to see that the man was actually in tears.

"I'm sorry, Mr. President. Sorry. You are right, sir. We can rally them."

Lincoln felt an infinite exhaustion. He thought of the pictures he had seen of General Washington, the forlorn hope of crossing the Delaware, of the bitter winter of Valley Forge when nearly all had given up hope. The mantle of that now rested upon him, the sacrifices made to create this republic now upon his shoulders.

He said nothing, features now stern, bony shoulders braced back.

"Let us just stay here," Lincoln said softly.

Heintzelman looked back up, nodded, and fell in by his side.

Men continued to pass, falling back, but at the sight of the two, here and there a soldier slowed, stopped, a few calling out Lincoln's name, others silent, as if ashamed. Gradually a cluster of men gathered around them. A flag bearer came out of the smoke, carrying the dark blue banner of Maine. The soldier stopped and without comment planted the staff of the flag in the ground and turned to face back North. Within minutes hundreds were gathering. There was no cheering, no singing, no heroic gestures, just grim determination.

As he looked at them he wept inwardly, struggling to hide his tears. Here was the republic, his country, which he had sworn to defend and which those men were now defending, without fanfare, without much hope of seeing the day through to the end, but which they would now die for. The cause of the United States of America was reduced to this band of nearly defeated men who were gathering new courage, reorganizing themselves, and beginning to gird for battle in front of his eyes.

He took heart from these rallying troops, as he had taken heart from a servant of a race who till now were exempt in the minds of so many from that solemn pledge that all men were indeed created equal.

Another flag bearer, from New York, fell in carrying the national flag. A militia regiment, easily distinguished by their bright, clean uniforms, came up the road at the double. Sweat streaked their faces; many were gasping for breath, many trembling with fear, and yet they swung into line.

Heintzelman looked over at Lincoln, nodded, and then, with proper flourish, drew out his sword and saluted.

Lincoln could only nod.

The ragged formation stepped off, following Heintzelman. They went back into the inferno. He caught glimpses of battle, his first sight of that blood-red banner of the South coming forward, a dimly seen line of men advancing. A round struck one of his escorts, the man swearing, turning away, clutching a shattered arm. The wounded trooper looked at Lincoln, then pushed his mount back into the formation around the president, reassuming his post.

The roar of battle swelled, expanding, racing outward to either flank, Union huzzah counterpointed by rebel yell.

And then they started to fall back, giving ground slowly, men dropping, but none running.

"Sir, we must move back. Now."

His attention was so fixed on the battle that he had not even noticed the captain by his side, reaching over to take his reins.

"Not yet."

"Sir, they're a hundred yards off, they'll be on us in a minute."

He shook his head.

The captain started to pull his mount around and Lincoln angrily jerked his reins back.

"We stay here," Lincoln said sharply.

The captain looked at him, wide-eyed, and then with a flicker of a smile raised his hand and saluted.

"Yes sir, Mr. President."

And then a distant cheer rose up behind them.

Lincoln looked back over his shoulder; even as he did so, another trooper of his escort collapsed, falling from his horse, dead. Behind them, though, he saw something coming. A column on the road from the city, running, bayonet points held high, tin cups and canteens clanging, an officer riding at the front ahead of the colors.

The officer came on fast, now urging his mount to a gallop and then reining in hard, and with an elegant gesture raised up his sword and saluted.

"Mr. President, I'm Col. Robert Shaw, Fifty-fourth Massachusetts."

"Colonel, it warms my heart to see you and your men; you may be just in time to save your nation's capital."

"Mr. President. We're from Charleston. We arrived at the naval yard two hours ago. My brigade commander, General Strong, ordered me to move my regiment to the sound of the guns. He and the rest of the brigade will be coming up shortly."

Lincoln looked back and saw the column of veterans beginning to shake out into battle line, the men professional-looking, moving sharply . . . and they were colored.

Unable to speak, Lincoln faced Shaw again.

Shaw could not help but smile.

"We loaded up from Charleston the day the message arrived about Union Mills. There's a full brigade of combat-experienced troops behind me, sir. Now just tell me where to go."

He still could not speak.

"To the sound of the guns, sir!" the captain exclaimed, reaching out to grasp Shaw on the arm.

Shaw saluted, turned, and galloped off.

A minute later the regiment swept past, and at the sight of the president, the men burst loose with a thunderous cheer.

"Lincoln . . . Lincoln . . . Lincoln!"

The charge went in.

He watched them go forward, still unable to speak. Behind them, back down the Seventh Street road, he saw more troops coming on at the double, a battery of artillery galloping across the open field beside the road, caissons leaping into the air.

He turned back to say something to the captain. But the saddle was empty, the young officer down on the ground, a couple of his troopers around him, kneeling, one looking up anguish-stricken at Lincoln.

He dismounted and knelt down by the captain. The man had been struck in the chest, was struggling to breathe.

Lincoln took his hand.

"Will we hold, sir?" the captain gasped.

"Yes, son, we'll hold. You have helped save the Union this day."

In Front of Fort Stevens

July 18, 1863
10:00 A.M.

G eneral Lee, I beg you, sir, call it off."

He turned to look at Longstreet and Hood, who stood beside him.

He could not reply.

"Sir," Hood interjected, "it's finished. They're closing the breech. They have a colored regiment in the line now; one of my staff says it's the Fifty-fourth Massachusetts. General Beauregard reported that same regiment as being in front of Charleston two weeks ago. It means, sir, that they have fresh troops, experienced troops in the city now."

"Can we not sweep them aside?" Lee asked, and even as he spoke he realized his own will was breaking, he was asking now for some final reassurance.

"Sir," Hood continued. "My divisions are a shambles, one of them my own former command; if they cannot take it, no one can."

Longstreet shifted uncomfortably at this unintended slight.

"General Longstreet?"

"I agree with General Hood, sir. I'm sorry, sir, but that road, in places the mud is knee-deep; we just can't bring men up fast enough to exploit the breakthrough."

"What about somewhere else along the line? They must have stripped their defenses to the bone elsewhere."

"Sir, we have no infantry along the rest of the line. We don't have enough men as is, even if we do force our way into that city. Sir, we've lost five, maybe ten thousand this day; we'll lose that much again, even more if we press it."

He paused, as if seeking a dramatic effect.

"Sir, we just might take the city by the end of the day if you press it, but the Army of Northern Virginia, our last hope, will be destroyed doing it."

"I beg you, sir," Hood cried, his voice close to breaking. "Stop it now, our chance has passed for this day."

Lee looked toward the fort, that accursed fort. Wounded, demoralized, pitiful fragments of broken units were coming back out of the smoke.

He lowered his head and nodded.

"Pull them back," he whispered.

He looked back to the southeast. The Capitol was still visible, its nearly completed dome standing defiant.

He turned and walked away.

Chapter Seven

G.S.A. General Lee walked with infinite sadness and weariness through the hospital area. As he passed, those around him, even the most hideously wounded, fell silent.

General Pettigrew had been found, just before dusk, when Lee had asked Heintzelman for a truce. Contrary to the first reports, the general had still been alive. He was no longer; Lee had held Pettigrew's hand as he died.

Perrin had been more fortunate, hit twice, in the arm and leg; the limbs had not been broken. Perrin had wept at the sight of his commander, asking forgiveness for not going in "more sharply."

How did one answer such a statement when it was obvious where the fault truly rested?

Lee finally broke the silence, looking over at "Pete" Longstreet, who respectfully walked by his side.

"It was my fault, General Longstreet."

"General Lee, you did all that any man could do."

"I should have waited another night. I attacked too soon, I asked too much of these men."

"Sir, the reason you attacked this morning was clearly confirmed. Reinforcements are pouring into that city." He nodded in the direction of

Washington. "If you had waited another night, the results would have
been the same, perhaps worse."

"Then I should have realized it was impossible."

"Sir, how? The only way to confirm the impossibility was to attempt
it. If we had not attacked at all, what would we have then thought? It
would have haunted us, the thought that we might have been able to take
it. It would have undermined morale. What would all have said across the
South if we had not tried?"

"A terrible confirmation, General," Lee sighed. "Eight thousand or
more dead, wounded, or captured. I might as well strike the divisions of
Pettigrew and Perrin off the roster. After the losses suffered at Gettysburg
and Union Mills, and now this, they are fought out."

Longstreet nodded in agreement. The two divisions, since July 1, had
sustained over eighty percent casualties. All of the original brigade commanders, except for Scales, were dead or wounded. All but three of the
regimental commanders were down as well. As fighting units, the two divisions were finished. They would have to be pulled from the order of
battle, rested, consolidated, and reorganized.

The two walked back toward the grove that had been his headquarters for the last two days. With the truce, the enemy had stopped shelling
the position, but when morning arrived Lee would have to move. As they
approached the roughly fashioned bridge of logs and barn siding, the two
stepped aside as a convoy of a dozen ambulances passed. The shrieks and
groans of the wounded within cut to Lee's soul and he stood with hat off
as they passed, in the darkness no one recognizing him.

The grove was illuminated by several dozen lanterns, officers and
staff standing silent. There was no frolicking this evening, no banter or
music. All were silent. All were oppressed by the cost of this day's fighting and the friends dead and dying. At his approach whispered commands echoed, men coming to attention, some taking off their hats,
others saluting.

He looked around at the gathering he had called—Longstreet, who
was already at his side, Hood, arm in a sling from a rifle ball that had
nicked his shoulder, Stuart, Walter Taylor, Jed Hotchkiss the cartographer, Scales as the senior surviving officer of the first two assault waves.
Staff retreated to a respectful distance as Lee stepped under the over-
hanging tarpaulin and sat down in front of the rough-hewn table that had
been dragged over from a nearby house.

"A terrible day, gentlemen," he opened without fanfare.

No one spoke.

"I take full responsibility for what happened here today."

"General, we all must take responsibility for it," Hood interjected.

"I will hear no more on that, General Hood. I ordered the attack, it was my decision and mine alone."

He held his hand up for silence and Hood lowered his head.

Yet Hood was right to a certain degree. It was his first attack as a corps commander. The assault waves should have been better coordinated, sent in directly one after another. The attack had kicked off an hour late, the second wave going in late as well.

Hood should have informed him of that confusion before the attack commenced. But on the other side of the ledger it was a night attack, something the Army of Northern Virginia had never before attempted, except after already being committed to action at Chancellorsville, and that was against a beaten foe . . . and in the confusion that action had cost him Jackson. The single road up was indeed a quagmire; the fog and friction of war were at play. He should have sensed that, made closer watch on the preparations, but he knew that he, too, had been exhausted and in his exhaustion had trusted the judgment of those beneath him.

That was his responsibility and his alone.

"There was no alternative," Pete said even as he puffed a cigar to light. "We had to try and strike before reinforcements came in. The men that counterattacked us in the final assault were veteran units pulled all the way up from Charleston. We knew they were coming and had to attack before they arrived. If they are moving the entire besieging force up from there, that could mean twenty thousand additional men are now in the city or will be within the next few days. General Lee, that is why you had to attack today, and not tomorrow. Today was our only hope of taking the city by a coup de main."

"Is it true there was a regiment of niggers with them?" Stuart asked.

Lee looked up at him sharply. "You know I don't like that word, General."

"I'm sorry, sir. Colored then."

"I saw them," Hood interjected. "It must be that regiment from Massachusetts. Now we must deal with that as well."

"If we take any of them prisoners," Lee said softly, "they are to be treated like any other soldiers. I want that clearly understood. I disagree with General Beauregard's statements and that of our government that they will be sold as slaves and their officers executed. I will not have that in my army and I want that clearly understood by all."

No one spoke.

"We drift from our topic, gentlemen," Lee announced. "And that is to decide our course of action."

He looked at the men gathered at the table.

"Two of our divisions are no longer fit for service, at least for a fortnight or more. What is left of Anderson's division is still in Virginia, escorting prisoners back. In our remaining six divisions of infantry I would estimate that we have barely thirty thousand men under arms."

He looked at Taylor, who sadly nodded in agreement.

"That does not include artillery and cavalry, sir," Stuart said.

"No, of course not, General Stuart, but when it comes to siege operations and assault, it is infantry we need."

No one replied.

"It is safe to assume that their garrison in Washington, now receiving yet more reinforcements, numbers at least thirty thousand, perhaps as many as forty thousand by tomorrow. Their heavy artillery, well, we saw what but three forts defended with heavy artillery can do to our men out in the open."

"Are you saying, sir, that the hope of taking Washington is finished?" Stuart asked.

"Do you see any alternative, sir?"

"They are still strung out defending thirty miles of front, sir. We can maneuver, feign, probe. Sooner or later, we'll find the weak spot and push in."

"That will take days, maybe weeks," Longstreet replied, "and every day means yet more men in their garrison to repulse us. They have the interior lines. Even if we did break through, they can muster a force sufficient to face us at the edge of the city or inside of it.

"I must say this now, sir," Longstreet continued. "Our army, unfortunately, is not an army that can fight a siege, or take a city the size of Washington; we are a field army that survives by maneuver, surprise, and agility. That other type of warfare fits our enemy, with their limitless numbers."

He sighed. "It doesn't fit us and never will."

"Then you believed we would not take that city?" Lee asked.

Longstreet hesitated, then finally nodded his head. "I didn't think we could take it if they were prepared to fight block by block and house by house."

"I wish I had heard that from you yesterday, General, or a week ago before we even marched down from Westminster."

Longstreet could sense the rebuke and his features reddened.

"We had to try, sir. After all, their army might have lost enough morale after their shattering defeat at Union Mills. The green troops in the forts might have broken down. The reinforcements might have come a day later. We had to try, General Lee. Maybe it was a forlorn hope, maybe not. But we had to try. Everyone, our men, the government, the people of the South, expected it and therefore we had to try."

Placated, Lee nodded and leaned back in the camp chair.

History would have expected it, he realized. After the triumph at Gettysburg and Union Mills history itself would have expected him to march on Washington and take it. He had to have tried.

The dream of taking Washington had been the goal ever since the start of this campaign, the thought that with the final defeat of the Army of the Potomac, Washington would fall and then it would be over. Was that itself an illusion?

If so, what now? Was everything this campaign was predicated upon an illusion? Was there nothing that could force the North to negotiate a peace?

Walter stepped away from the group for a moment and returned with a tin cup brimming with coffee. Lee nodded his thanks, lifted the cup, blew on the edge and took a sip, then set the cup back down.

Hotchkiss had already spread the maps of northern Virginia, Maryland, and southern Pennsylvania out on the table. Lee examined them. At Gettysburg this had been a defining moment, when the map seemed to come alive with movement, of troops marching on roads, enemy positions marked, all leading to a place where victory awaited.

But nothing stirred within his heart and mind. All was still and silent, except for the creaking of the ambulances passing nearby on the road, the distant cries of the wounded piercing the night.

"We have three choices," he finally said, rubbing his eyes then taking another sip of coffee. "We either stay here and continue the action or we pull back into Maryland, maybe toward Frederick, and in so doing reorganize, see to our logistical needs, and then perhaps consider Baltimore. We can also retire back into Virginia and reorganize and refit until Grant and his new army come after us."

He had laid it out cleanly and no one spoke, though he could see that all were now forming their responses, each ready to set forth his opinion.

"Continue it," Stuart said sharply. "I still maintain that we can maneuver, shift some of our forces toward Blandensburg, others down along the Potomac, stretch them out using my cavalry, then when the weak point is found, go in."

"Not again." This time it was Scales. Though he was only a brigade officer, now in command of a shattered division, all looked over at him respectfully. He was the only general to come back out of today's inferno.

"Go on, General Scales," Lee said politely.

"Sir, as you know, I was there today and saw it all. My men, sir, they did everything humanly possible, beyond humanly possible. They stormed through six rows of abatis, waded a moat, charged a muddy slope, and finally took Fort Stevens. We lost two divisions just doing that, and now it, too, is back in their hands.

"I actually thought that after two hours of firing, the garrison inside would run out of ammunition. I looked in one of their bunkers once the fort was taken, sir; they could have kept up that rate of fire with canister alone for another three or four hours, and with shell and solid shot for the rest of the day.

"Sir, taking those forts is pitting mere human flesh against earthworks and steel. Maybe if we had a hundred thousand more men, and, God forgive us, the cruelty to use them without thought or compassion, we could do it, but I for one, sir, could not give such an order ever again."

"I agree, General," Lee said softly. "I will not order such an assault, ever again, unless I am certain that the sacrifice is worth the final reward."

Stuart started to raise an objection, but Lee's tone indicated that this line of debate was finished. The attack on Washington was over.

He could see though that what he had just admitted was that the raison d'être of the entire campaign was now in question and he could not leave it there.

"If we had reinforcements, and with them the proper equipment to conduct a successful siege, only then would I now consider it. We took the gamble, we did our best, but things have come out against us."

A gloom settled over the group.

"I cannot believe," Hood finally interjected, "that to withdraw back to Virginia is our only remaining option."

Grateful for the comment, Lee nodded for Hood to continue.

"That would be the ultimate admission of defeat. All our people's hopes coming out of our triumph at Union Mills will be dashed if we now turn our men south, especially after this defeat. The Yankee press will crow that we've been turned back without hope of ever returning. It will give them time as well to rebuild the Army of the Potomac once more and to combine it with Grant's new force. I think, sir, if you do that now, you will lose the war."

"I agree," Stuart announced and there were nods around the table.

"We have good supplies here," Hood said. "If we can maintain ourselves here through the fall harvest, it will give all of Virginia, especially the valley, time to recover and then, if need be, support us through the winter and following spring. We still have a good stockpile of ordnance supplies taken from Union Mills as well, so there is no concern for that at the moment."

"Our numbers though," Longstreet said, and his words dampened the first sign of renewed vigor.

"Go on, General Longstreet."

"As we already discussed, we are down to roughly thirty thousand men in the infantry. We know that on the Yankee side thirty thousand or more are, or shortly will be, in Washington. Though we might scoff at them now, the Army of the Potomac will rebuild. Perhaps as many as thirty thousand got out and are somewhere north of the Susquehanna. They are undoubtedly funneling men into that army even as we speak. And then there is Grant. He is bringing in troops as well. We might very well be facing a hundred to a hundred and fifty thousand in fairly short order."

"Grant?" Hood snapped. "An amateur from the West compared to the caliber of what we have here in the East. At this moment, I think McClellan would be a bigger threat."

"An amateur who defeated Johnston and then took Vicksburg? I wouldn't call the victor of Pillow, Donelson, Pittsburgh Landing, and Vicksburg an amateur, General Hood," Lee commented.

"It will be months before he can marshal a force capable of meeting us," Hood pressed.

"General Hood, they brought up troops from Charleston in a matter of days. What is to prevent them from bringing troops to Grant from as far afield as Texas, Florida, or even his own army from Vicksburg, battle-hardened men fresh from a major victory?"

"That would strip every other front clean," Stuart replied, coming to Hood's support.

"This is the only front that matters now," Longstreet countered. "If we take back the Mississippi, New Orleans, and all of Kentucky, what does it matter if this army is defeated and, by logical deduction, Richmond then falls?"

"Then we take it to the hills, the mountains, and down into the deep south until they finally give up."

"A dozen or more years, is that it?" Longstreet snapped.

"Gentlemen," Lee interjected, extending both hands in a calming gesture.

The arguing generals looked to him.

"Both of you are right. We must be concerned about this Grant, the potential that he can form around him another army. But I do not see that happening tomorrow, or even in a month. We still have time to consider that when the time comes. Let us hold ourselves to the immediate, to our concerns of tonight and the next few days."

Hood and Longstreet gazed at each other and then looked back to Lee.

They both nodded in reply.

"I think, gentlemen, that we have some sense of things this evening. We cannot storm Washington, nor is retreat back to Virginia a viable choice."

No one raised an objection.

"Then let us rest our men in place tomorrow. General Longstreet, pass the word back to your corps to stop where they are on the road. General Stuart, continue to observe their lines to either flank; if something remarkable develops we will of course act on it, but by that I mean they all but abandon their lines. I do not want you to bring on any sort of general engagement without my direct orders."

He shifted and looked over at his aide.

"Colonel Taylor, meet with our medical staff and see to arrangements for the proper evacuation of our wounded. General Stuart, you will have to detail off at least two or three regiments to escort our injured back to Virginia. The truce along this front lasts till dawn and I expect all to observe that. Colonel Taylor, at dawn I want a letter to be sent to General Heintzelman extending my thanks for his courtesy. If need be, we might ask for a truce till noon but we'll decide that in the morning."

He looked around at the gathering.

"Any other questions?"

"Sir," Hood pressed. "I understand that we have decided to stay in Maryland, but to what end now, sir?"

Lee sat back with a sigh. In truth he simply didn't know. Ever since crossing the Potomac he had moved with the next goal clearly in sight, first to find the Army of the Potomac and position it on suitable ground for a decisive blow. After that to try and take Washington. That had been decided this day.

What next? Hold in place and hope they attack? They would be fools to do so until their strength is again overwhelming. Pull back up into central Maryland, toward Frederick perhaps? That would significantly shorten his lines of communication, but for the moment that was not a major concern. The windfall at Westminster, and the richness of the surrounding farmlands, could support them right into early autumn. Try for Baltimore? It would extend him, widening his flank to the north, and leave in his rear a gathering enemy strength in Washington. His instinct of the moment was to draw back toward Frederick, but he was not yet ready to give that order.

He could not decide that tonight, not after this bitter day.

"We'll talk again at dusk tomorrow, gentlemen," was all he could say. "I think we all need a day of rest."

One by one they saluted and stepped away from the table. He could see that Pete wanted to continue the conversation, but a gentle shake of his head was signal enough. Pete saluted and withdrew until finally only Walter was left.

"Sir, your bed is ready," Walter said. "May I suggest some sleep."

"In a little while, Walter."

Walter made as if to argue. The general touched his aide lightly on the arm.

"I think, Walter, I'm going to order you to bed. You can see to your duties before dawn."

"Yes, sir."

Walter knew better than to press the issue. He touched the brim of his hat and withdrew.

Alone, at least as alone as he could ever be with this army, Lee sat back down but then, after a restless moment, he stood up and walked out of the grove. The ever-present troopers who served as his escort stirred.

"Just walking," Lee said. "Stay off your mounts, let them rest at least."

A sergeant with the detail saluted, called for a dozen men, but then kept them back at a respectful distance.

Lee slowly walked up the slope. The tangled grass, brambles, and corn had all been trampled down in the assault, the debris making his footing somewhat difficult. As he went along he could see dozens, perhaps a hundred or more lanterns, now pale and ghostlike in the light mist that was rising, ambulance crews and stretcher parties sweeping the ground for the fallen.

In the faint glow of starlight he finally saw the outline of the fort, easy to pick out by the lanterns atop it, several signal flares sputtering on the breastworks, casting a sharp, metallic light.

He could hear distant moans, cries, a hysterical shriek, "Don't touch me! Don't touch me!"

He lowered his head.

"Merciful God, forgive me my many faults," he whispered. "Grant repose to those who fell here this day. Grant peace to the families of the fallen, and lay Your gentle hand of peace upon those who suffer this night. Forgive us, Oh Lord, for what we have done to each other this day. Amen."

He looked back up at the fort. Beyond it he could see the unfinished dome of the Capitol, the lights of the city. For a moment he wondered if a more distant light was the front porch of his own home, but knew that was fanciful illusion, though the thought of it caused his eyes to sting.

He turned and walked away.

Fort Stevens

July 18, 1863
11:45 P.M.

Lincoln slowed his pace as he walked into the fort. Now he was seeing it up close for the first time. Torches flickered on the parade ground, which had been turned into a temporary hospital, the men waiting for the ambulances that would take them back into the city and out of harm's way if the battle should resume tomorrow.

It was a charnel house, thick with the stench of torn flesh, vomit, excrement, gun smoke, with the faint whiff of ether and chloroform. He wanted to shut out the sound of a surgeon at work, taking a man's leg off, operating on a rough plank set up on sawhorses right out in the open, two assistants holding lanterns to either side of him.

He spared a quick glance; the surgeon did not even see him, so intent was he on his work, struggling to loop a string of catgut around a hemorrhaging artery. A male nurse, middle-aged, white-flecked beard, was beside the surgeon, ready to hand over more looped strings of ligatures. The man looked somehow familiar, and their eyes met. It was the poet he had heard so much about and read. The poet smiled, and the gesture was strange until he realized it was a look of encouragement, an almost fatherly gaze. Lincoln nodded and turned away, fearful that if he actually saw the operation in its entirety, the leg dropping off, he would become ill.

He carefully stepped around the wounded, most of them so preoccupied with their personal hells that they did not know who was walking past them. To the east side of the parade ground there was a long row of still forms, the dead; a couple of orderlies staggered by, carrying a body away from where the wounded were spread out. They dropped the body and went back, walking slowly.

He saw a knot of officers gathered on the parapet, and approached. One of them turned, whispered, and the others came about, coming to attention. He recognized Heintzelman in the middle of the group, arm in a sling.

He had not held much confidence in this man, and still had doubts as to his fitness to manage an independent command, but Heintzelman had proven in the moment of crisis that he had courage, personally going back in to lead the countercharge, getting wounded in the process.

Heintzelman fumbled for a second to salute, grimaced, letting his right arm drop back into the sling, and then saluted with his left hand as Lincoln carefully ascended the steps to the gun platform where the officers were gathered around the thirty-pounder.

"They're still out there, bringing in their wounded," Heintzelman said.

The president didn't need to be told. The ground before him at first glance looked like a summer meadow covered with fireflies. The lanterns swung back and forth, bobbing up and down, some not moving, resting on the ground, casting enough light to reveal a stretcher-team bending over to pick up their burden. Ambulances were lined up alongside a row of torches, men being lifted into the back. Cries of anguish echoed across the field.

Bright flares were set along the top of the fortress wall, illuminating the moat below and the wall of the fort. Men were sloshing through the muck, pulling out bodies, dragging them up the opposite slope.

"Sir, perhaps it's not wise for you to be this close. Those are rebs working out there," Heintzelman whispered.

A bit surprised, Lincoln suddenly realized they were indeed rebels, not thirty feet away, moving like ghosts in the dark. One was humming a hymn, "Rock of Ages," as he helped to pull a wounded man up out of the moat. But his hymn was all but drowned out by the low, murmuring cries, sounding like the damned trapped in the eternal pit below.

"I'm safe here," Lincoln replied softly. "General Lee is scrupulous about a truce, his men will honor it."

"Sir, I took the liberty of loaning them twenty ambulances with teams; they were short."

"Short?"

"One of their doctors told one of my staff that their army was bogged down on the roads, leaving all their baggage and nearly all their artillery behind. The ambulances were left behind as well. They only had a few dozen with them."

"It was right of you to do so, General."

It was an interesting bit of intelligence, explaining perhaps why they had not attacked with more strength.

"I also sent over several wagons of medical supplies. We've got warehouses full of ether, bandages, medicine; I just couldn't stand to see brave boys like those out there suffering needlessly now that they are out of the fight."

Surprised, Lincoln looked over at the general and nodded his approval.

"You did the proper thing, General, and I thank you."

He stood silent and no one dared to interrupt.

"If they want more time after dawn, do not hesitate to give it to them. The same stands for ambulances and medical supplies. I will not have wounded men out there suffering."

"Yes, sir," Heintzelman lowered his head, "and thank you, sir."

"Thank you?"

"This morning, sir. What you did on the road. The entire army is talking about it."

Lincoln felt himself flush. He had done nothing out of the ordinary and he was still a bit shocked by the terror he had felt when the enemy battle line came into sight, flags held high, that terrible screaming yell resounding. Certainly his three months in the militia years ago had not prepared him for this moment of crisis and the overwhelming emotions that came with it. That was play soldiering. This was the real thing. It was not just terror for himself, but terror as well that here was the ending of it, that he had lost the war, that the republic would be forever sundered, and centuries of division, woe, and yet more war were now the fate of this world.

He had hardly been able to think of anything else, even as the reinforcements stormed up the road, deployed, and then struck with such terrible fury, losing a third of their numbers, but hitting with such ferocity that the enemy attack had faltered and withdrawn.

He started to turn and leave but then recognized a diminutive officer standing at the edge of the group. He approached, the officer stiffening, saluting. Lincoln extended his hand.

"Shaw, isn't it?"

"Yes, Mr. President."

"I know your parents."

"Yes, sir, they are honored to have your acquaintance."

"As I am now honored to have yours, Colonel. Your men were magnificent this day. The entire nation shall know of them."

"Thank you, sir, but we were just one regiment out of many who did their duty here today."

He could sense that the other officers were watching. Some might be jealous of the attention, but Shaw's words had the proper diplomatic effect and he could see a couple of the generals behind Shaw nodding with approval.

"Your men proved something today, Shaw. In this time of crisis I hope we can raise a hundred thousand men of color in short order. Your example will open that way."

"Thank you, sir."

"Once the crisis of this moment has passed, Shaw, I'd like you and several of your enlisted men to visit me in the White House."

Shaw grinned.

"An honor, sir."

"I will confess to being exhausted tonight. I might forget this invitation, so please send a messenger to the White House. Have him ask for Mr. Hay, and an appointment will be made."

"Thank you, Mr. President."

Lincoln lightly took his hand, shook it, and then left the gun position. He could hear the chatter behind him, one of the generals offering Shaw a cigar, telling him that he was certainly the "trump card" tonight.

As he stepped off the ladder, the horror was again before him. Half a dozen ambulances were lined up, stretcher-bearers swinging their loads in, four men to an ambulance on stretchers, one or two lightly wounded sitting up and riding the buckboard, another upright wounded man forward on the seat with the driver. As the ambulances jostled into motion, cries and groans erupted. Men who had struggled so hard to hide their pain as they believed soldiers should, once inside the confines of the ambulance and concealed by the canvas walls, could at last give voice to their pain—and most did.

He took his hat off, watching as the ambulances moved out of the sally port.

"Mr. President."

He turned. It was the poet.

"Yes?"

"Mr. President, I was just helping a boy. He saw you come in and asked to speak with you. He says his ma knows your family."

The escort of cavalry that had trailed behind him at a respectful distance came in a bit closer. A lieutenant, who had replaced the young captain who was now dead, tried to interrupt.

"The president has had a hard day, sir, perhaps another time."

"Mr. President, he won't live much longer. I feared to leave his side to help that surgeon you saw me with even for a moment. He's dying, shot in the stomach."

Lincoln nodded.

"Yes," was all he could say, not sure if he could bear what was coming.

The poet led the way, weaving past hundreds of wounded lying on the ground, makeshift surgical stations set up under awnings, a pile of arms and legs stacked on the ground so that he slowed, wanting to offer a protest; decency demanded that these shattered limbs should be hidden away. But how can you hide away a hundred limbs when every second was precious, every orderly staggering with exhaustion, the surgeons slashing and cutting as fast as they could to stop hemorrhaging, plug holes in gasping chest wounds, dull the pain of a chest so badly shattered that the broken ends of bare ribs were sticking out, push back in loops of intestines, or still the hysterical babbling of a man whose brains were oozing out?

The poet slowed, then looked back at the president.

"Sir, one thing."

"And that is?"

"He's a Confederate soldier, sir."

Lincoln slowed, paused, and then nodded his head wearily.

"That doesn't matter now."

The poet offered a reassuring smile, took him gently by the arm, and guided him the last few feet.

The boy was curled up on his side, panting like an injured deer; in the flickering torchlight his face was ghostly pale, hair matted to his forehead with sweat. His uniform was tattered, his butternut jacket frayed at the cuffs and collar, unbuttoned. The boy was clutching a bundle of bandages against his abdomen. In the shadows the stain leaking out seemed black. He looked up, eyes unfocused.

"I brought him to you," the poet whispered, kneeling down beside the boy.

The boy looked around, a glimmer of panic on his face, and he feebly tried to move, then groaned from the pain.

"I can't see."

Lincoln knelt down, then sat on the ground, extending his hand, taking the boy's hand, touching it lightly. The skin was cold.

"I'm here, son, I'm here."

"Mr. Lincoln?"

"Yes, son."

"Private Jenkins, sir. Bobbie Jenkins, Twenty-sixth North Carolina."

"Yes, son. You asked for me?"

"My ma, sir. She was born in Kentucky. When she was a girl she took sick with the typhoid."

He stopped for a few seconds, struggling for breath.

"Your ma, Mrs. Hanks, helped take care of her. You were a boy then, sir, she told me, she remembered you bringing some soup to her. Do you remember her?"

"Of course I do," he lied. "A pretty girl, your ma."

The boy smiled.

"Mama," he gasped, and curled into a fetal position, panting for air.

"It hurts," he whispered.

Lincoln looked at the poet sitting on the other side of the boy.

"Anything for the pain?" Lincoln whispered.

"As much as we dare give him," the poet replied softly, leaning over to brush the matted hair from the boy's brow.

"In spite of this war," the boy sighed, "Ma always said you and your kin were good folk."

"Thank you, son, I know you and your ma are good folk, too."

"The man here, he told me I'm going to be with God soon."

Lincoln looked up at the poet and was awed by the beatific look on the man's face as he gently brushed back the boy's hair, using a soiled handkerchief to wipe his brow.

"I'm afraid, sir," the boy whispered. "Please help me. Will you write to her? Tell her I died bravely."

"Yes, son."

"Help me," the boy whispered, his body trembling. "I'm afraid."

Lincoln lowered his head, slid closer, and took the boy into his arms.

"Do you remember the prayer your mother taught you? The one you said together every night when she tucked you into bed?"

The boy began to cry softly.

"Let's say it together," Lincoln whispered.

The boy continued to cry.

"Now I lay me down to sleep," Lincoln began.

The boy's voice, soft, already distant, joined in.

"I pray the Lord my soul to keep . . ."

"If I should die before I wake . . ."

"I pray the Lord my soul to take . . ."

Even as the last words escaped the boy's lips, he shuddered, a convulsion running through him.

He thought of his own boy, of Willie, his last strangled gasp for air.

There was a gentle exhaling, the tension in the boy's body relaxing, going limp, his last breath escaping, washing over Lincoln's face.

He held him. He tried to stifle his own sobs as he held him. He knew others were watching, watching the president, not a tired, heartsick old man; they were watching the president, but he didn't care.

He felt a gentle touch on his shoulder, the poet, up on his knees, leaning over the body.

"I'll take him, sir."

He didn't want to let go, but knew he had to.

He leaned over and kissed the boy on the brow, the way he knew the boy's mother had kissed him every night.

"God forgive me," he whispered.

He sat back up, letting the poet take the body. The poet ever so gently closed the boy's eyes, folded his arms. He reached into his pocket, took out a notebook and a pencil. He scratched the name of the boy and his regiment on a slip of paper. He drew a pin out of the binding of the notebook and fastened the name on the boy's breast pocket. Lincoln realized that this little ritual was an attempt to identify a body so it would have a marker, something the poet had done innumerable times before. The boy, however, would most likely go into a mass grave with hundreds of his comrades.

The poet took another piece of paper and again wrote the boy's name and his hometown in North Carolina upon it, and handed it to the president.

"You promised him, sir," the poet said. There was no reproof in his voice, no questioning, just a gentle reminder.

"Thank you," Lincoln whispered.

The poet stood up and Lincoln came up as well. He looked around and saw that all were silent. Dozens had been watching, Union and Confederate, lying side by side, all silent, some weeping.

He lowered his head, struggling to gain control of his voice.

"Let us all pray together," he said, his voice suddenly calm.

"Oh, God, please lift this terrible scourge of war from our land. Let all here return safely home to their loved ones, and together let us learn to live in peace."

Chapter Eight

Harrisburg, Pennsylvania

July 19, 1863
3:30 A.M.

US The train drifted into the station, its bell ringing, the steam venting and swirling in the still morning air.

He sat hunched over, wrapped in thought, headache still throbbing. At least the trip was finished, eight hundred pounding miles, the incessant click-click of the track a numbing repetition, every bump of the train as it lurched its way through the mountains of Pennsylvania resounding in his head like a cannon shot.

Haupt, Washburne, and Parker were up, looking at him, and with a muffled groan he rose from his seat and went to the rear platform. A cloud of wood smoke washed around him as he stepped out. A small guard was waiting, a dozen men snapping to attention, a captain with drawn sword saluting as he stepped off the platform.

After more than two days on the train his legs felt unsteady, the ground shifting and swaying beneath his feet. A wave of nausea hit and he fought to keep it down; the last thing needed at this moment was to vomit in front of the men.

"Welcome to Harrisburg, sir," the captain said, voice quavering a bit nervously.

"Thank you, Captain."

"Sir, General Couch sends his regards. He regrets not being here to meet you but will report at your earliest convenience."

Grant said nothing. Couch was most likely fast asleep.

The rail yard was a bustle of activity with half a dozen trains being off-loaded, crates of rations piled up under an open-sided warehouse, horses being driven off boxcars, a dozen Napoleons on flatcars ready to be dragged off and then matched up with crews.

The captain reached into an oversized haversack dangling from his hip and drew out a sheaf of envelopes, bound with a coarse string.

"Sir, these letters are waiting for you."

The captain handed them to Grant.

"Any word from Washington?" Grant asked.

"They beat off Lee's attack. It's all in there, sir."

Grant took the package and looked around.

"Sir, there's a desk in the yardmaster's office." Leading the way, the captain took him across a set of tracks, around a locomotive that was ticking like a teakettle, with heat radiating from its boiler and into a well-appointed clapboard-sided office. The obligatory pot of coffee was brewing on a small wood stove and Parker immediately took down four tin cups from a shelf, filled them, and passed one to each of the travelers.

Grant settled into a wood-backed chair, laid the package on the open rolltop desk, took out his whittling knife, and cut the package open. Twenty or more letters and telegrams spilled out and he opened the top one.

He leaned back in the chair and a thin trace of a smile creased his face.

"What is it?" Washburne asked.

"The captain's right, Lee failed to take Washington. It's a report from Stanton. Heavy assault on Fort Stevens this morning, just before dawn. Estimate eight to ten thousand casualties for the rebels. Our losses estimated at four thousand. Reinforcements from Charleston decisive. Enemy driven back out of our lines by midday."

"Will they attack again?" Elihu asked.

He shook his head.

"I doubt it. Cut the estimate of their losses in half and it's still a devastating blow. If they couldn't take it yesterday, Lee knows it would be even worse today. I think that finishes their hopes of taking the capital for now."

He opened the other envelopes, scanning through them, lingering over one for a moment, then continued till the last was read and laid down on the desk. He finally took up the cup of coffee, which had cooled, and drained it in several gulps.

"Most are repeats of the same message. The rioting in New York, for the moment, has been suppressed. Haupt, your efforts are bearing fruit; we have trains ladened with supplies, rations, remounts, artillery, wagons, coming from as far away as Maine."

Haupt smiled and nodded.

Grant looked around at the small gathering.

"I'm to report to Washington immediately," he said and stood up.

"You just got here," Elihu said.

"I know. Stanton wants a conference and I'm to take the fastest train to be found down to Perryville on the Susquehanna, where a dispatch boat will be waiting to take me to the capital."

"Stanton?" Elihu asked cautiously.

"Congressman, I'd like you to accompany me," Grant announced. "Parker, I want you to stay here. The First Division of McPherson's corps should start coming in later today. Set up my headquarters. I want it in the field, not in town. Find an appropriate place. Haupt, I think it best if you accompany me as well."

"An honor, sir. I'll go over to the dispatch office now and clear a line for an express. We can take the same train that brought us here."

Grant picked up the first telegram he had read and reviewed it one more time.

So Lee had tried. Well, he had to. Even on the slimmest of bets, the chance to take Washington by a bold assault could not be ignored.

He might try again a few days hence, to probe around the fortifications and look for a blunder by Heintzelman. All Heintzelman had to do in response was to keep the exterior forts reasonably garrisoned and shift reserves along his own interior lines to wherever the threat might develop. A child should be able to do that, but then again, more than one general in this army had sunk below that level during the last two years.

The question is, what will Lee do next?

"Sir?"

He looked up. The captain of the guard detail stood in the doorway, holding another telegram.

"This came in for you. It was dated nearly six hours ago but was in code. Sorry, but it took a while to find the translator book."

Grant took the telegram and opened it. A message out of Greensburg, Pennsylvania, a hundred miles to the southwest along the Pennsylvania Railroad. The message was from a Pinkerton agent claiming to have come in from behind Confederate lines. . . . Jefferson Davis was reported as being seen two days ago at Greencastle, a small town in the Cumberland Valley, just inside the Pennsylvania state line, riding to meet Lee.

Now, if true, that was news, revealing much of what was to come. In fact, it was damn good news.

Haupt was back.

"I've ordered the line cleared. We can leave as soon as our engine is watered, oiled, and fueled."

Grant stepped out of the office, lit a cigar, and looked heavenward. It was a clear night, the stars were out, shining through the faint overcast of fog drifting up from the river.

"How's the headache?" Elihu asked.

"It's gone."

Three Miles North of Fort Stevens

July 19, 1863
2:00 P.M.

C.S.A. "General Lee, President Davis is on the road just north of here, he'll be arriving in a few minutes."

Startled, Lee looked up from the map spread out on the table. Having moved his headquarters out of artillery range, he had just settled in under an awning spread on the front lawn of a modest, two-story home facing the Seventh Street road. Under the shade of the awning he had been contemplating a nap after the sleepless night that had bedeviled and exhausted him.

"Are you sure it's the president?" he asked.

Taylor nodded excitedly.

"One of Stuart's boys saw him and galloped back here with the word."

Lee came to his feet, looking down at his uniform. His jacket was off, vest open, pants stained with mud. He felt clammy, sweat-soaked, realizing it had been a week or more since he had been out of these clothes. It was scorching hot out, and he dreaded having to get back into formal attire, but there was nothing else he could do. Taylor had already picked up his jacket and helped him get into it. Next came the boots, replacing the comfortable slippers. A black servant with the staff knelt to help him with his boots, then produced a stiff brush and worked on the trousers for a moment before helping him to wrap his sash and then snap on his belt.

He already felt confined, sweat breaking out. There was a flurry of activity up the road; on the low ridge a half mile to the north men were on their feet, a distant cheer echoing. It had to be Davis, nothing else could stir the men on this day of rest, of disappointment, and heat.

There was a momentary flash of frustration, even anger. There had been no notification that the president was so close, just a vague message after Union Mills that he would come north at his earliest convenience to inspect the troops and discuss future plans. It was obvious now that this visit by Davis was in anticipation of the news that Washington had already been seized, or was about to fall. Still, there should have been more formal notification so that he and his men could prepare.

"Taylor, get some sort of formal guard out there. Also, send messages to Generals Longstreet, Hood, and Stuart that the president is here and I expect them to report in as soon as possible."

Taylor, obviously a bit flustered for once, saluted and ran off, shouting orders. The headquarters company, Virginian cavalrymen, were already forming up, the rumor of the president's arrival having swept the camp. There wasn't time to saddle and mount, so the men simply formed up by the road, brushing off each other's uniforms as they waited.

A troop of cavalry were coming down the road, riding at a swift trot. Their uniforms of dark gray jackets and light gray trousers were stained and muddied from the long ride. The escort reined in, Taylor down on the road to greet them. Salutes were exchanged.

A second troop came in, and in their midst was Jefferson Davis, riding a black gelding, trailed by civilian staff. To Lee's surprise, Judah Benjamin was with them, the secretary of state for the Confederacy. He looked haggard, wincing with every jolt as his mare trotted behind the president's horse.

The group reined in. There was a flourish of salutes from the escorts, men racing up to hold the reins as the civilians dismounted.

Lee came forward, stopping a half dozen feet from the president and saluting. He wondered if Davis would feel some offense at the paltry nature of the greeting, no band, no flags displayed other than the headquarters insignia, no brigades of troops lining the road.

Davis stepped away from his mount, moving stiffly, looking around. He bowed slightly in acknowledgment of the salute.

"Mr. President, welcome to the Army of Northern Virginia, sir," Lee said formally.

"An honor, General Lee."

There was a moment of awkward silence. The other civilians were gathering behind Davis and Benjamin, jockeying for position, a couple of them obviously reporters, notebooks already out.

"My headquarters are rather spartan, sir, I hope you don't find it too uncomfortable."

As he spoke, Lee gestured toward the canopy of tarpaulins spread out on the front lawn of the house. A couple of servants were racing about, dragging more chairs out from the house, another setting out a fresh pot of coffee and tin cups and surprisingly a pitcher of what looked to be iced lemonade.

"Not at all, in fact this reminds me of my own days in the field during the war with Mexico. Lead the way, General," Davis said.

Lee guided them the few dozen feet to the table. The entire crowd of civilians tried to close in and follow. Davis turned to one of his military escorts and whispered a few words. The escort nodded.

"Gentlemen. The president wishes a few moments alone with General Lee and Secretary Benjamin. I believe General Lee's staff will offer some refreshments in the house."

"General Lee," one of the civilians shouted, stepping around the escort. "I'm with the *Richmond Examiner.* Is it true you were repulsed yesterday in front of Washington with heavy losses?"

Lee looked at the man out of the corner of his eye. Several others were crowding around behind the reporter, notebooks out as well.

"I first wish to make my report to the president, gentlemen," he said, forcing himself to remain polite. "I will be more than happy to talk with you later."

"Sir, just five minutes please. Will you renew the assault?"

He turned away, ignoring the man, who smelled of whiskey and bad cologne. Several guards from his own staff stepped between Lee and the reporter, there were whispered comments, and Lee inwardly smiled.

There were several muffled protests, but the reporters, staff, and hangers-on were led away.

Davis was already sitting in the chair Lee had occupied only minutes before. Benjamin was standing, looking down at the map.

Lee approached, glad to be under the awning, at least out of the direct sunlight, though the heat was stifling.

"Gentlemen, something cool to drink? Perhaps you'd care to rest a bit before we start?" Lee offered, even as he poured a cup of lemonade and offered it to Davis.

"I'd like to hear what happened first," Davis replied, looking up at him.

He wasn't sure if there was a tone of reproof in Davis's voice. He set down the cup that he had offered to Davis and then poured another for Benjamin, who gladly took it. Benjamin took his hat off and with a sigh pulled out a handkerchief and wiped the sweat from his brow.

"Thank you, General," he gasped and drained the lemonade in two gulps. Seconds later he winced, rubbing his broad forehead from the shock of the cold beverage.

He forced a smile.

"Foolish of me, should always take it slow," he said and then unbuttoned his jacket, removed it, and placed it over a chair. His shirt was plastered to his body with sweat, and as a soft breeze wafted by he actually sighed with delight.

"General, make yourself comfortable, sir," Judah said. "Our president has an iron fortitude, but I'll tell you, in those last ten miles I thought I would die from the heat. It is worse up here than in Richmond."

"I agree," Lee replied, glad for the moment of the small talk, which was customary and polite before getting to business. "Washington has its own unique climate, which in midsummer is worse than anything to be found farther south."

Judah poured another cup of lemonade and sipped it slowly. It was obvious that Davis wanted to press straight in, but Judah was diverting him for a moment.

Lee had always liked this man, and he could tell that Judah was trying to give him a few minutes to organize his thoughts.

"The ride up was grueling, General. Train to Winchester, where, I should add, we passed the convoys of Yankee prisoners from Gettysburg and Union Mills. I tell you, I've never seen such a sight. It was biblical in its proportions. I'm told there were ten thousand or more in that one column. Then by horseback up the Cumberland Valley and across to here.

"We dodged several of their units, mostly militia, but some regulars as well, cavalry patrols. That's why you didn't hear of our coming. We felt it best to keep such intelligence to ourselves."

Lee nodded, glad to hear the explanation. Of course it was obvious, the way Judah stated it, and he relaxed a bit; sending heralds ahead might only have served to alert a potential enemy. It told him as well that while he was focusing on Washington, his tenuous line of communications to the South was even more fragile than he had thought. There was really nothing at the moment to prevent enemy patrols from wandering freely right down into northern Virginia.

"Take off your jacket," Benjamin pressed, "let's get comfortable. If you keep yours on, sir, I will be forced to put mine back on, and that I would not care to do."

Lee smiled, and Taylor was quickly behind him, helping him to remove the heavy wool coat. He breathed an inner sigh of relief and nodded his thanks to Judah.

He beckoned to a chair and Judah took it. Davis, who had remained silent through the interplay, removed his jacket as well, having been outvoted on the dress code for the meeting.

"We rode past General Longstreet's headquarters about three miles north of here." Davis said, his voice quiet, even-toned. "General Longstreet was not there, but his staff told me that yesterday our army was repulsed in front of Washington with heavy casualties."

"Yes, that's true," Lee replied.

"What happened?"

Lee gave him a brief review of the action. He spared the details of Hood's failure to properly coordinate the attack. He knew Hood was a favorite of the president, and besides, it would be unfair to lay blame.

Davis listened without comment, taking a sip of lemonade while Lee talked.

Finished, Lee sat back in his chair.

"Can you renew the assault?" Davis asked.

"I would prefer not to, sir. I've asked for a full muster and review of all units, which should be in by the end of the day, but I think it's safe to say that we are down to roughly thirty thousand infantry capable of bearing arms."

"You came north, sir, with over seventy thousand men. What happened?"

"That was over seventy thousand total, sir, including artillery, cavalry, logistical support, medical personnel. Our victories at Gettysburg and Union Mills came at a price. Anderson's division, as you know, was fought out, and I detailed it to escort the prisoners back to Virginia. There have been the usual losses as well to disease, accidents, desertions, and just simple exhaustion. Just the march from Westminster to here cost us nearly five hundred men from accidents and the rigors of the road, and now the heat."

"If you did renew the attack," Judah asked, "what do you estimate our losses would be in order to press through and take the city?"

"I can't begin to even guarantee that another attack would take Washington," Lee replied. "We tried our best yesterday, lost eight thousand, and could not press it to a conclusion."

"To take the city, how much?" Davis asked, repeating the question.

Lee lowered his head.

"Perhaps half our remaining force," Lee finally replied. "With what little we'd have left, I daresay that within a fortnight we'd be forced to abandon the city and retire back into Virginia."

Davis looked over at Benjamin, blew out noisily, and sat back in his chair.

"I came north, General Lee, under the assumption that by the time I arrived you would be into Washington, and that our secretary of state here would be discussing terms of peace with the Yankees and opening negotiations with the various embassies of Europe. I am gravely disappointed by this turn of events.

"When you proposed this campaign to me back in May, it was to serve several purposes. One was to relieve Vicksburg, an intent that has failed. A second was to defeat the Army of the Potomac, and in that you succeeded brilliantly. Yet a third was to hopefully bring Washington into our grasp; it appears that has failed as well."

Lee listened, trying to maintain an air of patience and deference, but he felt an anger building. He knew he was tired and the day so hot that the heat was getting to him as well. He had to stay calm.

"Sir, are you dissatisfied with the results?" he asked.

"Let us say I expected more, much more, General Lee. The reports that came back to Richmond indicated that we were on the brink of a final victory that would conclude this war."

"I never said such a thing in my reports, sir. Perhaps public enthusiasm, generated by our friends of the press, elaborated on what I reported to you in my dispatch after Union Mills. I stated in that report that I would march on Washington and probe its defenses; never did I indicate that I felt confident that I could take that position."

"It was implied however, General Lee. Else why should I travel here, enduring the hardships of the road, and the unexpected threat of being captured."

"We had a bit of a skirmish near Frederick," Benjamin said. "Nothing serious, as it turned out, just some Union militia that stumbled into us, but they gave us a few minutes of concern."

"I'm sorry if you had such difficulties," Lee replied, "but I thought it would be evident that our lines of communication are by no means secure. What force I have left needs to be concentrated here, it cannot be spared elsewhere."

"I would think the security of the president of the Confederacy would be of some concern, General Lee."

"Sir, if I had been made aware of your intent to travel, beyond the rather vague dispatch sent up by the War Office, I would have detailed off the necessary men regardless of my needs here at the front lines."

He knew he had transgressed with that last statement. He caught an ever-so-worried glance from Judah. Davis's features darkened but he did not reply.

"I'm sorry, sir," Lee said. "Do not take offense. Know from my heart that if I was aware of your presence in Maryland, I would have moved to more closely ensure your safety. You are here safe, however, and I daresay the journey in and of itself will be noted and remembered as an adventure worthy of you."

He knew it was outright flattery but it had the proper effect. Davis seemed placated.

"Then back to the question of the moment," Davis replied. "Can you take Washington regardless of cost?"

"Sir, with but thirty thousand infantry, I believe we are, as of today, outnumbered. A day ago I might have questioned the fighting ability of their garrison troops, but no longer. They fought well; in fact, with courage and honor. You know as well as I the old adage that against a fortified position the attacker should outnumber the defender by at least three to one. That in a full assault the attacker can expect to lose a number equal to the total number of defenders. With those two factors alone, I would say the taking of the city would be impossible. We no longer have enough men."

"Suppose I ordered it."

Lee hesitated. Along the road he could see where hundreds of men had gathered, his headquarters company and Davis's military escorts forming a cordon to hold them back. Men were coming down from farther up the road to join the throng.

I cannot order these men into a fruitless attack, he realized. *They are too precious to spend thus, merely to demonstrate to Davis the impossibility of the task. They deserve better. I learned a bitter lesson yesterday in the assault; I will not allow another just to prove yet again the futility of it all to the president.*

"Respectfully, sir, I would have to refuse that order."

"If I made it a direct order?"

"Sir. Please don't do that. It would force me to tender my resignation. If I thought there was a semblance of hope that such an order would bear fruit, I would be the first to try, but I can tell you now, without hesitation, the opportunity of the moment has passed, unless General Heintzelman makes an extremely foolish mistake, such as venturing forth to try and fight us in the field, and I know he will not do that."

Davis sighed and poured himself another cup of lemonade.

"I had to be sure," Davis said. "I will confess, it was a grave disappointment to travel so far to find this failure."

"The army tried, sir, it did all that was humanly possible. And please do not dismiss the victory they brought us at Union Mills."

"The destruction of the Army of the Potomac. Yes, though I did hope for more results to emerge from that. It appears that Mr. Lincoln still will not waver from his course, regardless of how much blood he spills."

"Sir, we crippled the Army of the Potomac, have taken it out of action for at least a month, perhaps two, before it can reorganize, but it has not been totally destroyed. Except in the most rare of circumstances, that, sir, is impossible."

Davis said nothing and Lee felt his own frustration growing again. Who had been talking to this man? Never did he say in his reports back to Richmond that the Army of the Potomac had been totally destroyed. His after-action report made that clear enough. Yet again he could see how wishful thinking in the War Office and the government bureaus, combined with the press, was generating false assumptions. Yes, the news of July 4 was indeed heady stuff. It was fair to assume that it could be the forerunner of yet more victories, perhaps even greater ones, but to assume that it truly signaled the end of the war, that was foolhardy.

"A remarkable achievement, General Lee, your victory at Union Mills," Benjamin interjected. "It will stand in history alongside the victories of Wellington and Marlborough."

"Thank you, sir."

Davis stirred, looking over at Benjamin.

"I for one would like to hear the details from you, General, of how it was achieved," Benjamin continued, obviously enthusiastic, "but perhaps we should focus on the next step, given the realities you have just shared with us."

Davis nodded. Lee said nothing, waiting for the president to lead the way.

"I have given some thought to alternatives in case our hopes did not come to pass here."

"My staff and I opened discussions on that last night," Lee replied. "We were to meet again tonight to come to a firm conclusion. I thought it best to first give everyone a day of rest. Our activities have been nonstop since the evening of June 28. The men, their officers, my staff are all exhausted."

"And your thoughts as to what will come next?" Davis asked.

"Sir, it is obvious we must remain on the offensive and continue the campaign in Maryland, but to attack Washington is out of the question at the moment, given our numbers. To withdraw back to Virginia is out of the question as well. We cannot allow ourselves to fall back into a strategic defense and give those people the time to concentrate their forces and come after us again."

"What if I were to tell you that even now twenty thousand additional infantry and five thousand cavalry are mobilizing to come to your side?" Davis asked.

Surprised, Lee could not respond, and for the first time Davis actually smiled.

"I've ordered General Beauregard to bring up half of his garrison from Charleston. Additional troops are being drawn from North Carolina and Virginia, including the brigades left behind by Pickett. Governor Vance has pledged ten thousand men, including the releasing of significant logistical support. They should be here within a fortnight. I am strongly suggesting that Beauregard be given a corps command in your army."

A fortnight? Two more weeks. Even now the Union was moving tens of thousands of men in a matter of days. In one sense it gave him renewed hope. Twenty thousand, plus the return of some of Anderson's men and lightly wounded from the other divisions, could bring the active numbers back up to the strength prior to Gettysburg. Enough for one more good strike, even though the replacements, both in terms of men and officers, were not of the caliber he had two months ago. Perhaps there just might be a chance for renewed action against Washington. If the weather would clear up, the roads dry, he might be able to play out a campaign of maneuver against the capital that would draw the Union forces out.

If the reinforcements arrived in time and proved to be of sufficient caliber to stand in the line against veteran Union troops, he would actually be tempted to try a second assault on Washington.

There was no sense in playing that game at this moment. War is not won on "ifs." He had to focus on the here and now.

"So, your intentions, General Lee?" Davis pressed.

"We must maintain our presence in Maryland, if for no other reason than logistical ones. The supplies here are rich and the movement of the center of operations out of Virginia will give our farms time to bring in their harvests unmolested."

Davis nodded and Lee knew that his answer had been a weak one.

"Baltimore, General Lee, are you considering that?"

Lee did not reply for a moment. Yes, he had been considering moving on that city, it was to be the main focus of his conversation this evening with his staff and generals. He had hoped not to bring this conversation on prematurely with the president without careful analysis, but it was obvious that he could not avoid it.

"Yes, Mr. President, we were to discuss Baltimore as an option this evening."

"I'd like to discuss it now, especially in light of the fact that for at least the next two weeks Washington is out of the question," Davis replied.

"Sir, my first thought was to draw back toward Frederick."

"Why?"

"Several reasons. Primarily because it would shorten our logistical lines. From Frederick we might even be able to establish some rail connections, if only temporarily. The land and supplies there are good, not heavily foraged by either side. It would give us a secured area from which we could exclude Union attempts at intelligence-gathering, and from there we could respond to any movement toward Virginia out of Washington, or from farther north."

"And Baltimore?"

"I am quite open to that suggestion, sir. However, I should caution that I do not want to see our army enter into an urban battle for possession of a city. Second, it would extend us significantly, with a hostile force in our rear and the potential of those Union forces gathering north of the Susquehanna threatening us as well. Such a move would make our lines of communication vulnerable and would add upward of a week to the consolidation of reinforcements of which you have just informed me."

"But you are not adverse to the idea?" Davis asked pointedly.

"If it means a brutal street-to-street fight, we cannot afford such losses. I would also want to think through the question of the ultimate purpose and how long we would be expected to hold that city."

"Permanently," Davis replied.

Lee raised a quizzical eyebrow but said nothing.

Davis cleared his throat and nodded significantly toward Benjamin, who was watching the exchange with his usual soft genial smile.

"The president and I did discuss this eventuality as we rode north," Benjamin announced. "I will say that I for one was not optimistic that Washington would fall easily into our hands. Its fortifications may be the most formidable in the world. However, Baltimore does not have that kind of protection."

Lee wanted to offer his thanks for that comment but remained silent, pouring another cup of lemonade and sipping from it while Judah talked.

"Though Washington is out of the question at the moment, I believe that Baltimore is a viable target, the taking of it perhaps ultimately achieving certain political goals at a fraction of the cost in men."

"I'm intrigued, sir," Lee replied.

He had always liked Benjamin, angered at the low, anti-Semitic prejudices that far too many had demonstrated against this brilliant man. In his brief tenure as secretary of war, from late in sixty-one to the spring of sixty-two, Benjamin had tackled with ability the herculean task of marshaling the resources of eleven semi-independent states into a common cause, a task that by its nature had earned him the enmity of most of the governors.

Few realized that Benjamin's fall from grace as secretary of war had actually been a brilliant subterfuge. When Union forces threatened the coast of North Carolina, there were simply no resources available to meet them, other than a few state militia units. Rather than admit to the paucity of Confederate resources, Benjamin had silently accepted the blame and the charges that his incompetence had allowed a significant portion of the Carolina coast to fall without a fight. Militarily, the ground taken was next to useless anyhow, and it had preserved the secret of just how weak the South was at that moment. For his loyalty and silence, Davis allowed him to resign as secretary of war and then immediately appointed him secretary of state.

He was Davis's silent partner, constantly at his side, and though Lee would never admit it even to his most intimate of friends, if there were any really useful intellectual concepts or decisions put forth and then acted on, it was most certainly Benjamin who was behind them.

For that reason alone Lee was now more than glad to hear what this man had to say.

"I think we should look at Baltimore for several reasons," Benjamin continued, voice pitched low, as if sharing a deep personal secret.

"The political considerations first. On an internal level, meaning within this state, the taking of Baltimore, and with it a side action that took Annapolis, would give us a legitimate stance to declare a state convention and in short order establish a state government that would vote for admission into the Confederacy. Our base of support in Maryland is in the eastern region anyhow. Our presence last year in western Maryland aroused no support or even a remote opportunity to call for such a convention, as we then occupied the region that in fact is strongly Union in sentiment.

"Bringing Maryland into the fold would be a major coup, gentlemen, a crowning laurel for the Army of Northern Virginia, which of course will now be seen as liberators who have come to free their Southern brothers from the tyranny of Lincoln. It would be a political sensation."

He continued to smile and Lee found himself nodding in agreement. Yes, it would provide an immediate justification for this campaign and for the great victory won on the soil of Maryland.

"It would also present a major political and dare I say to you, General Lee, military setback as well for the Union. If Baltimore is taken, Washington will continue to be in isolation and threatened.

"The amount of supplies to be seized would be significant as well, undoubtedly enough to easily maintain our army for the remainder of the campaign. And, I should add, the industrial resources of Baltimore are almost beyond counting. Rolling mills, shipyards, iron mills, boiler works, foundries, all these resources can be brought into our efforts."

Lee nodded but felt he now had to raise a point.

"I've considered that very point, sir," Lee replied, "but the question would be, how to move those resources south. We don't hold the railroads and even if we did take a section of the Baltimore and Ohio and repair it, there is still no direct link back to our own lines. They would be useless to us in Baltimore, at least in the immediate future."

"If we hold Baltimore," Davis interjected, "and, when we reach an armistice, Baltimore and with it Maryland become part of the Confederacy, it will be invaluable to us. It will mean our hold on the Chesapeake is secure; we will have a major port and industrial base and the wherewithal to defend ourselves in the future if the Yankees should ever contemplate a second war against us."

A second war? That was too far in the future for Lee to even try to contemplate. His only concern now was the immediate, the campaign of this moment and the bringing of it to a successful conclusion.

"As to the primary consideration," Judah said, taking the conversation back from Davis, "it is the international one."

Lee nodded.

"When the culmination of this campaign results in the taking of Baltimore, I would be present as secretary of state. We, of course, would announce for all the world to hear that this indeed had been our intent from the start. The attempt on Washington was perforce necessary from a military standpoint, but we never seriously contemplated the taking of it. Baltimore from the start was our goal. Realize, sir, that in Baltimore, though there are no ambassadors there, there are several consular offices watching over trade issues and such. The French have a consulate there, as do the British. I would meet with them at the earliest possible moment and present yet again the case for their intervention.

"By international law the federal government cannot hinder their open communications with their governments. I can promise you that within three weeks after Baltimore is in our hands, lengthy dispatches from the president and myself will be in Paris and London. Couple that with the news of Union Mills, and the transfer of Maryland to the Southern cause will present an image of inevitable Confederate success to European statesmen."

He sat back, his perpetual smile turning into a broad grin.

"Sir, I think we would then stand a reasonable chance of recognition, at least by France."

This was indeed heady news, Lee thought, unable to hide his own smile of approval.

"England?" he asked.

Judah regretfully shook his head.

"There are other issues hindering us there."

As he spoke, he looked over at Davis, whose features were now wooden and unresponsive.

"Why France, then?" Lee asked.

"Because of the nature of their emperor, Napoleon III. We know he is trapped in a deepening quagmire in Mexico. That ill-advised campaign is going into its second year without any real results. Napoleon knows that a Union victory would result in an immediate turning of the wrath of the Yankees upon that troubled country. A war will result, and the Yankees will drive the French out and take the country for themselves."

"There is, of course," Davis added, "the simple desire of many European powers to meddle in our affairs in any way whatsoever to damage us, both North and South. But we can turn that to our distinct advantage at the moment, to play France in the same way our revolutionary forefathers did. Only a fool would think they aided us out of altruistic dreams to advance the cause of liberty. They did it to hurt Great Britain. But no one will intervene if we do not present them with the reality that we can indeed win this war. Taking Baltimore, bringing Maryland into the fold, and opening direct communications via their consulates from a city we've freed from Yankee tyranny will be of incalculable benefit to the cause. I think, General Lee, it will mean a final victory thanks to the brilliance of all that you have achieved."

"Is it realistic to think France will intervene?" Lee asked.

As he spoke, he looked past the two men to the road. A thousand or more troops were standing there. The men were his men, tough veterans even at the tender age of eighteen. Their features were sunburned, uniforms filthy; in the summer heat and mud many had taken their shoes and socks off, the precious footgear tied around their necks. They were watching this conference, hopeful, expectant, most of them knowing that without a doubt their own fates were being decided here.

I owe them everything, Lee thought. *Everything including my very life. They were the ones who stormed the cemetery at Gettysburg, then force-marched fifty miles and held the line at Union Mills. What we talk about now was created by their blood and sweat. I must not fail them. I cannot fail them.*

"General?"

It was Judah, looking at him.

"Just thinking," Lee said absently.

Judah looked over his shoulder at the troops watching expectantly, turned back to Lee, and nodded.

"We must see that their efforts are rewarded with final victory," Judah said softly and Lee smiled.

"In answer to your question about France," Judah continued, "yes, I think it is realistic, and it will bring immeasurable aid to those young men of yours. Troops from France? I doubt it. Logistically it would be difficult, and besides we don't need them, as General Washington once did. Our soldiers are the match of any Yankees we'll ever face, as long as they are backed up with sufficient supplies and equipment."

Lee nodded his thanks at this compliment.

"It is the breaking of the blockade that matters. The diversion of Yankee naval forces to counter Napoleon. If but one convoy of supplies got through to Wilmington or Charleston, loaded with artillery, ammunition, guns, medical supplies, that alone would be worth it.

"The political consternation it would create for the Union would be incalculable. It would exert profound pressure for negotiations on Lincoln and his government.

"The thought of the French ironclad *La Gloire* arriving off New York Harbor would send the entire North reeling and divert their assets from us. That, sir, would be a fitting result of your campaign against the Army of the Potomac. That would be the beginning of the end for Lincoln and his cronies. Congress would force them to seek an armistice with us."

He smiled softly.

"Perhaps even to then find a common front against a foreign foe."

He laughed softly and Lee could not help but admire the adroitness of this man's thinking. Yes, American self-centeredness and its ultimate distrust of Europe could very well engender a peace and then a common front afterward. How ironic, but also how sad.

"We must take Baltimore. That is the road to peace," Davis announced.

Lee stood up and as he did so there was an audible stirring from the men out on the road, as if they sensed a decision was about to be made.

He looked down again at the map. A two-day march would place them into the city, as long as there was no more rain. There were some fortifications to the southwest of Baltimore, but they were, at last report, manned only by some local militia. Yes, it was feasible, but would it also prove to be a trap? Once into the city, they were wed to it for the duration of the fight. Could he occupy it, but still maintain a presence in the rest of Maryland and facing Washington? But Davis had promised twenty thousand more infantry. If only it were forty thousand, he would not hesitate.

We must achieve something decisive here, he thought. And he knew that with Washington impossible there was now no other choice.

He leaned over, studying the map, nodding slowly. Details would have to be worked out this evening with Hood and Longstreet. Stuart's command would have to be split, half to stay here, shadowing Washington. A division of infantry would have to stay behind as well, to feign an attack. At least a division toward Annapolis, leaving five divisions in his main force, with the rest of Stuart's command racing back north to act as a screen and to scout out the enemy's dispositions. Supplies were not a concern at the moment and yes, Judah's assertion that there was a virtual cornucopia waiting in Baltimore was undoubtedly true.

Not given to hasty decisions, he knew that he must make one now. He would have preferred a day or two to contemplate this, for it was a profound shift in all his thinking of the last three weeks. It would tie the Army of Northern Virginia to an occupation role, and the effects of that might be profound. But there was no other choice. He could not pull back to Frederick and adopt a waiting-and-watching role, not after this conversation.

"We move on Baltimore tomorrow morning," he said, looking at Davis and Benjamin.

The two smiled and stood up. Davis, aware of the gathering crowd that was watching them, leaned over and shook Lee's hand. A wild shout went up from the watchers. From somewhere a band had come up and immediately broke into a slightly off-key rendition of "Dixie," which was greeted by the piercing rebel yell.

Davis came out from under the awning and walked toward the men, the crowd breaking through the cordon of escorts to surround their president. Lee, always uncomfortable with such displays, held back, Judah by his side.

"You really believe it can still be done, don't you?" Lee asked.

Judah smiled his inscrutable smile and nodded.

"With luck, General Lee. Tonight I shall appeal to my Old Testament God while you pray to your New Testament Savior. I don't think though that He takes sides based upon a few feeble prayers. So I shall have to trust in luck, your skill, and the courage of these men."

He hesitated.

"For if we appealed to Him on moral grounds alone, well, I think I would be concerned."

Startled, Lee looked over at Judah, who shrugged his shoulders and then walked off to follow his president. Not wishing to join in the display of exuberance, Lee stepped back and walked off in the opposite direction in order to contemplate what Judah Benjamin had just said.

Chapter Nine

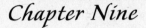The sudden lurching of the boat as it bumped against the dock roused him from a deep, dreamless sleep.

Ulysses Grant sat up and instantly regretted it, as he banged his head on the overhead deck. Softly muttering an obscenity, he lay back, disoriented for a moment. He was in a narrow cabin lit by a coal oil lamp turned down low. The space was little bigger than a coffin, just enough room for a bed, with the deck only inches from his face. Beside the bed was a small nightstand, with a basin of water on it. Under the stand was a chamber pot. In the corner sat a small chair with his coat draped on it.

Rolling over, he slipped out of the bed and found that even at his stature he could not stand upright. The boat swayed gently; topside he heard shouted commands, the scurrying of feet.

There was a knock on the door; it was Elihu.

"We're here."

"I'll be right out."

He splashed some water on his face, buttoned the plain four-button coat of an infantry private, and looked down at his uniform. The only mark of command was the hastily stitched shoulder boards with three stars. The third star for each shoulder had been cut out and sewn in between the existing two stars, since no official three-star insignia could be found. The uniform was stained, rumpled, smelling of sweat, both human and horse, but there was no changing to a fresh uniform now. In the hurried confusion in the dark at Port Deposit his trunk had never been transferred from the train to this courier boat. There was nothing to be done about it now, and he opened the door.

Elihu was hunched over in the corridor.

"What time is it?" Grant asked.

"Just after four Philadelphia time, not exactly sure what it is here. We really flew down the Chesapeake. That young lieutenant in command has nerves of steel; I couldn't see a damn thing and yet he was puffing along, boilers wide open."

The journey had gone by in a blur for him. Express train to Philadelphia, where they changed trains, and from there down to Perryville on the north bank of the Susquehanna, where they had transferred to a waiting courier boat.

"You get any sleep?" Grant asked.

He had felt a twinge of guilt when the young naval lieutenant in command of the boat insisted that Grant take his coffinlike cabin, leaving Washburne and Haupt to fend for themselves aboard the toylike boat.

"Haupt slept on the deck, in the pilot's cabin; I played cards with the crew."

"Win anything?"

"You know it's against regulations to gamble aboard a naval vessel," Elihu said with a grin. "How would it look for a congressman to be caught trying to take the earnings of our gallant sailors?"

He shook his head.

"They cleaned me out. I lost fifty dollars."

Climbing a half dozen steps up a ladder, Grant and Washburne came out on the deck. The open boiler aft was ticking and hissing, steam venting out. All was wrapped in a thick, oily fog, muffling sound; the dock they were tied to illuminated by gas lamps that cast a feeble golden glow. The air was thick with a fetid, marshlike scent, mingled with the stench of sewage.

The young lieutenant and his crew of five stood at attention by the narrow gangplank. Haupt was already on the dock, disappearing into the shadows.

Elihu stepped down the gangplank, two of the sailors grinning and winking at him. Grant followed, stepped on to the dock, and looked around. It was as if he had walked into a ghost land. A lone sentry on the dock was the only living presence, the sailor looking at him nervously and then snapping to attention.

"No one knows we're here," Elihu said.

"Fine with me."

They stood in the fog, Grant not sure at the moment what should be done next. Haupt returned a moment later.

"No one knew we were coming. It's a bit chaotic, casualties being brought in from the fight at the fortifications, but I'm having three horses brought to us. They should be here in a few minutes."

Grant slowly walked along the dock, hands behind his back, the point of his cigar glowing. A shallow draft ironclad was tied off just ahead of where they docked, guns protruding fore and aft, a wisp of steam and smoke venting from the stack. A detail of half a dozen sailors approached out of the fog, running hard, a naval ensign leading them. They drew up short, and the ensign saluted, the men coming to attention.

"Sorry, sir, no one told us you were coming," the ensign gasped.

"No problem, Ensign. What has been going on here?"

"The fight, sir?"

"Yes."

"We could hear it, hell of a barrage. Our artillery really put it to them. The barracks have been converted over to a hospital for rebel prisoners. A dirty lot, sir, covered in lice most of them."

Grant said nothing. The navy was used to a far different standard of living, and the sight of a real infantryman, who had been campaigning for weeks in the field, would of course come as a shock to them.

"Is it true, sir, you're coming from the West with fifty thousand men?" the ensign asked excitedly.

"You know I can't discuss that with you," Grant replied, a note of reproach in his voice.

"Sorry, sir. Just that's been the word around here the last few days."

There was a clattering of hooves, and several cavalrymen approached, leading their mounts. The sergeant in charge of the small detail did not look all that pleased.

"Are you General Grant, sir?" he asked coolly after saluting.

"Yes, Sergeant."

"Some general just came up and said he was requisitioning three horses."

"That's right, Sergeant. Don't worry, I'll make sure we get them back to you by midmorning."

"Sir, I don't like being dismounted at a time like this."

"I understand, Sergeant."

The trooper reluctantly handed over the reins of his mount, a towering stallion.

"He's a tough one, sir, sensitive mouth, so be careful."

Grant smiled, took the reins, and quickly mounted. The horse shied a bit, tried to buck, and he settled himself down hard in the saddle, working the bit gently but making it clear he was mounted to stay. The horse settled down.

Elihu and Haupt mounted as well. Grant looked around, totally disoriented.

"I know the way," Elihu announced.

The sergeant looked up at him, and Grant sensed the man was a bit disappointed, half hoping that the mighty general would wind up on his backside for having taken his horse.

Elihu led the way, moving at a walk down the length of the dock, passing another ironclad, this one rigged with lanterns hanging over the railings and boarding nets strung around its circumference.

They eased past a line of wagons, several carriages, and a couple of ambulances. The main barracks were aglow with a light that cast dim shafts of gold out the windows to dissipate in the cloaking fog. From within he could hear low groans, a sudden cry of pain. Naval sentries, half-asleep, stood outside the building, leaning on their muskets. Four bodies were lying on the lawn, bare feet sticking out from under the blankets, the corpses, like all corpses, looking tiny and forlorn.

Elihu broke into a slow trot as they went through the gates of the naval yard, the sentries looking at them wide-eyed as they passed.

"Hey, was that Grant?" one of them asked as they passed, their conversations muffled and then lost in the fog. They trotted up a broad avenue, passing a convoy of wagons parked by the side of the road. No one was about. The streets were empty, the soft glow of streetlights marking their way. Two- and three-story houses lining the road were dark. Several street corners had small patrols stationed, three or four men. Some were up, standing, more than one man curled up, sleeping in a doorway while a lone comrade fought to stay awake, keeping watch.

A black cat darted across the street in front of Grant, causing his horse to shy, and he fought it back down, urging it forward.

Elihu chuckled.

"Not superstitious, are you?" he asked.

Grant said nothing, letting go of the rein with one hand to reach into his pocket, pull out a match, and strike his cigar back to life.

A wagon rumbled past them, going in the opposite direction. Inside, piles of newspapers were stacked high. The road slowly climbed up a slope, the narrow confines of houses giving way to a broad, open expanse of lawn. He didn't need to be told; it was the Capitol.

Dim lights glowed from within, the fog breaking up slightly to reveal, in the first early light of dawn, the great iron dome that was still under construction.

Elihu slowed a bit, reined his horse in, and stopped for a moment.

"No matter how many times I see it, it still gives me a lump in the throat," he whispered.

Grant said nothing, looking up at the towering heights. Even now, at four-thirty in the morning, the building was open. A row of ambulances were parked in front of the east portico, stretcher-bearers carrying their burdens up the steps. Civilians were coming in and out, some moving slowly, wearily, after what must have been a long night of labor, others hurrying in.

He was tempted to stop, if only for a few minutes. It had been years since he had trod these halls, and within were men who had suffered, some enduring the final agony of having paid the ultimate price for the preservation of what this building represented. But other matters pressed, and he slowly rode on.

They skirted around the south end of the Capitol, dropping down to the broad, open, almost marshy ground below the building. Directly in the middle he stopped again and looked up.

The structure towering above him was imposing, solid, conveying a sense of the eternal . . . the temple of the republic for which he fought.

Whether it would one day stand as a hollow testament to the failure of the dream, or remain the central hall of freedom, now rested squarely upon his shoulders. It was a responsibility he had not sought, but which fate seemed to have thrust upon him. Strangely, he found himself wondering how this place would look fifty, a hundred and fifty years from now. Would it be barren, a city abandoned like so many capitals of the ancient world, or would it be vibrant, alive, the dream continuing, a place of pride, a republic that would endure this time of crisis and emerge yet stronger?

He pressed on, following Elihu, who had slowly ridden ahead, Haupt at his side. They reached Pennsylvania Avenue and turned left. There was a light scattering of traffic, the first streetcar of the morning slowly making its way up the hill to the Capitol. A company of troops marching in route step passed on the other side of the road, rifles slung over shoulders, the men bantering among themselves, barely noticing the two officers and a congressman trotting past. A barricade blocked off most of the street farther on, with two twelve-pound Napoleons deployed behind it, sentries standing at the narrow opening. No comments were exchanged as they rode through, though one of the men looked up curiously at Grant as he saluted.

As they dropped down off Capitol Hill, the fog thickened again. Riding in the middle of the street, they could barely see the buildings flanking either side. A drunk sitting on the curb was being soundly dressed down by a policeman who was hoisting him to his feet. A few ladies of the evening, or in this case the early morning, loitered under a streetlamp, looking over hopefully as they passed, but offering no comments.

They passed by the bright lights of the Willard, a small crowd gathered outside, mostly officers, but none looked over at his passage. He was glad of that, otherwise the rumor would explode like wildfire. With his private's sack coat, collar pulled up against the morning damp, he was barely distinguishable, except for the three stars on each shoulder.

Directly ahead was the War Department, Elihu leading the way. In the fog he caught a glimpse of the White House, troops deployed on the front lawn. The sky was brightening, shifting from indigo to a sullen gray.

They reined in before the dark somber mass of the War Department building. The sentries out front, in spite of the hour, were well turned out, uniforms smart, brass polished and reflecting the glow of the streetlights.

As he swung down off his mount, several orderlies came out of the doorway and at the sight of him slowed, stiffening to attention.

"General Grant?" one of them asked.

He returned the salute and nodded.

"Sir, the secretary of war is in his office; he told me to escort you in the moment you arrived."

Haupt dismounted with him, but Elihu stayed on his horse.

"Think I'll wander over to the White House," Elihu announced.

In spite of the hour, Grant knew that Elihu would rouse the president, and he was grateful. Stanton had no real love for him, and at this crucial first meeting it would be good to have Lincoln present.

Grant followed the orderly into the building after telling one of the sentries to find a way to return the horses back to the cavalrymen at the naval yard.

The corridors were brightly lit with gaslight, the floor beneath his feet sticky with tobacco juice, cluttered with scraps of paper, and even what appeared to be splotches of blood. Even at five in the morning it was bustling with activity, staff officers running back and forth; a lieutenant with his arm in a sling—the blood on the floor obviously from the leaking wound in his elbow—leaned against a wall, pale-faced, not even noticing as Grant walked past him. In his good hand he was clutching a roll of papers.

They went up the stairs, turned down another corridor, the air a bit stuffy and damp, and without fanfare were ushered into the outer office of the secretary of war.

A well-dressed colonel, sitting behind a desk, stood up as Grant and Haupt came in.

"Good morning, General, we were expecting you," the colonel announced in a soft, silky voice. "The secretary is asleep but I have orders to wake him the moment you arrive. Please make yourself comfortable."

The colonel slipped through a doorway, barely opening it, and the etched glass panes of the inner office, which had been dark, now glowed from a light within.

There was muffled conversation. Grant settled back in the leather-bound seat and looked over at Haupt, who was obviously exhausted.

They didn't wait long. The doorway opened, the colonel beckoning for them to enter.

Stanton was up, hair rumpled, feet in carpet slippers, an unmade day-bed in the corner, with blankets kicked back. He wheezed slightly as he came up and shook Grant's hand.

"You made good time, sir."

"General Haupt is to be thanked for that. We had an express with track cleared all the way from Harrisburg to Perryville."

Stanton beckoned to a couple of seats across from his desk as he settled down. The colonel reappeared bearing a silver tray with a pot of coffee and one of tea. He poured the tea for Stanton and coffee for Grant and Haupt, then withdrew.

Stanton opened a desk drawer and pulled out a pocket flask.

"Would you care for a bracer in that, General?" he asked.

Grant, features expressionless, shook his head. Stanton put the flask back in the desk.

"Give me a minute to wake up, General," he said, and leaning back in his chair, Stanton noisily sipped on his cup of tea, draining it, then refilling it.

Grant waited patiently.

"Did you hear what happened here the last two days?" Stanton asked.

"Just the telegrams you sent up to me and the usual newspaper reports."

"We bloodied them. Two divisions, Perrin and Pettigrew, were all but destroyed. It was a major defeat for Lee and his men."

"That's what I heard."

"We have some reports that Jefferson Davis is in their camp."

"I heard that as well, sir."

"If he's there, I think that means he will renew the attack."

Grant said nothing, making no comment about Stanton's observation.

"We are getting stronger pretty fast," Stanton continued. "All of Strong's brigade is up from Charleston. Two more brigades are slated to arrive today, along with some additional units out of Philadelphia and several ninety-day regiments that were mustering in New Jersey. I hope the rebels do try it again."

"I don't think they will," Grant ventured.

"Why?"

"If Lee failed in his first assault, and did so with the casualties you are reporting, I cannot see him trying the exact same attack again. One attempt against a fortified position might be justified, but a second one on the heels of a failed attack would be folly. And Lee is not given to folly."

"Are you certain of that?"

"No one can ever be certain in war, but it's what I would do and I think Lee is a professional who avoids self-destructive mistakes."

"Suppose Davis orders another attack? He obviously came north to be here and gloat over their final victory. I cannot see him turning away from us now. The political repercussions would be significant."

"I think, sir, that General Lee would resist any such order. In spite of their victories of the last month they cannot afford any more serious losses. If he takes Washington but drains his army's manpower, it will be an even worse defeat in the end."

"And you are certain of that?"

Again Grant shook his head, knowing right here at the start that Stanton was trying to force him into a commitment to his own vision of what would come next.

"And again, sir, nothing is certain in war."

Stanton coughed noisily and then looked over sharply at the cigar in Grant's hand.

There was an ashtray at the corner of the desk and he put it out.

"Do you know why I summoned you here?" Stanton asked.

"I would assume, sir, to review the plans of the forthcoming campaign."

"Yes, General. Since your appointment to field command of all armies, I have not the slightest inkling of what your intentions are."

"Sir, I thought it best not to entrust such delicate information to either the telegraph or dispatches. I was going to prepare a full report for you once I was in Harrisburg."

"Why Harrisburg?"

"Sir, I plan to make that the base of my operations."

Stanton coughed again and then poured another cup of tea.

"You did not get my approval for making that your headquarters."

"I know that, sir."

Haupt stirred uncomfortably by Grant's side and Stanton looked over at him.

"What is it, Haupt?"

"Sir, Harrisburg is an ideal location to constitute a new field army. Its rail connections are some of the best in the North. It offers easy access not only to Upstate New York and New England, but to the Midwest as well. We will have to run literally thousands of trains in the next month in order to create this force, and I suggested Harrisburg almost immediately as the place to marshal. Besides, though not a field commander, I think it is evident that by organizing at Harrisburg, we maintain a potent position to strike into the rear of Lee's lines of communication, thus ultimately forcing him to battle."

"Thank you for that analysis, Haupt, but there is another consideration that carries far more weight, and that is the political consideration of maintaining Washington no matter what the cost."

"Mr. Secretary," Grant interjected, glad that Haupt had offered a moment's diversion with a very pointed and cogent argument, "I think it is fair to state that Washington is secure now."

"Are you certain, General Grant? We've had reports that a massive Confederate column, maybe upwards of fifty thousand strong, is already marshaling in Richmond; advance elements even now are moving into the Shenandoah Valley, coming up to reinforce Lee or to act as an independent striking force."

"And who commands this?"

"Our agents report it is Beauregard."

Grant said nothing. He had faced Beauregard once before, at Shiloh, and did not hold him in the high regard that others did.

"I would think they are destined to merge with Lee's forces," he finally offered in reply.

"Whether with Lee or not, such a force could very well tip the scale and take the capital."

"I would not place this new force in the same caliber as the Army of Northern Virginia. They are scraping the bottom of the barrel. Chances are many of the units are state militias, about as useful as our ninety-day regiments. It could take them weeks, a month or more, before their numbers will even be noticed."

"Sir," Haupt said, pressing back in to the conversation. "The Confederate railroad system is a shambles. Several different gauges on their lines hinder any transfers when moving long distances. They have to stop and transfer men and equipment between trains every time they encounter a

new gauge. Last winter, when the Army of Northern Virginia was encamped in front of Fredericksburg, they could barely move half a dozen
supply trains a day, forcing Lee to scatter his forces across hundreds of
square miles for forage. The task of moving that number of men north, if
that is indeed the number, will strain them to the breaking point."

"The number is valid," Stanton snapped.

"As reported by whom?" Grant asked.

"I've sent Pinkerton agents into Virginia."

Again Grant did not reply. Some of the agents were good, obviously
the one who had sent the message to him about Davis was doing his job,
but most of them were amateurs when it came to doing field reconnaissance. It was similar reports, early in 1862, claiming the rebels had two
hundred thousand in front of Richmond, that had crippled McClellan. In
his own mind, he cut the numbers in half. At most Lee would get twenty-
five thousand.

"I think, General Grant, that you should stay in Washington, establish
your headquarters here, and make this your main base of operations. Sickles, up on the banks of the Susquehanna, is even now reorganizing the
Army of the Potomac. Between your force and his, Lee can be trapped."

"Sickles? Dan Sickles?"

"Yes, Dan Sickles. I signed the order this afternoon promoting him to
command of the Army of the Potomac."

He felt his face flush at this news.

"Sir, as commander of all forces in the field, I feel I should have been
consulted on this."

"General Grant, you've been incommunicado ever since this debacle
unfolded. I was forced to act and act I did."

Before I could countermand it, Grant thought.

"Why General Sickles?" he finally asked.

"I don't like him any more than you do, Grant," Stanton replied. "But
he has powerful friends in Congress. We need the continued support of
the Democratic Party and he is firmly in their camp and now their hero of
the hour. His after-action report for Gettysburg and for Union Mills has
been printed up and circulated, even the newspapers have it."

"I've yet to see this report, who was it forwarded to?" Grant asked.

"It came straight to me. With Meade dead, he had the excuse to by-
pass proper channels. Copies were leaked as well. I do have to admit that
the man had a point about Gettysburg. If Meade had allowed him to go
forward on July 2, he would have plowed straight into Lee's flanking
march and perhaps destroyed it. He argued as well that if he had been allowed to march to the support of Fifth Corps in front of Taneytown, rather

than ordered to proceed to Union Mills, he could have turned Lee's left flank and forced the rebels to withdraw. It's causing an uproar. He was scheduled to appear before the Committee on the Conduct of the War to testify."

"But if he was appointed to command of the Army of the Potomac that hearing would be canceled?" Haupt asked.

That ploy was something he had never considered, and Grant shook his head. Yet again, the political maneuverings. Command in the East was clearly much more political and complex than command in the West. Distance from Washington might have been a bigger advantage than he had thought.

"Yes, something like that. He won't have time to testify now.

"Besides, he suppressed the rebellion in New York City and even the Republican papers are hailing him as the savior of the city."

Grant looked at the crushed cigar in the ashtray, wishing he could relight it.

"You are stuck with him, Grant," Stanton said.

"But nevertheless he will still answer to my orders," Grant said softly.

"In proper coordination with this office," Stanton replied.

Even though Grant's thinking rarely turned to outright guile, he could see that Stanton was trying to outmaneuver and box him in. He wondered if perhaps his old foe, Halleck, licking the wounds of public humiliation at his dismissal from supreme command, was even now lurking in a room down the hallway, waiting to rush in once this meeting was over.

The doorway opened and he almost cried out with relief. Elihu was there with President Lincoln behind him.

Obviously a bit flustered, Stanton stood up as Lincoln came in. His features were pale, eyes deep-set with exhaustion, black coat rumpled as if he had been sleeping in it, trousers stained with mud.

"Mr. President, General Grant and I were just discussing the forth-coming campaign."

"Yes, I can well imagine," Lincoln said.

He looked over at Grant and a genuine smile wrinkled his face.

"General, so good to see you," and he extended his hand.

His contacts with Lincoln, up to this moment, had been only remote. He had never stood like this, so close, almost a sense of the two of them being alone. He looked straight into the man's eyes and liked what he saw. Homey, down-to-earth, the prairie lawyer without pretense.

The handshake was firm, strong, with a touch of an affectionate squeeze just before he let go.

The colonel in the outer office came in, dragging two straight-backed chairs, hurriedly deployed them, and left, closing the door.

Lincoln went to the window and looked out. Dawn was breaking, wisps of fog curling up, the sky overhead visible now with streaks of pink and light blue.

"A long night, gentlemen," Lincoln said, and then turned back, "but hopefully a better day now. General Grant, I'm delighted to see you at last."

"I am honored to be here, sir."

"Tell me of Vicksburg and your journey to here. I need to hear some good news for a few minutes."

Grant briefly reviewed the climax of the campaign and his hurried journey east, Lincoln smiling and nodding as if all other cares had disappeared for the moment.

"Remarkable, when you think of it, gentlemen. When I first came to Washington almost twenty years ago, the trip took weeks. When I was a boy, my trip to New Orleans, traveling with a raft of cantankerous hogs, took well over a month. And now we can all but leap across the country in a matter of days."

"After this war is over, sir," Haupt said proudly, "we'll go from Chicago to San Francisco in less than a week."

"Think of it," Lincoln said with a smile. "I read in *Scientific American* just a few weeks back how some tinkerers are talking about balloons powered by steam engines that will traverse the skies, perhaps even crossing to England in a matter of days. I would love to see that."

Stanton coughed and shifted uncomfortably in his chair.

"Our good secretary is reminding us, gentlemen, that we must deal with business before we can play with our dreams. Is your health well this morning, Mr. Secretary?"

"No, sir. The cursed asthma again."

"I'm sorry to hear that, but yes, down to business."

"Mr. President, I was just discussing with General Grant our wish that he establish his headquarters and operational base here in Washington. It will serve to defend our capital, but also has a logic in terms of logistics, with our superior water transport moving the men and equipment he might desire."

Lincoln nodded thoughtfully, crossing his legs to reveal a pale white shin, his sock having slid down to pile up atop his shoe.

"And, General Grant, your opinion on this? I should add that though the secretary speaks in the plural with his statement as to 'our' wishes, I will admit to not having discussed this with him yet at length."

Stanton bristled slightly and Grant saw the interplay between the two, and the opening Lincoln was providing him.

"Sir. I think Harrisburg is the better choice."

"Enlighten me."

He presented his argument in a concise, clear manner, both in terms of the plan he was formulating and the logistic issues, which Haupt weighed in on. Concluding his presentation, which took no more than five minutes, he fell silent.

"I think, sir, that establishing the base in Harrisburg would be redundant," Stanton replied sharply. "We already have Sickles north of the Susquehanna. It would divert from him resources and rolling stock needed for his own efforts."

"I thought all efforts were for the same goal," Lincoln said softly, looking back out the window.

"A renewed Army of the Potomac, a hundred thousand strong, coming down out of the north," Stanton pressed, "with General Grant here in Washington acting as the anvil, would force the conclusion we want."

Lincoln looked back at Grant.

"Your reply to that?"

"A hundred thousand for the Army of the Potomac?" Grant asked.

"They are the army of this theater, sir," Stanton replied.

"And have lost," Grant said quietly without condemnation, just a simple statement of fact.

"Are you saying they should be disbanded?" Stanton asked heatedly.

"No, sir. They have a role, which I've already mentioned just now to the president. But a hundred thousand strong?"

"You disagree with the number?" Lincoln asked.

"Sir, you've appointed me commander in chief of all forces in the field. To do that task I must be in command, and in the field, not trapped in a besieged garrison. Washington will hold just fine for the moment. If another crisis appears, I can quickly shift men here as needed. But if I stay here, I will be cut off, only able to communicate with all the other field commands by a tenuous line of courier boats racing from here up to Perryville and back. The delay will be crippling in and of itself, and will render me ineffective in my post."

"You answer to the War Department, General Grant," Stanton said heatedly. "General Halleck found it workable to run things from Washington. If you do not like that arrangement, sir . . ."

And his voice trailed off as Lincoln held up his hand for silence.

No one spoke as Lincoln stood back up and walked to the window.

He gazed out for a moment. Grant looked straight at Stanton, who was obviously angry, breathing hard, each breath a labored struggle.

Lincoln finally turned.

"General Grant, I give you full discretion."

Stanton shifted, looking over at Lincoln, about to protest.

"Mr. Secretary, you've done an admirable job these last two weeks."

Grant could detect a certain strain in Lincoln's voice. He knew of the controversy that had blown up about the contradictory orders sent by Stanton and Halleck to Meade, after Lincoln had ordered Meade not to risk his forces recklessly in an attempt to reestablish contact with Washington. He could see that there was a complex battle now brewing between these two men, and his own position was a major piece in that fight.

"Sir, I must protest," Stanton replied.

"And your protest will be duly noted. You are right that General Halleck managed things from here, but he did not win from here. I want General Grant out in the field. It's good to hear for once a commander asking for that, and not hiding behind his desk. I think General Grant is right: if he stays here in Washington, his position will be rendered ineffective, and we do not want that now, do we, Edwin?"

The secretary, flustered, was unable to respond.

"Good then, that's settled. Gentlemen, I've been up all night and would like to find some sort of breakfast. So if you will excuse me."

The group stood up as Lincoln headed to the door. He stopped and looked back.

"Grant, would you care to join me?" he asked.

"Mr. President, I have numerous details to go over with the general," Stanton protested.

"I think General Haupt could be of more assistance to you at the moment. Don't worry, I'll have our commander here back to you later today."

Without waiting for a reply Lincoln was out the door. Elihu beckoned for Grant to follow.

Lincoln waited in the hallway as the door closed behind Grant. Not a word was spoken as they went back down the stairs. The corridor was packed, word having raced through the building that the president and Grant were in with Stanton. Men snapped to attention, saluting, Lincoln smiling, shaking a few hands until they were out in the street.

To Grant's dismay he saw several reporters racing up, notebooks out, shouting questions. A provost guard was waiting, however, rounding the reporters up, pressing them back against the wall of the War Office. The press howled, especially when a captain of the guard shouted a reminder that the city was still under martial law and they were to keep quiet about whom they saw, under penalty of arrest.

Lincoln set off at a brisk pace, crossing the street, heading back to the White House, a mounted guard detail forming a circle around them, but moving at a discreet distance, allowing the three to talk without being heard.

"Well, that was interesting," Elihu offered.

"Stanton wanted to chain you to that building," Lincoln said, shaking his head. "He wanted you where he could watch you and control you. You would think that we all would have learned by now."

"I smell Halleck in this," Elihu replied angrily.

"All of them are jealous," Lincoln said, shaking his head. "Grant, I'm afraid there are some here who are not pleased by your promotion."

"I'm sorry if that is the case."

"Don't be. It's not a time to be sorry about stepping on toes. Especially big toes sticking out from under the safety of their desks."

"Yes, sir."

"I think I'm going to like working with you, Grant," Lincoln replied. "You're from the West, as I am; we see things differently. None of this flummery and posturing. I'm sick to death of it, while good boys are dying. Why everyone needs so dang much gold braid to play dress up for what is after all the business of killing is beyond me."

Grant spared a glance down at his own soiled tunic and trousers. He had been a bit embarrassed while riding through the city. He was glad now his dress uniform had been left behind.

"Smoke, if you feel like it, Grant; I know it bothers our poor secretary with his lung sickness, but it's fine by me. When we meet Mrs. Lincoln, however, I'll ask you to refrain."

"Yes, sir."

He reached into his breast pocket, pulled out the last of his cigars, and paused for a second to strike a match on the side of his boot. He puffed it to life and nodded his thanks.

"That's Grant. I know it!"

The streets were beginning to fill with early-morning traffic. Several companies, in columns of fours, were marching by in the other direction, and a cheer went up for Lincoln and Grant.

Grant did not acknowledge it; it was something he hated and it was clearly evident these men had never served under his command. Lincoln tipped his hat, nodded, and pressed on.

The last wisps of morning fog were breaking up, the sun hot and low on the eastern horizon, casting long shadows.

They approached the front entrance to the White House. The troops who were camped on the ground were getting rousted out, the word of who was approaching obviously having raced ahead. Orders were shouted, men falling into ranks, forming twin lines across the front lawn and snapping to attention. Lincoln stopped and put a hand on Grant's shoulder, causing him to turn.

"A few comments and questions before we go in," Lincoln said softly.

"Anything, sir."

"You are to be in sole command, General. We have lacked that for too long. To be frank, I felt that General McClellan saw the armies as nothing more than his personal escort. I made mistakes as well then; I was patient when I should have interfered and I interfered when I should have stepped back. I think any president would be tempted to do so, but I've learned my lessons. I think as well I should have been far more forceful in finding a general that would fight, then letting him go do his business. You are my expert at battle, so unless there is a profound issue that cannot be avoided by me, I will stand back and let you see to your business."

Grant could not reply to that. The reality was simply too startling. But three short weeks ago he was handling a siege on the Mississippi, all that he commanded almost within direct view at any given moment. Now every soldier as far afield as Texas or the Indian Territories was under his command.

And yet it did not overwhelm him. He thought of the many cold, rainy nights, sitting alone with Sherman, talking of how the war should be fought, how if allowed to do so they could bring the bloodletting to an end. The price, up front, would be cruel, and yet in the end it would spare all of the nation endless years of half measures and unrelenting agony. This president had just given him that power.

"The secretary is not happy with your appointment. Frankly, it was done without serious consultation with him. Some claim it was the spur of the moment, the night I learned of the destruction of the Army of the Potomac. Maybe so, but I will tell you, Grant, that the thought had been building for some time."

"I appreciate that confidence, sir; I hope I can live up to it."

"All right, then. To speak bluntly and no whispers on the aside. I know about your problem with drinking."

Grant flushed and lowered his head.

"I know as well that you have kept it under control in spite of the vicious rumors launched by your enemies, including some back in that very office we just left.

"I'll only say this once and the matter will never be spoken of again. Until this war is finished, not another drop, sir. If you shall fail in that pledge, your enemies and mine will howl for your head and I doubt if even I will be able to save it. I have placed a confidence in you and I expect it to be observed."

Grant looked back up into his eyes and saw there was no recrimination. The gaze was almost fatherly as Lincoln reached out and squeezed his shoulder.

"You have my word of honor on that, sir," Grant replied humbly.

"Good. Nothing more will be said on that," and Lincoln smiled.

"Now, establish your headquarters where you will. If Harrisburg is your choice, so be it."

"And General Sickles, sir?"

Lincoln sighed.

"My hand was forced on that point. He might be a thorn in your side, the last of the old guard of McClellan's time, but then again, he seems to have conducted himself well in division and corps command. And like it or not, he was right about the second day at Gettysburg. If he had been allowed to advance, the same request he had made at Chancellorsville, all might be different now."

Lincoln smiled.

"Perhaps we would not even be meeting like this if he had been listened to. Some philosophers muse on the idea that history can take many paths, and perhaps that is true. It might very well have been the case at Gettysburg. So General Sickles now has his chance, but he is to answer to you."

"And if I find it necessary to relieve him?"

Lincoln sighed and looked away.

"Grant, you are the supreme military commander, but in this one case I will have to ask for your forebearance. Can I ask you to trust me on this score? The ramifications would, unfortunately, go far beyond the military issues and affect our entire war effort. I hope you understand."

He could not refuse the request as Lincoln had just made it, as if he was a neighbor asking for a favor.

"Yes, sir. Whatever you wish."

"Fine then. Are you hungry?"

Grant smiled and nodded his head.

"Yes, sir, to tell the truth I'm starving."

"We have an excellent cook. Perhaps some flapjacks with maple syrup, a good slice of fried ham, and some coffee?"

"I'd be delighted."

"We'll talk more later, when we are alone. But let's relax for the moment. I just met this remarkable fellow I'd like you to meet. Hope you don't mind that he's colored."

"Of course not, sir."

"Been learning a lot of history from him these last few days; he's known every president since Madison. Has some delightful insights."

"It would be a pleasure to meet him."

"Good then. Elihu, I know you're looking for a meal as well at taxpayers' expense."

"Thank you, Mr. President."

Lincoln started to lead the way again, but then stopped and it seemed as if a visible weight had suddenly come back down upon his shoulders. He looked back at Grant, eyes again dark, careworn.

"May I ask a question, General Grant?"

"Yes, sir, anything."

"Can we win? Can we end this madness before it destroys us all, North and South?"

The intensity of the question, the look in Lincoln's eyes struck him. Rarely given to sentiment, he found his own voice choking for a moment, and he was unable to speak. It was as if a mystical bond was, at that moment, forged between them. As if in whatever way possible, he had to lift some of the infinite burden off this man's shoulders, and even as that thought formed he felt the weight, the awesome responsibility of knowing that the republic, its very survival, its fate over the next hundred years, rested on him as well.

He slowly nodded his head, looking straight into Lincoln's eyes.

"Yes, sir, we can win."

Chapter Ten

Near Leesborough, Maryland

July 20, 1863
2:00 P.M.

C.S.A The last of the storm was passing to the southeast, dark clouds bristling with lightning. Stepping down off the porch of a pleasant frame house whose owner had offered him coffee and biscuits while waiting out the blow, Lee stretched, looking around, breathing deeply of the cool fresh air that came sweeping down out of the northwest.

After three weeks of unrelenting heat, humidity, and rain, he could feel that the weather had indeed changed, that this last blow had swept the air clean. The rain had come down in torrential sheets for a half hour, swamping the road, but now, as a column of men from Pickett's division were filing out of the woods where they had sought temporary shelter from the blast, he could see their renewed vigor. The temperature had dropped a good fifteen to twenty degrees, the air was crystal clear, sharp, a pleasure to breathe. It sent an infectious mood through the men, who were joking, laughing, splashing around in rain-soaked uniforms, boots tied around their necks. For a few minutes they seemed almost like schoolboys again.

He mounted Traveler, staff falling in around him. He waited patiently for President Davis and Secretary Benjamin to come out of the house, the two climbing into an open four-horse carriage that had been "borrowed" from a wealthy landowner near where they had camped the night before. The owner was furious about the requisitioning until he heard who would be using the carriage, then simply asked for a receipt, along with an affidavit to be given back with the carriage, confirming who had ridden in it. It was obvious he planned to make a commercial venture out of the carriage when it was finally returned.

Lee edged out onto the road, Traveler kicking up muddy splashes. Behind him the lead brigade of Pickett's division, Armistead's men, were forming up. Turning, he headed north, the road clear for several hundred yards ahead. His staff, the headquarters wagon, and the president's carriage followed. With Taylor and his guidon-bearer just behind him, he urged Traveler to a slow canter, enjoying the ride, the cooling breeze, a shower of heavy droplets cascading down around him as he rode under a spread of elm trees that canopied the road. Reaching a gentle crest he saw the village of Leesborough, a small, prosperous community with several stores, a couple of dozen homes, rich farmland surrounding it. The winter wheat had been brought in, but the orchards, especially the peach orchards, had been severely damaged by the passing army, nearly every tree plucked clean. Fences were broken down and gone as well, wet circles of ashes and partially burned wet wood marking where men had camped the night before.

At the intersection with the Rockville Pike in the center of town a regimental band stood, playing patriotic airs. A spotter for the band, having seen the approaching cavalcade of the army headquarters and the president, was running back to the center of town, waving his arms.

Lee slowed, looking over at Walter.

"It's good for morale," Walter said with a smile.

Lee nodded and waited, letting his staff ride on, then edging back on to the road alongside the presidential carriage.

"It's turned into a lovely day," Benjamin announced, gesturing to the sparkling blue sky overhead.

"That it has, sir. By evening the roads should dry out a little, and hopefully tomorrow we'll make good time."

Up ahead the band struck up "Bonnie Blue Flag," and a cheer rose, a regiment that had been coming down the road from Rockville stopping, men spilling out of column to swarm behind the band.

Lee said nothing, though this would play havoc with the marching order, stalling the troops farther up the road, but it couldn't be helped now. Besides, Walter was right. They needed a boost after the misery and frustration of the last week.

The reporters traveling with Davis were off their mounts, notebooks out; one of them produced a large sketch pad and, with charcoal stick in hand, began to furiously scratch at his paper.

Lee fell in behind the carriage, Walter at his side, as they rode into the small village. Cheer upon cheer greeted them. From the rear, Armistead's men were splashing through the mud, coming up on the double to take part in the show, slowing at a respectful distance, breaking ranks, holding caps in the air, and yelling.

Davis, obviously pleased, ordered the carriage to stop in the middle of the intersection and stood up. Lee reined in behind him, and troops from the two columns edged closer, yelling and waving. Davis held his hands out and the men fell silent.

"Gallant soldiers of the Confederacy. I salute you!"

Another roar went up, the roads now clogged with men breaking ranks, pushing in closer.

"You, the victors of Union Mills, have crowned your reputation with undying glory. You march now to yet a greater victory. A victory that shall soon end this war. And then, as conquering heroes you can return to your homes and loved ones, where you shall be forever honored for what you did here."

Yet more cheers greeted this statement. General Longstreet approached the edge of the crowd from the west, coming down the Rockville Road. He pushed his mount through the crowd, falling in alongside of Lee, saying nothing, but his gaze was anything but happy over this disruption. Lee smiled softly and said nothing.

"I have a request of our wonderful band," Davis cried.

The bandmaster saluted with his staff.

"An honor, sir. What do you request?"

"In honor of our gallant friends, who even now are rallying to the cause of Southern freedom, I would appreciate hearing 'Maryland My Maryland.'"

The bandmaster turned with a flourish, passed the command, instruments were raised, and the band began to play. It was obvious after several measures that they were not as well practiced with this tune. Davis stood solemn, listening, ignoring the more than occasional off-key notes. The newspaper artist, standing on a porch, sketched away furiously.

The band finished. Davis was about to continue to speak but Longstreet, with less than the required diplomacy and politeness, loudly cleared his throat. Davis looked out of the corner of his eye toward Old Pete and then Lee.

"Perhaps our gallant General Lee would care to address you," Davis offered, pointing toward him.

More cheers erupted, and under the cover of the noise Lee moved to the side of the carriage.

"Sir, I think General Longstreet was reminding us that we have an army on the march and this crossroads needs to be cleared if we are to continue."

Davis flushed slightly but then nodded. Benjamin, obviously enjoying himself, just smiled and said nothing.

Davis extended his hand again; the men fell silent.

"God bless and keep all of you." He sat back down and told the driver to move on. The driver hesitated and looked at Lee, obviously not sure of what direction to take.

"North," Walter said, and with a crack of reins the carriage passed through the crossroads, escorts and guards galloping ahead.

Longstreet turned to a provost guard standing mud-splattered in the middle of the road.

"Clear the rest of this division from Rockville," Pete said angrily, pointing back to the west. "Then, have General Pickett file in behind it."

The provost saluted and started to turn.

"And tell that damn silly band they can play but get the hell off the street, move them out of the way."

Anxiously, the provost saluted again and ran off, shouting orders.

"Shouldn't be too hard on them today," Lee said.

Longstreet shook his head.

"The roads are still a mess and we're funneling not just my corps, but Hood's as well through here. That little demonstration tied things up for a mile in each direction."

"Still, the men needed it and so did the president."

"Sorry, sir. I think once we're clear of here, I'll feel better again."

"I know. I feel the same way. It was a bitter march to here and a bitter defeat, but now we are moving again, doing what we do best."

He could again see the movements on the map engraved in his mind's eye. The army was reduced to but six divisions, and all of those were under strength to varying levels. Longstreet, with four divisions, Pickett, who was coming up even now, McLaws, who was behind Pickett, Johnson, and Doles, commanding the division coming down from Rockville, formerly Rhodes's division (Rhodes died in the final moments at Union Mills), were to push on toward Baltimore until twilight. Once they had cleared Leesborough, Hood would follow, leading Early's tough veterans and Robertson, who was now in command of Hood's old division. Hood's corps would turn east from here, move to Beltsville astride the Baltimore and Ohio Railroad, turn north, then east again to Annapolis.

The shattered remains of Perrin's and Pettigrew's divisions would stay behind just north of Fort Stevens as they were being reorganized into a single division under Scales.

Stuart's command was being split up as well. Half his strength was to shadow Washington, probe, demonstrate. The other half was to sweep north up the two lines of advance, cutting telegraph lines and securing the way clear up to the outskirts of Baltimore and Annapolis.

He looked back up at the sky. If the weather should hold like this, sunny with a dry, cool evening, by midmorning tomorrow the roads should be dry enough to swing his massive artillery reserve, usable guns captured at Union Mills, and his regular artillery train on to the roads as well. He could have them in position to bombard Baltimore's defenses by nightfall.

The march would be a leisurely one, only thirty miles in two days, nothing at all like the blistering pace of the previous campaign. Officers had been told not to push the men hard, keep a standard pace of two miles to the hour, with ten-minute breaks. Forage parties were to move ahead and, following proper custom, offer payment vouchers for any supplies taken. His general order of the previous evening had emphasized that yet again. They were here to entice Maryland into the Confederacy, not to come at bayonet point, strip away its rights, and then rob it, as the Yankees had done throughout Virginia.

He hoped that Baltimore could actually be taken without a fight. Once his lead division was in place, a message would be sent in to the mayor offering full protection to the city if the civil authorities would surrender without a fight. He knew the army garrison would most likely refuse, but directing his appeal to the civilians might help win their support when they pushed in.

The band, now standing in a field at the edge of the village, broke into a cheery polka. Longstreet looked over at them with displeasure.

"Rather see them carrying rifles. Better use of those men than their tooting away like that; they can't even carry a tune."

"They're hospital orderlies when the fight is on," Lee said soothingly, "and besides, the men do like them."

Longstreet shook his head.

"I'm going to push on, sir, move up to the head of the column. My staff will be back here to keep an eye on the crossroads."

"I'll ride with you then, General Longstreet."

"A pleasure, sir."

He looked over at Longstreet and felt a surge of approval. Old Pete was now the aggressive one. The victory at Union Mills, with praise heaped upon him for the brilliance of the flanking march throughout the South, was overshadowing the legend of Jackson at Chancellorsville. This last campaign had transformed the man. He was more confident, aggressive in movement, hard-driving the way Jackson had been.

Hood would still bear watching. Like Ewell and Hill before him, he was new to corps command. He was a brilliant division commander in the field, but his fumbling before Fort Stevens, though by no means entirely his fault, meant he was still not up to corps command. Lee had given him the Annapolis assignment for two simple reasons. First was the route of march. He wanted Pete's greater striking power to hit that major city. Pete had to clear the road up here to Leesborough before Hood could even begin to move. Hood's actual fighting strength was barely half that of Longstreet's, with two of his remaining divisions under strength and a third division detailed off to Virginia. His Fourth and Fifth divisions, Pettigrew and Perrin, were being left behind for now. Annapolis was obviously suitable for Hood's smaller formation.

The second reason was that it would give Hood a chance at a semidetached command in an operation that was not all that crucial. If he won, it would reinforce his confidence and serve as a good test. If he failed, it would reveal his faults, which, if serious enough, would mean he would have to be relieved; yet such a defeat in and of itself would not be a threatening or terrible blow.

The two generals rode on, the day an absolute delight. An actual coolness was in the air as the last vestiges of the storm raced southeastward, the trees swaying, leaves rustling in the breeze. The fence rails flanking the road were piled high with weeds and honeysuckle. The pastures beyond, though empty of cattle and horses, were rich, the tall grass flattening down before the wind.

Several children were sitting atop a fence, wide-eyed as they approached. One of the boys, standing, balanced himself, saluting. Smiling, Lee saluted back. Two girls, giggling and blushing, stood at the gate to a farmhouse, both of them waving National Flags of the Confederacy. This time Longstreet tipped his hat, as did Lee. An infantryman, sitting on the side of the road, barefoot, nursing what looked to be a broken ankle, looked up balefully as the two approached.

"Sorry I can't stand and salute, sirs; it's broke. Fell out of a tree picking peaches."

"An ambulance will be along to see to you," Lee said in a kindly voice. "But next time, son, don't go foraging like that. Take it as a lesson."

"Give it to 'em in Baltimore, sir," the boy shouted as they continued on.

"They weren't supposed to know where we were heading," Longstreet said, apologizing.

"No matter, any man who knows his geography can figure it out now.

If we'd turned west at the Rockville Road, it would've meant western Maryland or back to Virginia. That's why their spirits are up; they know we're not retreating."

He caught a glimpse of the president's carriage just ahead around a gentle turn in the road, guards trailing behind.

He slowed his own pace, not wanting to catch up quite yet.

"Strange to have him marching with the army," Pete said.

"To be expected now."

"I could tell he wanted Washington. In fact, he assumed he could ride straight in."

"God willed differently."

"I don't think he likes God's will," Pete replied.

Lee did not respond to what could be considered to verge on blasphemy.

"Frankly, I wish he had stayed back till we finished the job," Longstreet persevered.

"I will admit the thought," Lee replied. "However, Mr. Benjamin's arguments for taking Baltimore were cogent and persuasive."

"It's just that we should be clear to do our job without someone second-guessing our decisions, or, for that matter, countermanding them."

"I don't think the president will do that. He is an old military man himself, remember. He will stay back and only observe. He'll leave the job to us."

"I hope so, sir."

"Let's not be troubled by it now," Lee replied soothingly. Catching up to the rear of the president's cavalcade, Lee reined in, and returned Old Pete's salute as his second in command spurred his mount and continued on.

It was a most pleasant day, and for the moment he rode alone, glad to not be noticed, glad to just enjoy the cool, windswept afternoon.

Port Deposit, Maryland

July 20, 1863
6:45 P.M.

The train glided into the station, bell ringing and whistle shrieking. A full brigade, his old Excelsior, was drawn up along the siding to greet him. Though standing at attention, the men let

out a tumultuous roar of approval as he stepped out on to the back platform, eyes sparkling with delight.

Gen. Dan Sickles had returned to his beloved Army of the Potomac.

The brigade broke ranks, swarming around the train. Grinning, he
waved for them to gather in, ignoring this breech of discipline. Scarred
battle flags were held aloft and waved overhead, the cool evening breeze
rushing down the Susquehanna Valley causing them to snap and flutter.
He held up his hands for them to be silent, but the cheering continued,
climaxing with a rousing three cheers for "Old Dan!"

Finally they fell silent, looking up at him, some with visible tears in
their eyes.

"My comrades, my friends," he began, and for a moment his voice
choked, so he lowered his head. A bit of it was required melodrama, but
in his heart, it was real as well. These were the men he had recruited back
in sixty-one, and how few of them remained. How many ghosts now stood
around them. He truly loved this brigade, and he would see that now it
was done right, that they would be led to the victory they deserved.

He raised his head again.

"As you know, yesterday I was appointed to command of the Army of
the Potomac."

Again three cheers greeted him and he basked in the glow of it.

"And yet I must now ask. Where is the Army of the Potomac?"

His words were greeted with silence, many of the men standing stock-
still, some lowering their heads.

"Where are our gallant comrades of the old reliable First Corps? Our
brothers of the Second Corps, who we watched go bravely forward at
Union Mills? The men of the Fifth? The Eleventh, which, better served,
could have shown their mettle, and the Twelfth, who valiantly charged on
that terrible Fourth of July. Where are they?"

No one spoke.

"You and I would willingly give our lives for that dear old flag," and he
pointed toward one of the national colors, a regimental flag, torn, battered, stained.

"We would do so without hesitation if we knew that our lifeblood
would nourish it, protect it, and cause it to be raised high in final victory.
That we would not hesitate to do!"

A ripple of comments greeted him, but no cheers. These were veterans who had seen far too much.

"Perhaps, my comrades, you and I are fated to fall, but here and now,
I promise you this, I promise you that if that should be our fate, it shall

happen as we charge forward to our final victory against the traitors and not ignominious defeat and withdrawal as we have seen too often in our past!"

The men looked up at him, nodding in agreement.

"For too long our beloved Army of the Potomac has borne the weight of generals' follies upon its shoulders. And I tell you this plainly. I stand here to declare, before the entire world, that the fighting men of our gallant army have never lost a battle!"

For a moment there was confusion over his words. For, after all, what of Chancellorsville, of Union Mills? And then the meaning of what he said was realized and a deep, throaty roar of approval greeted him.

"You, my dear comrades, have never lost a fight. It is others that lost it for you. Those of you who stood with me at Gettysburg, who marched across that field on the morning of July second, who saw the chance for ultimate victory, and then saw it torn so basely out of our hands when we were ordered to pull back, you know what I mean and you know who lost it!"

The men looked at him, stunned. Never had a general spoken so plainly to them, spoken the very words they had shared around the campfires and on the march. Their cries now knew no bounds, as if the frustration and rage of the previous two years were at last given vent. He let them roar for more than a minute, then held his hands up again.

"I promise you this. The Army of the Potomac even now is forming its ranks again. Those who are left, our old brothers from other corps, who cut their way out of the debacle, even now are rallying back to our side. The vacant ranks will indeed be filled.

"And I promise you this as well. Soon, far sooner than many ever dreamed of, we shall march forth. This time no one will hold you back, because I will be in the fore as your commander. There shall be no hesitation. No doubting. No stab in the back.

"We will show the world, we will show the North and the South, we will show all those who ever dared to doubt us, that the Army of the Potomac will drive the enemy before it, not just back to Richmond, but clear down to the Gulf of Mexico. And upon your heads shall be crowned the laurels of the final victory!"

He finished his words with a flourish, arms held wide, and the men went wild, hats in the air, the cheering breaking into a steady chant . . .

"Sickles . . . Sickles . . . Sickles!"

He stepped down off the train. Staff officers were waiting for him, including Meade's old chief of staff, Dan Butterfield, who looked at him coldly. Sykes was there as well, as was Howard of the Eleventh Corps, whose gaze was icy. Sedgwick was nowhere to be found. He had already been relieved.

Butterfield pointed the way toward the station. Sickles was glad to see his surviving division commanders waiting for him at the doorway to the station. He paused, looking out over the expanse of the Susquehanna. Ferries for bearing entire trains were docked on the north side, as were tugs, lighters, and barges. Half a dozen small gunboats and ironclads were drawn up in midriver, pennants fluttering in the stiff evening breeze, the broad expanse of the river covered in whitecaps.

He walked into the station, the other officers crowding in, one of his staff closing the door. Without preamble he turned to Butterfield.

"Your report, sir."

"Which report, sir?" Butterfield replied coolly.

"The current status of the Army of the Potomac."

Butterfield looked around the room, like a man on the docket.

"Sir. I have the returns and after-action reports from all surviving units," and he pointed to a leather-bound case on the table in the middle of the room.

"In your own words, and briefly."

"The only viable fighting units left are your corps and the Fifth Corps with a strength of less than forty percent, the Sixth Corps with about the same numbers, and the Eleventh Corps at fifty percent. It is my advice that the First, Second, and Twelfth Corps be disbanded, the men consolidated into other units.

"We have less than eighty guns that are serviceable; nearly the entire Artillery Reserve was captured. Of cavalry, we still are not sure, but I would say less than forty percent are effective. Your total strength therefore is at approximately forty thousand men, that is for all three branches under arms.

"As for support services, we have none. Our entire baggage train is gone, medical supplies all but gone, along with every ambulance. Specialized units, such as pontoon trains, engineering, they are gone, too."

Sickles nodded, his gaze cold, unwavering, as he struck a match and puffed a cigar to life.

"Thank you, General Butterfield. I will read your reports tonight. You are relieved from duty, sir."

"General?"

"Just that. You'll have new orders in the morning. Hold yourself available for a briefing with my new chief of staff later this evening. Good day, General Butterfield."

Butterfield looked at him without comment, eyes narrow, features flushed.

"Yes, sir," he finally snapped. Saluting, he turned on his heels and walked out, slamming the door.

Dan looked around the room, his gaze fixing on Howard.

"You, General Howard, are relieved. Thank you for your service. You as well will receive new orders in the morning."

"On whose authority?" Howard replied softly, speaking each word slowly.

"On my orders."

"I understood that General Grant is now the commander of all forces in the field. The decisions regarding who shall command corps must therefore be in his realm."

"I am commander of the Army of the Potomac now. You are under my authority, and by that authority I am relieving you. You have a choice now. You can take that removal with my blessing, thanks, and recommendation for further posting. Or you can choose to fight me. But by God, sir, if you try to defy me, I will destroy you. You failed your men at Chancellorsville and failed them again at Gettysburg. I wouldn't give you a regiment after that, but perhaps the War Department will see it differently."

"How dare you?" Howard's features were flushed, eyes wide, his one hand resting on the table, drawn up in a fist.

"How dare I? Easy. I am now in charge here. That's how I dare. Now we can do this as gentlemen or we can do it another way."

"You, sir, are no gentleman."

"You're damn right I'm not," Sickles roared. "I'm sick to death of all this damned talk about gentlemen while those good soldiers outside die in the mud. To hell with gentlemen, sir, and to hell with you if you don't obey my orders now!"

Howard drew his balled fist up and slammed it on the table.

"You are a reckless amateur. You think you know how to fight Lee. Maybe so, but I truly doubt it. I daresay it was luck more than anything else that got you as far as you have. Luck and politics of the lowest sort. God save this army with you in command."

"You are relieved, General Howard," Dan said coldly, stepping toward Howard so that his old division commanders moved to his side, ready to restrain him.

Howard looked around the room.

"God save us all if this type of base man is the one that we feel can lead us to victory."

Howard stepped past Dan and went to the door. With his hand on the doorknob, he turned and looked back.

"God forgive me for saying this. But with a man such as you, a man who would gun down your wife's lover on the street while he was unarmed? And now you are in command? I think it is time I do retire."

"God damn you!" Sickles roared, turning, fists raised.

Staff gathered around him, holding him back as Howard gazed at him coldly, waiting several seconds as if ready to accept the challenge to a fistfight or a duel. Finally he opened the door and left.

All were in stunned silence as Sickles, breathing hard, was pushed to the far corner of the room by his staff. He struggled for composure. No one in this army had ever dared to fling that at him. In any other position he would have challenged Howard to a duel on the spot, but now he knew he could not. One of his men drew out a flask, and, angrily, he shook his head, returning back to the table. Sykes stood silent, watching him.

"And am I to be sacked, too?" Sykes asked.

"Hell, no," Dan growled. "You, sir, put up one hell of a fight. The type of fight I want to see. By God, if I had been allowed to march to your aid at Taneytown, we'd have finished Lee then and there."

"I'm not sure of that, General Sickles."

"I am. You are a fighting general, like me. I respect you, General Sykes, and forgive me for what had to be done here."

Sykes said nothing and Dan smiled.

"I want this army ready to march within the month," Dan said, "and your corps will play a leading role."

"In a month? I would think it will not be until fall before we can even hope to have things reorganized. Beyond our loss of men, over half our brigade, division, and corps commanders fell in the last fight or were captured. The army is a shambles, sir."

"Not for long," Dan said. "And besides, some of those generals are no real loss as far as I'm concerned. I will fill the vacant slots and then we shall see how they fight."

He drew out a sheaf of papers from the haversack at his side and tossed them on the table.

"On the train ride down here I've been drawing up the reorganization. The First and Second Corps, God bless them, will unfortunately have to be disbanded. The men will be consolidated into my old corps and yours. The men of the Eleventh and Twelfth will be organized around the Sixth Corps. After its streak of hard luck, the Eleventh must be disbanded. We had too many corps in this army anyhow, some barely more than the size of one of Lee's divisions. We were cumbersome, slow to move and act. We'll take that leaf from Bobbie Lee's book and use it. It will be a more effective command structure, fast-acting and -moving. We were cumbersome in weight as well. The loss of the Artillery Reserve was a terrible blow, but we can live with it."

He paused and looked over at Henry Hunt, who stood in the corner of the room.

"I have no complaint against you, Hunt. But the artillery reserve is finished. All artillery is to be operational at the corps level with only a small reserve left under my direct command. Do you have any objections?"

Hunt shook his head slowly.

"Sir, I think we should talk about this later."

"I assumed that's how you would feel, Hunt. No insult to you but I feel that General Grant, if he ever arrives and builds an army, will need a good artilleryman to advise him. Would you care to be transferred?"

Hunt was silent for a moment and then wearily lowered his head.

"Yes, sir, if there is no Artillery Reserve I no longer see a role for me here."

"Fine then, Hunt, report to my headquarters in the morning and I'll see what I can do for you."

Glad to be rid of that minor detail, Dan turned back to the rest of the gathering without waiting to hear Hunt's reply.

"We have a lot of work cut out for ourselves, gentlemen. First I want the Army of the Potomac concentrated here. There is to be no siphoning off of units into the command that Grant is supposedly trying to form up at Harrisburg. I repeat, that is final, not one man wearing the corps insignia of our gallant old army is to be taken. As we get the lightly wounded and missing back into our ranks, they will rejoin their old regiments.

"For the morale of the men, even though four of the corps are to be disbanded, they will retain their old corps badges. Regiments are to be consolidated into new regiments from their home states and will retain their colors. I know these men, and those badges and their flags are sources of pride that must be honored by us."

The men gathered around him nodded with approval.

"I want the best damn rations down here now. None of this hardtack and salt pork while we are in camp. I want good, clean field kitchens; I want fresh food; I don't care how we get it, but I want it. The men are to have fresh bread daily, all they can eat, fresh meat on the hoof; by God we have the transportation here with the railroads and rivers, and I want it. Nothing is to be spared.

"One out of every ten men from each regiment is to be granted two weeks' furlough. Three weeks for our regiments from the Midwest. The enlisted men of each regiment will select among themselves who receives these furloughs. For every recruit they bring back from home their company will be given a cash bonus of fifty dollars, the men of the company to spend it as they see fit."

"Where are we going to get that kind of money, sir?" one of the staff asked.

"Don't worry about it. I have friends in the right places. If we bring in five to ten thousand that way, it will be worth it. The new recruits will be men from hometowns standing alongside their neighbors and kin in the next fight, not the riffraff to be found by the draft boards. It will play well with the veterans, who will look after them and teach them the traditions of the Army of the Potomac.

"I want a liquor ration to be given every Saturday night as well. Half a gill of rum or whiskey per man."

"The temperance crowd will scream over that one," someone chuckled.

"To hell with the temperance crowd. These men have been through hell and deserve a touch of liquor. To be certain, it might cause a few problems, but it will bind them to us the stronger.

"I've got more orders as well, regarding sutlers, equipment, outfitting of select regiments with breech-loading rifles, new uniforms, shoes, drill, reviews. We have thirty days to build this army back into a fighting force, and by God we will do it."

No one spoke.

"Fine, then. Staff meeting at eight in the morning."

His tone carried a note of dismissal.

"General Sickles," it was Sykes. "Did you see the latest dispatches from Baltimore?"

"Not since I left Philadelphia just after noon."

"It's reported that Lee is abandoning his position in front of Washington."

"What?"

"Civilian reports only. President Davis is confirmed as being with him. Baltimore and Annapolis are in a panic. It appears that Lee is marching north."

Dan grinned.

"Good! Damn good! My one fear was that he would slink off before we could give him the treatment he deserved."

"Also, General Grant came through here late yesterday and took a courier boat to Washington. There's been no report on him since."

Sickles's features darkened.

"Who was with him?"

"General Haupt and Congressman Washburne."

"Who saw him?"

"Just the guard detail down at the wharf."

"Did he ask for me?"

"No sir, not a word. He got off the train and was on the boat and gone within five minutes."

Dan nodded.

With luck, Grant would be ordered to stay in Washington. More than one of his friends would be pulling strings for that even now. If not, it would mean he would return through here. That was worth knowing, and of course Dan would make sure he was unfortunately unavailable when Grant came through. The last thing he needed now was for that man to be interfering in his own plans.

Everything would fall into place in due course, of that he was certain.

Washington, D.C.

July 20, 1863
8:00 P.M.

"Come in, Elihu," Lincoln said, waving for the congressman to sit down in the seat across from his desk.

Elihu, moving slowly, obviously beaten down with exhaustion, exhaled noisily as he took the seat. Lincoln smiled, stocking feet up on his desk.

"Did you see him off?"

"Yes. Both he and Haupt are on their way. Same courier boat that brought us here."

"And the meeting with Stanton before he left?"

"Tense, to say the least. It's obvious Edwin wasn't pleased with how you outmaneuvered him."

Lincoln chuckled softly and shook his head.

"Edwin means well, most of the time. It's just that Grant is not part of his circle. He felt a need to control him."

"'Means well most of the time'? I do think that Edwin believes he is running the war by himself. He'll try to somehow knock Grant off his tracks."

"One of the advantages of being a city under siege," Lincoln replied. "Communications between us and Harrisburg will be difficult for now. Grant can do as he wishes with my authority behind him."

Lincoln sighed, looking up at the ceiling.

"I would have thought that by now we would all see the situation clearly and bury our differences. In the next eight weeks we will either win this war or lose it. Gettysburg and Union Mills focused that clearly for me. The crisis has come. We're like the two farmers who hitched two sets of mules to a wagon pointing in opposite directions and then fell into arguing about it for the rest of the day. We've got to get them all pointed in the same direction, with only one driver on top.

"Grant sees that. In the East he will point everything at Lee, and Haupt will give him the means to do it. In the West we stand in place on the Mississippi, just hold what we have for the moment. Any thoughts of taking Mobile, Charleston, Texas, and Florida are to be abandoned, the men shipped here. The second big effort will be with Rosecrans on Chattanooga and then Atlanta. Once Sherman has consolidated our hold on Vicksburg, he will join Rosecrans and take command. That will be it. No other campaigns this summer and fall. Every available man here, to face Lee and no one else. If we lose some gains elsewhere, that will be in the short run.

"Grant understands this new kind of war, Elihu. It's frightful. War is now a machine, a steam-powered juggernaut. God save us, in a way, the old image of war did have its appeal, even though boys wound up dying, often in droves. Grant can guide this juggernaut, pushed by a thousand factories and locomotives. It's ghastly, but if in the end it saves this republic, and perhaps scares everyone so badly that we will never see a war here again, then the sacrifices will be worth it."

Lincoln sat back, precariously balanced with feet up on the table so that his chair almost tipped over. He pulled a small paring knife out of his pocket, opened it, and went to work on his fingernails.

"And yet the political games still play out," he sighed.

"It's always been that way, sir. We're no different from the Romans, the Greeks. Remember Alcibiades? Even though the city-states knew they were collapsing under the weight of their wars, still Athens worked at cross-purposes with itself and squandered its best generals. We're no different."

"I hoped we could be. I believe we can be," Lincoln said softly. "A fair part of the world, at this moment, wishes us to fail. They are praying even now for it, because we represent something different. A belief that the common man is the equal of any king, of any despot, of any fanatic claiming that God is behind him. If we fail now, if we let this continent sink into divided nations that ultimately will fight yet again and divide yet again, then the dream of our forefathers will be for naught."

He shook his head and chuckled self-consciously.

"Sorry for the speech, Elihu."

"I rather like them at times, Mr. President. When they come from the heart they remind me of why I first got into politics."

Lincoln chuckled.

"I wonder at times how many out there believe that idealism did drive some of us to this path. To hear our opponents and the press behind them, one would think that we did it simply to grasp for power and money. I'll be hanged, Elihu, but if I wanted that, I'd have stayed in my practice and charged the railroad companies exorbitant fees."

"It's always that way, sir. When they can't fight you on principles, the only recourse is to smear you or to kill you."

Lincoln said nothing for a moment, slowly nodding his head.

"Do you think Grant will measure up to the job?" Lincoln asked.

"Yes, I do believe he will. His record already indicates that. As you asked, I observed him closely the last week. There was no puffing up the way so many would have, like McClellan or Hooker. He took his responsibilities calmly, without pomp or fanfare. You saw that touch of his private's uniform. It wasn't posturing; it's just the man is so simple in that sense that he believes that is how he should dress and behave. I like that."

"So do I."

Lincoln smiled and nodded to his stocking feet on the tabletop.

"Mrs. Lincoln is always telling me that George Washington never would have put his bare feet up on a table, but Elihu, I think he did."

Elihu laughed softly in reply.

"Well, sir, when it comes to George Washington, honestly I can't see him in stocking feet. Andy Jackson, of course, but not Washington."

Lincoln smiled.

"Grant's staff, the generals under him, they worship the man," Elihu continued, "but he will tolerate no open displays. As you said, he sees this war as a grim, filthy business. And the quickest way to resolve it is to apply every ounce of strength we have into one terrible blow at the key point. We talked a lot about that. He says that war has changed forever. It is now an entire nation, its industry, its strength, applied to the battlefield. He grasps that our strength might not be in terms of certain generals, such as Lee, but rather in an unrelenting combination of manpower and industry. That he sees as the key to victory."

"You like him, don't you?"

"Yes, I do. I remember him from before the war. Poor man, washed up from what had happened to him. We talked several times; he was gentle, quiet, soft-spoken; hard to believe he had been trained as a soldier. I think he was haunted by what he saw in Mexico, and frankly I liked that, in spite of his turning to the bottle as an answer.

"He hates war. He hates the waste and the blood. Someone told me that in one of his first battles in Mexico, a close friend, standing by his side, was decapitated. It has given him nightmares ever since."

Lincoln said nothing.

"There is no talk of glory in this man the way we heard with McClellan, Hooker, Pope, and too many others."

"Will he see it through and not lose his nerve?"

"Sir. The question is more will *you* see it through?"

Lincoln looked at him quizzically.

"Many of the papers up north are howling. The riot in New York was a near run thing, as were the riots in Cincinnati and Philadelphia. If we lose one more fight like Union Mills, you might be facing a collapse, the Democrats in Congress will call for a meeting with Davis, who, as you know, is this night not a dozen miles from here. If you refuse, they might seek to impeach you, and I fear that more than one member of your Cabinet would go along with it."

Lincoln shook his head.

"Thank God for the Founding Fathers," he said softly.

"Sir?"

"In their wisdom they gave the executive four years in office. Until that term expires, I will hold the course. I swore an oath before God to defend our Constitution and I shall do it. Congress can howl, they can scream. I don't care what they say now. Congress might be swayed by the passions of the moment, but I will not be. If my Cabinet turns against this course, I will fire them. If need be, I will stand alone. As long as Grant can field an army, I will support him and I will hold this course. If the people, in their wisdom, or because of the fears and lies of the demagogues, should vote me out, then so be it, but until then, I will plow the furrow I am in."

Elihu smiled.

"Then Grant is your man."

Baltimore, Maryland

July 20, 1863
11:30 P.M.

C.S.A.   The knock on the door was in code—three taps, three times. Sitting in the semidarkness with George Kane, one of the city's former commissioners of police, ex-mayor George Brown looked up nervously. He moved to blow out the coal oil lamp on the table between them, but Kane shook his head.

"Do that, and they'll come barging in."

"What if it's Federals?"

Kane forced a smile.

"Then it's back to prison. Go answer the door."

Brown stood up, his wife standing at the top of the stairs looking down at him, eyes wide.

"Stay up there," he hissed.

He went to the door, checked to see that the chain latch was hooked in place, undid the bolt, and cracked it open.

"The Honorable George Brown?"

The man standing on the steps was wrapped in a dark cloak, broad-brimmed hat pulled down low over his eyes. He smelled of horse sweat.

"Who is asking for him?" Brown asked.

"A friend."

"How can I be certain?"

"Mr. Brown, I don't know any of the damn silly passwords, but I beg you, let me in."

"I'm armed," Brown said.

"You should be, on a night like this; now please let me in."

He hesitated, the man in the doorway looking around nervously. A patrol marched with shouldered rifles, passed on a side street, a crowd of several dozen behind them, shouting, obviously drunk.

"Damn it, sir, don't leave me standing out here."

The stranger opened the top button of his cloak and Brown caught a glimpse of a uniform collar. It was light-colored, not the dark blue of a Union jacket, which looked black at night.

Brown unhooked the chain and opened the door wider. The lone man slipped in, Brown latching the door shut behind him.

"This way," Brown announced and pointed to the parlor. Kane was on his feet, hand in one pocket of his trousers.

"Who is it?" Kane asked.

The man stood in the doorway and looked around cautiously.

"Sir, I will have to ask who you are first."

"This is a friend of mine," Brown interjected, "and you are a guest in my house. So please, no more tomfoolery, identify yourself."

"Sir, I am Lieutenant Kirby of General Stuart's staff and with the First Maryland Cavalry, Confederate States of America. I grew up here in Baltimore; my father worked on Mr. Howard's newspaper as a typesetter. If you wish for verification, I know where Mr. Howard is and will find him, but I would prefer not to be back out on the street."

Kirby unbuttoned his cloak, revealing a stained jacket of the Confederate army, and reached into his breast pocket. Kane stiffened slightly at the move. Kirby slowed and drew out a sealed envelope, with several matches welded to the paper in the wax seal so that it could be destroyed quickly.

"Sir, this is a letter of introduction from General Stuart. It is not addressed to you for obvious reasons, but I was instructed to place it in your hands."

Brown took the envelope, broke the seal, and read the contents. It was the standard sort of letter, asking for the kind reception of the bearer, some general platitudes, nothing more. Brown looked carefully at the signature.

"I regret to say I do not know General Stuart's hand," Brown said cautiously.

"We didn't expect you to, sir."

"How did you get here?" Kane asked.

"I was part of a troop sent forward to gather information about the defenses of this city. The men are all Marylanders and we know this place well. My orders were that, given the opportunity, I was to try and slip into the city and establish contact with you."

"In uniform?" Brown asked, a bit incredulous.

"He's no fool," Kane interjected. "If captured, he's a soldier and cannot be hanged as a spy. Most likely your cover was that you were just sneaking through to visit a dying mother or auntie. Is that it?"

Kirby grinned boyishly and nodded.

"And your passage in here?"

"Sir, I don't think I should tell you my exact path. But as a boy I used to come out of the city to hunt and fish, so I know my way about. It didn't get dicey until the last ten blocks or so. Loyal League patrols are out in force, raising a ruckus, many of them drunk. I bluffed my way past one group; it cost me the bottle of whiskey I had in my pocket. I fear though there could be violence before much longer; they seem frightened."

"They are frightened, Lieutenant Kirby, and perhaps you can enlighten us as to why. We were visited by the guard this afternoon and ordered to stay inside after dark under threat of arrest. If more than two of us are seen together, we will be arrested as well for conspiracy to incite rioting."

"The real message is a verbal one, Mr. Brown. I am ordered first of all to find out whatever you and your friends can share with me about the current state of military affairs in Baltimore. Size of the garrison, state of readiness, and armaments. The political situation as well. And finally to ask if you would be willing to place yourself at the disposal of our forces for a service, which as of yet cannot be discussed."

Brown finally started to warm to him. The young lieutenant looked and sounded sincere; his enthusiasm for this shadowy work was clearly evident.

"What news, first?" Kane asked, warming up as well.

"We're coming," Kirby said with a grin. "I can't tell you exactly how or when, but the army is on the march, heading straight to Baltimore. By this time tomorrow this city will be free of the Yankee tyranny."

Brown and Kane looked at each other and broke into grins. Brown, with a flourish, opened a sideboard and produced a thick-cut glass decanter and three heavy tumblers. Pouring three shots of brandy, he passed them around and silently held his glass aloft.

"To hell with the ban on saying it," Kane snapped, "here's to the glorious Confederacy."

Brown looked over at Kirby. If this was indeed some sort of elaborate trap, to get the two of them to utter a so-called traitorous oath, Kane had just done it. Kirby simply grinned.

"To the glorious Confederacy," the lieutenant said, drained the glass, then was hit an instant later by a spasm of coughing.

"To the glorious Confederacy," Brown whispered, still not quite sure if he could believe what was happening. A little more than two years ago he had been dragged out and arrested, his right to habeas corpus denied, incarcerated without charges in Fort McHenry, and then transported, like a common slave, to Fort Warren up in Boston. There he had languished for over a year before finally being released last fall. Never an apology, never a comment about what he had been charged with, just sent home with a stern warning that if he ever uttered a word against the Union, it would be back to prison, and this time they would throw away the keys.

Hundreds of others in Baltimore and eastern Maryland had endured the same fate, recalling to many of them the worst of the tyranny of kings, and a stunned disbelief that the principles of the Constitution could be so basely abused. If anything, the Federal government's abuse of power was proof positive of the righteousness of the Confederate cause.

It had, up to this moment, broken the spirit of the city of Baltimore, a place of fear, with armed bands patrolling the street, a place where ruffians lorded over them, their women were insulted in the street, and none dared to speak in what was now a Southern town under the fist of a foreign power.

God willing, that was about to change at last. The day of liberation was at hand. The city had been seething with rumors ever since Union Mills, waiting, hoping. Though all understood the need to take Washington first, still there had been consternation that not a single brigade of Jeb Stuart's famed cavaliers had made the attempt to free Baltimore as well. If this boy was to be believed though, they were coming at last!

He set his glass back down.

Kirby nodded.

"Now please tell me what you think might be helpful to General Stuart."

"The guard," Kane started. "The Loyal League. I would guess it numbers around five thousand. They're good at beating up defenseless old men and terrorizing women, but against any kind of disciplined military force? They'll scurry like rabbits."

"The garrison?"

"What little was here was all but stripped out and sent down to Washington last week. There's the First Connecticut Cavalry based at Federal Hill, several other regiments scattered around the city. It's been hard to keep track of things the last week. Anywhere we attempt to go we are followed by traitors and spies. We are stopped far outside the range of any of the forts or headquarters."

"The hospitals are packed with wounded coming in from Gettysburg and Union Mills," Brown interjected. "A thousand or more, I heard. Also, there are maybe five hundred paroled Union prisoners downtown as well, waiting for the final paperwork for their exchanges along with several hundred Confederate prisoners. At Fort McHenry at least a hundred civilians are being held under guard as well."

"So your estimate of the fighting strength?"

"As I said," Kane excitedly jumped back in, "some of the troops were ordered down to Washington by General Heintzelman. I'd estimate roughly two to three thousand infantry, the regiment of cavalry, some heavy artillery, and that's it."

Kirby smiled and then gladly accepted a second glass of brandy poured by Brown, but this time only sipped from it.

"We heard you attacked Washington but not a word of the results. All telegraph lines into and out of Baltimore in every direction are down. Did you take it?"

Kirby shook his head.

"I rather assumed that, given you were coming here," Brown interjected.

"Tell General Stuart this," Kane said forcefully. "Come on quickly. There are rumors that the Army of the Potomac is reorganizing at Perryville. If they have word of your coming, they could rush trainloads of troops down here in a matter of hours, man the fortifications, and it will be a bloody price to get in here."

Kirby smiled.

"We're aware of them, sir."

"I'll sketch out the fortifications for you if you want, son," Kane said.

Kirby shook his head.

"Sir, I was told not to be caught carrying any maps or such on me, so I think I'll refrain from that. Just what I can carry in my head. But if you'd draw some rough sketches, I'll try and remember the details."

Kane nodded and, returning to the table, he called for Brown to bring some papers and a pencil. Minutes later he had produced rough sketches of the primary fortifications guarding Baltimore, Kirby leaning over the table to examine them carefully.

"There are over seventy heavy guns in Fort McHenry, a dozen heavy guns on Federal Hill," Kane said. "The garrisons are definitely not frontline troops, but behind fortifications they could be formidable."

"Suppose rioting should break out in the city?" Kirby asked. "We don't want anything serious, I'm told to convey that to you. Nothing that could get out of hand, but sufficient to clog roads, prevent the movement of troops, perhaps spread panic with the garrisons."

Kane looked over meaningfully at Brown.

"Yes, there are thousands waiting for this day."

Kirby said nothing more, and the two civilians looked at each other and smiled.

Chapter Eleven

In Front of Baltimore

July 21, 1863
3:00 P.M.

"**G**eneral Longstreet, what is the situation?"

General Lee, reining in Traveler, looked expectantly at Old Pete, who had been busy shouting orders to several staff officers. The staff, clearly aware of Lee's arrival, hurriedly saluted, turned, and galloped off.

"McLaws's division is deployed for action, sir," Longstreet yelled, in order to be heard above the thunder of a battalion of artillery that was firing less than fifty yards away.

The battalion was wreathed in smoke; General Alexander, newly promoted to command of all artillery for the Army of Northern Virginia, was racing back and forth along the line of guns, motioning another battery into place along the low ridge.

On the flank of the guns, McLaws's division was ready to go, haversacks and equipment dropped in regimental piles, battle lines forming up, officers pacing back and forth nervously. Having ridden up from Ellicott Mills, Lee had just passed Pickett's division, coming on at the double across the open fields.

"Jeb did his job here," Longstreet announced. "You can hear his skirmishers forward even now, probing their line."

"Taking the bridges at Ellicott Mills was a feat," Lee said in agreement.

His young cavalier was at his best again, the failure before Gettysburg still a goad, a blemish to be redeemed. In a predawn charge he had personally led a brigade into Ellicott, seizing the town, leaving garrison and bridges intact, a feat that had laid Baltimore open to them. Throughout the day the men of Longstreet's corps had been storming across the bridges, deploying to approach Baltimore from the west side of town.

He raised his field glasses. The town was clearly in sight, high church spires, smokestacks of factories, warehouses, rich homes, all of it wreathed in smoke.

"Is the town burning?" Lee asked.

Longstreet nodded.

"Started around noon."

"Who started it?"

"It wasn't us, sir. I've held fire back to hit just their fortifications. It must be inside the city."

"We've got to get in there before it goes out of control."

"Here comes Jeb," Longstreet announced.

It was indeed Stuart, riding hard on a lathered horse, staff trailing behind him, plumed hat off; he was using it to strike the flank of his horse. Troops seeing him approach let out a rebel yell in greeting.

Grinning, he reined in before Longstreet and Lee.

"A lovely day!" Stuart exclaimed, waving his hat to the sparkling blue skies overhead.

"They're abandoning the lines, running in panic, General Lee! Some of my men are already into their fortifications. We need that artillery fire lifted, General Longstreet."

Longstreet shouted an order to a waiting staff officer, who ran off toward Alexander.

"One of my young spies just came through the lines," Stuart announced, pointing to a sweat-soaked lieutenant behind him.

"Lieutenant Kirby, sir," and the boy saluted with a flourish.

"Your report, Lieutenant?" Lee asked.

"Sir, it is chaos in the city. The panic started midmorning with the reports that Stuart's cavalry was in sight. I tried to get back through during the night, but got trapped in an attic loft when I was chased by one of their Loyal League patrols. Fortunately I knew the neighborhood, and a friend of my family hid me. I'm sorry I didn't get back through earlier."

"That's all right, son. I'm glad you are safe."

"Sir, their garrison is not more than several thousand, but a panic just exploded around noon. Deserters are pouring into the city, many of them heading down to Fort McHenry. Word is the commander there is threatening to shell the city."

"He wouldn't dare," Stuart grumbled. "That's against all rules of civilized warfare."

"He just might," Longstreet replied.

"Is that what started the fires?"

"I couldn't tell for sure, sir. I did hear some artillery fire. The family that was hiding me, they said that fighting is breaking out in the streets between the Loyal League and those on our side. It's getting ugly."

"How so?"

"Burning, sir. Hangings, executions."

"General Stuart, did you leave the northern roads open as ordered?"

"Yes, sir. I have patrols watching them, but there are no troops moving in."

"I want those roads kept open. If we cork the bottle, those people in there just might turn and fight. I want them to know there is a way to get out safely. We can chase their infantry down later, out in the open, but I don't want them barricading themselves into the city."

"I'm certain it is still open, General Lee."

"Sir," Kirby interrupted. "I urge you to go in now. It is getting out of control in the city. Your presence will stop it; otherwise all of Baltimore might burn to the ground."

Lee nodded, looking over at Longstreet.

"Send McLaws in now, General Longstreet."

"Sir, I'd prefer to have Pickett up on the line before we attack."

"There is nothing organized in front of us to attack," Stuart announced. "As I said, my boys are already into some of their fortifications."

Longstreet nodded toward Lee.

"As you wish, sir."

He urged his mount away from the group and raced off to where McLaws and his staff were waiting. Orders were shouted. Thousands of men stood up, rifles flashing in the brilliant afternoon sunlight. Drums rolled, officers, most of them mounted, riding up and down the lines, waving their swords.

The division lurched forward, five thousand strong; as the men cleared the crest, passing through Alexander's guns, which had fallen silent, a cheer went up.

Caught up in the moment, Lee fell in on their flank, standing in his stirrups, urging them on.

The day was glorious, bright, crystal-blue sky, a touch of breeze whipping out the flags, men cheering, the city of Baltimore before them.

First Church of the Redeemer (AME), Baltimore

July 21, 1863
3:15 P.M.

US John Miller stood in the nave of the church along with many of the other elders, his wife and three children gathered fearfully around him.

It was chaos. The small, clapboard-sided church was packed beyond overflowing, hundreds more gathered out in the streets and yard around this center of their community. A white officer from the army was up at the pulpit trying to be heard, Miller and the other elders shouting for those around them to fall silent, to hear what was being said. The officer looked down at Miller, exasperated, and then actually motioned to his revolver, as if ready to draw it and fire it into the ceiling. John shook his head, pushed his way up to the side of the pulpit, and cupped his hands.

"Everyone! Shut up!" he roared.

His tone, his bull-like voice, a voice of command gained from years working in the heat and thunder of the Abbot Rolling Mills, cut through the chaos. At this moment, the shy, soft words of a preacher just would not have done it. The church fell silent, though the tumult out in the street still rolled in to them, counterpointed by the distant rumble of artillery fire.

Children and some of the women continued to cry.

"Either silence those little ones or take them outside!" John roared.

A few looked up at him, startled at his imperious, harsh tone, but mothers struggled to comply.

He turned back to the army officer.

"Please continue, Major," John said.

The major looked out over the assembly.

"I felt it a personal obligation to come to you," the major said, voice near breaking, "to tell you that the army is abandoning this city."

Cries started to rise up again; those were the same words that five minutes ago set everyone off. Miller held a hand up, and the crying subsided.

"Why?" John asked, looking up at him with an almost accusatory gaze. "Why is the army running?"

"This is not a raid attacking us. It is the entire Confederate Army of Northern Virginia. We cannot hold against that. Even now the garrison is pulling out. I felt it my duty to come and warn you before leaving."

"Thank you, Major. Now what should we do?"

The major lowered his head.

"I'm not sure," and to John's surprise, the man was in tears.

John looked back out over the assembly, the upturned faces. He could see the fear in many eyes. Many here were freemen, sons and even grandsons of freemen; more than a few were slaves, some still held by their masters in town, others men and women who had drifted into the city after the start of the war, escaping and fleeing out of Virginia.

The stories were already well-known in their community, though the newspapers reported little of it. During the campaign of the previous year in central Maryland, more than a few black folk—escaped slaves, owned slaves, and freemen—had been taken back into Virginia by the army or by the frightful slave catchers, who trailed along at the edge of the army, like carrion eaters following a hunter. The same had stood true over the last month.

There were near fifty thousand men and women of color in Baltimore. What was to be their fate? No one said. Some of the Loyal League, the pro-Union militia that had taken over the city, claimed that black men would hang from every lamppost in Baltimore if the rebels came. John knew that was just talk to stir up passions, but there might be a grain of truth to it. More than one whose loyalties were with the South had said the exact opposite, that all would be as before. There were some though that muttered that "the niggers had gotten the upper hand," and a day of reckoning would come.

He looked at his friends and neighbors, his own family huddled in the crowd, and knew something would have to be done. They could not just stand here like sheep waiting for the slaughter, praying that the good mercies of their white neighbors would see them through. Yes, most of them were good neighbors, but one lone wolf could still slaughter them all or take them back into slavery.

He had never known that bitter bondage. He was a skilled man, helping to oversee one of the rolling mills that turned out iron plate for the navy. He would die before a slave catcher would ever place a hand upon him, or his skills would ever be turned to feeding the Confederate cause.

"Major, which way is your army fleeing?"

"Some to McHenry, others on the road north, following the tracks of the Philadelphia and Wilmington Railroad. Why?"

"I'm leaving," John announced, his voice raised so all could hear. "I'm taking my family and going north."

The major looked at him and then nodded with approval.

"Don't go down to the Fort. There will most likely be fighting there. Boats are already taking many out; I doubt though if they will allow you colored to board. Get on the road north and stay on it. There are some troops moving on it who should protect you."

"We'll protect ourselves," John said harshly. "Some of us have guns."

"Don't do that; you know what will happen if you are caught with weapons."

"Major, if you were me, wouldn't you carry a gun?"

The major, taking no insult as some white folk would have, looked at John and then smiled.

"The army, as you know, is recruiting for colored regiments. Go to Wilmington. Better yet, Philadelphia, where the recruiting and training camps are for the colored regiments. Go there, become a soldier, then come back and fight to liberate Baltimore from the Confederates!"

John listened but said nothing. For the moment all he cared for was to get the hell out of this town and move his family to safety.

John left the pulpit, gathered his wife and three children under his arms, and headed for the door.

"I'm leaving now," he shouted. "Any who want to go with me, pack up some food, leave everything else behind, and let's get out of this God-cursed city before the rebels get here."

Near Federal Hill, Baltimore

July 21, 1863
3:45 P.M.

Brown, things are getting out of control!"

Former police commissioner Kane came staggering into the hotel lobby they had established as temporary headquarters for their new "Sons of Liberty" militia.

Hundreds had rallied to their call in the hours just before dawn. Street fighting had erupted almost immediately. At first it was nothing more than scuffles, taunts, which had then moved to boys throwing "horse apples," to an occasional brick, and in short order had escalated to showers of rocks, men armed with clubs, and in the final step to pistols, rifles, and now several artillery pieces taken by both sides from the regular troops who were now only themselves trying to get out of the way.

The sound of glass shattering was a continual accompaniment to the cacophony of noises, intermixed with gunfire, screams, the panicked braying of mules, the pitiful shrieks of wounded horses, one team trapped under an overturned carriage that had crashed into a building burning across the street.

Kane stood in the doorway, blood pouring down the side of his face, which was puffed up, swollen from where he had been struck by a piece of cobblestone. A bullet nicked the frame of the open doorway, splinters flying. Another round hit the chandelier over Brown's table, shattered crystals raining down.

A volley erupted, ragged, the report greeted by guttural cheers. A group of men stormed out of an alleyway alongside the hotel, charging across the street, colliding with a mob of Loyal Leaguers, who turned and started to run. Brown stood up, watching the mad scuffle, musket and pistol butts rising and falling. A giant of a man armed with a pickax handle fighting like Samson in the middle of the fray, going down, a moment later his body rising back up, held aloft by half a dozen men, several boys looping a coil of rope around his neck, throwing the other end over a lamppost and then straining to hoist the dying man aloft.

Disgusted, Brown turned away.

"It's this way all over the city," Kane gasped. "Murders, beatings, reports of rape; entire blocks are burning now. My God, the city has gone insane."

Brown, obviously overwhelmed, could not speak. He knew this was far beyond anything he could have ever imagined. Yes, there would be fighting, but these were neighbors before the war, friends even. *Have two years of this war so coarsened all of us that we have sunk to this?* he thought. All the talk of glory and freedom now tasted bitter and stale.

"Can't we stop it?" Brown asked weakly.

"Not now," Kane shouted as an explosion down the block rocked them, flames gushing out of a tavern. Several men were running out of the open doors, as if emerging from the pit of hell, their entire bodies on fire. They ran shrieking, flailing, then collapsing.

"Hate, liquor, half the mob out there is drunk, the other half drunk on blood."

Brown lowered his head.

"What are the Yankee troops doing?"

"Fort McHenry is threatening to open fire. The road down to the fort, however, is packed with refugees."

A "Son of Liberty," Brown recognized him as a former police captain, came through the door, eyes wide, the stench of liquor on his breath.

"The niggers are rioting," he shouted. "They're killing white folk!"

Brown looked at him, incredulous.

Before he could even respond, the man was back out the door, holding a pistol aloft, shouting for men to follow him.

Brown retreated back to his table in the corner of the lobby and slumped into his chair, covering his face.

If this was war, he wanted nothing to do with it. It had all sounded so bright and wonderful last night. In his fantasies, it would be done with chivalry, a few dead perhaps, but done cleanly, the cowardly Yankees fleeing under a gauntlet of taunts, the Loyal League retreating to their basements to hide, the gallant Army of Northern Virginia, with Lee at the fore, riding into the center of town, where he, as the provisional mayor, would ceremoniously hand him the keys to the city.

Another explosion rocked the room, but he did not even bother to look up.

Outskirts of Baltimore

July 21, 1863
4:00 P.M.

General Lee, I think we should hold back here for the moment," Walter Taylor announced, coming up to the general's side.

Reluctantly, Lee found he had to agree. They were into the edge of the city, a district of neatly built homes. He did not recognize the neighborhood; it must have been built after his tenure supervising the building of fortifications for the defense of Baltimore. So ironic that the very defenses he helped to build and upgrade were now the object of his attack.

If the fortifications were properly garrisoned, he knew there would be a formidable battle ahead. So far, however, his hope that the outnumbered, second-rate garrison would take flight seemed to be coming to pass.

He always had a fondness for this town, Southern in so many ways, but also bustling, sophisticated, with orchestras, theaters—a place of culture. It had been a comfortable posting.

He did not recognize any of it now.

Crowds were out in the street and panic was in the air. McLaws's men had stormed up and over the outer perimeter of fortifications with ease; barely a shot was fired. The men were exuberant, for the works were indeed extensive though nowhere near as well designed as Washington's, and to the last instant there had been fear that somehow it was a trap, that the guns, visible in their emplacements, would suddenly open up, turning an easy advance into a shambles.

The only Yankees to be found were drunks and a few sick and injured who had been abandoned by their terrified, retreating comrades. There had been a few shots from houses at the edge of town, the advance line of skirmishers rushing in, the shooters bursting out of the homes, casting aside their rifles, and running for their lives. He had already intervened personally at the sight of a couple of young boys, not more than fourteen or fifteen, surrounded by an angry knot of his soldiers. The boys had apparently decided to try and hold back the Confederate army on their own and shot a soldier, fortunately only a graze to the arm, but the wounded man's comrades were getting set to string the boys up.

"Give them a good spanking," Lee had announced good-naturedly, his suggestion breaking up the angry mood. "Then send them home to their mama."

He could hear the two boys howling as the men set to them with a will.

But as they got a few more blocks into the city, the mood turned darker. Several houses were burning, no one bothering to try and put the flames out, the owners standing outside, shocked, one shouting to the passing troops that the damn Loyal Leaguers were burning the town, a half block farther on another victim hysterically screaming imprecations at the soldiers and at "all goddamn rebels."

An occasional report of a rifle or pistol echoed ahead. Walter and his guard detail looked around nervously. Though Lee hated to put a special distinction unto himself, he felt the need for it now. He had no hesitation about riding into the storm of battle; there were times that he sought the challenge or knew that his duty required it, but to be gunned down by a hidden assassin lurking in a darkened window struck him as obscene, and inwardly he had to admit that it did frighten him a bit. Somehow he still clung to the notion that battle should be fought in open fields and woods. There it was pure, no innocents caught in the middle, the only ones present men who had volunteered to be there, and who in general fought with honor. To die at the hands of a drunken assailant was not a worthy death.

He reined in and waited, his guards, with pistols and carbines raised, forming a tight circle. Down the middle of the street a regiment from Pickett's division came by on the double, Virginia state flag at the fore.

"Your orders, Colonel?" Lee shouted as the regiment came abreast of him.

Startled, the colonel looked up, saw Lee, stepped from the front of the column, and saluted with a flourish.

"We're leading Armistead's brigade, sir. Our orders are to occupy Federal Hill."

"Carry on."

The men cheered as they passed, more regiments coming around a bend in the road behind them.

Their enthusiasm was overflowing, the men yelling, cheering, drummers struggling to keep up while at the same time beating out the pace. A troop of cavalry riding on the sidewalk across the street trotted by, pistols drawn.

The wind shifted slightly, carrying smoke on it, a distant rumble, almost like battle but not quite.

A courier came tearing back up the street, lashing his mount, shouting for the infantry to clear the way. He rode straight past Lee, went half a block, then reined in hard, horse skidding. He turned his mount and came racing up to Lee, breathing hard.

"General McLaws's compliments, sir. He begs for you to come forward with as many men as possible."

"What is wrong? Are the Yankees standing?"

"No, sir. It's the civilians. Sir, it's a riot like nothing we've ever seen. I'm supposed to find General Longstreet and report this, sir."

"How bad is this riot?"

"Sir, I've never seen anything like it. Whole blocks are burning; there's people a-hanging from trees. They're fighting so hard neither side will stop."

"Our men?"

"They're trying to stop it now, sir, but we're getting hurt some. General McLaws got hit by a rock and is down."

A thundering explosion suddenly washed over them. Startled, Lee looked up to see a massive fireball climbing heavenward, mushrooming out. Windowpanes farther down the street shattered, glass tinkling down onto the street.

"Longstreet's farther back," Lee said, pointing back up the road. "He might be riding with Pickett's headquarters."

The boy saluted and galloped off.

He took a deep breath.

"We better go in."

"What was that?" Taylor asked, pointing at the still-mushrooming cloud.

"Might be the powder reserves at Federal Hill; if so, there's going to be a lot of damage down in the center of town," Lee announced.

Taylor shouted for the guard to keep a sharp watch, and Lee did not object as several of the men moved in closer. He knew he had to put on an imperious air, to project a calm authority, but still he found himself looking nervously about. After so long in the field this environment was alien, disquieting.

Crowds were out at every street corner, some cheering the passing troops, others standing by, sullen and quiet. Confederate flags appeared at some windows and porches. A lone defiant girl stood in her doorway, holding a Federal flag up in her hands, weeping.

Moved by her bravery, he saluted, then told Taylor to detail off a soldier to gently take the girl inside for her own safety but offering his compliments as well.

They turned the corner in the road leading down to Federal Hill, and he reined in again. The scene was apocalyptic, something from the Bible. Fire was soaring up from the center of the old fort, buildings beyond the fort shattered, in flames. But what he saw at the next street corner truly sickened him. A body was dangling from a tree, another lying in the gutter. The house the bodies were in front of was engulfed in flames, the side of the neighboring house already scorched and smoking.

The body hanging from the tree was a black boy, not more than twelve or thirteen, the body in the gutter a woman, her throat cut, blood spilled out in a dark, ugly pool.

Sickened, Lee looked over at Taylor.

"Damn it," he shouted, "this will not be tolerated!"

The use of even a mild profanity startled Taylor, who, ashen-faced, stiffened in the saddle.

"I want the provost guard in this town, in force now! This will not be tolerated! I want that boy cut down. His family and that of the woman to be found, our condolences offered, and funerals paid for! I want someone to find out what happened here!"

Angrily he turned Traveler away. His fear of the moment before gone, he pressed farther into the city.

Even as Pickett's regiments stormed along the street beside him, he caught glimpses of side streets and alleyways. Some were empty, others lined with nervous groups of civilians watching, and then the next one would reveal a raging battle, mobs swaying back and forth, storefronts being broken into, looted, crowds fighting with each other, bricks flying, rifle shots echoing. The column of infantry suddenly stopped, half a dozen blocks from the center of town, the men who were now stalled leaning over, panting hard, looking around nervously, not sure of what should be done next.

"General Lee!"

McLaws, with Stuart by his side, was forcing a way through the columns of infantry. The main thoroughfare just ahead was littered with debris, a rough barricade blocking half of it, a storefront burning. A man came running out of a building directly behind Stuart and began to raise a rifle, aiming at Stuart's back, incredible, since dozens of Confederate infantry stood only feet away.

A flurry of shots dropped the man in his tracks. Stuart, not even bothering to look back, approached Lee, unaware that in another second he would have been dead. Lee's escorts, seeing the drama, became more tense, most of the men now cocking their revolvers, looking around warily.

Stuart came up, features pale. McLaws by his side had a bandage around his forehead, left side of his face puffy and swollen, with his eye half-shut.

"There's hell to pay up there," McLaws shouted. "It's madness. You'd think the entire city's sold itself to the devil."

"What is the situation, gentlemen?" Lee asked sharply.

"To be honest, sir, we're not sure," Stuart interjected. "We got in without a fight, as you saw, but about four blocks back it started getting ugly. The fort blew a few minutes ago; guess you saw that. The garrison is making a run for the harbor."

"I no longer care about that!" Lee snapped. "I want this city intact, not a smoking ruin. And I want it done peacefully. What I've seen so far is barbaric."

"It's not us, sir," Stuart said defensively. "It's these damn civilians, both sides. You think all the hatred these last two years is boiling out. They're killing each other without mercy."

"I want it stopped now, General Stuart. Now!"

He shouted the last word, half standing in his stirrups.

"Get your men fanned out along every street and thoroughfare. I want the word passed that everyone is to return to their homes. The city is now under the martial law of the Confederacy and a twenty-four-hour curfew is in place. I want that done now."

"Sir. I don't think many will listen."

Lee looked around, exasperated. From a block away, up a side alley, he saw two men pointing toward them. One lowered a pistol and fired several shots. At such a range, of course, the rounds missed, but two of his guards set off in pursuit. He wanted to shout for them to come back, but they disappeared around a corner. More shots, and no one came back.

His army was not trained for this, had no experience at all in how to take a city and then control it. Even as he thought that, one of his attempted assailants stepped back from around the corner, making a rude gesture and a defiant wave. This time he had a carbine and lowered it to take another shot. A volley from some of Pickett's men dropped him.

We are out of our depth here, Lee realized. For the first time in a very long while he was flustered, not sure how to act, what orders to give. This was not as easy as simply ordering a division out of line and sending them in. They'd done that a hundred times; everyone down to the dimmest private knew his role. But here?

"General Stuart. Cavalry to stay together in troops; do not let your men split up or get lured off. Infantry to move in company strength. I'll establish headquarters . . ."

He hesitated. Where?

"Mount Vernon Square. It's half a dozen blocks from here. I'll be at the center of the square. General McLaws, you are to advance down to the harbor. I want a courier sent down to Fort McHenry. We will offer a temporary truce. Ask the commander to please cease any thoughts of firing upon the city and to aid us in containing the fires and the rioting. Any Union troops still in organized formations and attempting to maintain order will be granted free passage back to their lines once order is restored."

"I doubt if he'll go for it, sir," McLaws said. "He's a real firebrand."

"Then that is on his head, not ours. If he goes for it or not, any Union troops you see in formation or attempting to control this madness, grant them a truce, assistance if they need it, then the right to leave."

"With arms?"

"Yes, with arms," Lee replied, exasperated at such a picky detail. "They'll need them against this madness. I want those fleeing to be aided and assisted with safe passage."

"Sir, what about the . . ." Stuart began, than hesitated, "the colored?"

"The what?"

"The colored, sir. Some of my men just reported that thousands of them are fleeing north. Many of them are slaves, sir, or runaways from Virginia. By right they should be returned to their masters."

"Like the two I saw several blocks back?" Lee asked.

"Sir?"

"I just saw two dead Negroes, one of them a boy hanging from a tree, the other a woman with her throat cut; is that what you mean?"

Stuart lowered his head and said nothing.

Another explosion rocked the plaza ahead, debris soaring heavenward, tiny fragments raining down around them long seconds later.

"I want the colored left alone. Let them flee if they wish."

"But the slaves?"

"General Stuart, just how in God's name will you tell the difference?"

All were again startled by his rage.

"I don't know, sir," Stuart said woodenly.

"Then don't bother with it."

"Sir," Taylor said softly. "Remember, the president is just outside the city. If he hears you've willingly allowed slaves to escape, there could be problems."

"Then, sir," Lee snapped, "I suggest you go back out of this city, bring the president here, make sure he sees that hanging, and let him pass the order as to what to do. We are a Christian army that has fought with honor, and I still propose that we maintain that honor. I will not tolerate what we just saw back there."

Taylor, absolutely crestfallen, lowered his head.

Lee took a deep breath. The fear of earlier, the confusion as to what to do in this strange, new battlefield, then the outrage had overtaken him for a moment. He turned away, mastering his passion, and looked back.

"I apologize, Walter. You were doing your job."

"No apology needed, sir."

Lee leaned over and in a gesture of remorse lightly patted him on the arm.

"Gentlemen. Remember, we are gentlemen," he said softly. "I want this city brought under control. As I said, I will establish headquarters at Mount Vernon Square. General McLaws, pass the message to the commander down at Fort McHenry. General Stuart, start moving your men out as ordered. Taylor, locate General Longstreet and ask him to come to my headquarters. Finally, locate Pickett and order him to start spreading his division out and make sure they understand my orders as well."

The gathering looked at him for a moment, trying to process all that he said. Again there was a flash of exasperation.

"Move!"

The group scattered.

With his escort pulled in tight around him, Lee pressed into the city.

Baltimore

July 21, 1863
5:00 P.M.

"Hey, niggers!"

John Miller slowed. At the street corner ahead, a cordon had been set up. A rough barricade of torn-up cobblestones, an overturned delivery wagon, and bits of lumber blocked the way. Behind him hundreds of blacks from his community were surging forward. Behind them the city looked like something out of the Bible, of Sodom and Gomorrah, flames soaring heavenward, explosions rocking the harbor, and now this line of men armed with clubs and guns.

To his dismay he did not see any indication that they were the Loyal League, who had freely let them pass several blocks back, though more than one taunt was hurled about a black Moses leading his children.

He slowed.

"Where you going, boy?" one of the toughs asked, stepping out from behind the barricade.

"Out of this city. We're going north."

"Oh, no you ain't. You're runaways. Now git back home where you belong."

"We're freemen, and we can go where we please."

"Don't back-talk me," the man came forward, raising an axe handle threateningly.

All was silent for a long moment.

"We're leaving the city," John said quietly, looking the man straight in the eye.

"God damn you!"

The handle came down. The man was clumsy, obviously not used to the type of dark-alley brawls that John had grown up with. He easily dodged the blow and with a single strike from a curled-up fist knocked the man flat.

"The son of a bitch hit George!" someone screamed from behind the barricade.

John looked up and saw a rifle being leveled, aimed straight at him. Before he could even begin to react, the gun went off. He heard a scream, looked, and saw his young son stagger backward from the blow.

A wild madness now seized him. He raced the dozen feet to the barricade, reaching into the haversack by his side, drawing out an antique pistol, an old flintlock that his granddaddy claimed to have carried against the British in 1814. He cocked it even as he ran. Stopping on the far side of the barricade, he leveled the piece straight at the man who had shot his son, and squeezed the trigger. The gun went off with a thunderous report, kicking his hand heavenward. The rifleman seemed to leap backward.

The next couple of seconds were mad confusion. Hundreds charged around him, swarming up over the barricade. Shots rang out; the flash of knives glinted in the sun; rifle butts were raised, slammed down; the wild, hysterical crowd pushed forward, clearing the barricade.

Stunned, he just stood alone and then looked back to where his wife, Martha, knelt in the middle of the road, keening softly, cradling the body of young John, his two daughters standing wide-eyed, looking down at their mother and dead brother.

He walked back to her as if in a dream, taking her by the shoulders and pulling her back up.

"We have to go," he whispered.

"No!" She started to flail wildly at him.

"For our two who are still alive we've got to go! We stay here now we'll all be killed."

She stiffened, nodded, but her face was still buried in her hands.

He knelt down, picked up his boy, and carried him to the side of the road, to the entry of a livery stable. A couple of hands in the stable looked at him nervously, bitterness in their eyes.

He gazed at them, saying nothing as he reached into his haversack, drew out a pad and a pencil, wrote the name of his son and their address on it, then tucked the paper into the boy's breast pocket.

In a way he could not believe what he was doing, so casually marking the body of his son before walking away. He folded the boy's hands and kissed him lightly on the forehead, drew out five dollars from his pocket, nearly all he had, and put it into the boy's pocket, then stood back up.

"His name is John Miller Junior. I put five dollars in his pocket for his burying."

"So what?" the younger of the stable hands growled.

John looked around meaningfully then back to the two.

"If you have any Christian sense to you, you'll see that my son is buried proper."

"And if not?" the young one laughed.

"I'm going to join the army now. And after this is over, I'll be back. If he isn't buried as I want, I'll track both of you down and kill you."

The older of the two, gaze lowered, nodded his head.

"I'll see to it. I'm sorry for your loss."

"Thank you."

John turned without looking back down at his boy. He knew if he did so he'd break, and there was no time, no luxury for that now.

He gathered Martha under his arm, his two sobbing daughters clinging to her skirts.

Hundreds were still passing over the barricade, which was carpeted with a score of dead and wounded, black and white. Lying on the ground was a rifle, a new Springfield. He looked down at it, and the man still clutching the weapon, the man who had killed his son. He picked the gun up, testing its heft, then bent back over to pull off the cartridge box the man was wearing, the brass plate on its side an oval with US stamped in the middle. He put it on, picked up the cap box, and slipped it on to his belt.

He had seen it done often enough. He drew a cartridge, tore it open, poured in the powder, rammed a ball down, half cocked the gun, and capped the nipple with a percussion cap.

Some had stopped to look at him, wide-eyed. None had ever seen a colored man do this or seen a colored man with a cartridge box stamped US on his hip.

He scrambled over the barricade, then turned to help his wife and daughters. Shouldering his rifle, he headed north.

Mount Vernon Square, Baltimore

July 21, 1863
6:30 P.M.

"You, sir, have let this go out of control," General Lee snapped, looking up at the quaking civilian standing before him.

The Honorable George Brown stood crestfallen, shirt open, tie gone, fine broadcloth jacket streaked and burned.

"Sir, if only I could explain."

"You've tried to explain," Lee said, "and I find your explanation unacceptable.

"Young Lieutenant Kirby here tells me that you were told to help us enter the city but to keep things under control. Do you call that control down there?"

Lee pointed back down toward the center of the city, which was a raging inferno. Fort McHenry beyond was concealed in the smoke.

"General Lee, we did not want this, either."

"I should hope not."

"Sir, you have not been here these past two years," Brown said defensively. "It has been a place seething with hatred, with midnight arrests, a city under occupation. The passions simply exploded, sir."

Lee sighed wearily. He had no authority to deal with this man, but if he did, he'd have him under arrest, if for no other reason than to set an example.

"I want you to go back out there. General Stuart will provide you with an escort. You are to try and help us stop this, because if you don't, my provost guards most certainly will. I have issued orders to shoot to kill anyone caught looting or setting fires, and I don't care which side they are on."

"What about the Loyal League?" Brown asked. "Aren't you going to arrest them?"

"No, I will not. Do you want to set off yet another explosion? They are to go home. Tomorrow I will offer them amnesty if they turn in their arms."

"Amnesty, sir? They should be thrown in jail the way we were!"

"Don't you understand, Mr. Brown? I am trying to restore order here. I will not follow the practices of the Lincoln government in the process. If we act with forebearance now, it will reap rewards later. As long as they comply with military law, they and their property will not be harmed."

"At least round up their ringleaders. I have their names, sir," and Brown fumbled in his pocket, pulled out a sheet of paper, and placed it on Lee's desk, which had been set up under an awning right in the middle of the square.

Lee angrily brushed the note aside.

"No, sir. No! I want their help at this moment. If they will help us to restore order, no matter how naive that might sound, then they are free to live peacefully. I would think that together, both sides would wish to save this city before it burns down around your ears."

Brown said nothing.

"Now go do your duty, sir."

Brown, obviously shaken by the interview, withdrew.

Lee stood up and walked out from under the awning. The city he had loved so much was going under. The entire central district was in flames, the fire department all but helpless to contain it, since so many of the firemen had fallen in with one side or the other during the rioting.

He now had most of Pickett's division either fighting the fires or struggling to suppress the rioting. A report had come in of one company from the Fourteenth Virginia all but wiped out in an ambush, dozens more injured or killed fighting either the rioters or the flames.

It was early twilight, and as he watched the fire, he wondered if this was now symbolic of their entire nation, North and South, so consumed with growing hatred that they would rather destroy all in a final orgy of madness than band together to save what was left.

If this is indeed what we are sinking to, then we are doomed, he thought. *Even in victory we will be doomed, for God will surely turn away from us.*

We have to retrieve something out of this, he thought. *There has to be something saved out of these ashes. I must still set the example and lead if we are to restore what we have lost.*

Chapter Twelve

Harrisburg

July 23, 1863
8:00 A.M.

The constant stream of engines pulling the long convoy of trains coming down through the gap above Marysville, Pennsylvania, filled the Susquehanna Valley with smoke. The shriek of train whistles echoed and reechoed. The mood all along the trackside was jubilant, civilians out to watch the spectacle, boys waving and racing alongside the long strings of flatcars and open-sided boxcars packed with troops.

The veterans of McPherson's corps, riding east to save the Union, seemed to be delighted by the spectacle as well. Regimental flags were unfurled, hoisted up, the staffs tied securely in place, each train thus festooned with battle-torn standards from Illinois, Iowa, Michigan, Wisconsin, Ohio, Indiana, emblazoned on them in gold letters the names of campaigns that to the Easterners were a mystery, except for the freshly lettered, triumphant VICKSBURG.

Rumbling down out of the mountain gap toward the broad, open plain of the Susquehanna Valley just ahead, the veterans looked about with approval at the rich farmlands, the open vista, the cool air of the mountains wafting down around them. It was indeed a far cry from the heat, swamps, ague, and snake-infested landscape of the lower Mississippi. These farms looked much more like the neat, well-kept farms of their Midwest.

They were, as well, coming now as saviors and heroes, and they basked in the glory of it. At crossroads and whistle-stop stations young women waved, sang patriotic airs, and passed up baskets of fresh-baked bread, biscuits, pitchers of cool water and buttermilk, and older men, with a glimmer in their eye and a wink, would hand off bottles of stronger stuff. The reception across the Midwest had been a warm one, especially when a regiment was passing through its home state, but here at the edge of the front lines the outpouring of enthusiasm was bordering on the ecstatic. These were the men who were going to save central Pennsylvania from the Confederate army, and the local citizens were thrilled by their arrival.

The trains passed over the massive viaduct that spanned the Susquehanna a dozen miles north of the city. Earthworks and freshly built block-houses guarded the approach to the bridge on the western shore. Fortunately, this bridge had not been dropped, the furthest advance of the Confederates stopping down at the gap just above the city.

Along the narrow road just south of the bridge more fortifications were in place, two batteries of rifled pieces guarding this precious crossing in case any rebel raiders should now try to attack.

The river beneath the bridge was still swollen and turbulent from the torrential rains of the previous three weeks, the water dark, littered with debris that tossed on the waves. As the lead train shifted through a switch and on to the bridge, they passed out of the morning light on the west bank of the river into the shade on the steep slopes of the eastern side, the air cool and refreshing.

Spirits were up. The word had passed that their journey of almost a thousand miles was at an end. Fifers picked up songs. Here and there men joined in, some of the tunes patriotic, more than one off-colored, with loud coughs and throat-clearing at every sight of girls lining the track. A group of young women from a nearby female academy, dressed in patriotic red-white-and-blue dresses, triggered an absolute frenzy of coughing, cheers, and more than one friendly, ribald comment that set the girls to blushing but also giggling in response.

The train thundered out of the pass into the broad, open panorama of the Susquehanna Valley, directly ahead the dome of the state capitol, church spires and factory smokestacks of Harrisburg. All could see the flame-scorched piers of the destroyed covered bridge dropped during the Gettysburg campaign, and the approaches to the pontoon bridge that had been swept away in the flood. Several artillery batteries lined the bank of the river, the guns well dug in, the crews lounging about, waving as the first train passed, the veterans replying politely but holding themselves a bit aloof. For, after all, they were fresh from victory, and the ones waving were not. The armies of the West were now here to teach them how to do it right.

Interestingly, a small knot of horsemen were stationed on the far bank, sitting in a clearing partway up the slope of the mountain . . . advanced rebel scouts, signal flags fluttering. The Confederate outpost had been dislodged several times by small raiding forces coming over from Harrisburg, but as quickly as the Yankees withdrew, the rebs came back to continue their observations of the goings-on inside the state capital.

At the sight of the rebs, the men stood on the flatcars, taunting and waving, shouting that Grant's boys were now here to set things right. Several of the rebel cavalry waved back.

The lead train began to slow, the engineer merrily playing his whistle with a skilled hand, trying to squeeze out the opening bar to "Rally Round the Flag." The tune didn't carry too well, but the rhythm was plain, and some of the men picked up the song, though this was an army that didn't hold much with such patriotic mush. And anyway, in their minds that had been a marching song of the Army of the Potomac and not of the armies of the West.

The crowds along the siding were increasing, people rushing down side streets, cheering, waving, Union infantry joining in, their greeters dressed in bright, new, unstained uniforms.

In contrast, these boys of McPherson's corps were a hard, grizzled lot. Uniforms had long ago faded in the harsh Mississippi sun, the color all but bleaching out to a light, tattered blue. Pant legs were frayed; many had patches sewn on thighs and knees and had backsides stained darkly from countless nights of sitting around campfires. Headgear was nondistinct; few wore kepis, most favoring broad-brimmed hats of brown, black, or gray, which were just as faded and holed as the uniforms.

Hardly a backpack was to be found, the men having long ago adopted a simple horseshoe collar roll of vulcanized ground cloth, with a shelter half, one blanket, and a few changes of socks and a shirt rolled inside. Haversacks were stuffed with some rations; extra food—such as a heavy slice of smoked ham, or a chicken waiting to be plucked—was tied to the strap of the haversack. Of course cartridge boxes were crammed with forty rounds, ten or twenty extra cartridges stuffed into pockets. Maybe a Bible was in the breast pocket of their four-button wool jackets, sometimes riding alongside a deck of cards, a flask of good corn liquor, or some of the new picture cards from Paris. Given the largesse of civilians along the way, most canteens were filled with a mixture of water and whiskey, rum, applejack, or, from the hills of western Pennsylvania, a good solid load of clear, white mountain lightning.

They were veterans, easy in their self-confidence, inured to hardship, long ago disabused of any vague dreams of glory. They had seen what glory led to. They knew their job and would see it through to the end, but they would do so with a quiet, no-nonsense determination. They had signed on for three years, back in the heady days of 1861. Shiloh, Corinth, Fort Donelson, the swamps of Louisiana had forever dimmed the visions and dreams of those early days. What compelled them now was the pride in their regiments and the friendship of their comrades, and no vainglorious words of beribboned generals would sway them one way or the other. It was their job and that was it. War no longer held any illusions for them.

These veterans of the West held the eastern soldiers who were greeting them with a sort of bemused contempt. Granted, they were on the same side in this war, but it was beyond their understanding how anyone could let a rebel drive them out. Where they came from, it was the rebels who did the running, and so it would be here as well. They had come to save the East, and they found that concept amusing. They would lord it over the eastern boys as was their right, but then they would see it through to the finish.

They held Grant in supreme confidence. He was one of them. In the shadows of evening, when he would at times walk through their camps, few would actually notice his passing. He was as rumpled as they were, unshaven, battered hat pulled down low, a man you would never notice in a crowd, the only giveaway the almost-permanent cigar clenched in his teeth, glowing like a smokestack. As quickly as it burned to a stub, another would be lit. On a rainy march you might see him sitting astride his horse by the side of the road, eyes watchful, hat brim soaked and dripping, silent, perhaps offering an occasional word of encouragement, but woe betide the man who cheered him; the response was always an icy stare.

He gave no speeches, disdained reviews, which to both him and them were a waste of time, dealt summarily with fools in command, and though they knew he would not hesitate to feed them into the cauldron, he would do so only when there was something to be gained. Their lives, they thought, did mean something to him.

They were of the armies of the West, a different kind of American than those who dwelled in these lush farmlands and burgeoning cities. Many had helped their fathers to clear land on the edge of the frontier. If they were born in Ohio or Illinois, the stories of Indian raids, of virgin forests, and trackless wilderness were still real to their families. If they were from western Minnesota or Iowa, the frontier was indeed real to them; just beyond the western horizon was a limitless world yet to be explored. Such a vista affected a man, how he thought, what he believed, what he knew he could do, what a hundred thousand thousand of them could do if ever they set their minds to it.

Most had schooling, but not much. Perhaps, like their president, a few months in "blab school." They usually had four, maybe six years tops in a one-room structure that they walked miles to each day. A few, very few, were schooled in the classics and spoke almost like their cousins in the East. Some of these were now officers, but they learned quickly to speak like the men they commanded, to think like them and respect them, or they did not last for long.

Some came from the emerging cities of Chicago, Springfield, or Indianapolis, while others came from the new factory cities springing up around the Great Lakes, and in those regiments could be found mechanics, iron pourers, toolmakers, men who could fashion anything the army might need, or fix anything broken or taken in conquest. Men like these could put twenty miles of track back in operation in a matter of days, salvage a locomotive, restore a gasworks, or repair a burst steam boiler.

A sprinkling of Irish were with them, laborers who bent double fourteen hours a day in prairie heat or driving snow, laying the track that was lacing the country together, and some were river men, working the steamships, or guiding the flatboats on the Mississippi, the Missouri, and the Ohio. From the far north, more than a few only spoke German, or Swedish, or Norwegian, farmers who had cleared the cold northern land or lumberjacks still felling the great, silent forests. Their new country reminded them of ancestral farms back in northern Europe. Such men were inured to the harsh winters they had always known in both the Old and New Worlds.

Until the start of the war few had ever traveled farther than their county seat to attend a fair or a Fourth of July parade, and nearly all could remember at least one old man riding there in a carriage, eyes dim, but proud and erect, a man who had so long ago marched with Washington, or Wayne, or Morgan.

They were used to vast, open vistas, the limitless plains, or the deep northern woods. This East was almost a different nation, cities to be mistrusted or hated, rich merchants and countinghouses of the railroads, which even at this time were wringing the profits out of their farms.

Ironically, if given a choice, they would have felt far more in common with their foes from Tennessee, Arkansas, and Texas than their comrades from Boston and New York City. The southern boy might sound strange, but still, he could talk of crops, and raising hogs, and trying to spark a girl behind the barn at a cornhusking, and knew the feel of the damp, rich earth on bare feet when you did your first plowing of spring.

If they had their eyes set anywhere for when this was finished, it was not to the east but always even farther west, maybe mining in Colorado, or perhaps all the way to California. The East was the past, the West was the future, and they were eager to see this war done so they could embrace that future.

There were no illusions now among them. Losing was a concept that was all but impossible for them to contemplate, but they knew the vagaries of battle might bring hard losses. Yet they would see it through even as they knew victory would carry a price. Comrades laughing beside them might be dead in a month; for that matter they themselves might be dead, but at this moment it seemed almost worth it. They were free of the heat and stench of Mississippi, they were back north, treated as saviors, and, as veteran soldiers, they knew how to enjoy the moment.

The lead train drifted into the rail yard, bell ringing, whistle blowing. Behind the lead train were fifty more, spaced at ten-minute intervals, the convoy stretching clear back nearly to Pittsburgh, an entire corps with its artillery.

Few contemplated all that had gone into this move, brilliantly designed and orchestrated by Herman Haupt. Entire trainloads of firewood had come along the track ahead of them, replenishing stockpiles at fueling stations. Where it was felt that watering tanks could not fill the need, hundreds of buckets had been left for the men to haul water up from the nearest stream. Patriotic civilian committees had been raised to bake bread, set out food, pack hampers to greet the soldiers at each of the refueling stops along the way, all of it choreographed so that a train could pull into a siding to take on wood and water and back out in the required ten minutes. Replacement steam engines had been set at major rail yards, ready to rush out and clear the track of breakdowns. This had only happened twice in the long journey. Countless chickens had been slaughtered, fried, and packed, tens of thousands of loaves of bread baked, barrels of fresh drinking water delivered, beeves by the hundreds slaughtered and cooked over open fires alongside the station. Hospitals had been established to take care of the sick or injured, of which there were more than a few. Guards had been posted at key bridges. All of this under the watchful gaze of Herman Haupt, who sat for endless hours by the telegraph in Harrisburg, monitoring every step of the great movement. This was the largest, fastest movement of men and equipment in human history and Haupt was determined to make it work.

Supply wagons, ambulances, and nearly all horses and mules had been left behind. Remounts, mules, replacement wagons were coming in from other sources to meet up with this corps, the logistics of it far easier than shipping the same all the way over from Mississippi.

It had come together smoothly, and now the first of these trains could slow to a stop.

General McPherson stepped down from a passenger car at the front of the lead train, stretching, looking around, accepting the salute of the guard detail and then smiling as he saw Grant approach, hat brim pulled low, cigar clenched firmly in his mouth.

"General Grant, it is a pleasure to report to you," McPherson said. "My entire corps should be here by the end of the day."

Grant offered nothing more than a salute, a nod of approval, a brief "welcome to Harrisburg," and, turning, led McPherson back to his headquarters. It was the type of greeting McPherson expected, and he smiled at the unpretentious simplicity of it.

Baltimore

July 23, 1863
Noon

C.S.A The band, the same one that had serenaded the troops at Leesborough, was yet again playing "Maryland My Maryland," though it was evident that they had spent quite a bit of time practicing since their last performance.

The carriage bearing President Jefferson Davis, Secretary of State Judah Benjamin, and Gen. Robert E. Lee came down the thoroughfare, which was lined shoulder to shoulder on either side by the men of Pickett's division. The troops looked exhausted, uniforms filthy, soot-stained, more than one of the men with blistered hands and face.

Smoke still coiled up from dozens of fires, sometimes an isolated house that had been torched through accident or the ire of a neighbor. But in the downtown district entire blocks were gone. Smoke still coiled heavenward, and over the entire city there hung a pall, bits of black ash covering houses, streets, and even trees.

The troop of cavalry riding escort was strictly adhering to orders, riding almost nose to tail, two ranks deep around the carriage so that Davis grumbled more than once about not being able to see anything.

"Sir, I am responsible for your security and I felt it prudent to exercise caution," Lee replied calmly.

The fact that Jeb Stuart had been winged by a bushwhacker only that morning had sobered everybody. The bullet had narrowly missed the bone in his upper arm, causing Lee to remember how a similar wound had taken Jackson from him.

The assailant had not been caught, and it took serious restraint and the arrest of several of Stuart's troopers to prevent the burning down of the entire block where the attack had occurred.

The carriage turned on to North Holliday Street and stopped in front of City Hall. Cavalry troopers lined the approach from the street and up the front steps with carbines drawn. The ceremonial guard was at attention, but behind them dozens more faced outward, eyes on the windows of buildings up and down the street, and yet more men, selected sharpshooters, were atop the roofs.

A small gathering of well-wishers were out in the street, the band thumping away as the carriage came to a halt, a feeble cheer going up, small Confederate flags fluttering. Twelve girls dressed in white stood on the steps of the building, each wearing a sash hastily lettered with the name of one of the states of the Confederacy; the twelfth, wearing the sash of Maryland, curtsied and gave a bouquet of flowers to Davis, who formally bowed and then kissed her hand, the girl blushing and drawing back.

The president had already been briefed in the strongest of terms by Lee and did not pause on the steps, instead going straight inside, the foyer of the building cool after the noonday warmth of the sun.

An escort led them down the main corridor and into a side office. The table before them was neatly arranged with flowers, pitchers of lemonade, and an ornate coffee-and-tea setting in silver. A black servant stood at the ready, softly asked what each gentleman would prefer, poured the refreshments, and left. Davis settled down at the head of the table, Benjamin at the middle, and Lee across from him.

"General Lee, I will confess to expecting a bit more ceremony on our triumphal entry into Baltimore. We arrived almost as furtively as Lincoln did when he passed through here two years ago."

"Sir, I would rather err on the side of caution this day. You already know about what happened to General Stuart."

"Yes, how is he?" Judah Benjamin asked.

"He'll mend. It is a clean wound. Several inches more to the left, however, and we would have lost one of our best generals this morning. If there is one man gunning for General Stuart, I daresay a dozen, a hundred would be aiming at you, sir."

"But nothing happened," Davis said a bit peevishly.

"Because, sir, you had a full division of my finest infantry on guard. This city is not yet secured and will not be so for at least a fortnight."

"And the delegates?"

"Sir, the former mayor, the former chief of police, half a dozen former state legislators, various citizen groups are waiting for you in the next room."

"Good. I look forward to meeting with them. The news this morning, in spite of your caution here, has been fortuitous beyond our dreams of but three months ago. We need to act swiftly."

Lee nodded in agreement.

"And the state of the city?" Benjamin asked. "I can barely hope to carry on negotiations if we are in the middle of a battle zone. It would not look good at all; I hope you understand that, sir."

"Yes, Mr. Secretary, I do understand, and am making every effort to facilitate your wishes.

"I've sent another envoy to the garrison at Fort McHenry this morning. I have begged the indulgence of the commander there to refrain from any consideration of shelling the city. To do so would only damage civilian property and not serve his cause. I've offered him, as well, free passage out of the fort, troops to bear arms and colors. Union soldiers waiting for parole are to be free to go as well, along with any Union soldiers that sought refuge there, without need for parole."

"Generous terms, General Lee."

"Yes, sir, but necessary. If I took you down near the waterfront, you would see half a dozen gunboats in the harbor."

"What about the guns we captured at Federal Hill? I understand we have six eight-inch Columbiads."

"Yes, we do, sir, but precious few men trained to man them. To begin a formal siege will be an exercise in yet more bloodshed at a time, I would hope, when we both should be looking to stem that flow."

"There are over seventy guns in Fort McHenry, General Lee," Davis retorted. "Heavy siege guns. If we could seize them intact, they just might be the key to taking Washington."

"I know that, sir. That was one of the terms, that the guns in Fort McHenry are not to be spiked or damaged. But I think that will be a sticking point. It would give us a fort that controls Baltimore and armament that would threaten Washington. Sir, he will not surrender the fort, of that I am all but certain."

"Then we must storm it and take the guns by force. Their garrison surely cannot be strong enough to withstand you."

"At a cost of yet thousands more, which we simply cannot afford," Lee replied forcefully. "I lost nearly three hundred more killed and wounded taking this city."

"A small price."

"Not if you have General Lee's numbers," Benjamin said quietly.

Davis nodded reluctantly.

"The state of the city, General Lee?"

"Sir, there are still scattered pockets of rioting and looting, but no organized resistance. It should be noted that the retiring Union soldiers behaved with honor and I was more than happy to grant them free passage. Several of their companies, when they realized they would not be taken prisoners, pitched in with helping to contain the rioting and put out the fires. We then escorted them to the north side of the city and set them on their way."

"Why did you leave the roads to the north open?" Davis asked.

"Sir, never trap an opponent in a place you want to take. Give them a way out and they will take it. The capture of several thousand more soldiers would have served us little, and in fact burdened us with yet more men needing to be guarded."

"I understand though that tens of thousands of civilians are fleeing as well, that many of them are escaping slaves."

Lee said nothing. It was a topic he was hoping to avoid.

"This newspaper from Philadelphia came through our lines this morning," Lee said, reaching into his dispatch pouch and placing it on the table. The headline proclaimed that the rebel army was looting and burning the city.

"To be expected."

"Still, sir, it is not the image we want with the world at this time. We need to show forebearance now."

Benjamin cleared his throat.

"I would suggest that we allow some members of the Northern press to enter the city and interview civilians who witnessed the rioting," the secretary of state declared. "There are no real military secrets we need to conceal now. Perhaps, Mr. President, you should agree to an interview as well, to lay out our proposal for peace talks."

"I'll consider that," Davis replied.

Davis shifted back to face Lee.

"But I am disturbed that valuable property is escaping north. These are people that we can put to work helping our cause. Many of them are able-bodied men, and the Yankees will press them into their colored regiments."

"Sir. There have been a dozen or more incidents of hangings, rape, torture, outright murder in the colored community. I would much rather see those people leave this town than to have the stain of blood on our hands by forcing them to stay."

"I heard a report that some colored killed white citizens."

"Yes, only after they were attacked."

"Nevertheless, that is intolerable."

"Perhaps intolerable, but I would say intolerable on both sides. Sir, I beg you. Declare an amnesty in this city. It will stand well with the European press and derail the efforts of the Northern press. Declare that all free blacks are to be unmolested as long as they obey martial law. All slaves to stay with their owners."

"And the contraband, the runaways from Virginia?"

"I beg you, sir, do nothing about that now."

Davis looked over at Benjamin, who nodded in agreement with Lee.

"Let it rest for now, sir. Let it rest. To do otherwise will trigger yet more panic and rioting."

Davis said nothing.

"The city itself?"

"I think we can have the fires under control by this evening, as long as Fort McHenry and the gunboats do not shell us. We've captured dozens of factories all but intact, including the Abbot Mills. Thousands of colored work in them and we need them to get the mills back in production, yet another reason to go easy on them. There's enough food to sustain our army for months. Thousands of rifles, artillery, powder, shoes—more shoes than we ever dreamed of. I've ordered our quartermaster to take control of one of the printing presses and print up vouchers for all supplies taken. What we have here, on top of the supplies taken at Westminster, can sustain the Army of Northern Virginia clear through the winter."

"Good, General Lee, very good. Do you see now why taking this city was crucial?"

"Yes, sir. The question though is how long can we hold it?"

"Why, until peace is negotiated, General Lee."

Lee said nothing, hands folded, looking down at the desk.

"You look distressed, General. What is it?"

"Sir. It'll take at least two divisions, for the next fortnight, to keep order here until we can turn it back over to a reorganized police force. Ten thousand or more are homeless and it is our Christian duty to give them aid and help find shelter. My army is a field army, not an occupation army. There is still the question of the reports of the Army of the Potomac reorganizing on the Susquehanna and the reports that Grant is mobilizing a force at Harrisburg. I must have the latitude to maneuver with my forces if need be."

"Baltimore is our key now," Davis replied forcefully. "Mr. Benjamin will reinforce that, won't you, sir?"

Benjamin nodded reluctantly.

"I'm preparing dispatches to be given to the French consulate here in Baltimore, outlining our position. We cannot just seize Baltimore, send the dispatches, and withdraw. We must be here for the replies. The factories here can be of incalculable service to our cause. We must hold this city, and perhaps, with the armaments taken, renew the threat on Washington.

"The political situation is ripe as well. The fall of Baltimore, the third largest city in America, will reverberate across the North as well. I think, General Lee, we are here for the duration."

"Is there any chance you can get the B&O line reestablished back over to Harper's Ferry?" Davis asked.

Lee had never seriously thought of that. It would speed up communications to Richmond and help as well to bring up reinforcements.

"I don't have the railroad people. I wish I did," Lee replied, "but I will see what I can do. Yet again, it will stretch us. We'll need to garrison key points, draining yet more men, but yes, it would be a great help."

"If you could open that line all the way back to Winchester, it would mean little more than a day's journey back to Richmond. It would be a major statement as well that Maryland is now firmly linked to our South.

"The news you gave me this morning from General Hood, that Annapolis has fallen, the governor and his pro-Yankee lackeys in the legislature fleeing to the east shore of Maryland, has set the stage for us. Tomorrow I will call a convention for the establishment of a new state-governing body for Maryland with its capital here in Baltimore, declare the prior state administration as illegal and disbanded, and appoint a provisional governor. It is my intent that within the week this new legislature will declare for the Confederacy. If we do that, General Lee, I can promise you twenty thousand more troops within the month, rallying to defend their home state."

"Sir, that would be a boon, but nevertheless they will be barely trained militia."

"Men, nevertheless."

"Yes, sir."

Lee sat back wearily in his seat. All was happening far too fast. The city was barely under control; there was the threat that the gunboats and fort might open fire. It was not as easy as Davis wished.

"General Lee," Benjamin interrupted. "I received a most gracious invitation this morning from Rabbi Rothenberg of the local Jewish congregation. Would you be interested in joining us for dinner? I think your presence would be of interest to him and the congregation, and helpful as well."

"Me, sir?"

"You are noted for your piety, sir; a visit with one of the leaders of the Jewish community would be a positive example."

"Yes, sir. But of course."

"He has invited us to dine with his family tomorrow night. I think you would find him remarkably interesting and the meal more than adequate."

"If he is a friend of yours, I would be honored to join you," Lee replied.

Davis looked at the two, obviously wondering for a second as to why he was not invited.

"The delegation is waiting in the next room?"

"Yes, sir."

"Then let's get started," Davis announced. "This should be most interesting."

Richmond, Virginia

July 23, 1863
6:00 P.M.

CSA   Gen. Pierre Gustave Toutant Beauregard paced up and down the railroad siding, his anger clearly visible to all who were watching. He pulled out his pocket watch, snapped it open, at least the tenth time he had done so in the last hour, and then snapped it shut.

"Just where the hell is my damned train?" he snarled, looking at his thoroughly harassed staff.

"It's coming," one of the staff replied woodenly. "The dispatcher said that once they get the broken switch repaired, it will be here."

Beauregard looked at the milling crowd of spectators who had gathered at the station to see him off. The afternoon had gotten quite warm, and the group was beginning to thin and drift away.

The send-off was to have been a grand affair, band playing, troops lining the track, his departure in command of what he already called the Army of Maryland a major social event.

Troops had been slowly streaming into Richmond for the last week, more than five thousand following him up from Charleston, eight thousand more from garrison duties in North Carolina and southeastern Virginia, several thousand more dragged in from state militias as far as Georgia. He judged about half of them to be fit for combat; the others were going to have to learn, and damn quickly. The two brigades that had been detached from Pickett prior to the invasion were already up in Winchester, waiting to move forward.

Except the damn railroads were failing to deliver as promised. Engines were breaking down; sections of track were in such an abysmal state that the trains could barely move at ten miles an hour; the new uniforms and shoes promised by Zebulan Vance of North Carolina had yet to materialize. Again, because of supposed "problems with shipment," no artillery was available, and the remounts for cavalry were one step removed from being converted into rations as an act of compassion.

Yet still it was *his* army. He had exulted when the telegram came from Davis, ordering him north, to leave as soon as it was evident that the Union was abandoning the siege of Charleston.

Technically his rank was equal to Lee's, and while the implication was that his command would constitute a new Third Corps for the Army of Northern Virginia, he just smiled at that assumption. There would be more than enough room in Maryland, both politically and militarily, to assert his own position. His arrival would be seen as that of the savior sent to bring succor to the battered Army of Northern Virginia in its hour of need. He alone of all the generals in the East had faced Grant and knew his ways. That expertise could not be denied, and he would make the most of it.

The shriek of a whistle interrupted his musings. A lone train was coming around the bend into the station, and on cue the band struck up "Dixie." The crowds, which had been drifting off, came hurrying back, children waving small national flags.

Wheezing and hissing, the locomotive drifted into the station, behind it three passenger cars for himself and his staff.

He climbed aboard, remaining on the rear platform of the last car as staff and an escort of a company of infantry scrambled on to the train. It was already more than an hour late, so there was no time for final, lingering farewells. The last man barely aboard, the train lurched, a shudder running through the three cars. The band struck up "Maryland My Maryland," a tune that everyone seemed to be singing these days.

Striking the proper pose on the back platform, the South's "Little Napoleon" set forth for war in Maryland, the train forcing itself up to ten miles an hour as it left the station, and then settling down to the slow, monotonous pace, railings clicking, cars swaying back and forth on the worn rails and crumbling ballast.

Chapter Thirteen

C.S.A. "I hope, General Lee, that you would consider attending our Sabbath day service this Friday. My congregation and I would be honored by your attendance."

Lee smiled warmly at his host and nodded his thanks.

"Rabbi, I would indeed be honored."

"Please, just Samuel, General Lee."

Lee could not help but respond to this man's natural, warm hospitality. In spite of his preference for formality and tradition in nearly all social occasions, he felt he should let it drop this evening.

"Then Robert for myself, sir."

Rabbi Samuel Rothenberg bowed slightly while remaining seated, then offered to refill Lee's glass of wine. Lee motioned for just a small amount to be poured, but the rabbi filled the glass nearly to the brim anyhow.

"What did you think of dinner, General Lee?" Judah Benjamin asked.

"Delicious. I'm not paying a false compliment when I declare it is the best meal I've enjoyed since the start of this campaign."

Judah laughed softly.

"So we have converted you to kosher cuisine?"

"Sir?"

"Everything tonight was kosher."

"I am relieved not to have to eat salt pork for once, sir, if that is what you mean."

"Not in this house, sir," Samuel laughed, holding up his hands in mock horror.

"Well, sir," Lee grinned, "I wish you could teach our army cooks a few things. I think the Army of Northern Virginia could benefit from a kosher diet."

The three laughed good-naturedly at his joke.

As Lee looked over at his host sitting at the head of the table, and his attractive wife at the other end, their two young children sitting wide-eyed and respectful to either side of their mother, he was warmed by the situation. It was a blessing to sit in a friendly home, tastefully decorated, the food well prepared, the host and hostess so congenial, cultured, and well educated.

The children had been a relaxing pleasure, quickly warming to him when he expressed interest in their studies, and he had sat, fascinated, when the elder of the two recited from the Torah in Hebrew, the boy obviously delighted by the attention, while the younger was beside himself to talk about trains and all the names of the locomotives he had seen. It had been a wondrous predinner diversion and he had insisted that the parents not interfere for, in fact, he was truly enjoying himself.

Prior to his arrival, under a heavy escort that even now loitered outside, guarding the house, he did have to confess to a slight trepidation over this engagement that Judah had so casually offered him. He had never taken a meal in a practicing Jewish household, and he wasn't sure what to expect. The prayer, however, except for no mention of Jesus, was familiar and comfortable to him, drawing on the Psalms. The conversation over dinner was sophisticated, urbane, with the rabbi quickly sharing memories of New York City and his knowledge of military history, which was quite extensive, especially when it came to Napoleon's campaign of 1805.

The house was appointed with a bit of a Germanic Old World touch to it, the rabbi having emigrated from Prussia during the unrest of the 1840s. At times his English did have a slight accent, but his command of his adopted language was superb. He could claim acquaintances with a number of noted personages in America, including several senators, both North and South, and was proud of the literary discussion group that he hosted each month.

Samuel was fascinated by a poet and short-story teller of whom Lee had heard, a washed-out cadet from the Point who had attended the Academy shortly after Lee graduated and who had taken to writing tales of the macabre until his premature death from excessive drinking. The rabbi even had one of his original poems, unpublished, which the poet had given him as a thank-you for a weekend's lodging and several meals shortly before his death. The work, "The Nightmare of the Wandering Jew," was interesting, but upon reading it when Samuel showed it to him before dinner, Lee felt it to be somewhat overblown, yet out of politeness he expressed admiration for this rare literary item.

"Samuel and I go back some years," Judah declared as he accepted his second glass of Madeira. "I tried to convince him to come to Richmond to help me when the war started."

Samuel laughed and shook his head.

"Come now, Judah. Two Jews in the Confederate government? Some would say it was an outright conspiracy of our people to take over."

"Still, you have a sharp mind, Samuel; I could use some of your advice now and again."

"Such as tonight?" Samuel asked with a smile.

Judah fell silent and looked over at Lee.

"I think it is time that you gentlemen excused us," Mrs. Rothenberg announced. "The children need to do their evening studies and then to bed."

Both instantly raised vocal protests, but, smiling, she rousted them out of their chairs. Lee and Judah stood, both bowing to Mrs. Rothenberg and then taking delight in shaking the hands of the two young boys. One embarrassed both his parents when he blurted out that he wished for General Lee's signature; the other then demanded a keepsake as well. Lee, grinning, pulled out his pocket notebook and addressed a brief note, formally commissioning Lt. Gunther Rothenberg to his staff, and then did the same for David. Clutching the notes, the boys bounded off to their rooms; their mother followed.

"Thank you, Robert, they'll treasure that forever; in fact, our entire family will treasure it."

"You have sons to be proud of, sir. And I thank God for you that they are still young enough not to be in service. My own boys are a constant source of worry."

"Yes, I heard about your son being taken prisoner."

"I pray there are some of my old friends on the other side who will see after him."

"This tragedy dividing my adopted country," said Samuel as he shook his head. "I fear if it does not end soon, the only thing both sides will gain is a divided and hate-filled land, setting the stage for a repeat of Europe, states constantly warring against each other."

"My fear as well, sir," Lee replied forcefully. "That is why I pray that the successes of the current campaign will soon bring the fighting to an end, and then calmer heads, such as my friend Judah here, can negotiate a peaceful solution that is fair to all."

"May I speak freely, gentlemen?" Samuel asked and Lee sensed a touch of nervousness in his voice.

"Samuel, when did I know you not to speak freely?" Benjamin said, chuckling softly. "That's why I came here tonight and brought my friend along. You are a leading citizen of this city and we've known each other for years. I want to hear what you have to say about our cause, how we can bring Baltimore into that cause, how we can win and achieve a peace that is just and lasting."

"You might not like what I have to say."

"When did that ever stop you, Samuel?"

Samuel was quiet for a moment, and lowered his head, as if praying, then raised his gaze, fixing Judah with it.

"It has not been easy the last two years," Samuel said, his tone suddenly serious. "As a leader of my community, a community as divided as all others in this city, I've tried to maintain a neutral position, and, as you know, to be neutral often antagonizes both sides. The position of my people, in spite of the promise of this country, can be a precarious one at times, and thus one must tread softly. I do see both sides of the issue though. I chose to live in the South, I understand many of its ways, and I do agree with the argument that the economic inequities between the two sections needed to be addressed."

"So at least you are with us on some points then," Benjamin interjected.

"Of course. But I don't think you wish for me simply to sit back now and offer platitudes when I suspect, my dear friend Judah, that you've come to me wanting something else."

"Samuel, whenever I come to you, I expect a sharp lesson at some point."

"I hope it is not too sharp," Samuel replied.

"Please, Samuel, go ahead," Judah said.

"You're going to lose the war unless you take radical steps," Samuel said, almost blurting the words out.

Lee settled back in his chair, not letting any reaction show. Samuel looked over at him nervously, as if expecting some sort of angry or defensive response.

"Please continue, Rabbi," Lee said quietly. "I am eager to hear your reasoning."

"I will not delve into any philosophical debates here. I think too many focus on the rightness, or wrongness, of their causes, and thus waste effort that should be devoted, instead, to the far more pragmatic question of simply how to win."

"Your reason for predicting our defeat?" Lee asked.

"You will fail because of three central points—material, numbers, and, most important, the fundamental moral issue behind this war."

Lee said nothing, looking over at Judah, who had settled back in his chair.

"When it comes to material, you feel you have gained a momentary advantage, which indeed you have. The supplies you garnered in the last month must seem as if you have indeed stumbled into the Garden of Eden before the fall."

"Not quite that good," Lee said with a smile, "but yes, it can sustain our efforts through the rest of the year and give Virginia time to recover from the Union depredations of the last two years."

"And yet such a loss for the North, their supply depot for an entire army, this city, which is the third largest in the nation, the riches of the state of Maryland, do you think it affects them at all? Will one of their soldiers go hungry or shoeless because of your brilliant successes of the last month? Does it even matter to them?"

Lee reluctantly shook his head.

"Yet if a similar blow was inflicted upon you, it would have spelt the doom of your army."

Lee did not reply, but he knew it was true; to have lost his supply train at the start of the campaign would have been a disaster almost impossible to recover from.

"Gentlemen, I think that tells us volumes about which side is better suited to war, a new kind of war that Napoleon never dreamed of. If you were fighting fifty years ago, I would say your victory would be assured. Perhaps even ten years ago, but railroads and industry have changed all of that forever. Your opponent can overcome his tactical weaknesses in the field by the mobilization of his masses, wherever he might so desire. That is something the legs and courage of your men can never overcome."

Lee did not reply. It was a sharp analysis, plainly spoken, but he had just spent the last year overcoming this disadvantage through the courage and the legs of his men, shifting the war from the banks of the James to the banks of the Susquehanna. Politely he shook his head.

"I might disagree, sir, but continue."

"I will be the first to express admiration for the prowess of you and your command, General Lee; it is the wonder of the world, and even your opponents admire you for it. But how long you can sustain that, General, is open to debate. Imagine Napoleon with all his brilliance, facing a

Prussian or even an Austrian army that could move a hundred thousand men at will from one front to another in the twinkling of an eye. I think you know what would happen in the end, even with him."

"Yet, was it not Napoleon who said that morale was more powerful than any other factor upon the field of battle?" Lee replied, his voice calm and even, in spite of the tension he felt. "Every army they have thrown against us, in the end it was the morale of my men that was crucial."

"And, sir," Samuel interjected, "your leadership, which helps to bring that morale into play."

Lee nodded his thanks.

"That is why we hope that Union Mills, and now the fall of Baltimore, will be defined by some as our Saratoga," Benjamin interjected.

Samuel frowned, looking down at his glass of wine, tapping his fingertips together.

"You mean the intervention of France, or perhaps England?"

Benjamin laughed softly.

"I don't wish to be quoted on such issues at the moment, Samuel, not even in confidence to you."

"Still, it is evident. I've heard rumors you will meet with the French consul for Baltimore tomorrow morning."

"Do you know everything in this city?" Benjamin exclaimed.

"Almost everything," Samuel grinned. "And yes, the analogy is a good one, your hoping that like the victory at Saratoga during the Revolution, Union Mills and the capture of Baltimore will bring France and others into the war. What our valiant General Lee and his doughty warriors achieved this month stands alongside Napoleon in his march from the Rhine to the Danube or Washington in his move from New Jersey to Yorktown. Union Mills has achieved a profound military victory of the moment. The question unanswered though is, Will it break the will of the North to continue the fight? Whatever happens next on the battlefield, realize this, that for the next year it comes down to but one man, and one man only."

"Lincoln," Benjamin sighed.

"Yes, Lincoln. The entire Congress could turn on him, most of the state governors as well, but as long as he maintains his will, if but twenty percent of the populace and the troops in the field stand by him, the war will continue until the next election. The army, especially this Grant, will stand by him and thus the war will indeed continue."

Lee said nothing. This man was sharp, clear in his logic, and also disturbing. He had struck to the core of his own campaign, to break Lincoln's will to fight.

"Now to the third part of my thesis," Samuel said. "It is the moral issues but relates to numbers as well."

He shifted slightly, fixing his gaze intently on Judah.

"You must mobilize Negroes into your army, offering those who serve immediately freedom, full rights of citizenship, including the right to vote, hold property, and hold public office. That freedom must also be extended to their wives and children. As for the rest of your population in slavery, you must offer a solemn pledge of manumission once the crisis of the war has ended."

There was a long, almost stunned silence, as if the unspeakable had just been pronounced.

Lee sat silent. The conversation had turned to a political issue and as a general in the field, he was solemnly bound to leave such issues to his government, regardless of personal feelings.

Judah shook his head wearily, as if a sudden weight had been dumped upon his shoulders.

"I've heard this before," Judah replied. "General Cleburne, a brilliant field commander in our Western armies, said the same thing last year. It forever ruined his career in the army, and it will never happen as long as this war continues."

Samuel looked over at Judah.

"My friend, I know that somewhere hidden within you, you've entertained the exact same thoughts."

Judah nodded in agreement.

"Several months back, when it was evident that Vicksburg would fall, and after the terrible casualties from Chancellorsville, I ventured this proposal, in private, to one of our senators, who shall remain nameless," Judah said. "His response, 'My God, Judah, if we maintain that the black man is only fit to be a slave, and then give him freedom and arm him, what will that say of everything we once believed in?'"

"I am urging you to reconsider the very core issues some on your side believe in," Samuel continued. "For if you do not, I predict ultimate defeat. You will be forced, at bayonet point, to change anyhow. Why not do it now, on the crest of the incredible victories General Lee has given you? It would change the course of the war; in fact, I predict it would end the war."

"To turn that into a political reality?" Judah asked and shrugged his shoulders. "Do you realize there would be some who would actually suggest secession from the South if our government tried that move?"

Samuel chuckled sadly.

"Once the precedent has been set, it is hard to stop. If that was threatened, then I would urge you to face it down, to challenge them to go. Their will would collapse and reality would be faced.

"The tens of thousands of colored who have fled Baltimore these last few days, how many of those young men will wind up in Union army recruiting depots?" Samuel asked. "How many will come back here in a month, two months, rifles poised, men filled with a terrible resolve."

"Some have said that the black man would not make a good soldier," Judah replied.

Samuel shook his head.

"Any student of military history would tell you different. Would you not agree, General Lee?"

Lee was silent, not wishing to get drawn into this conversation, which had turned so political.

"The reports I received of the black regiment in the defense of Washington indicated they fought with ferocity and were a crucial element in our defeat," he finally replied. "My own father spoke of the role played by men of that race in the Revolution. No, sir, I think if motivated, they will fight. There are thousands of freemen and even slaves in our ranks now, usually as cooks, teamsters, and servants for officers, but more than one has stood on the volley line."

"Some point to the anarchy in Haiti as an example of how the black man can never be trained to be an efficient soldier and have an effective army," Samuel interjected. "But then again, one could point to a hundred wars where white soldiers were rabble or worse. But in direct response the black men of this country were good enough to fight for America in 1776 and 1812. They have served by the thousands in our navy with valor since the first days of the republic. Elite units in many of the nations of the Middle East are made up of Africans. I could offer yet more examples but I digress.

"Judah, in direct response to those who question my proposal, I would reply they are placing the cart before the horse. Recruit them, train them, put them into battle, and then judge the results. If they then fail, the argument would, in fact, be settled forever. But if they succeed? Then you will have not just divisions but entire corps of men equal to any soldier of the Army of Northern Virginia, or more important, the Army of the Potomac."

Lee looked at the two and shifted uncomfortably. Was this conversation real, or in some way was Judah playing a subtle game, to impact on his own thinking about the war?

"Why was the president not invited to this conversation?" Lee asked.

Samuel and Judah looked at Lee.

"Let's just say it would inhibit conversation. Besides, he has other duties to attend to this evening," Judah replied. "Discussions about the new state legislatures, appointment of a provisional governor."

"My sense of duty obligates me to raise a question about the appropriateness of this conversation. It is not the place of a soldier to discuss politics."

Judah laughed.

"Tell that to, let's see, Braxton Bragg, our dear friend Beauregard, for that matter, nearly every general under your command. There is a difference, sir, between the ideal and the real in this war, as there is in every war."

"Nevertheless, I prefer to hold myself above that."

"General Lee," Samuel said softly, "if ever there has been a political war in history, it is this one. It is the heart and soul of this conflict."

"I cannot do that, sir," Lee replied sharply. "What you suggest has the taint of Napoleonism in it, and I would rather die than see my army become a tool of that kind of thinking."

"Do not misconstrue Samuel's words," Benjamin continued. "I, sir, in spite of your gallant record, would urge your removal from office if ever I even suspected you were breaking the code of the professional military officer. Nor is there that faintest suggestion that you dabble in politics, as too many of your brother officers do, but perhaps we should hear Samuel's arguments nevertheless, purely as an intellectual exercise, a chance to hear the views of a learned man who has lived behind the enemy's lines for two years."

Lee nodded and settled back again. If anything, curiosity now compelled him to hear, even more than Samuel's challenges, the reply of the secretary of state of the Confederacy for which he fought.

"Go ahead then, gentlemen."

"General Lee, I hope I have not offended you in any way," Samuel said, his concern obvious and heartfelt.

"No, sir, I always prefer plain truthful speaking, and it is obvious to me you are a man of courage to do so."

"Thank you, General. May I continue?"

Lee reluctantly nodded agreement.

"The North has outflanked the Confederacy on two points in relationship to the black man," Samuel continued. "First, and most clearly evident, Abraham Lincoln's decree of emancipation, whether it is legal or not, has redefined this war from one that is a constitutional question to a more fundamental question that I think goes back to the Declaration of Independence. . . . Are all men indeed created equal?"

"Lincoln's political maneuverings are a fraud, sir," Judah replied sharply. "It is a diversion from the real issues of this war, the constitutional issues that created this fight."

"Yes, in some ways, it is a fraud, for if the full intent was equality, it would have applied to all states where slavery exists, including here in Maryland and Delaware. It does not, but that point is moot."

"How so?" Judah asked.

"Because Lincoln has created a new moral perception, a different reality. The North, with that one act, with one signature on a document, has changed the political and moral dimensions of this war. One must admit that prior to the proclamation, the argument was almost an abstraction. Yes, men of both sides could rally to the cry for a single Union or Southern Independence, but the deeper complex issues evaded the minds of many."

"I'll consider that point," Judah replied, "but it is simplistic to think that slavery alone caused this war."

"Consider the Talmud."

Judah smiled.

"Remember Samuel, I am a Jew by birth but have not devoted myself deeply to the teachings of my faith."

"I wish I could change that," Samuel replied. "You're a good challenge for a rabbi."

"Perhaps after this war is over," Judah said with a smile, "I will come and sit in your library, and you can attempt to bring me back to my roots."

"'Talmud'?" Lee asked. "Please enlighten me, sir."

"Writings of learned Jewish scholars. It is fascinating stuff, the most complex of arguments, page after page on the most minute of topics. Learned men devote their entire lives to but one passage of Scripture and the arguments that could be derived out of it.

"I find it fascinating, but ultimately, what will God ask of me and of all those brilliant scholars when we stand before Him?"

"I don't follow you," Judah said.

"Will God ask of me, 'Samuel, did you study Talmud?' or will he ask, 'Samuel, were you a good man and did you honor God?'

"Too many of my friends, great thinkers, become caught in the arguments of the Talmud, forgetting that ultimately the question God will put to us is, 'Are you a good man, did you honor God, and did you lead a righteous life?'

"The same is true of the causes of this war. Right or wrong, the complexities of the Constitution, the issues of States' Rights, the wishes and desires of the Founding Fathers, the legality of secession, all of it is moot compared to the more fundamental question, 'Is this morally right and is it good for the common man?' All the other arguments are like the Talmud when compared to that most basic question of all. For, my friend, the founding of America is based upon that, the dream that it is a nation for the common man."

No one spoke for a moment.

"Whether Lincoln's proclamation is a fraud or not," Samuel continued, "whether it is sleight of hand, whether he believes in it or not, though honestly I am convinced he does believe in it, Lincoln has seized the moral initiative of this war. He is now asking his own countrymen, does the founding document, the Declaration of Independence that we all hold sacred, have meaning? Do Jefferson's, and for that matter Locke's, immortal words about the equality of man carry with them a fundamental truth?

"I remember one of Lincoln's speeches before the war, and I will confess it stirred me. He raised the question as to what the words 'all men are created equal' actually meant. He then reasoned that if we, in America, created exceptions, by saying that all men are created equal, except for Negroes, then what was to prevent us from saying that all men are created equal except for Irish, Catholics, or Jews. Lincoln asserted that if such was the case, he would rather go to Russia, where he could breathe the air of tyranny free of the taint of hypocrisy."

"Words when compared to the reality of what Lincoln has forced us to, the devastation he has wrought against hundreds of thousands of common men of the South," Judah replied sharply.

"Words are weapons in war, just as the bayonet or gun. It is with such words that Lincoln will bring hundreds of thousands of men of color into the ranks of his legions, while the South continues to bleed itself dry."

"So, to cut to the core of this," Judah replied. "You are actually proposing our own Emancipation Proclamation."

"Exactly. Do that, gentlemen, and you will have cut out the props from under Lincoln. You will have a profound impact on foreign intervention, and you will bring to your ranks hundreds of thousands of men of color, who will see that here is their chance for honorable freedom and a future in the South as equal citizens. You could mobilize hundreds of thousands of fresh troops within months. That answers then the other point, the one of numbers.

"I daresay, gentlemen, it would bond the men of the South, black and white, into a bond of blood that will forever change the social dynamic of your newly freed country. When men bleed side by side on the battlefield, they become brothers in peace."

Lee sat silent, gaze fixed on Judah. Till this moment he had never considered the issue in this light. For a brief instant he let his imagination run with it; a hundred thousand fresh troops, even fifty thousand at this moment, would most certainly tip the scale once and for all to his side. But the barriers . . . and as quickly as his mind turned to those realities, the dream flickered and died. Davis and the Confederate Congress back in Richmond would never agree.

"Let me finish quickly, my friends, for I know the hour is late," Samuel said. "I asked my servant to take some coffee and biscuits out to your guards, but I can imagine those young lads are weary and would like to return to their rest, so I shall try to keep it short."

Lee looked out the window and saw that his troop of cavalry escorts were, indeed, enjoying coffee served on fine china, while out in the street a small crowd of the curious had gathered.

"Thank you for seeing to my men," Lee said. "Such kind treatment will be remembered by them and by me. I must add now, sir, that I am posting several of them here for the next few days, just in case our visit should cause subsequent problems."

"If it was only myself, I would insist against it, but I know Sarah was worried about this, so I thank you, sir."

Samuel sighed. "Tragic isn't it that we must take such precautions in these times?"

"I hope soon that we will not," Lee said with a smile.

"I will raise another point that stops us," Judah interjected. "The slave owners themselves. They are a minority in our country but a powerful one. I do not see them readily agreeing to this."

"I've thought of that as well," Samuel replied. "First off, ask them to speak to the slave owners in what is now territory occupied by the Union. They have lost what they held forever. That tidal wave is coming down upon the rest of the South, a storm that cannot be stopped. So I would argue that now, before it is too late, you should offer them compensation."

"With what?" Judah asked. "We are bankrupt as it is."

"Think creatively, Judah. I daresay you might even be able to get foreign funds for such a venture; the liberals of England would rejoice at such a pronouncement, perhaps even be willing to fund some of it. Your economy is stagnant because of the blockade. After such a proclamation France will undoubtedly come in, and, I think, England as well. Trade will generate some of the funds necessary."

"This stays here," Judah replied, "but I think we will see that anyhow."

Samuel sniffed and shook his head.

"Too little, too late. France? Their only concern is expanding their empire in Mexico and doing what damage they can to both of us, North and South, to prevent our intervention after our own war is over. The impact of France, at best, would be limited.

"It is England you want, and as long as you embrace slavery, nothing you achieve on the battlefield will bring them to your side. Besides, I think they see that as long as Lincoln stands firm, the war will continue. No, shake Lincoln with your offer of freedom. England will see the Union cause tottering and at that moment, they just might consider breaking the blockade. If for no other reason than to win your gratitude once the war was over.

"The sale of the tens of millions of dollars in cotton rotting on our wharves could be used to help offset the temporary financial loss of the slaveholders and keep them in your ranks.

"The South must make some hard decisions within the next few weeks if it is to survive," Samuel said, pressing his argument. "Perhaps, if both sides have declared for emancipation, then what the North now claims is one of the fundamental issues of the war has been resolved. Doing it now, at a moment of strength, on the coattails of victory, will add even more weight, rather than to do so as a final act of desperation.

"You can then argue that there is no longer any point to the war. Lincoln altered the terms; you have agreed to those terms; the issue is settled. I daresay that the will to continue the fight on the side of the North, to venture yet another battle with your army now reinforced with tens of thousands of black soldiers, will evaporate."

Samuel spoke now with open enthusiasm, as if his proposal could actually become a reality if the three of them sitting about the table would agree.

"Our government will never accept it," Judah replied, "more so even now because victory seems all but assured."

"You mean President Davis will not accept it."

Judah shook his head.

"Samuel, you have been my friend for fifteen years, but you must know that there are lines drawn by my office, and I will not discuss that here."

"And my suggestion?"

"The realist in me knows that our president, our Congress, and those in power will not yet agree to such a measure."

"As I feared," Samuel said wearily.

Lee stirred, sliding his chair back. He had listened to the debate with interest, and he knew it would trouble his thoughts, but the more immediate concerns of command called, and the hour was late. His gesture was a signal to both.

Samuel stood up and bowed graciously to Lee.

"I hope, sir, that two old friends talking politics have not dulled the pleasure of this evening."

"On the contrary, sir, you have been a wonderful host."

Samuel guided them to the door, on the way pointing out several small items of his collection: documents signed by Napoleon, Wellington, a framed locket of Napoleon's hair.

"I will pray for both of you," Samuel said. "Know that my heart is with you."

Samuel opened the door and the three stepped out. The guard detachment, who had obviously been enjoying themselves, surrounded by admiring citizens and more than one attractive young lady, quickly snapped to attention. The captain of the guard called for orderlies to bring Judah and Lee's horses.

The two mounted, bid their farewells to Samuel, and rode off, the detachment surrounding them.

"Gentlemen, just a little room please," Lee asked. "The secretary and I need to talk for a moment."

The captain of his guard detail looked over at Lee with concern. The street was dark, there was no telling what danger lurked in side alleyways, but Lee's forceful gaze won the argument and the detachment spread out. Lee brought Traveler over closer to Judah's side.

"Any thoughts, General Lee?"

"Sir, respectfully, but I must ask, was part of that conversation staged for my benefit?"

"What do you mean, General Lee?" Judah asked innocently.

"Sir, you are noted for your subtle abilities."

Judah laughed softly.

"I am not sure if I am being complimented or insulted."

"A compliment, Mr. Secretary. But the question I raised earlier, about the president not attending, and now my question for the reason I was invited at all."

"I wanted you to meet Samuel. He is a sharp wit. In less troubling times, I know the two of you would have enjoyed talking history."

"But we are in troubled times, sir. I wonder how much you knew about the direction tonight's conversation would take."

"Oh, I assumed it would go in the path it took. I've had several letters from my old friend come through the lines since the war started."

"Then why was I there?" Lee asked, and there was a slight touch of anger in his voice. "You placed me in an uncomfortable position. I will admit, I was quite taken by our host and his family. I would love to sit with him again, but to talk of other things. I am a field commander who must answer to my government. It is not my position, sir, to discuss the policies of our government."

Judah held up an apologetic hand.

"Do not chastise me too harshly, General Lee."

"I am not chastising you, sir. Merely making a point, a tradition that any general must maintain."

"General Lee, some words from my heart."

"Go on, sir."

"You have become the soul of our cause."

Now it was Lee's turn to hold up his hand, shaking his head as if not wanting to hear what would be said, for the words, as always, were a burden he did not want.

"Hear me out, please. You are the soul of our cause. Every Southern household hangs on your exploits. Where we face defeats on so many other fronts, you bring victory. You have built perhaps the finest army in history and led it to victories unimagined. The survival of our cause now rests with you. Not with the president, nor our Congress, nor my own feeble attempts at foreign policy. It rests with you."

"It rests with the men of the army, sir. Always it rests with them," Lee said forcefully. "It is their blood that will buy us liberty."

"I know," Judah said sadly. "But the blood of how many men? We know it cannot go on much longer. We have only so much of that blood to give. There isn't a home in the South that has not paid for this damnable war. And we are running out of that blood.

"Samuel was right. Even as we bleed, and prepare to bleed again, Lincoln holds fast. I fear sir, he has indeed seized the moral high ground from us. He has shifted the reasons for this war far beyond what many of us believe started it. Samuel proposes a way to put an end to it, and, perhaps, as well to end the division of the races in our homeland. I would like to think that if the black man were given his chance, in defense of the South, it would change forever how we see each other. Perhaps it would give us a chance to rebuild a nation together. And in so doing, give to you two, maybe three, more corps of men for the battles yet to be fought."

"It is not my decision, sir," Lee replied sharply, a touch of anger in his voice. "It is the president's and yours, not mine."

"I know, General Lee. But I must say this. Perhaps, someday, the burden will be yours. That is why I asked you to join us tonight to hear what someone who is astute has to say, and also what I have dwelled upon since this conflict started."

"Sir? You have felt this all along?"

"Just that, General Lee, but I think I've said enough for one night."

The two rode on in silence, disappearing into the night.

Chapter Fourteen

Harrisburg, Pennsylvania
Headquarters Army of the Susquehanna

August 3, 1863
10:30 A.M.

Grant looked around at the gathering in his oversized command tent. A photographer from Brady's had just finished taking several images of them outside, and now from a distance was doing a fourth and final shot of them gathered in the open-sided tent. The group remained still until it was done and the photographer ran off to his black wagon to develop the plate as an assistant picked up the heavy camera and lugged it away.

The day was warm, another heat wave setting in, and his officers were grateful to get their jackets off, sitting about the long oak table in shirt-sleeves and vests.

Maj. Gen. Edward Ord, who had arrived only yesterday with the last of the men from his Thirteenth Corps, was relaxed, sipping from a tall glass of iced lemonade. Beside him was McPherson, commander of the Fifteenth Corps, the first unit from the West to arrive in Harrisburg. Burnside, who had reassumed command of his old Ninth Corps, which had served in part of the Vicksburg campaign, sat quietly to one corner. He had arrived ahead of his two small divisions, which were still crossing Indiana and Ohio. Couch, commander of the twenty thousand militia and short-term regiments that had gathered in Harrisburg at the start of the Gettysburg campaign, was fanning himself with an oversized, wide-brimmed hat. Several divisional commanders and the usual staff were gathered as well, while in the far corner sat Ely Parker, Grant's adjutant, taking notes. Beside him sat Elihu Washburne, who had arrived from Washington only within the last hour.

"It's time we started laying out our plans," Grant announced, "and I want to know our state of readiness."

"My men are ready any time you give the word, sir," McPherson said confidently. "But it is a question of supplies, remounts, support equipment."

The other generals nodded in agreement.

Grant looked over at Haupt. The general was actually dozing and Ord, smiling, nudged him awake.

"Sorry, sir."

Grant smiled indulgently. Haupt was working himself into a state of collapse. He had lost weight, his features pale, the dysentery draining him of all energy.

"Are you ready to report, sir?" Grant asked.

"Yes, sir."

Haupt stood, leaning against the table for support, and pointed to the map of the entire eastern United States, which was spread on the table.

"We've moved over forty thousand men east in the last three weeks and I must say that it is a unique accomplishment in the history of warfare. It has of course created certain problems, which my staff did anticipate but could do nothing about during the movement of forces, and now it will take some time to straighten out."

"What problems?" Burnside asked.

"Locomotives and rolling stock. We commandeered over two hundred locomotives from different lines and over two thousand flatcars and boxcars. Repositioning them back into useful service after their express run east is taking time. I could not ship them back while the entire road, involving several different lines, was cleared for eastbound traffic. Therefore these last two weeks have created some depletion of available trains in the West. Once the last of Burnside's men are in, we need to take a breather, to reposition that rolling stock back to their owners, who are screaming bloody murder."

"Can't they wait?" Ord asked. "We still need to bring more men in, tens of thousands more."

"Yes and no, sir. We will continue to bring in troops. I'm preparing for the next big transshipment of Nineteenth Corps from Philadelphia as they arrive by sea from New Orleans, but in order to keep other activities moving, including industrial and even commercial movement, we have to slow the pace slightly."

He paused, looking over at Grant, who nodded his approval.

"Go ahead, General. I'm in agreement. Our presence here, at this moment, has at least alleviated any defensive concerns; in that capacity we are fully ready to fight. It was beyond my hope that General Lee might actually attempt to sally forth from Baltimore and try to strike us here. We knew that wouldn't happen, but our friends over in the state capitol building are now relieved. We are not yet, however, an offensive army."

Ord grinned, chewing meditatively on a wad of tobacco, leaned over, and spat on the ground.

"Tell that to my boys; they're eager to get at it, sir."

McPherson grinned and nodded in agreement.

"Our little skirmish a couple of days ago got their blood up, sir; I kind of agree with Ord. Perhaps a demonstration down towards Carlisle?"

Grant shook his head.

"General McPherson, your men did admirably driving back Stuart's pickets. One brigade across the river, to deny them the ability to see us, is sufficient for now. We move when ready, and not before."

"I concur," Haupt said, taking out a handkerchief to wipe the sweat from his face.

"The big problem of logistics now is horses. As General Grant said, we are a defensive army at the moment; we can fight in place, but to move? Not yet, I am sorry to say."

"How soon?" Ord pressed.

"Sir, we need over twelve thousand more horses and at least six thousand mules for our supply trains, and we don't even have the wagons yet for the mules to be hitched to.

"Moving men is simple in comparison. Pile a regiment on a train, get patriotic civilians to pass up hampers of food at every stop, have wood and water in place for the locomotive, and you can go clear from Wisconsin to Maine in a week if you wish. Horses are a hell of a lot more difficult.

"At best we can maybe load a hundred horses to a train, but that is pressing it, a hell of a lot of weight for the steeper grades. They have to be unloaded every day, exercised, fed, watered. We can't go too fast. A bad bump or shift, and you have a trainload of horses with broken legs. A trip of three days to move five hundred men will equal a week or more with five trains with incredible amounts of fodder placed along the way. Then, once here, sir, ten thousand horses means four hundred thousand pounds of fodder a day. Granted, we can pasture a lot of them in nearby farms, but they'll eat that out in a couple of weeks."

He shook his head wearily.

"How many of our own horses from Vicksburg will come up?" Ord asked. "A lot of my men in the cavalry and artillery are upset about losing their old mounts and trace horses, which are trained to their tasks."

"I'm having near five thousand moved by steamers up to Wheeling. From there they'll be loaded on trains. That cuts six hundred miles off the train run, but it's a lot slower and the Ohio is still in flood from all the rains, so it's even slower than expected. The first trainload should be coming in next week."

"And the others?" Grant asked.

"I'm ordering in trainloads of remounts from as far as Maine. It's a little complex, since the actual purchasing of horses is not in my department, only the transporting of them. I can have a procurement officer in Vermont tell me that he has a hundred mules, the train gets there, and half of the poor beasts are on their last legs, shipping them here a waste. The system is riddled with corruption, paybacks, purchasing of animals just about ready to drop; it's a nightmare."

Grant tossed down the butt of his cigar after using it to puff a new one to life.

"When?"

"I think by the end of the month, sir."

Grant exhaled noisily.

"I'd prefer sooner. That gives me only four to six weeks of campaigning weather before the onset of autumn."

"I know that, sir; I'm moving hard on it."

"I know you are, Haupt. What else?"

"Sir, with the delay we'll need to start shipping in fodder as well for the horses already here, not much at first but it will quickly increase to ten to fifteen trainloads a day. Three to four times that amount if we are stuck into late fall. Purchasing agents are combing Upstate New York for fodder, which is our best route for bringing it down to here."

"We won't be here by late fall," Grant snapped and then nodded for Herman to continue with his list.

"We need fifteen hundred wagons for supplies. Again that has to go through a different department than mine. I can cram twenty-five of them onto a train. We have orders in to factories and suppliers across the country. I think we can make good on those in short order. Fortunately there's a lot of wagon-makers right here in Pennsylvania and we're offering a premium for quick delivery. There's a purchasing agent in Reading buying them up now. He's efficient, and as fast as a trainload of them is assembled, they're shipped here. We also need three hundred more springed ambulances, twenty more forge wagons for the artillery batteries, roughly a hundred wagons for headquarters baggage, and, most important, two hundred heavy wagons for the pontoon trains."

"Why so many?" McPherson asked. "We never had that many down in Mississippi."

"I want two pontoon bridges across this river when we move," Grant interjected, "and I want enough bridging material together to throw two more bridges across the Potomac. If the campaign then presses into Virginia, we will need additional bridging for half a dozen rivers from the Potomac down to Richmond."

"You plan to go that far this fall?" McPherson asked, surprise in his voice.

Grant looked up at him and shook his head.

"I'm not ready to discuss that yet, and let me remind all of you here that what is said in this tent stays here. I misspoke to even mention the bridging requirements."

Haupt, who by the simple process of planning the transportation of supplies already had a good sense of what Grant was indeed planning, lowered his gaze for a moment. He knew men like Ord, McPherson, and Burnside were burning with curiosity about the forthcoming campaign, and though he could surmise what was to come, he would never breathe a word or give something away. Haupt knew Grant would reveal his plans in his own good time, and he was not about to risk Grant's wrath by hinting at anything.

There was some grumbling, but all three of the corps commanders knew the issue was closed.

"The army has orders in for the necessary pontoon boats with shipbuilders on the Hudson and along Lake Erie. Filling the order is relatively easy, but they are big, cumbersome affairs and only ten will fit on a train. I should have them down here though, at least enough for two bridges within three weeks."

"Good work, Haupt," Grant said. "Anything else?"

"Yes, sir. Railroading equipment."

"Railroading equipment?" Burnside asked, a bit surprised. "For what railroad?"

Haupt looked over at Grant, who nodded his approval.

"The Cumberland Valley Railroad ran from here clear down to Hagerstown," Haupt said.

"That's gone now," McPherson replied. "I understand the rebs are tearing up the rails, hauling them south to repair their own lines."

"If, gentlemen, and I have to emphasize the word 'if,'" Haupt continued, "our primary axis of advance is down the Cumberland, I propose to repair the line as rapidly as possible. The rebs cannot destroy the grading. As for every bridge on the line, fortunately the management of that line has records stored here in Harrisburg, so we have the specifications, and I'm ordering replacement bridges to be precut and ready to be loaded for the entire length of the line. I believe that if we advance down the Cumberland Valley, within two weeks we can have the entire line up and running again as long as I have the necessary manpower of trained personnel."

"You'll have them," Grant said sharply. "We must have a couple of thousand men in our ranks who've worked the rails before the war; we can temporarily detach them."

"That's a lot of manpower," Burnside interjected.

"Well spent," Haupt replied. "Twenty trains a day on that line could sustain the army while it advanced, cutting down drastically on our need for wagons and mules. I'm stockpiling over a hundred miles of track, twenty thousand ties, material for water tanks and switching. The Cumberland line managed to get five of its locomotives back here before the bridge was burned, and we'll get additional rolling stock and locomotives from the Pennsylvania and the Reading. The bridge a dozen miles above Marysville is still intact to the west shore, thank God, so we can run supplies directly down to you once the campaign starts.

"If, and again I'm only saying if, the campaign takes us down to the Potomac, once into Harper's Ferry, your new supply line can run out of the west from the Baltimore and Ohio. I'm stockpiling replacement bridges for that line as well. I only wish I had enough men and material. I think I could throw a connecting line from Hagerstown across down to the B&O in less than a month if I had five thousand men."

"We'll see," Grant said with a smile.

This man was the type of soldier he liked, and he was amazed that Haupt's skills were never fully appreciated here in the East. Haupt had only confessed to him the day before that he had been seriously contemplating retiring from the army, fed up with its bureaucracy and backstabbing. Fortunately Grant had been able to convince him to stay on to the end of the campaign, promoted him to major general, and given him complete control of all military operations on all railroads in the country.

And Haupt was indeed right. If the campaign did take them to the Potomac and beyond, it would be worth the effort to run a railroad track from Hagerstown the twenty miles to a hookup with the Baltimore and Ohio. Such an accomplishment would give him a link from Harrisburg to Harper's Ferry, and from there clear down to the Shenandoah Valley, linking as well back to the Midwest. It was the type of project undreamed of five years ago, to run a line twenty miles in one month, solely for the purpose of supporting an army in the field. Today, if need be, it could be done, and if he gave the order, it would be done.

"Other supplies?" Grant asked.

Haupt stood silent for a moment and seemed to sway. Grant looked over nervously at Elihu Washburne, who sat quietly, unobtrusively, in the corner of the tent. Elihu and Haupt had formed quite a bond over the last month. The way Haupt had stood up to Stanton had won his admiration, along with the wonders he had created in terms of bringing this army together.

Elihu shook his head.

"Perhaps later, General Haupt."

"No, sir. Just a minute more, and then, yes, I think you will have to excuse me."

Haupt took a deep breath, sweat glistening on his face.

"Ammunition. Enough stockpiled now for a strong defensive action but sustainable for only two days at most. Just over one hundred rounds per man in the ranks, two caissons of assorted solid shot, shell, and canister for the field pieces. The suppliers in New York and Massachusetts are working twenty-four hours a day, and we should be up to the levels you will need in four weeks as well.

"Artillery. You have a hundred and ten pieces with you now, a mix of Napoleons, three-inch ordnance rifles and Parrotts, two batteries of twenty-pounders, and one battery of thirty-pounders. Again, you should have a hundred more guns in a month."

"Billy Sherman is up to his ears in guns," Ord interjected. "He must have three hundred pieces with him between the guns we left behind and the ordnance captured at Vicksburg."

"Too difficult to ship now. I'd rather use the shipping for horses and get the guns from New York," Haupt replied.

"What about all that artillery still down in Mississippi?" Ord asked. "Surely Sherman can't use all of it?"

"I told him, if it's a burden, put what he can on boats to haul north and dump the rest in the Mississippi," Grant replied coolly.

No one spoke. Such a profligate waste of material, perfectly good field guns, shocked none of them anymore. If the guns were dumped, others could be made.

"Rations?" Grant asked.

"That's going ahead of schedule; it's convenient that we are near Philadelphia and New York. Hardtack is almost up to the level to support us for a month in the field, the same with salted pork, coffee, sugar, to-bacco, tea. Farmers from as far away as Berks County to the east are driv-ing in herds of cattle and swine; we'll have a good supply of food on the hoof. Medical supplies as well are more than sufficient."

He hesitated for a moment and again seemed to sway.

"I talked with the head of your medical corps this morning. Hospitals sufficient for twenty thousand casualties will be constructed here in Har-risburg. Mostly open-sided sheds and tents to start; bedding is being shipped in; volunteer nurses are being recruited through that Miss Barton that everyone is talking about."

Twenty thousand casualties. No one spoke. Though they were hard-ened by the campaign for Vicksburg and even Shiloh, the sheer magni-tude of so many wounded and sick was still daunting, but after Union Mills, the larger number had to be anticipated.

"Another reason I want the railroad repaired," Grant interjected. "We had hospital boats for our wounded at Vicksburg. Hauling wounded men back on a hundred miles of dirt road would be a nightmare."

"The other supplies—ether, chloroform, morphine, medical tools, stretchers, bandages, splints, crutches—all of it should be in place."

Haupt fell silent and looked over at Grant.

Grant could see that the man was about to have another violent attack.

"General Haupt, you are excused, sir, and please, will you get yourself over to my doctor and then take some rest?"

"Yes, sir," Haupt gasped and, bent over slightly at the waist, he stag-gered out of the tent.

Grant followed him with his gaze. Over two years of war he had learned to become hard when it came to the using of men. He had looked into the eyes of far too many, knew he was ordering them to their deaths or the destruction of their commands, and then told them to go, never hesitating, never showing sentiment. War had no room for that, no matter what it might do inside his heart. Haupt was valuable, far too valuable to use up, but it was obvious that the dysentery that was tormenting him was beginning to drain his life away. And yet he had to continue to use him rather than order him back to a hospital in the rear. He had tried that once, and the following morning he had found the man in the telegraphy station, dictating orders as fast as four scribes could take them down, his mind some sort of strange calculating machine that could not stop whirling.

Grant looked back to his three corps commanders and the various staff and division commanders gathered around the table.

"I want this army ready to move within a month," he announced.

There were nods of agreement, though he could see that Ord, if given the order to jump into the Susquehanna today, would do so.

"We are constrained, as are all armies, by our supplies. General Haupt is doing his best to see us through."

"And additional men?" Burnside asked. "I am still one division short of a standard corps. I would have liked to have brought along the Twenty-third Corps from my old command in Kentucky."

"I understand, Burnside. I would have preferred it as well, but we have to maintain some kind of force in Kentucky. You will receive an additional division by the end of the month."

"From where, sir?"

Grant hesitated for a brief instant.

"Eight colored regiments, currently being recruited in Ohio, New York, and Pennsylvania, are to report here. They'll be at nearly full strength. That should be six thousand additional men. Do you object?"

He watched Burnside carefully. More than one general would flatly refuse such an offer, even if it meant his command remained under-strength.

"No problem with that at all, sir," Burnside said and then he actually smiled. "Freemen or slaves?"

"Mostly freemen from the North, though we might have a regiment or two of untrained refugees from Maryland. Why?"

"Slaves are used to the toughest work; army life is a picnic in comparison."

"Until the minié balls start whistling," McPherson interjected.

"Still, I think the black man will prove to be a tough soldier. I'll take 'em."

"Fine then, they're yours. You appoint the division and brigade commanders. Make sure they are of like mind and can inspire these men. I suspect the president will be watching this closely. I don't want these men held back, nor do I want them thrown away as a sacrifice, but they will be expected to fight when the time comes."

As he spoke, he looked over at Elihu, who nodded in agreement.

"What about the Nineteenth Corps?" Ord asked.

The men around Ord nodded in agreement and anticipation. Nineteenth Corps was a familiar command to all of them. Though unfortunate to be under General Banks, they had campaigned well farther south on the Mississippi, misused at times by their leader, but good fighting men, nearly all from New England and New York. It was ironic that they, rather than western troops, had wound up on the lower Mississippi, a fate decided by the ability to ship them from northern ports to support Farrugat's naval assault up the river. The men had suffered terribly. For every battle loss, half a dozen were felled by ague or yellow fever. The men were ecstatic to be coming back north again, and would be eager for a fight on familiar terrain rather than the muddy swamps and bayous, which had bedeviled them for over a year.

Even now the convoy bearing them was coming from New Orleans, supposedly to begin docking at Philadelphia in a matter of days. The original command had close to thirty thousand in their ranks; a brigade of infantry, the locally recruited Corps d'Afrique, and some other militia to be left behind to garrison New Orleans. The famed Grierson, commander of their cavalry, a match for Stuart's men, was coming with his brigade as well, to be remounted in Philadelphia once they arrived.

Their arrival would increase his army by over thirty percent, giving him four solid corps of combat-experienced troops, all of them used to victory.

"The Nineteenth will fall in on Harrisburg within the week. We have to be careful with all these forces coming from the western theater. I don't want any slacking off over this next month," Grant said, and now his voice was sharp. "I've seen a bit of it already, some of the men swaggering around, lording it over the militia and the ninety-day regiments."

As he spoke, he turned and looked straight at old General Couch, who had come to him repeatedly with the complaint. There were still twenty thousand militia with him in Harrisburg, and the old general wanted to take them into the field, to convince as many as possible to reenlist for the duration of the campaign, or "the current emergency," as he was calling it. A number of fistfights had already broken out between the western veterans and the green recruits from the East. The camp of one Pennsylvania militia regiment had been raided only the night before, the men actually stripped of their uniforms, shoes, rifles, tentage, and choice rations, with the culprits running off into the night, hooting and laughing. The hospital was filled this morning with several dozen cases of broken bones and one man lingering near death with a fractured skull.

"Well," Ord interjected, "the boys have a right to be proud."

Grant glared at Ord. Damn! Ord knew it was his boys and was trying to cover up for them.

"I want an army that is united," Grant snapped. "It's why I left the name Army of the Tennessee behind when we got off the boat at Cairo. This is a new army. Do you understand that, a new army, the Army of the Susquehanna."

Everyone was silent.

"Do we understand each other? Any more thievery, any more brawls like last night, and I'll have the culprits bucked and gagged, then drummed out of the army, their regimental commander stripped of rank, and right up to corps someone will pay for it."

No one spoke, even Ord lowered his head, though Couch did smile, but his grin disappeared when Grant caught his eye.

"And by heavens, General Couch, if you can convince your men to sign on for the duration, enough to field another corps, they will march and they will fight like soldiers. I rode past your camp yesterday, and a pig wouldn't live in it. As for your men, if that is how they plan to look and fight, I'll ship every last one of them across to the rebels and have them sign up with Lee. With men like that in his command, it will only help us to win."

Now it was Couch's turn to look crestfallen.

"You have commanded a corps in the field, General Couch. I understand your reasons for resigning because of General Hooker. Given your experience, I expect you to whip your men into shape; militia, ninety-day regiments, I don't care. They are to be turned into soldiers ready to face Hood, Pickett, Scales, and Early. You've faced them before, Couch, and I'm asking you now, will your men be able to stand on the volley line a month from now? I know the mettle of the rest of my men, but yours I am not sure of, and by God if they break and we lose this war, I will hold you responsible."

Couch nervously looked around the room, the other three corps commanders all glaring at him.

"I will do my best, sir."

"You haven't answered my question, General."

Couch hesitated, cleared his throat, then finally nodded.

"I will have them ready, sir."

Grant turned away from him.

"Remember, we are one army now, all of us. There will be no room for mistakes either on your part," and he paused for a moment, "or mine."

He caught Elihu's eye, the congressman sitting intent, soaking up every detail.

"Our republic cannot sustain another Gettysburg or Union Mills. If this army is destroyed, our cause is finished. We are stripping every available soldier from our other fronts for this action. We might very well lose some of the gains made in the past year, perhaps a length of the Mississippi, maybe even New Orleans. But that, at this moment, is not of consequence to us. I have for us one goal and one goal only, to destroy General Lee's army in the field and to take Richmond."

No one muttered an approbation, or, worse yet, gave some sort of foolish patriotic reply. All were silent.

"Gentlemen, when we cross that river and move, I do not ever want to hear again someone worrying about what Lee is doing. I want Lee to worry about what we are doing. I do not want anyone worrying that an action taken might lose a battle, and thus the war. I want everyone focused on one thought, that the actions we take will win the battle and win the war. Do I make myself clear?"

Again no response, only a few nods, though a subtle smile did crease the faces of McPherson and Ord, men who had been with him for over a year.

"I've said enough. I want full drill every day except Sunday. I expect to see the roads east of here filled with men marching daily, full packs, good march discipline, and the men in shape. They've had their time to relax, and that is finished. I want to see good food and plenty of it, but no waste. The discipline against strong drink is to be kept in force, and that goes for my officers as well."

His glare moved from man to man; some met his eyes, some lowered their heads.

"We meet again three days from now, same time. Dismissed."

The men cleared the tent; outside he could hear them immediately start to talk, comments about the "old man's ready for a fight." Ord's distinctive, high-pitched laugh about a good chewing-out making a few men nervous.

"That certainly had some heat to it."

Grant looked up to see Elihu smiling at him.

"It was needed."

Grant extended his hand and stood up. Elihu had arrived just at the start of the meeting, fresh from the arduous roundabout journey to Washington and back.

"Tell me everything," Grant said, motioning to the chair by his side.

Elihu, who had sat through the meeting in formal attire, gladly took his jacket and tie off, his finely ruffled shirt plastered to his body with sweat. He groaned with delight, took a glass of lemonade, the precious ice long ago melted, and drained it off before sitting down.

"Some good, some bad."

"Go on."

"As you ordered, I brought Dan Sickles up here with me," Elihu said. Grant nodded.

246 NEWT GINGRICH AND WILLIAM R. FORSTCHEN

"His reaction when you told him you were escorting him to meet me?"

"He wasn't pleased, tried to beg off, said duties of command, all the usual. I handed him your written order and that took the wind out of his sails, though he did mutter about having to check with Secretary Stanton."

"And?"

"The letter from the president informing him he was to comply with all your orders settled his hash. He's waiting in a tent just down from here."

Grant looked over at his adjutant, Parker, who had remained silent in the corner of the tent throughout the meeting.

"Give Mr. Washburne and me about ten minutes, then go fetch General Sickles for me."

Parker grinned.

"Yes, sir." And he left the tent.

"How are things in Washington?"

"In an uproar. The siege is wearing nerves thin."

"They're most likely facing no more than one division of infantry and some cavalry."

"Still, Heintzelman is ordering all troops to stand in place within the fortifications; he fears a ruse and Stanton agrees."

Grant nodded his head.

"Fine for the moment but he should still be probing, making Lee a bit nervous, maybe forcing him to send some troops back that way."

"I carried that suggestion to the president; he said it's like watching a blind woman trying to catch a goose and cut its head off."

Grant chuckled softly.

"But Heintzelman did put up a good fight defending the city."

"Yes, he's good for a defensive fight," Grant said softly.

"Any thoughts on that?"

"Not yet, perhaps later. But what else?"

"You heard about President Davis and the state convention in Baltimore?"

"Just that they were meeting yesterday."

"The rebels have convened a new state legislature. It was sworn in late last night. Its first act was to officially declare that Maryland has withdrawn from the Union and joined the Confederate States of America. Adm. Franklin Buchanan was appointed provisional governor until an election can be held. Judge Richard Carmichael is provisional lieutenant governor and acting as governor until Buchanan can come up from Mobile."

"Interesting turn of events," Grant said noncommitally.

"A smart move by Davis. Carmichael is held in high regard, even by some pro-Unionists. I don't know if you are aware of this, but he was the presiding judge of the Seventh Circuit Court. Some damn coward and two of his cronies pistol-whipped the man nearly to death because of his pro-Southern leanings. It was an outrage felt across the entire state. He's acting as governor for the moment until Buchanan, who is a Maryland native and the highest ranking officer in the Confederate navy, comes up to take the post."

"The fact he commanded the ironclad *Virginia* will play well with some. Besides, I heard he's an able administrator."

"Exactly. You have a war hero with naval tradition that appeals to Baltimore. In fact, the man was born there, and is a well-respected judge who can work the political angles. A smart move by Davis."

"What about Fort McHenry?"

"Still holding out. That's a strange truce neither side wants to break at the moment. If Lee tries to seize it by a frontal attack, he'll lose thousands; the garrison is well reinforced now. On the other side, President Lincoln has ordered the garrison commander not to fire unless fired upon. If we set off another conflagration in Baltimore, it only will serve the other side."

"The heavy artillery captured around Baltimore?"

"Hard to get accurate reports on that. Some say the guns positioned up on Federal Hill are now all 'Quaker guns,' just painted logs, but with so many civilians around that would be hard to conceal. There are some reports that Lee will dispatch the heavy-siege equipment toward Washington; others say he'll finally be forced to try and reduce McHenry."

"Frankly, I hope he fires on McHenry."

"Why?"

"The symbolism of it, General Grant. The site of our gallant star-spangled banner remaining defiant against the British. Every artist and editorial writer in the North will have a field day with that one."

Grant had never really thought of it in that light. As for the song, he found it far too difficult to follow, the latter stanzas rather overblown.

"So far the news you bring is bearable; what's the bad news?"

Elihu smiled and shook his head.

"Lee is reportedly starting to get reinforcements. The first of Beauregard's men are reported to be in Baltimore. There are accounts he'll get upward of thirty thousand fresh troops."

"We'll see," Grant replied without any emotion.

"We know as well that he is absolutely burdened with artillery. His standing force, the guns taken at Union Mills that weren't spiked, additional field pieces at Baltimore. Word is he has two hundred and fifty guns and the ammunition to keep them firing for days. They're converting some of their infantry over to artillerymen."

Grant said nothing. In an open-field fight, the type of terrain to be found in a fair part of Maryland—expansive fields and pastures—combined with good roads to move the guns rapidly, this could be a problem.

"Sickles," Elihu continued. "He's cut up a fuss with Stanton that the Nineteenth Corps should be incorporated into his command, and Stanton agrees."

"Damn him, Stanton has to quit interfering," Grant muttered softly.

"The president said it's up to you though, since you have direct command in the field."

"Thank God for that."

"Sickles is also diverting trainloads of equipment and supplies, at least that's the rumor. His Tammany friends have raised five regiments; they paid a lot for them, too. The governor of New York, when he had them sworn in, specifically stated they were taking duty with the Army of the Potomac."

"We're going to put a stop to that."

"Be careful, Sam. Even Lincoln conceded that for the moment Dan Sickles cannot be touched, so I have to ask that you tread lightly."

"I know, I know."

"That's it in rough form. The president is keeping his nerve up to the hilt. At least fifty papers up North have already declared, or will after to-day's announcement of Maryland's secession, that the president should negotiate a cease-fire with Davis."

"His response?"

"In confidence?"

"Of course."

"He said he wished it was winter; that way he could use the papers as kindling to warm his feet."

Grant could not help but laugh at the image it conjured.

Elihu grinned.

"He made another reference to how he might use them as well, but good taste forbids me from citing him."

"More in line with what I was thinking."

"I won't quote you, either, General."

Both men smiled, the interlude interrupted by the clearing of a throat outside the open flap of the tent. It was Parker, General Sickles by his side.

Grant took a deep breath and stood up.

"General Sickles, please come in and join us."

His tone was neutral, not genial, nor cold in the manner in which he had just addressed some of his closest companions only minutes before.

Sickles stopped at the entryway and formally saluted, Grant returning the salute then motioning for the commander of the Army of the Potomac to come in.

Elihu went through the motions of being a proper host, pouring a glass of lemonade and offering it to Dan, who politely refused.

"If you don't mind, sir, after such a hot and arduous trip up here, I'd prefer something a little stronger."

"We don't serve liquor at this headquarters, General."

"Oh, really. Too bad. If you should need some, sir, do let me know; I keep an excellent selection at my headquarters. It is good for morale at times."

Dan reached into his hip pocket, pulled out a flask, picked up an empty lemonade glass, poured several ounces of brandy, and took a drink.

Grant said nothing, eyes cold.

Sickles drained half the glass and put it back down, his features going slightly red, and he smiled.

"It is good to see you, General Grant."

"I'd like a report, General Sickles, on the status of the Army of the Potomac."

"It is moving along, sir, but slowly, I regret to tell you. As I indicated to you in my report filed last week, the army has been reorganized into three corps, the old Third, the Fifth, and the Sixth. I have a little more than thirty thousand men now under arms, nearly all of them veterans of the best sort. I have eighty guns, four thousand men mounted."

He fell silent.

"That's it?"

"Yes, sir, there is not much else to say. The men are still recovering from the, how shall I say it, mishandling they suffered from last month, but morale is improving, the men training for the next campaign. May I ask when that will begin?"

"When we are ready, General Sickles, and not before."

Sickles nodded thoughtfully, on the surface taking no offense from the obvious rejection regarding a discussion of operational plans.

"You heard about the traitors in Maryland switching sides," and Sickles looked over at Elihu.

"Yes, the congressman just told me."

"Some sort of demonstration, perhaps on your part," Dan offered, "might be of advantage now, to show them we will not take this lightly."

"As I just said, General Sickles, when we are ready and not before."

Sickles nodded and drained the rest of the glass. He started to open his flask again, but the look in Grant's eye made him stop.

"Is there something you wish to tell me, General Grant? I have traveled a long way to meet with you, time that frankly I had hoped to spend with my command."

"My command," Grant said softly.

Sickles froze, eyes unblinking.

"Sir?"

"The Army of the Potomac is my command as well, and will obey my orders to the letter."

Dan forced a smile.

"Sir, but of course. However, you being new to the East, sir, I daresay that there are unique aspects to the Army of the Potomac that will take time to fully understand."

"It is but one component of the armies of our republic. It will be run like any other army, will fight like I expect every army to fight, will answer my commands, and will see this war through to its proper conclusion."

Sickles said nothing, the smile frozen on his face.

"You, sir, have direct field command; that was the decision of the secretary of war and President Lincoln. I hope, sir, that you fully understand that responsibility and live up to the obligation of your command and the obligation to lead your men properly."

Sickles's features darkened.

"Sir. I fought with those men through the Peninsula and every campaign since right to Union Mills," his words coming out forced, through clenched teeth. "I think, sir, I do not need to be lectured on my obligation to my men."

Grant sat back in his chair, the silence in the tent chilling.

"I don't think General Grant meant any offense to you personally," Elihu interrupted.

"I should hope not. I know my men and they know me. If I had been listened to at Chancellorsville, at Gettysburg on the second day, at Union Mills, we would not be in the fix we now find ourselves in."

"I will not dispute your suggested decisions in those battles, General Sickles," Grant replied. "I am just stating that in the future you will coordinate your actions with my direct orders. If we understand that, sir, I know we will work together well."

"Fine then, sir," Sickles responded, voice still strained, "I understand what you are saying. Is there anything else you wish to discuss?"

"Regarding the Nineteenth Corps."

"Sir?" Now his features shifted in an instant to open-faced innocence. "Is there a problem with their shipment to Philadelphia?"

"No. It is just that they will be detailed to this army here in Harrisburg."

"Sir. Is that prudent? I am outnumbered and Lee's army is little more than thirty miles away while you are here, a hundred miles from the front."

"You have the mile-wide Susquehanna between you and him, that river patrolled by gunboats. I doubt seriously if General Lee will make any demonstration against you, and the men you have, who as you said are all veterans, would certainly be more than a match if he tried to force a crossing. I am confident you can hold with the numbers you have."

Sickles's features were again frozen, as if he was calculating his chances of winning the argument.

"I understand, General," he said quietly.

"Fine then, I hope you may join my staff and me for dinner tonight."

"Yes, thank you, sir."

Sickles stood up to leave.

"And, General Sickles, one more thing," Grant said casually, as if he was about to address a minor issue.

"Yes?"

"A week and a half ago I passed through Perryville after my visit to Washington. I went looking for you, in order to have this meeting. Your staff claimed you could not be found."

"Sir, I was surprised to hear that you were in the area. I was out inspecting units in the field. I hurried back but you had already taken train and left."

"Next time, sir, when I visit the Army of the Potomac, I expect to see its commander as well."

"I apologize for the failure of my staff, sir."

"Fine then, that's all."

Sickles stiffened, features red, saluted, which salute Grant returned while remaining seated, and left.

Elihu exhaled noisily.

"I hate to say it, Grant, but even I could use a drink after that."

Grant looked over at him coldly, and Elihu smiled in apology.

"Well, you certainly blistered the paint off of him."

"Had to be done. Let's hope he toes the line now. In private I'll admit he has the makings of a good general in him, a good tactical sense. I studied the reports on Chancellorsville, and the man was indeed right. If he had pushed forward as he wanted, he'd have taken Jackson apart on that flanking march. He has the stomach for a fight.

"But he's too much like our old friend McClernand; he doesn't know when to keep his mouth shut and is always looking for his own political gain."

"And you fired McClernand," Elihu said.

"I hope that was different. Frankly, if I could bring that man to be part of my command, he might prove his mettle as well. At least he fights, and that's more than can be said for a lot of corps commanders. I'm willing to give him his chance. He had the guts to give it back to me a bit, which I respect. Let's see if he can give it back to Lee when the time comes."

"That comment about the liquor, that was uncalled for," Elihu replied sharply.

"You just asked for a drink yourself."

Elihu shrugged.

"Sorry."

"No need to apologize. I'm past that now. Remember, I made a promise to Lincoln on it, and I find he's one man whose respect I want."

Elihu smiled.

"I know what you mean. He's grown. He's not the same man at all I put up for nomination three years ago. He's only seven years older than me, and yet I feel like he's ancient now."

Elihu looked off and smiled.

"I know you won't lose your nerve. I think that in what's to come, their president really doesn't matter. It's down to Lee or Lincoln and who will break first. That's what will decide it."

Grant said nothing. His cigar had gone out and he tossed it aside, fished in his pocket for another, and, striking a match, he puffed it to life.

"It's going to be a hot day," he said quietly.

Chapter Fifteen

Baltimore

August 9, 1863
3:00 P.M.

The band played "Dixie" for what must have been the tenth time as the last of Beauregard's men marched past, hats off, cheering. As Lee watched, yet again he was caught up in that fleeting moment when war did indeed have glory to it.

The Army of Northern Virginia, except for Pickett's division, which had been assigned garrison duty within the city, and Scales's, which still shadowed Washington, was encamped in the fields west of Baltimore, along the line of fortifications that had been so easily pierced three weeks before.

The parade ground for this grand review had been carefully chosen by Walter Taylor. A gently sloping ridge, where the famed divisions of the Army of Northern Virginia could deploy across a front of nearly two miles, regiment after regiment, the hard-fighting battalions from Virginia, Georgia, Texas, the Carolinas, Florida, Mississippi, and Alabama. The heroes of Fredericksburg, of Gettysburg, and of Union Mills. Shot-torn standards were proudly held aloft, whipping in the stiff afternoon breeze. The day was still bathed in sunlight, though the western horizon was dark with approaching storms.

Before them, across the broad, open valley, the twenty thousand men that Beauregard had brought to Maryland had advanced in columns of

company front, the men in general ragged and lean, veterans of the hard-fought campaigns in the swamps around Charleston, their uniforms sun bleached to light gray or butternut. A few regiments were neatly attired, militia units from Georgia and North Carolina that till now had known only soft duty, the occasional chasing down of deserters or Unionist bushwhackers up in the hills. These men were dressed in solid gray, carried backpacks, their muskets shiny.

The arriving units had paraded down the length of the Army of Northern Virginia, passing beneath sharp, hardened eyes, veterans, some only seventeen years old but still veterans, who looked appraisingly, nodding with approval at the boys from Charleston, remaining silent at the sight of the militia, in their hearts concerned but also smugly glad because the stay-at-homes were now going to see the "elephant" for real.

The unwritten orders from Lee's headquarters had been sharp and clear. The men of Beauregard's command, now officially the Third Corps of the Army of Northern Virginia, were to be greeted as brothers, no taunts, no airs; if victory was to be finally theirs, their blood would be needed as well.

As the last of Beauregard's men marched the two-mile length of the review, Wade Hampton's brigade put in their appearance, Jeb Stuart in the lead, his arm still in a sling from the bullet taken in Baltimore. The troopers deployed out, drew sabers, forming a battlefront a quarter-mile wide, keeping alignment, advancing first at walk, bugles sounding the walk to trot, and then a canter. The waning sun, disappearing behind the roiling storm clouds, reflected off a thousand drawn blades.

"Charge!"

Stuart was in the lead by half a dozen lengths, hat blown off, mouth open, shouting the command, then roaring with delight as the troopers, leaning over in their saddles, blades pointed forward, broke into a mad gallop. A wild rebel yell erupted from the charging line, to be greeted by the enthusiastic roar of the watching army, tens of thousands of voices commingling, battle flags held aloft, waving back and forth, the music of the band drowned out, even the musicians now lowering their instruments and joining in the cheer, the music far more piercing and soul-stirring than anything they could ever hope to create.

On the slope above the army, tens of thousands of civilians from Baltimore, who had come out to witness the show, joined in the cheering as well.

Unable to contain himself, Lee stood tall in his stirrups, Traveler's head up, ears pricked back, as if ready to join in the mad dash sweeping before them, the thunder of the charge echoing, and then drowned out as ten batteries, deployed to Lee's left, fired a salute of fifty guns, the thumping roar booming down the line, the cheering of the men redoubling at the thunder of the guns, stirring the blood, filling all with the vision of all that they had done, and all they would still do when next the guns fired for real.

The last echo of one of the heavy thirty-pounders drifted away. The smoke swirled and eddied eastward, driven by the wind of the approaching storm, the distant heavens matching the reports with the roll of thunder, the shimmering golden light of the sun now disappearing behind the dark, gray-green clouds.

Stuart, turning out from the charging line, cantered up to Lee, sweat glistening on his face, and with drawn saber he saluted; his mount, with a gentle urging, lowering his head and lifting a front leg in salute as well.

Grinning, Lee returned the salute.

"Magnificent, General Stuart," he proclaimed, "a fitting climax to a glorious day."

All along the two-mile line, commands echoed from division generals, to brigadiers, to regimental commanders. Hundreds of fifers and drummers picked up the beat, music playing, regiments forming into dense columns to march back to their encampments. Those closest to Lee, parading past, holding hats aloft, cheered him and the president of the Confederacy by his side.

Lee looked over at Davis, normally so sphinx-like. He was smiling, breathing hard.

"By the Almighty, General Lee, with an army such as this we can lick the world," Davis proclaimed.

And for a moment he believed it as well, swept into the passion of it all, the tens of thousands of his men, rested, fit, well fed, eager now to go back into the fray and finish it. They had never known real defeat, they had taken Baltimore without effort, they had brought another state into the Confederacy, and now they were reinforced back up to a strength of over fifty thousand rifles and two hundred and fifty artillery pieces. He knew that in the next action they could sweep the field again. He could see it in their eyes, these men confident of victory. And their spirit leapt into his soul. They were ready.

A pavilion of open-sided tents had been set up atop the slope, the tents linked together to form a vast covered area that could accommodate several hundred people. Tonight there would be a ball, the finest of Baltimore invited to attend with their ladies. Dinner would be a "special repast in the tradition of the Army of Northern Virginia"—fried and basted salt pork served with a sprinkling of ground hardtack, the first sweet corn of the season, and "Confederate coffee" made with chickory. It would be seen as delightful and quaint, the talk of a city so used to dining on far better fare. The cooks, of course, were substituting fresh bacon for the salt pork, the topping was made with real bread crumbs, and since the army was awash in captured coffee, the real treat would be provided instead, but still the officers and guests would wink at the substitution. One of the famed Booth family, who by chance was in Baltimore when the city was taken, would provide the afterdinner entertainment with dramatic excerpts from Shakespeare's plays, and then the Regimental Band from the Twenty-sixth North Carolina would offer a selection of waltzes, polkas, and reels.

Lee with Davis, Beauregard, Benjamin, and Stuart at his side rode up to the pavilion. Longstreet and Hood, coming over from their respective commands, arrived at the pavilion just behind Lee.

Hood was positively beaming; he had always been one to enjoy such pageantry, and for once the mood between him and Stuart was openly jovial. Dismounting, Lee looked over at Longstreet, who stood to one side, and approached.

"Did you enjoy the parade?"

"You know I find them to be a bit tiresome, sir. Rather have the men out drilling."

"Still, it's good for their spirits. It boosts morale to see the army assembled and a proper greeting to General Beauregard's men."

"We're as ready as we'll ever be," Longstreet replied. "You could see that today."

Lee smiled; it was a concession that on Old Pete's part that the grand review had caught his soul as well.

Yes, they were ready; the question was, To do what?

One corner of the pavilion had been set aside for Davis, Lee, and his staff to have a private repast before the beginning of the afternoon's and evening's festivities. Orderlies from his staff, well turned out in new uniforms, waited, the table already spread with the finest Baltimore could offer—oysters, champagne, fried clams, half a dozen selections of wine, crabs freshly boiled and spiced crab cakes, French brandies, thinly sliced beef, sweet corn, and, of course, fried chicken.

For once he did not feel guilty as he looked at the cornucopia of food spread upon the table. His men had been indulging in the same, except, naturally, for the spirits, eating as the Army of Northern Virginia had not eaten since the hard, bitter days before Richmond, the year before.

Already spoiled by Yankee largesse in their march north to Chambersburg, and then to Gettysburg and beyond, they had known true luxury the last three weeks. With President Davis ready to sign a voucher order, the warehouses of Baltimore had been stripped clean of anything that would feed and boost the morale of this army. The men had marveled at the cans of condensed milk issued to them to lighten their coffee. And coffee! Not just any coffee, but a selection of beans from Jamaica, Brazil, Colombia, so that a lively trade had developed between regiments issued one or the other.

Every man now had new shoes, hats, blankets, even trousers and jackets, the milliners conveniently ready with gray dye to convert trousers that only the month before had been destined for the armies of the North. Canvas for tents had been found, including the very canvas that now covered the pavilion, along with hundreds of saddles, wagons that had escaped from the rout at Westminster, ammunition for both artillery and rifles, two hundred additional ambulances for the medical corps, thousands of mules, yet more remounts for the cavalry, forge wagons for artillery, even portable bakery wagons containing ovens and steam engines "borrowed" from fire departments, which might prove of use in some unexpected way.

For an army that had marched for far too long on lean stomachs it was as if they had gone to heaven while still alive. Bullocks by the hundreds had been driven into the camps; each night the regiments offered choices of fresh beef until they could eat no more. Wagons loaded with sweet corn came in from the countryside, and fresh-faced girls made it a practice to visit the camps, bearing loaves of home-baked bread, cakes, and cookies, greeted with reverent respect, at least on the surface, by these hard-fighting veterans. They had endeared themselves to the citizens of Baltimore, who were now eager to compare the valiant and yet humble Christian boys of the South with the hawk-faced Yankees of Massachusetts and New York.

Far more than any diplomatic efforts of Benjamin, or cool leadership of Davis, the ordinary rank and file of the Army of Northern Virginia, so hard and remorseless in battle, had shown themselves, at heart, to be really nothing more than boys and young men, desperate for home, for the simple things in life, and in so doing had won Baltimore back to the South.

Already dozens of requests for the right to marry had come up from the ranks, and Lee had been forced to pass a strict injunction that such things would have to wait until the war ended, unless it could be proven that the couple had known each other before the war and were now, by this circumstance, reunited. As a gesture of this new joining of Maryland to the cause, both he and Davis had attended a wedding only the day before, between a young boy on Stuart's staff, the same Lieutenant Jenkins who had infiltrated into Baltimore, and the object of his affection, the charming young daughter of a Methodist minister, the couple separated for two long years. Their wedding had become the social event of the month and was widely reported in all the newspapers.

As he looked around the pavilion he saw young Jenkins, still dressed in his formal uniform, and as he caught the boy's eye, he smiled as the young man blushed and lowered his head, having come from his all too brief honeymoon to participate in the review.

The entourage settled down under the pavilion, the breeze sweeping in now cool, the storm front approaching. Orderlies and staff scurried about, offering fresh pastries, coffee, wine, raw oysters, and even small, crystal shot glasses of brandy.

President Davis, showing his delight at the proceedings, accepted a glass of French wine and raised the glass high.

"To the success of our cause," he announced.

The group stood, Lee taking a glass as well, though merely swallowing a drop or two for the toast.

"And to France," Benjamin added. "May they soon stand by our side."

"To France!"

The group sat down, and for a moment there was only polite conversation, commentary about the grandeur of the review, and anticipation for the evening's festivities.

Davis, sitting beside Lee, leaned over.

"I must say, never have I seen the men so fit, so eager, General Lee."

"Thank you, sir, the past weeks have indeed been a tonic for them. Our boys deserved it after all they have accomplished."

Davis nodded, sipping from his glass of wine.

Benjamin came around the table to join them.

"The French consul is waiting to see us, sir," he said.

"In a few minutes, Judah. After all, we can't go running to him."

Judah smiled.

"He finally shared with me the dispatch he sent to the Emperor Napoleon III."

Davis, eyes sharp, looked up at Benjamin.

"I transcribed it as best I could after meeting with him this morning."
Judah reached into his breast pocket, pulling out a sheet of paper, which
he then handed to Davis.

"His report predicts that by the middle of autumn the Army of Northern Virginia will meet and defeat the new army being created by Grant. He
also predicts that General Johnston in the West will recapture Vicksburg."

Davis said nothing. The report had just come in the day before that
Johnston had indeed ventured such an attack, now that most of the Army
of the Tennessee, except for Sherman's corps, had come east. Sherman
had handed Johnston a stunning defeat, routing his army and driving it
clear across Mississippi and into northern Alabama.

"Well, the dispatch went out a week and a half ago," Davis said.

"Fortunately. I think that the dispatch, combined with the dozens of
newspapers, both north and south, which were sent along with it, might
do the trick. Napoleon's forces are stuck in Mexico. His promises to the
Hapsburg have drawn them into the fray; there are even regiments of
troops from Austria being dispatched to Mexico. If ever he has a chance to
ensure his success and prestige in both Europe and the New World, it is
now, at this moment. He will commit to us because a Union victory would
be a disaster for French policy. They would be forced to abandon Mexico
if Lincoln wins. We are their only hope."

Lee shifted uncomfortably. The thought of European soldiers again
tramping across the Western Hemisphere left him uncomfortable. It
struck at the almost hereditary spirit, inculcated into his blood, that this
hemisphere was a world to be left alone by the monarchies of Europe.

Davis smiled as he scanned Judah's notes.

"How long?" Davis asked.

"It went out under a fast packet, flying French colors so it could not
be stopped by the blockade."

With that, Judah grinned. Fort McHenry still held, a ring of Union
warships lying out in the harbor. No ships had been allowed in since the
city fell, but through a nice sleight of legal hand, a ship's ownership had
been reassigned to a French company, and by international law it could
not then be prevented from sailing. The incident two years earlier of
Confederate diplomats being stopped on the high seas by the Union navy
aboard a ship flying English colors had almost precipitated war, and since
then the Lincoln administration had been careful to a fault to avoid a repeat. The ship had been allowed to pass, with the consul's assistant on
board.

"The ship should arrive within the week in France. Maybe as early as
three or four days from now if the passage is smooth. We paid extra for the

fastest ship in the harbor and a full load of fuel on board. A month from now we might hear the results."

A group of civilian well-wishers came down and the president stood up, extending his hand, Lee standing as well and then backing away from the crowd, though for several minutes he had to endure a small crowd of young ladies who gathered around him, beaming, pressing him with questions, which he politely answered until Walter came up to him with the "usual" excuse that there were some "urgent issues that needed to be addressed."

Grateful as always for Walter's tactful help, he moved away from the crowd. Benjamin detached himself as well and walked over to Lee's side. Without comment the two drifted away, walking down to the line of artillery pieces, the gunners swabbing the bores clean. At Lee's approach a gunnery captain sensed that the general wanted some privacy, and detailed the men off. Lee returned the man's salute and nodded his head in thanks.

The storm from the west was coming closer and the other gun crews were laying tarps over limber chests and gun barrels. The breeze was cool, refreshing.

"I assume the president told you he is returning to Richmond tomorrow?" Benjamin asked.

"Yes, he mentioned it just before the review."

"But I'll be staying on for a while."

Lee smiled. He had developed a genuine affection for Benjamin, whereas the presence of Davis had seriously disrupted the routine at headquarters and imposed significantly on his own time, with Davis asking for daily conferences, discussions, and meetings with various representatives from Maryland. It was a political side of his job that he was glad to be freed from.

Lee looked across the field. He was used to a large degree of independence in his operations, answering to no one, and to have Davis now sitting in on every council of war, and attempting to be, at times, part of the planning, had made things difficult.

"Impressive review today, General Lee."

Yes, it had indeed been impressive, and for a moment he had allowed it to sweep him away. There was something about tens of thousands of troops, massed together, the cheering, the music, the precision of columns on the march, that stirred his soul like nothing else. At such moments one did indeed feel invincible. War had changed so much since he had taken the oath on the plains of West Point so many years ago, but the moments of pageantry had not gone away, and they masked the illusion of what the real purpose was.

He had agreed to the pressure exerted by the president to make another try on Washington, though he felt it would be an exercise in futility, except for one hope, that by threatening the capital yet again, it just might dislodge Grant, Sickles, or both from their inaccessible enclaves north of the Susquehanna.

The ring was beginning to tighten and Lee knew it. Davis had impressed upon him for the last three weeks that the thought of Baltimore falling back into Union hands was intolerable, and he had to agree, that now, after taking it, after the public joining of Maryland to the Confederacy—though there had been no real benefit from that so far other than grist for the newspapers—they could not let it fall.

That meant he was tied to this region and now to an essentially defensive posture of holding the city, but at the same time forced to make another try on Washington.

And every day, he knew, the Union forces were getting stronger in spite of Union Mills, in spite of the riots, in spite of the governor of New York declaring that his regiments would only go to Sickles. In spite of all that, Grant was building.

The first heavy drops of rain came down, carrying with them that warm, rich scent of an approaching storm. Flashes of lightning snapped across the sky, the rolling booms of the thunder coming now like a counterpoint to the salvos fired by the guns.

Lee looked around; he did not want to go back to the pavilion. A headquarters tent for one of the batteries stood just behind a row of Napoleons, and the two made for it. Yet again, the men, seeing Lee approach, stiffened, saluted, looking deferential.

He hated to roust them out of their shelter but he wanted a few minutes alone with Judah before the party. He knew Judah would enjoy himself tonight, and he wanted the man now, when his mind was still clear.

Lee made eye contact with a major, who stood before him nervously.

"Major, I truly hate to disturb you," Lee said quietly. "But may I ask your indulgence? The secretary and I need to talk."

"An honor, sir," the major said, obviously delighted that his tent had been so chosen, and he guided his men off.

Lee and Benjamin stepped under the awning and faced the storm, watching as the wall of rain approached, lashing the opposite crest.

"I'd like to talk frankly, General Lee," Judah said, looking straight over at him.

"I hope you would do just that."

"I believe France will enter the war, but any hopes for England I doubt now, and they are the strength we really need. If Napoleon III comes in, the English will just smile and sit back, waiting to see him take a major defeat. The Prussians would enjoy that as well. The effect you created at Union Mills will have far-reaching consequences, General Lee."

"The maneuvering between European powers was never part of my intent. All I want to do is finish this war."

The rain swept across the field, driving the two back into the tent. From the pavilion they could hear shouts, laughter, some cries of distress.

"The conversation with Rabbi Rothenberg," Lee said, lowering his head. "I've dwelt on it ever since."

"I have, too."

"Did you broach the subject to the president?"

"Yes, I did. Twice now. He has categorically refused to even consider it. He says that we are on the edge of a final victory. To make such a concession now would actually be a sign of weakness, according to him. He even suggested that some states might even secede from the Confederacy if we attempted it."

Lee sighed. That thought had of course occurred to him. What an absurdity, but then again, what was to prevent it? After all, once the Union was broken, the precedent had been set. Yes, perhaps several of the states, so dependent were they on the slave economy, just might do that. One final suicidal gesture.

"All my arguments failed, even the foreign policy advantage with England, which I pushed the hardest. He is confident the war will be resolved by October, and even if we did what the rabbi said, it would be six months or more before it would begin to impact the British government, while on the other hand Napoleon can pretty well do as he pleases, whenever he wants."

Lee put his hands behind his back and gazed out at the storm now lashing the open fields, gusts of wind causing the tent to billow and flutter.

"I've been ordered by the president to allow owners to repossess escaped slaves hiding here in Maryland."

"I know."

"Slave owners here may also lease their slaves to the Confederacy and send them south."

"And what will you do?" Judah asked. "You know what will happen; free blacks by the hundreds, maybe thousands, will be kidnapped in all the confusion."

Lee shook his head.

"I keep thinking of the logic of what Rabbi Rothenberg said. I will confess I find it difficult to imagine the black man as my social equal. But before God? That is what troubles me. Where would the Savior stand upon this question? That song the Yankees love to sing, 'as He died to make men holy, let us die to make men free.' It does have power to it, even if it is nothing but rhetoric."

"And the president's orders?"

Lee said nothing for a moment.

"I'm sworn to obey all orders of my government."

"And will you?"

Lee looked over at Judah.

"Please don't press me. I find the order repugnant. But can I refuse, then expect the unswerving obedience of my own men? For in battle that is what I will need if we are to win."

"You can do so as a moral statement," Judah said.

Lee looked at him appraisingly. Then he smiled and said nothing.

"Perhaps we can still resolve this issue by finishing the fight as quickly as possible," Lee finally replied.

"Do you honestly think you can do that?"

"Mr. Secretary, if I were not confident that I can still win, now there would indeed be a moral question. I would have to tell the president that, and I have not done so. Yes, the odds are steep; their strength is gathering yet again. But on the other side, it is no worse than it was seven weeks ago when we crossed into Pennsylvania. I will have to face two armies. One, our old opponents, the Army of the Potomac. After Union Mills they will be off balance, terribly off balance, and nervous. I can exploit that. The second army? It is an unknown, but then again so are we to them. They are in strange territory as well.

"Tomorrow Wade Hampton will take his brigade north. I need to know more about Grant. We have newspaper reports, but they are unreliable, as you know. The position of their Nineteenth Corps is a crucial piece of information. Which army they are positioned with will indicate much."

"Wouldn't it be easier just to get some spies up there, or scouts? Though I'm no tactician, sir, I'll be the first to admit."

Lee smiled. It was an obvious reference to Davis's daily interference at the staff meetings, urging positioning of regiments, wishing to move them like chess pieces. Davis, as a former brigade commander himself in Mexico, and as secretary of war in the previous administration, did have a good head for things military. He had, in fact, been far less interfering than Lincoln. But in this campaign, sensing that victory was near, he had taken to interfering more.

"Please, sir, your advice is always welcome to me," Lee said.

"I'm uneasy about this raid you are ordering north of the Susque-hanna."

"Why?"

"The river is still swollen, places to ford are few. Just a thought on my part, sir."

"I want to stir them up. If we can penetrate, get the information I seek, then perhaps push farther, threaten Lancaster, or even Reading, or the outskirts of Philadelphia, it will trigger another panic, possibly renewed riots. I think it is worth the risk."

"Rabbi Rothenberg, with his love of Napoleon, told me that the Army of Northern Virginia is like Napoleon's army in June of 1815."

"How is that?"

"Wellington and Blucher's armies. Together they would outnumber us. If you can drive a wedge between them, defeat one, and then turn upon the other, there is still a chance."

Lee smiled and said nothing. The intensity of the storm was at its height, sheets of cold rain lashing down, and he stood by the entrance to the tent, looking off, flashes of lightning arcing the sky.

Philadelphia

August 11, 1863
4:00 P.M.

Cpl. John Miller stood at attention under the blazing sun. He and the men of his company had been standing thus for the last ten minutes as their white drill sergeant paced up and down the line, delivering a lecture as old as the armies of Caesar, discussing with them their lineage, legitimacy, how "his" army had indeed fallen on hard times if the men before him were now part of it, how the best thing possible would be their complete slaughter on the first volley and other such minor threats.

The sergeant did not really know his audience. Most of the men around John had known nothing but a life of abuse and denial. Most of them were freemen, born in the North or in Baltimore. Nearly all had been laborers, farmhands, dockworkers, mill workers. For John, this session under the sun was a minor annoyance compared to being in Abbott's mill in July, when the hot iron was going through the rollers, sparks flying.

His body was a crosshatching of scars, deep burns, so many in fact that his white lieutenant, seeing him one evening with his shirt off, came up and sympathically asked if his master had whipped him. The young man was embarrassed when John told him about the scars, actually concerned that he might have insulted him by implying he had been a slave. That

conversation, talking about his work in the mill, his being foreman to twenty colored workers, his knowledge of writing, even some of the literature he took pleasure in, resulted in the two stripes on his sleeve the next day and an increase in pay, which meant that Sarah and the children, staying with her sister, would no longer be dependent on kin for charity.

"All right, you benighted bastards, let's do it one more time," the sergeant roared.

"Forward march!"

The company line, eighty men formed in two ranks, stepped off, moving like an undulating wave across the parade ground. John, as corporal, on the right of the line, kept looking toward the center, carefully measuring his pace to match the sergeant's.

"Keep watching the center, keep watching the center," he hissed, reaching out to push the man next to him up. The line buckled and wavered, keeping some semblance of formation.

The sergeant, now marching backward, kept up a steady cadence count; most all the men had finally mastered that, the steady tramp of left, right, left, right. . . .

"Company, by the right wheel, march!"

John instantly stopped in place, the man behind him almost banging into him as he took one more step.

The line started to turn, again wavering, one man tripping in the front rank, stumbling, breaking up the center.

"Move it, double time, double time!"

The line swung, bent like a snake, almost disintegrated.

"Halt!"

"God in heaven above, preserve me," the sergeant cried, taking off his hat and throwing it on the ground. One of the men actually stepped forward to pick it up for him.

"Get back in line there! You're a soldier, not my goddamn servant. If I want my hat picked up, I'll order you!"

John could not help but grin slightly. The sergeant had not even realized he had just complimented them. He had called them soldiers, not servants. The finer nuance was not lost on many of the men, who, even while the sergeant was swearing, had been looking sidelong at each other, a flicker of a smile on more than one face.

If this sergeant wanted to stand them under the sun all day, swear and roar, march them back and forth, that was fine with them. Dawn to dusk in a mill in July—this was like Sunday in comparison.

John knew that there was far more, however, than simple physical endurance that would be the final issue here. This new regiment had to learn to march, live, and fight as one. Just as in the mill, where a single misstep by one man could kill an entire crew. Something he had seen beyond counting, men turned to cinders by a blast of molten iron, caught in rollers, crushed in presses. Death and hardship were no strangers to him nor to the rest.

His only fear, the fear of all the men standing there beneath the hot August sun, was that it might be over before they were ready. The regiment had only started to form less than two weeks ago. They had come some distance in those two weeks; uniforms had been issued, shoes, which had caused agony for many of the men until the sergeant had shown them how to break in the heavy leather "brogans," as he called them, by first soaking them in hot water and then putting them on, so that the shapeless form molded somewhat to their feet.

They had yet to receive their rifles though, and rumors were sweeping the city and the newspapers that another great battle was brewing. The horror for all of them was that Lee might be defeated and they would not be there to do their part.

The men from Baltimore were imbued with a dream, that they would march in triumph back into their city. And yet he knew as well how much of a dream that might be. In his walk from Baltimore to Port Deposit he had seen the panicked Union troops falling back, running blindly whenever there was a report that rebel cavalry was closing in. He had seen it after finally crossing the river, where to his amazement a church group was helping to provide transport for colored refugees to Wilmington or Philadelphia. What had been the Army of the Potomac was gathering there, and though they were impressive at first sight, it was evident that they were but the survivors of a beaten army.

And then there was the other talk, that Lee just might win yet again, and if so, the war would definitely be over. If that was the case, he wondered if this could even be his country, North or South.

"All right, you bastards. One more time. Company forward march!"

The ragged line stepped off yet again, the hot sun blazing down, passing dozens of similar companies parading back and forth. The steady "left-right" cadences shouted by white sergeants with Irish brogues, thick German accents, Midwestern twangs, and deep New England drawls, echoing across the field.

Near Gunpowder Falls, Maryland, Fifteen Miles North of Baltimore

August 11, 1863
6:00 P.M.

General Lee rode with Longstreet by his side, staff, including Jed Hotchkiss, and a heavy security patrol of an entire regiment of cavalry spread out before them.

The evening was turning cool, after a warm day of riding. They had set out shortly after dawn, riding with President Davis for several miles until he had continued on to the west, this time escorted by a full regiment of Stuart's best and a section of light guns. Once the president was out of sight, he had told Pete that they would spend today riding north, to explore the land a bit. They had advanced up the road toward Bel Air, nearly halfway to the Susquehanna, then swung about, heading down toward the Chesapeake, following an open river valley with the ironic name of Gunpowder.

Reining in to rest Traveler, Lee dismounted, loosely holding his old friend's reins, Traveler cropping noisily at the tall, rich grass. Pete dismounted, stretched, and lit a cigar.

"Beautiful evening," Lee said softly.

"That it is, sir."

"We do love these moments. If other parts of our task could forever be put aside, if we could have but this, riding reconnaissance, watching our army on the march, now there would be something to enjoy."

Pete nodded.

"But there is something about the sting of battle," Pete replied, "just before you go in, that is stirring as well, when we are driving them, and the men are shouting to go forward."

"Yes," and though he felt uncomfortable admitting it, that was true for him as well, the vast battle lines deploying out, the thunder of artillery, flags held aloft, the long, long battle lines charging forward, that piercing yell reaching to the heavens. Those were good as well, except for the price that came afterward.

"I'm not given to religious philosophy as you are, sir," Pete said. "But I remember the Norse mythology. Perhaps our Heaven, our Valhalla, will be just that, a warrior's heaven, where we will march and fight forever, and at dusk the dead will rise to feast together, friend and foe, throughout the night until the coming of the next day's battle."

It was a thought Lee did not wish to pursue; he had dwelled too much on philosophy, on moral questions, these last few weeks; to debate now the nature of Heaven would reawaken those other thoughts as well, and he needed to again focus on the now.

"You realize the president expects us to end this within another month," Lee replied, changing the subject.

"I think we can do it," Pete replied forcefully. Pete had stood to one side while Davis had given his final admonition, that with the reinforcements that had just arrived, he expected Washington to be taken.

"We can win," Lee said quietly, shading his eyes to look off to the west. He said, letting go of Traveler's reins, "But not with another attempt on Washington, as the president expects."

Longstreet grinned.

"Glad to hear you say that, sir. Dare I assume that is the purpose of our ride today?"

Lee smiled and nodded.

Davis, unknowingly, had at least given him some wiggle room with his closing statement that he expected the Army of Northern Virginia to force Lincoln into capitulation. He cited a pledge, printed in all the Northern newspapers, where Lincoln declared that the city is invulnerable and that he would stay there no matter what happened.

"He cannot run now," Davis said. "Storm the city, capture the scoundrel, and I will be back to deal with him."

He did not exactly say that the city was to be stormed within the next two or three days, though one would have to admit that the president fully expected that outcome.

"I can see the way you've been looking at ground today," Longstreet pressed. "It's like the old days, when we had a chance to look things over before picking our spot."

Lee smiled, his attention diverted by the approach of Taylor and the army cartographer, Jed Hotchkiss.

"Beautiful ground, sir," Jed Hotchkiss announced, a flat board balanced on the pommel of his saddle with a sketchbook pegged to the board. Throughout the day he had been feverishly sketching away, turning out one map after another.

"May I see your work, sir?" Lee asked.

Grinning, Hotchkiss handed the sketch board down.

"Just rough drafts, sir," he said, offering the classic excuse of all artists and writers. "Once back to headquarters I can run off better copies."

Lee took the board, turning slightly to orient himself toward north, Pete coming up by his side.

"We have two good roads coming north out of Baltimore," Lee said, thumbing back to one of the earlier sketches, putting on his reading glasses so he could figure out the finely written details of distances, prominent buildings, and types of terrain.

"The first road toward Bel Air," Lee said, pointing to the map, "the second, the one we are on now, down closer to the bay and parallel to the railroad, which could be used as well for infantry if the weather turns bad."

"North rather than Washington, sir?" Walter asked tentatively. It was unusual for him to venture a question, but Lee did not reproach him. The excuse of their just "going for a ride after seeing the president off" was just that, an obvious excuse after nearly ten hard hours in the saddle, crisscrossing the landscape.

Lee did not reply to Walter's query, instead concentrating on the sketches, turning the pages, pausing occasionally to ask Jed to explain some detail, comparing relative heights between the low-lying ridges.

He could sense the mounting excitement of the other three. The weeks of idleness at Baltimore, though a wonderful chance to relax, reorganize, and refit, seemed out of place for a field army during the height of the campaign season. Battle, of their own choosing, was again in the air.

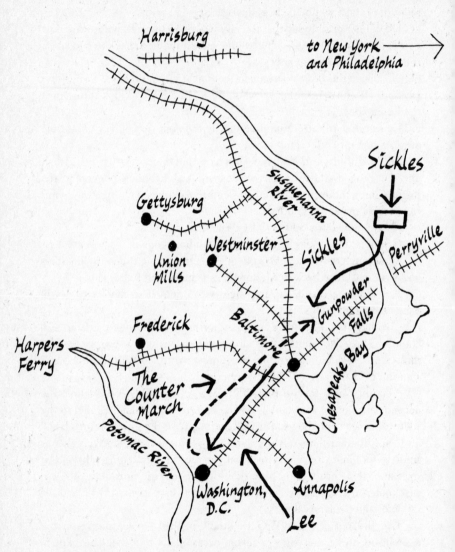

Harrisburg

to New York
and Philadelphia

Sickles

Gettysburg

Susquehanna River

Westminster

Sickles

Perryville

Union Mills

Baltimore

Gunpowder Falls

Frederick

Harpers Ferry

The Counter March

Chesapeake Bay

Potomac River

Washington, D.C.

Annapolis

Lee

The Plan to Bring Out Sickles

He reached the last map, the one that sketched this line along the Gunpowder River for nearly ten miles of length. Hotchkiss was obviously tired; he had gone through three horses during the day, covering two miles or more at a gallop for each one Lee had ridden at leisure. He alone knew the full details of why they were riding thus.

Their cavalry escort ringed in a bit closer as the four stood examining the maps, forward pickets a good three or four miles ahead of the main body . . . and not a single Yankee, not even a few scouts, had been seen all day, a clear sign that Sickles was keeping to the north side of the river.

Lee studied the last map intently, the shadows around them lengthening and then disappearing as the sun set, summer twilight settling over them.

"I think it will be here," he finally said.

"Good ground," Pete replied. "We can ring our guns along this side of the stream, force them to cross; this is very good ground."

Lee shook his head.

"No, I think we'll give it to them."

"Sir?"

"A friend of mine, a man Judah took me to share dinner with, made a good analogy of our army's situation. He said we're like Napoleon before Quatre Bras, several days before Waterloo. Napoleon was trying to force a break between the allied army and the Prussian army. As you know, he failed to do so, and the defeat at Waterloo was the result. We're like Napoleon at this moment, but it's not two armies we must force apart, it is three."

"We do have the advantage of being in the middle," Pete offered, "Washington garrison to the south, Sickles to the northeast, Grant to the north."

"And if they should all squeeze at once, we have a problem. No, we must lure one of the three out, defeat it without question, then turn on the second force and defeat that in turn. Once two of the three are destroyed, the third will be broken morally and then we finish it up. I think we can do that, but it will require audacity."

"We never lacked that," Pete said with a grin.

"If we offer battle to Sickles but then dig in here, on the south side of this stream, I think even he will hold. He talks big, but he also has the memory of Union Mills fresh on his mind. He will stop, probe, try to flank us, and in the interim I would suspect Grant will either order him to retire or come down upon our flank and rear and we will be forced to withdraw."

He smiled, pointing at the ground around them.

272 NEWT GINGRICH AND WILLIAM R. FORSTCHEN

"No, I want Sickles alone, I want him overly confident, I want him advancing rapidly. If I give him this ground—after a fight, mind you, but not a real fight, just a demonstration—I think he will come on with a vengeance, thinking we are on the run, and then we jump him. Conceding this ground at the start will embolden him to push on toward Baltimore and then we spring our trap several miles to the rear."

Pete grinned.

"Fine, sir, now how do we get him here?"

"We set him off half-cocked. Tomorrow afternoon the army will leave Baltimore and advance on Washington with all proper fanfare. I want it done publicly. Let the rumors fly. We don't press the men, however; we save their strength. How we arrange the marching order will be crucial. I want Hood on the left, Beauregard on the right, and you acting as a reserve in the rear, but instantly ready to turn around.

"Leave your strongest division here in Baltimore as a garrison."

"That would be Pickett and, as usual, he'll chafe."

"Let him. No one is to know of this plan other than the four of us here. I want no lost orders like we had at Sharpsburg. We can tell the others when the time comes."

"Thank you for the confidence, sir," Longstreet replied.

"Pete, I have to tell someone, in case anything happens to me."

"Just mind the heat, sir," Walter interjected protectively.

"Thank you, Walter, and remember, no written orders regarding this place here. I want all to appear as though we are marching on Washington with the full intent of storming it within three days."

"Yes, sir."

"We engage in front of Washington, make all appearances of preparing to attack. Now, if by some rare chance the opportunity does arise to take the city, we will venture it, but I don't see that happening, at least not without a bloody cost. Our threat, however, will trigger yet another panic in that city and in the North."

"But Grant did not even budge last time," Longstreet said, "and we've seen the reports about his statements, along with our observations near Harrisburg of his army building there rather than shipping it all to Washington."

"Sickles is the one," Lee said emphatically, "he is the one I'm playing this game to. We know the divisions between Grant and Sickles. It's the same as it was with Pope and McClellan at Second Manassas. We threaten Washington and I am all but certain that Sickles will find an excuse to bring his army, ill prepared, across the Susquehanna. At the very least he'll see the chance to grab back Baltimore, but I suspect that ultimately he will seek to strike us in the rear; at least he will think he is striking us in the rear."

Lee smiled, turning to walk back over to Traveler's side, gently rubbing his old friend's forehead.

"Once we know he is across the river, we move, countermarching back, and when I say move, we will do it with utmost speed, the same way you marched to Westminster, General Longstreet. Here is the place we drive for, especially after Sickles has gained it.

"We'll work out the details tonight. I think we'll camp near here, gentlemen, I'd enjoy a night away from the city."

Walter nodded and rode off, calling for the cavalry to circle in and to find a tent.

"We play this for Dan Sickles," Lee said, still smiling. "Bring him down here and let him think he is winning, then close in like a vice, taking him on the flank when the time comes. It will call for careful coordination, Pete. Stuart will observe, skirmish, and offer some delay, acting as if he is trying to buy time, thus causing Sickles to press harder. We then send Pickett up to delay, but not too much, a different kind of fight for him, but it's time he proved himself at it. Then, when the moment is right and all our forces have marched back up from Washington, we hit Sickles with a concentrated attack and finish him."

"Grant and the Washington garrison?"

"That's one of the reasons I'm sending Wade Hampton across the river between the two armies. Yes, I want to know exactly where the Nineteenth Corps is before we start this fight. If they do move with Sickles, we might have a bigger fight than anticipated. But the broader plan is for Wade to disrupt communications between those two armies and sow panic, perhaps even to lead Grant to think I'm preparing to cross the river farther up. I want Sickles cut off as much as possible from Grant to give him the latitude to move without being restrained. As for the Washington garrison, they will stay stuck behind their fortifications, as always. They are not a factor in this. Ultimately it will first be Sickles, and then Grant, but a Grant weakened when a third or more of those people north of the river cross over and then just disappear."

"Sir, a concern," Hotchkiss interjected.

"Go on."

"The main body of our army countermarching back up from Washington will have to march nearly three miles for every mile that Sickles makes."

"It will have to be done. We cannot allow Sickles to actually get into Baltimore. Once there, he'd be behind the fortifications and our chance to catch him in the open will be lost. If we beat him south of Baltimore, yet again he could fall back to Baltimore and dig in. No, we must fight him here, on this ground."

"That will be one tall order, sir, when it comes to the distance our men must cover before going into a fight," Hotchkiss pressed.

"Then we march through the night and into the next day," Lee said quietly, looking over at Pete.

"General Longstreet, do you think you have another Union Mills in you?"

Longstreet grinned.

Chapter Sixteen

August 14, 1863
7:30 A.M.

C.S.A "They're coming, I tell you!"

Sergeant Hazner wearily looked up at the excited young private and fixed him with a cool gaze.

"So what if they are?" he growled, shifting a wad of tobacco in his cheek and spitting.

"It means we'll finally take that damn city," the boy answered enthusiastically.

He pointed south, where, on the horizon, the unfinished dome of the Capitol was in clear view.

The others around the campfire were reacting in mixed ways to this tidbit of information, which a young headquarters cook had brought to them.

Rumors had been rampant for more than a week that something was about to happen. Ever since the bulk of the Army of Northern Virginia had marched off, what was left of Pettigrew's and Perrin's old divisions—now combined under the command of General Scales—had hovered at the edge of Washington. It had taken time to sort the battered regiments out, reorganize them into four effective brigades, and there had been much grumbling and arguing when a number of old glorious regiments had been disbanded, the men placed into other units from their home states. They had been allowed to keep their flags, but it had been a tough blow to many, for in this army, like all others in this war, regimental identity was a powerful force.

Even after the reorganization, the division was a light one, not much more than five thousand men under arms. Although lightly wounded men had been coming back into the ranks, there was still the daily toll from disease and from the incessant skirmishing along the fortification lines. Scales had taken to his job of "demonstrating" with a will, moving his men back and forth between the Seventh Street road and the Bladensburg road, probing, making feints at night, detailing experienced riflemen to harass the Union forces. The Yankees had refused to budge from their fortifications, a response that had become a source of derision with wags sneaking out at night and putting up signs made out of bedsheets, taunting the Yankees to come out and fight. But then again, none of them could blame the defenders of Washington; they were behind heavy fortifications, well fed and housed, and if they had advanced, Scales's division and his two brigades of cavalry would have of course pulled back on the double. Their job was simply to shadow and harass, not seek an engagement where they would be outnumbered six or seven to one.

Morale in the new division was down for more reasons than simply the recombination of units. They had taken a brutal pounding in the campaign from Gettysburg to Union Mills, and finally the debacle in front of Fort Stevens. The graveyard established back behind the lines on the Seventh Street road now had over a thousand crosses and more were being added daily. In the last two weeks some of the Yankees apparently had been issued heavy Sharps rifles, others the deadly, hexagonal-bore Whitworths, which could kill at a thousand yards. More than one incautious Confederate was dead, with a hole drilled into his head when he peeked up over a ditch. One poor soul, hunkered down next to Hazner, died when he had kicked up a nest of yellow jackets, stood up shouting, jumping, and dancing about as he tried to knock off the stinging insects, and seconds later collapsed back into the ditch, a bullet through his chest. That had set up a howl of protests, since it seemed so damn unfair, but then how were the Yankees to know that the poor boy was getting stung and that's why he was dancing around?

The men with Scales had also missed out on the glory of taking Baltimore. Rumors came back of the feasting, the girls, the easy duty, and though the tales were most likely exaggerated, at least the men hoped they were, still it set them to grumbling against the high command for leaving them out here all alone, missing all the fun.

And now it seemed the Army of Northern Virginia was coming back to gather its lost souls back into the fold.

There was a commotion on the road back toward the cemetery, and

Hazner casually stood up to take a look. Men were coming out from their encampments under the trees to watch the approach, and those who had been gathered around the campfire with Hazner went off, with the excited young private leading the way.

Though curious, Hazner waited a minute or two, feigning disinterest. That of course was part of his job, never to let the men see him getting excited. Finally he could bear it no longer, and he casually made his way up the slope and into the crowd.

Around the bend of the road he saw a team of mules, a long train of them, over twenty at least, straining at their load. Strapped to a heavy wagon behind them was a monstrous gun—from the looks of it, a heavy, eight-inch Columbiad. Behind the first gun was another team of ten mules pulling its carriage, which was resting atop a second wagon, and then yet more mules pulling, limber chests most likely filled with ammunition.

"It took 'em a week to get them down here," the private said proudly, behaving like so many who were the first to announce news, acting as if they were somehow the agents of the event.

"There's six of 'em, six big monsters to knock a hole right through Fort Stevens," the private continued. "Mortars as well, some thirty-pounders; a regular show it's gonna be."

Hazner spat and walked away.

A regular show all right. It meant that there would be another throw of the dice, another attack, this one most likely as bloody as the last. And their target would be stronger than last time as well. The fortifications had been all but impossible last time. Now that the defenders of Washington were literally staring the Confederate army right in the face, the Yankees had set to work with a will to make their positions even stronger. Night after night, when the wind was right, you could hear them digging out there, each morning revealing more abatis, deeper ditching, higher walls, and reserve lines going up behind the main one.

Hazner went back to his camp, which was all but empty, looking out through the trees toward the distant dome of the Capitol.

Didn't Lee see this? Surely he understood it. If there was a chance to take this city, it was in the days right after Union Mills and even then the chance was slim. In fact it had turned out to be no chance at all. Now an attack on these reinforced fortifications could be nothing but a suicidal gesture.

He leaned against a tree, studying the Capitol dome, the distant line of fortifications. Up at the front line, a half mile away, there were occasional puffs of smoke, the distant crack of a rifle. A mortar round arched up, sputtered, and plummeted down, exploding without effect. He heard a derisive hoot. It was almost a game, though every day a dozen or so soldiers paid the ultimate price for that game. But overall, nothing was happening. Nothing had happened here for the last three weeks.

Surely Lee would not throw them against those now-impregnable fortifications in yet another frontal assault. The Columbiads might excite the fervor of amateurs, but against heavy fortifications they would have little if any effect. Nothing more than a lot of flash and noise.

Though the generals might not realize it, after two years of war there was many a sergeant or corporal who knew how to read a map, could surmise much from little, and figure out what the bigwigs were thinking far better than the reporters, the armchair generals back home, and even some of the generals themselves.

"Hazner."

He looked up and smiled. It was Colonel Brown coming up to join him.

Brown had figured out long ago what had happened at Fort Stevens, how Hazner had knocked him cold with a single blow and dragged him from the line. The colonel still had an arm in a sling from that fight, the wound healing slowly. The only comment he had ever made on that terrible day was an offhand "Hazner, at times you are one hell of a headache," a tacit acknowledgment and no more that Hazner's direct action had undoubtedly saved his life.

"Lot of hoopla down on the road," Brown ventured.

"Yes, sir, the heavy-siege train is here."

"Took long enough."

Hazner chuckled. A cavalryman had joined the regimental mess for dinner one night and regaled them with stories about the serpentlike crawl of the heavy guns, the need to rebuild bridges so they could pass, the endless delays, all this effort to drag half a dozen guns only thirty miles to the front line.

"Think we'll attack?" Hazner asked.

Brown smiled and shook his head.

"Sergeant, perhaps I should ask what you think."

"Sir, you're the colonel; I'm just a sergeant."

"You have as much sense of all this as I do, Sergeant; please educate me as to your opinion."

"Well, sir," Hazner began expansively, inwardly delighted at the deference Brown now showed him, "there's only eight rows now of abatis to go through, a ditch half a dozen feet deeper than it was before, fortress walls half a dozen feet higher, and maybe fifteen thousand more Yankees behind it. Do you honestly think, sir, that General Lee will go straight in again?"

Brown smiled.

"The Yankees could have moved those guns in a couple of days," Brown said, thinking of the power of the Union railroads and steamships.

"That's the Yankees, not us."

Brown shook his head.

"Damn war, thought it would be over by now."

"We all thought that, sir," Hazner said absently, chewing and spitting a stream of tobacco juice.

He remembered his old friend, killed at Union Mills, his journal still in his haversack. How together they had marched off two years ago, two boys ardent for some desperate glory, believing that it would be over by Christmas and they'd come home heroes. His friend was dead, buried in some mass grave in front of Union Mills, and now he stood here, looking at the Capitol dome, so close and yet such an infinity of death away.

"Maybe those six heavy guns will start something," Brown opened. "I just pray to God it doesn't mean we go in against that fort again."

"Amen to that, sir, amen to that."

Washington, D.C.
The White House

August 15, 1863
3:00 P.M.

 President Lincoln turned away from the window and looked back at his Cabinet. Another thumping sound struck the windowpane, rattling it, all else in the room silent.

The bombardment had been going on since dawn, every two to three minutes another salvo, deeper-sounding than the fire of the previous weeks, clearly the pounding of heavy artillery against Fort Stevens. At night the sky to the north flashed and glowed from the bombardment, civilians out in the street, gathering in small knots, looking expectantly northward, talking nervously.

The city had been under siege for nearly a month and the strain was showing in every face. Every day rumors swept the city that the rebs had broken through, were falling back, had crossed the Susquehanna, had retreated back to Virginia, that renewed riots were sweeping the cities of the North, that France had declared war . . . and throughout it all he had learned to remain calm, sphinxlike, detached from both the rumors and the emotions.

He returned to his chair and sat down. Beside him Stanton rustled some papers and Lincoln nodded for him to continue.

"As I was saying, Mr. President. It appears that General Lee is advancing on Washington with his entire army now reinforced with the men brought north by Beauregard."

"And you anticipate an attack?"

"Yes, sir."

"How soon?"

"Within two to three days. Their siege batteries are giving an unmerciful pounding to Fort Stevens."

"How unmerciful?" Gideon Welles, secretary of the navy, asked.

"Several guns have been dismounted."

Welles sniffed derisively.

"Edwin, modern weapons simply are not effective against well-dug-in positions. Fort Pulaski in front of Savannah proved that older masonry forts are vulnerable to rifled guns, but a heavy earthen position, you can waste twenty tons of powder and shell against it, and in a single night a regiment of engineers armed with shovels can make it right again. I think we are overreacting."

"I beg to differ," Stanton sniffed.

"Gentlemen, we've conducted a dozen such operations with the navy since the start of this war, and always the situation favors the defenders," Welles replied forcefully. "Until someone comes up with a new way of attacking or a new explosive that can level forts like Stevens, this is an exercise in futility, and I don't see General Lee engaging in such futility."

"So why would he bother then?" Stanton replied heatedly.

Lincoln held out his hand for silence.

"Gentlemen, we are at the crisis," he announced.

Gideon Welles smiled and nodded in agreement.

"Indulge me for a moment, please," Lincoln continued.

No one spoke.

He settled back in his chair, tempted to put his feet up but in such a formal setting that was of course impossible.

"Some thought that Gettysburg and Union Mills were the crisis, but I realize now that they were not. Terrible as those four days were, they were but the opening of the first act in the confrontation that will decide this war.

"Yes, the Army of the Potomac was savaged in that fight, and God forgive us, ten thousand or more families will forever mourn those terrible days, but that was not the confrontation that would decide this crisis. It is now, this day and the next month, that will decide it."

"Sir. There might very well be seventy thousand or more rebel troops just outside the city this morning," Stanton announced. "In that I agree with you, the crisis has arrived, but I must beg to ask, what do you propose to do?"

"Nothing."

Stanton, flustered, set the papers he was holding back down on the table.

"We have forty-three thousand troops in the city, nearly a third of them well-seasoned veterans from Charleston. Frankly, if they can't hold the city, then I would venture to say we don't deserve to hold this city or win this war."

Gideon smiled in agreement.

"And those men are backed up by a dozen ironclad gunboats, a thousand marines, and three thousand sailors," the secretary of the navy threw in.

"And I still maintain that we should shift the Nineteenth Corps down here," Stanton replied heatedly. "They are doing nothing but lounging about up on the Susquehanna and I don't see Grant using them to any effect."

"I queried General Grant about their use in my last letter," Lincoln replied calmly, "and he said he preferred to keep them under his direct command. Gentlemen, I will not gainsay our new commander of the armies on this issue."

Stanton started to open his mouth to speak, but a sidelong look from Lincoln stilled him.

"That is final," Lincoln said softly.

Stanton nodded, crestfallen at this near-public rebuke.

"Anything else? I'd like to go up to Stevens to have a look around and then to the hospitals."

"Mr. President, the French," Secretary of State Seward said.

"Go on."

"We know for a fact that the French consul in Baltimore sent a report out under a French flag. It should be in Paris by now."

"Wish we had that ocean telegraph line up," Welles interjected. "I'd love to know what is happening over there today. Perhaps the dispatching of some of our ships to the coast of France as a show of force might be required."

"I would advise against that at the moment," Seward replied. "It would only serve to provoke."

"Provoke, is it? He's the one meddling in Mexico. The English and French are helping to keep the Confederacy alive. Talk about a provocation!"

"Go on, Mr. Seward," Lincoln interrupted.

"Sir, I think we'll be at war with France by autumn," the secretary of state replied.

"How so? All based on one letter?"

"The news for Napoleon from Mexico has not been good. He thought he could seize the country in a quick coup and then put his puppet on the throne. Part of his or his wife's dream of a renewed Catholic empire. A mad delusion, but it has gained a following in France and Austria. The campaign has not gone well. Juarez, though still bruised, at this moment is gaining strength in the back country and within a year, two at most, he will be ready to counterattack in strength. Especially if we can help him. Napoleon must see, at least from his reasoning, that if ever there is a hope for him in the New World, it is now, this moment. Union Mills and Baltimore will give him the pretext to recognize the Confederacy, and I suspect he will do it."

"Napoleon's half-mad," Stanton sniffed.

"We all know that," Seward replied.

"Where will he intervene then?" Lincoln asked. "Texas?"

"That would be my assumption. I don't see them trying a main force attack on the blockade at Charleston or Wilmington. I would venture at Brownsville, right at the border. First land some heavy guns on the Mexican side and establish fortifications. Then the main fleet moves in to engage ours. There'll be the usual claim of a provocation of some sort. Once Brownsville is secured, they'll try to roll our blockading force off the coast, clear up to New Orleans. For the French, a so-called liberation of New Orleans would have a special symbolic meaning as well, having once been French territory."

Lincoln turned to Gideon.

"Your response?"

"I'd love nothing more. Rear Admiral Farragut's job is done on the Mississippi, though he'll need to hold some forces at New Orleans to support the weakened garrison there. But we could have him shift down to Texas now. Some of our new oceangoing monitors and ironclads could move down there as well. I doubt if the French would risk their new ironclads on a transoceanic voyage. If not, our navy could pound theirs to splinters. Once that was finished, I'd love to see a blockading force off Le Havre."

Lincoln smiled.

"One thing at a time, Gideon. First, all our efforts must be to win this war. Second, to block the French if they should be so foolish as to join in. And, Mr. Seward, the English?"

"Still the same, as I said before. The sticking point is still slavery.

That, and frankly, if I were the English, I'd love nothing more than to see the French make that sort of foolish mistake. We keep the war out of European waters, bloody the French noses here in ours, and it weakens Napoleon at no cost to the English. I say, let them come, and the English will stand back. Besides, they don't want to risk Canada, or some of their holdings in the Caribbean, which we would most certainly move on if they should try to challenge us. No, the English will stand clear, unless the campaign of the next month presents them with a foregone conclusion."

Lincoln nodded approvingly.

"Insightful as always, thank you."

Again the windowpanes rattled and all looked up.

"I still don't like our loss of Port Hudson," Stanton grumbled.

Lincoln nodded. Word had just arrived this morning of that reversal on the Mississippi. Such setbacks were to be expected with the concentration of forces here in the East.

"What good will it do them?" he replied. "They can't ship supplies across the Mississippi. Our navy will continue to patrol the river."

"Still, to have taken that ground and then lost it."

Lincoln, feeling exasperated, lowered his head, not letting the outburst come.

He had learned that as well in recent weeks. To concentrate solely on what was of the moment, and what would win this campaign and, from that, the war. Grant had impressed that upon him. Hundreds of thousands of troops had been used up these last two years in scattered operations that in the long term might bring results, but as of this moment were nothing but wasted efforts. So what if Port Hudson fell back into enemy hands? The statement had already been made that, so willing, the Union could take the entire Mississippi basin and do it again. A thrust by a desperate force might for the moment look fancy in the newspapers, but better for the Confederacy if those ten thousand men involved were here, in front of Washington, or at least moving to contain Sherman, who continued to sweep through Tennessee, bent on linking up with Rosecrans.

As for this defense of Washington, the panic of the previous month had faded. Food moved freely up the Potomac, as did troops. Gideon's brown-water navy moved up and down the river at will. There had been some concern that Lee might try to cut down to the east, to place Alexandria under bombardment, but again it was Gideon who pointed out that half a dozen Columbiads could do little, and to move his forces in that direction would place him twenty miles farther away from Baltimore, from Sickles, and from Grant.

Heintzelman had also been in a bit of a panic over that threat. Lincoln had said nothing, but his patience was indeed wearing thin with the man. His last dispatch to Grant had expressed that, and he sensed that when the time came, Grant would address that problem as well.

The Cabinet started to talk among themselves again, used now to his silent lapses, filling the space until he bestirred himself again.

Finally he looked up.

"Gentlemen, I think that is all for today. If Lee should launch an all-out assault, I will call for you to discuss the situation, but I seriously doubt that will happen now. Yet again I must caution you. Calmness, gentlemen, calmness at all times. Remember, how we act is observed by others. If we should appear rattled, it would spread like a flash throughout the city, and we do not want that. Regardless of what the newspapers say, what Congress says, what anyone says, it is our example at this moment that will set the mood for this city. Go about your business as usual."

The group stood up to take their leave. Lincoln made eye contact with Stanton and nodded for him to stay. The secretary of war came over to the chair by Lincoln's side and sat down as the others left, several of them looking back, curious as to what might transpire.

Lincoln smiled, trying to set him at ease.

"I'll come straight to the point, Edwin. I feel you do not like our General Grant and his plans."

The secretary of war ruffled slightly.

"Honestly, Mr. President, I don't. He is taking a risk here."

"Edwin, it has always been you who told me war is risk."

"Yes, sir. But to risk the capital? Twenty thousand more men in this city would secure it beyond all doubt."

"I do not want Washington secure beyond all doubt," Lincoln replied calmly.

"Sir?"

"Just that."

"I don't follow you."

"Ever watch a cat in the barn, sitting on a beam, waiting for a mouse?"

"No, sir," Edwin replied coolly. Obviously he was not one to appreciate Lincoln's homespun examples.

"He only sits there because he thinks he can get the mouse. If there were no mouse, he would not stay."

"Sir?"

"We're the mouse, Edwin. If Lee did not feel that he had some hope of taking this city, he would not be here. That is what we want. Heaven forbid if after all this, come autumn, Lee withdraws back into Virginia. He will escape, having savaged the Army of the Potomac. He might even detach Longstreet or Hood to regain the situation in Tennessee. And then we face another long, hard campaign next spring. Given the reversal at Union Mills, if we face a protracted campaign next year, I daresay that you, I, the whole kit and caboodle, will be out come next November. Our political opponents, both North and South, see that now.

"In the South they are hoping for a victory by the end of autumn. They thought they might have had it on that terrible night of July 4, but we stayed the course. Grant and that railroad man Haupt have worked a miracle across the last five weeks. Now we must continue to stay the course. We have shown Lee that even if he defeats an army, it does not mean he has won the war.

"The days of single great victories deciding wars are forever over. War now is the will of nations, of ordinary people. Granted, few in the North fully endorse our efforts. Many would rather walk away, but as long as we can hold but a quarter of the populace to our side, as long as we can hold four hundred thousand patriots in our ranks, we can prevail. But that means risk as well, and I'm willing to gamble Washington for that chance."

"Has Grant shared his thoughts with you?" Stanton replied sharply.

"Not fully. He was willing to, but I told him I trusted his judgment.

"As long as he holds the trust I've given him, I will leave him to do his job unless he obviously fails. Our job at the moment is to take the heat. If some senators want to run off, half-cocked, crying about defeat, let them. And let us hope that come next election, after we have won, their cries are remembered."

"If there is a next election."

Lincoln raised a quizzical eyebrow.

"There is the smell of Napoleonism around Grant," Stanton said sharply. "He keeps his own counsel. He has followers in the ranks that are too worshipful. I prefer to know what he is doing."

"Edwin. Say that about McClellan or even Hooker, and I might have listened. But not Grant. He is as common as prairie dirt. The same as me."

Lincoln chuckled softly at the analogy, and Stanton did not reply.

"I will ask you a direct question, Edwin, and will only ask it once."

"Sir?" There was a slight nervous tone to his voice.

"Will you support me, and will you support Grant to the utmost in the weeks to come? The crisis is upon us. In the next six weeks we shall either win or lose this war. There can be no half measures. General Lee is a formidable foe. He might not follow at all the path we assume. He rarely does. If Lee should at least hold even in the coming battles, or even escape back into Virginia, there to present a strong front yet again, I fear that the defeat at Union Mills, and what Seward has told us about France, might collapse our political base once and for all. It might prove to be impossible to sustain the fight come next spring, and the bitter harvest of death that more fighting will create. So, my friend, will you support me?"

Edwin sighed.

"Of course, sir."

"Good then."

Lincoln studied him carefully. The look in his eyes, the flat crease of his lips—he wondered what Edwin might say later to Seward. But at least he had wrung out of him this concession of the moment. Though he did not voice it, nor would he voice it to anyone, he had reached a decision about Stanton: Either he fully supported the campaign to come, or he was out of a job, no matter what political heat that might generate.

The windowpanes rattled yet again from the bombardment, and neither man spoke.

Along the Susquehanna

August 15, 1863
7:30 P.M.

The coup had gone flawlessly. A dozen of his troopers, posing as farmers driving cattle, accompanied by several patriotic young women of Baltimore dressed in homespun and acting like frightened young wives, had come to the southwest bank of the river in midafternoon. They had signaled the ferryman on the opposite shore, who had, at first, refused to cross over. One of the men had then swum the river, and, gaining the northern bank, had offered the man five dollars in gold to help save their cattle from the "damn rebels." The man had complied and, once on the southern bank, was confronted by a dozen grinning troopers with revolvers.

The first dozen went across, seized a second ferryboat, and by dusk an entire regiment was across the river, fanning out, setting up a cordon. A third ferry had been seized as well, which even now was bringing over a battery of horse artillery.

Wade Hampton, standing on the north bank of the Susquehanna

River, was filled with pride. His boys had pulled it off without a shot being fired. Even now, the town of Lancaster, but a dozen miles away, was unaware of what would come sweeping down upon them by dawn, a full brigade of Confederate cavalry, hell-bent on raiding, disrupting, and sowing panic.

The campaign was on again, and after the bucolic three weeks in Baltimore he was eager for the fight. His orders from General Lee personally had been clear and concise. They were no longer in need of supplies, Maryland had yielded up her bounty to them, and the lean, hungry Army of Northern Virginia was a thing of the past. His job, first and foremost, was intelligence, to ascertain what exactly Grant was up to in the Harrisburg area. Was it merely a marshaling area, or was it to be a platform for him to try and sweep down the Cumberland Valley, and perhaps march on into Virginia. Next task for him would be their old adversary, the Army of the Potomac. It was time to rattle them yet again, a task he looked forward to with pleasure. Finding the location of the powerful Nineteenth Corps was high on the priority list as well. If they were with Grant, that would indicate much as to the possible Union actions. If not, it would mean they could support a renewed thrust by the Army of the Potomac. Though there was the chance now, with Lee marching toward Washington, that the Yankees, always in panic over their capital, would ship that corps down there by water to reinforce the defenses of Washington. Finally, Lee had emphasized his role of disruption, to cut telegraph lines, to spread rumors, and to work to isolate Sickles from Grant.

Of course, though he had not discussed it too much with Lee, now was the chance to win some glory as well. Lancaster would be in their pockets tomorrow morning. A day's hard ride could even take them to Reading and what a treat it would be to cut the major junction of so many rail lines, in effect all but isolating Grant from the Eastern seaboard. It would be a whirlwind of chaos for the Yankees, exceeding anything Jeb had done the year before in the Peninsula. To think even about venturing into the outskirts of Philadelphia was not beyond reach, tearing up tracks and burning bridges as they advanced. His boys would certainly enjoy the ride in such a rich countryside, and enjoy even more the chance to wreck some locomotives along the way.

The ferryboat down below on the river docked, and twenty more of his troopers got off, leading their horses, whooping and hollering as they mounted and galloped up the slope.

It was a grand day to be in the cavalry and Wade soaked up the moment with joy. The campaign had begun.

Paris, France

August 16, 1863
3:00 A.M.

Emperor Napoleon III studied the dispatch carefully, sitting alone. There would be time later to sit with advisors, his wife, and confidants to discuss all that it implied. The dispatch had arrived from the coast only the hour before; advance word of its coming via the semaphore link to Le Havre had kept him awake in anticipation.

News had come at the start of the month about Lincoln's defeat and the shattering of his army. The newspapers, as usual, had overblown the details but he could surmise that though nothing could ever rival his uncle's victory at Austerlitz, still it was a worthy victory for the Southern cause.

But this news now, of the fall of the Union's third largest city, the secession of yet another state, that was news indeed. Could it finally signal that the Yankee cause was unraveling?

He sipped from his glass of wine, reading the dispatch yet again, the evaluation of the Confederate army, the appraisal of President Davis and of this General Lee. Yes, he would have made a worthy marshal of the empire. He had breeding, strength, audacity, and luck.

He knew what his own generals and admirals would say. That there was too much risk. That Mexico was proving harder than first anticipated, that other countries in Europe might take advantage of the situation if France committed more resources to the Americas.

Did that ever stop his uncle? The name of Bonaparte was not made through caution.

He could see it clearly. Here was a chance to forever establish French dominance. Help the South, let them win, and that contemptible American nation divides and in short order divides yet again into internal squabblings. Within a generation, a new empire of his own creation would flourish, as that of the old empire should have flourished fifty years ago.

As for the Yankees' much vaunted ironclads, they had yet to meet a true ship of Europe. *Le Gloire*, the pride of the French navy, and her sister ships, ironclads as powerful as anything the Yankee tinkers might fashion, would leave nothing but wreckage in their wake. Land a few brigades of troops, engineers, artillery on the border with Texas, and there build a base to operate from. Then sweep northward.

Perhaps even Spain could be coaxed into the coalition. Cuba could offer a fine port to help sweep the arrogant blockade from the coast of Florida and perhaps even as far as South Carolina.

He smiled as he contemplated all that was possible. A new coalition, Catholic Austria and Spain, with France in the lead, reversing all the misfortunes that had befallen the world since 1815. For the slaveholding South he cared not a whit; they were just a means to an end, a humbling of England, a realignment of the balance of power. His fleets, operating out of Vera Cruz, Brownsville, Havana, would reestablish the glory that should be France's. The other European powers, except for England, would see the rightness of this as well. Russia, which had sent its pathetic fleet to New York City the winter before, would stand back, not wishing to risk yet another humiliation like the one he had dealt it in the Crimea. Those tradesmen across the Channel, so intent on their profits, would not stir. *They will not come into the fight for the South, but they most certainly will not align themselves with that damnable uncouth lawyer from the frontier. They will sit it out and by the time they realize their folly, it will be too late. Mexico will be taken, perhaps even gains in the Caribbean.*

Yes, he would commit to this. It was time.

In Front of Fort Stevens

August 16, 1863
8:00 A.M.

General Lee looked around at the gathering of officers. They were camped in nearly the same spot that had been his headquarters the month before. Yet the feeling was different now. The men were rested, the weather fair, though promising an intense heat by later in the day.

Longstreet had just ridden in; Beauregard and Hood were already present. Stuart was fifty miles to the north, deployed towards the Susquehanna. He had privately given Jeb his orders the night before, the cavalier grinning as he rode off.

Lee smiled as Longstreet rode up and dismounted.

"Good marching weather," Pete said, coming under the awning and taking a cup of coffee. "Roads are good, weather's fine, the men know something is up."

"It's hard to keep it hidden at times," Lee replied.

He looked around at the gathering and began.

"We're not going to attack this city again," he announced. Beauregard stirred in his seat but held back from comment.

"I know this seems like an elaborate effort for nothing, putting all but one division on the road again. At the very least, let us say it's given our army a chance to stretch its legs again, to not turn into garrison troops. But an attack on Washington is out of the question now."

"Then I hope you will inform us as to your intent, sir," Beauregard said calmly, looking straight at Lee.

"Yes. I think I should. We will demonstrate along this line today, tomorrow, and the day after, if need be. I want increased activity. I want all three of you to move cautiously when it comes to your personal safety. The Yankees have sharpshooters in their works, yet I want you to be seen, as if surveying the line for an attack. I want night probes; don't hesitate to burn off some powder; we have plenty of captured Union powder in reserve now. I want them to think that we are preparing a full-scale assault across the entire front."

"Sir, if we should see some promise of success, I'd counsel going in," Beauregard offered. "Perhaps another night attack; my boys are up to it."

Lee emphatically shook his head.

"General Beauregard. We have no more reserves. I will not venture the horrific casualties it will take to storm this city."

"Even if we did take it now," Longstreet interjected, looking at Beauregard, "we couldn't hold it for long."

Lee nodded his thanks. The relationship with Beauregard had been stiff ever since the man's arrival. Though Davis had made it clear that Lee was in command of this campaign, Beauregard was already chafing at being subordinate to a man he had outranked little more than a year ago. Twice he had requested independent command since his arrival, and each time Lee had reined him in, the first time with soft diplomacy, the second time more sharply, with a clear statement of who was in command. It would be like Beauregard to let a probe or reconnaissance turn into a full-pitched battle, and Lee looked straight at him.

"My orders are clear. Absolutely no general engagement is to be initiated. Demonstrations only. I don't want some hotheaded brigadier or division commander getting carried away, and, gentlemen, I will hold the three of you directly responsible if such a situation does develop. Do I make myself clear on this?"

Again the harsh tone that since Union Mills and the firing of Dick Ewell had become more and more his way of managing this army. He looked straight into the eyes of each man and waited until they nodded in agreement. Beauregard nodded and lowered his head.

"Then why?" Beauregard finally asked.

"I'll discuss the details in due time, gentlemen," Lee replied.

Longstreet, ever the poker player, revealed nothing. Hood simply smiled, used to how Lee preferred to run things.

"For the moment, gentlemen, demonstration only. You are not to discuss anything with your subordinates other than the orders just given.

"I want all of you to be ready to move at a moment's notice, to move fast and light."

"I think I know what's coming," Hood finally ventured.

"In due time, General. We all learned our lesson last fall at Sharpsburg when it came to the security of our operations. This next effort might entail a serious risk. Do not think my reticence is out of mistrust; rather it is simply out of concern for our safety and ultimate success."

"I wish we had thirty thousand more men," Hood said quietly.

"We don't," Lee snapped. "All we will ever have is what now marches in our ranks. There is no sense in wishing for more. We have a preponderance of artillery now, and I plan to see that used." He looked around at the gathering.

"Any questions?"

No one spoke.

"Fine then, gentlemen. Let us see to our duty. The moment I feel that all is ready I will pass to each of you detailed orders, which are to be followed to the letter. Remember though, when it starts, it must be done with speed."

He stood up, indicating that the meeting was over.

The generals walked off, all except Longstreet, who lingered by the table.

"I think you ruffled up Beauregard," Pete said.

"Perhaps, but all it takes is for one loose-mouthed staff officer to spread the word; it leaks into Washington, and then an order goes out forbidding Sickles to move. I'm hoping now that the exact opposite will happen, that Sickles might very well get the order to move, and when he does, we are ready. Walter and Jed have done a magnificent job of drawing up routes of march, deployment of supplies, even possible positions for the bulk of our artillery so they can move quickly to where they are needed. This one is well planned, General Longstreet; all I have to do is give the word to go. I'm confident on this one."

Longstreet nodded back to the map and pointed at Harrisburg.

"Suppose he doesn't do what you expect. Then what?"

"Sickles?"

"No, Grant, sir. That is now our main concern."

"He will," Lee replied. "Grant will hesitate, caught off balance by

Sickles, and then the administration will force him to detach troops to cover here. No, they will tie his hands as they have all the others."

"I hope so," was all Longstreet could say.

Harrisburg, Pennsylvania

August 17, 1863
9:00 P.M.

H aupt, good to see you."
       Grant came out of his chair, extending a hand as the frail figure of Gen. Herman Haupt stood by the open flap of his tent.

The appearance of the man shocked him. He was wasting away by the day; by the light of the coal oil lamp he had a pale, yellowish cast to his skin, his cheeks were hollow, eyes sunken.

As Haupt took a seat across from Grant, the general made a decision, uncharacteristically, without reflection or contemplation of the impact it might have on his plans.

"Haupt, I think I should relieve you of your office. Send you home for a month or two."

Haupt looked up at him angrily and shook his head.

"I respectfully decline, sir."

"Damn it, man, you are dying."

Haupt smiled.

"Not yet, and besides you need me."

"Yes, I need you, but a lot of good you will do me or the army if you are dead."

"Not by a long shot yet, sir. Give me a few more weeks, let me sort out a few things, and then I'll take the leave you suggest."

"Suppose I order you to go home now, tonight?"

Haupt chuckled.

"I'd refuse. And then what? Court-martial me for insubordination?"

Grant shook his head and laughed softly.

"No, I'd never do that, Herman."

"It's getting better, sir."

He could see the lie in that but decided that for the moment he could not push the issue further.

"What do you have for me?" Grant asked.

"I barely got through. It's chaos not fifty miles from here. Hampton's taken Lancaster and is even now riding toward Reading. I'll confess, he's made a mess of things for us. He caught a number of supply trains in the rail yard at Lancaster. Wrecked nine locomotives."

Grant could see that such wanton destruction of his precious machines troubled Haupt. At heart he was a builder, not a destroyer.

"We'll take care of him. But what else?"

"I've got ten more batteries of guns coming down from Albany. I'm routing them around Lancaster and Reading and they should be here late tomorrow. Remounts are still coming in via the Pennsylvania railroad."

Haupt paused for a moment, reached into his haversack, and pulled out a notebook, thumbing through the pages.

"Let's see now. Two thousand, three hundred and fifty horses from Ohio, eight hundred and seventy mules from Ohio and Indiana as well. Seventy-five more wagons out of Lancaster before Hampton hit it. Two regiments from Illinois and one from Indiana should arrive here in three days. The colored regiments from Philadelphia will transfer here starting tomorrow. I'm routing them up to New York and then across to the Pennsylvania and Susquehanna through Pottsville, yet again to avoid Reading. Replacement bridging is in place at Wheeling for the Baltimore and Ohio, and a million rations should be stockpiled there by the end of the month. Vouchers to all the rail lines involved have been drawn as well."

He thumbed through his notes.

"Shoes. I've got fifty thousand more coming down from Massachusetts and Vermont, but that will take another week. We're still short of tentage; one of the trains Hampton took was loaded with them, and of replacement rails and some bridging material."

"The pontoon bridges?"

Haupt shook his head.

"Only enough for five thousand feet so far. I'm pushing it hard, sir, but the routing of trains is still something of a tangle from the Midwest. We've yet to successfully shift all the rolling stock back out there, and it's causing problems."

Grant extended his hand and patted Haupt on the arm.

"You're doing fine, just fine, Haupt."

Herman said nothing, eyes glazed as he stared off.

"I'd like you to get some rest, Haupt. If I lose you, I lose the one man I'm relying on most right now."

Haupt's shoulders seemed to sag, as if the words of comfort had placed upon him an additional burden.

"Sorry, sir. Sorry I took sick at this time."

"No apologies should be offered, Haupt."

"I'll be on the pontoon bridges first thing in the morning."

Grant sighed. There was no way he could simply detach this man, to send him home, to let him take a month to recover from his bout with dysentery. Even if he wanted to, he could not, not tonight.

"Go and get some rest, General. And that is an order."

"Yes, sir."

Haupt, legs visibly trembling, stood up and saluted. Grant guided him out of the tent and watched him walk off. As Haupt disappeared, he caught Parker's eye.

"Call for my surgeon again," Grant said. "I want that man taken care of."

Parker saluted and followed Haupt.

Grant stood by the open flap of his tent. The night was cool, pleasant, a gentle breeze wafting in as he lit another cigar, coughed as he drew the first deep breath, inhaling the soothing smoke.

In the open fields beyond, hundreds of campfires illuminated the night. He could hear distant laughter, songs, a banjo playing. Nearby several officers were passing a flask, laughing.

It was all so soothing, and in this moment, alone, he realized yet again that in spite of the horror, the tragedy of it all, he did love it. The scent of wood smoke on the breeze, mingled with the rich smell of hay, horses, a gentle August evening camped in the fields of Pennsylvania. Better, far better than Mississippi with its hot, sultry evenings without a breath of fresh air. This was good, a moment of pleasure regardless of all that had transpired in the last day.

As he looked out over the encampment, the men, his men, victorious veterans of so many hard-fought campaigns, he was captivated yet again by the sense of destiny, of power.

He knew they were ready for the task ahead. It was strange how one could sense such things, as if the will of seventy thousand could become but a single voice, a voice that said that together all would see it through to the end, no matter what the cost.

He closed the flap to his tent and returned to his desk. The urge for a drink was suddenly upon him. Strange how it would come when unexpected, unanticipated. Just one drink, a soothing taste to relieve the tension.

But he had made the promise to one whose trust he desired, and though he knew that he could find the bottle easy enough, hidden away in his trunk, he gave it not a second thought.

The latest dispatch from Washington had come in just before sunset. Enemy fire all along a five-mile front, heavy artillery bombardment, fear that a night assault might be launched.

A copy of the *New York Herald* was on the table, declaring that Washington was on the brink of collapsing, a paper from Philadelphia decrying the continued slaughter, calling for Lincoln to meet with Davis to end the war.

It was strange. He and Lincoln were separated by not more than a hundred and fifty miles, but they could, in one sense, be as far away as if Lincoln was in China. Dispatches had to be routed through Philadelphia, to Port Deposit, and then by courier boat to Washington. Here again Haupt had set up such an efficient system that the secured envelopes moved efficiently, for their communications could not be trusted to any wire, where along the way a telegrapher could accept ten dollars from a reporter to divulge what the two were saying to each other.

And yet it was as if Lincoln was sitting with him now, in this tent, telling him to stay the course, to hold fast, to do what they had discussed in their brief meeting of a month past.

If anything, the cutting off of Washington was perhaps one of the great blessings of this campaign. Unlike McClellan, Burnside, Hooker, or Meade, he was, in fact, free. He was not tied by hourly telegraphs bombarding him with orders, counterorders, demands, and entreaties. And yet he knew that something had changed in Lincoln as well. He remembered sitting in the White House, the two of them talking, Lincoln sharing the story of the colored White House servant who wanted to fight.

"That man focused the war for me, Grant," Lincoln had said. "He had not lost his nerve. He had seen the history of our republic across fifty years. He had seen the failure of the promise, but also the hope of the promise. I learned from him that we cannot fail, we will not fail, as long as men like him are willing to stand for what they believe in, to give the last full measure for what this dream of our republic can be."

And in that meeting he had learned that Lincoln's will, combined with his determination to see it through no matter what the cost, could indeed prevail.

Lee might very well attack Washington within the next day or two. He doubted that the man would take the risk. If the situation was reversed, he knew he would attack, regardless of loss, but the South could no longer afford that. But even if Washington did indeed fall, he would stay his own course and within a fortnight he would be ready to proceed.

He chafed at the waiting. Ord, Logan, Burnside, even Banks were ready to go, but it still depended on Haupt, the gathering of the supplies, of horses and mules, wagons and limber chests. Lee had the preponderance in artillery, a strange reversal of the moment, but even that could be overcome.

The waiting was painful, but it had to be endured till all the pieces were in place.

Only when all was ready would he move. He would not make the mistake he had made last autumn in front of Vicksburg. Lee was too savvy an opponent to give him that opening. When the time came, Lee would have to be so soundly defeated, in the field, in an open fight, that the hopes of the South would be forever dashed. It was not just a battle on the field of action; it was a battle that would have to shatter, once and for all, their will to fight. Otherwise this conflict could drag on for years, fought in the mountains and bayous, a bitter fight that would forever pollute any hope of reconciliation.

He had to win, not just the battle, but the peace as well.

Chapter Seventeen

G en. Dan Sickles sat alone, contemplating the goblet of brandy in his hand, swirling it, letting the thick drink coat the sides of the glass, inhaling the fragrance, then taking a sip.

The moment had come. It had arrived faster than he had anticipated; another week, two weeks would have been preferable. He could still use another ten thousand in the ranks, some more guns. The Army of the Potomac was barely fifty thousand strong, two-thirds of them the old rank-and-file veterans, the remainder new troops, many of them ninety-day men. His recruiting effort had paid off handsomely, with returning veterans bringing four thousand new men into the ranks of seasoned regiments.

The new regiments he had distributed into hardened brigades, and he hoped that something would rub off on them. He had less than twenty batteries of artillery, many of them just three or four guns, but the crews were the pick of the old Army of the Potomac, consolidated out of many of the old artillery reserve units. Of cavalry he was very short as well. Stoneman could barely put five thousand sabers into the field.

All day long courier boats had scurried in from Washington. He had tried to intercept the dispatches destined for Grant, but they had been carried by men from Grant's headquarters who couldn't be swayed to reveal the contents.

But the news was clear enough and he didn't need to read the dispatches and secrets of Grant. He had so conveniently set up a telegraph station and announced it was open to whomever needed it on "vital business of the public interest" that reporters from the New York papers and the Associated Press were hurrying back to use it.

Thus he knew a heavy bombardment had been going on for nearly two days; the rebels were firing off artillery ammunition with abandon, shelling the Washington fortification line along a seven-mile front. A dozen shots from the heavy guns had been dropped into the edge of the city. There was a report that one shell had burst on the Capitol grounds itself, killing a horse.

Some reported an air of panic, especially among the colored of the city, who were desperate to get out, but passage on boats was forbidden except for military purposes.

One report stated Lincoln had been wounded when he had gone up to watch the bombardment of Stevens, and that had created a true panic, only to be negated when the next dispatch boat anchored, the reporters on board dismissing the claim.

All were convinced though that Lee was preparing an all-out assault, one that would strike perhaps within the day.

Next there was the news of Wade Hampton. That had been confirmed when in a delightful display of arrogance Hampton personally sent a dispatch to the *Philadelphia Inquirer* via telegraph from Lancaster, inviting them to come and give an interview, or, if the paper desired, he would visit their offices within the week.

Hampton had actually created a wonderful situation for the Army of the Potomac. Dispatches and orders between Harrisburg and Washington now had to be routed through New York and it was causing delays, confusion. . . . It was wonderful. And Sickles was determined to take advantage of it.

"General Sickles, the dispatch from the War Department is here."

Dan looked up; the sentry had opened the tent flap. A young captain, one of his own staff, entered and saluted, handing a sealed dispatch from Stanton. It was a private arrangement the two had agreed to the week before, and all day he had been anxiously awaiting what he hoped would be orders.

Dan motioned for the man to wait and opened the envelope, recognizing Stanton's bold handwriting. He scanned the letter, then reread it again carefully, smiling.

"How were things when you left?" Dan asked.

"Sir, everyone's on edge. There was a report of an attack column being seen forming up along the Blandenburg road. Word is the rebels will attack this evening."

Dan nodded, studying the dispatch. It was a copy; the original was already on its way to Grant, but he would not receive it until some time tomorrow. It was an appeal to Grant from Stanton to consider releasing additional reinforcements for Washington, but far more important, it was a request to authorize the Army of the Potomac to make a reconnaissance in force on Baltimore, by land, sea, or both, to ascertain if Baltimore could be retaken, and, if possible, to do so and from there to threaten Lee's rear. In addition there was a second note, in Stanton's hand, directed to Sickles. The wording of it was important and he studied it carefully.

> *All indications are that the rebels will storm the capital today, or no later than tomorrow. This is based upon reliable intelligence gathered from deserters and observations of their movements. One of the primary missions of the Army of the Potomac since the start of this conflict has been the protection of this city and the Administration. Though final orders for troop movements must come from the General Commanding, nevertheless I believe it is within your authority to exercise the traditional role of the Army of the Potomac and to find some means to exert pressure upon the Army of Northern Virginia and divert them from this impending attack. . . .*

It was precisely the excuse he had been looking for, an idea that had been well placed with several congressmen and senators across the last week and Stanton, as to be expected, snapped at the bait.

He dismissed the staff officer and settled back in his chair, pouring another drink, then lighting a cigar.

Yes, there was an opportunity here that could come perhaps only once in a lifetime. It was fraught with peril, but then again, what opportunity did not also pose a risk? He could steal the march and have the bulk of his forces across the river before Grant was even aware of what he was doing. He could, as well, then delay the recall, which he knew would come, doing so by the time-honored tradition of "lost" dispatches, misinterpretations, and claims that communications had been cut. If cornered, he had this letter, direct from Stanton, as his defense, but by then he would already be into Baltimore, and at that point not even Grant would dare to venture a recall. Instead the general from the West would have to march to his support or appear to be the one playing politics, risking the Army of the Potomac out of a fit of pique that he had not achieved what this army of the East, phoenix-like, had done on its own.

Lee would not take this lying down. If already in the city of Washington, he would most likely try and hold that position, then turn with part of his force to engage. The numbers then would be almost even, forty-five to fifty thousand on each side. Lee would have to leave at least one of his three corps behind, most likely Beauregard's, to occupy the city. Then it would be an open stand-up fight.

And if ever he had confidence in his boys, it was now. They had tasted the most bitter of defeats. The cowards, the shirkers, had all deserted, and though many a valiant lad and many a good senior officer had fallen in the last campaign, the core that was left was as tough as steel, wanting nothing more than revenge, to restore their honored name.

With that victory his own place would be assured. Grant would be forced to treat him as a co-commander, and that upstart, so unfamiliar with the finer nuances of politics, would soon be left in the dust and it would become clear to the public that he, Sickles, had won this war.

He savored that thought. The chance to prove his own mettle was here at last. The life of a ward heeler, of a mere congressman, of the snickers behind his back over that ridiculous Key affair, would be finished forever. Most important, the 1864 campaign for president loomed ahead.

There was, as well, within his soul, a still loftier ambition. His love of his country could not be questioned by any who truly knew him, though his vision of what that country was, and should be, might differ greatly from those of the ones born to wealth and position. He had clawed his way up, and he knew that nowhere else in this world could one such as he have reached the heights he now occupied. This country had to be saved, its brawling energy, its factories and urban power, and all that derived from that power, expanded to encompass the Western world. Too many good comrades had died for that end. He wanted their deaths to be worth something.

As he contemplated his brandy, tears came to his eyes, for despite his public bluster and bravado, he was at heart a sentimentalist, so typical of his age. The sight of the flag, shot, torn, fluttering in the wind, could still move him to tears. For his army, his Army of the Potomac, he felt a love deeper than any he had ever known. They were his boys, his men. He loved them with a passion, and they knew it, returning his love. They knew him first as a brigade commander, then division, corps, and now finally army, never afraid to stand on the volley line, a fighting general who had all but begged across two years to be unleashed and bring victory.

Victory, in a week I could bring victory.

He drained the rest of his goblet and poured out the remainder of the bottle.

Faces drifted before him, so many comrades gone, men of the old Excelsior Brigade, his first command, bled out in the Peninsula, at Antietam, Fredericksburg, Union Mills. Without hesitation they had gone forward on every field, always following the colors, the flag, always the flag going forward, God bless them.

He remembered a flag bearer from the city, the scum of the gutter before the war, ennobled by it in the end. It was at Chancellorsville, that ghastly, obscene debacle that he could have so easily reversed into a Union victory of historic proportions. They were retreating, and a flag bearer staggered to his side, looked up, and gasped, "Sir, I just want you to know, the flag never touched the ground."

The man collapsed, dying, and yet still he struggled to plant the staff in the ground, to keep the colors aloft.

A dozen of the dying man's comrades gathered around him, taking the colors from his cold hands, holding them aloft, weeping, begging to be ordered back in to restore their honor.

"My God," he whispered, "with such men, how can we fail."

He looked back down at his drink. No more, and he tossed the goblet to the ground, crushing it under his heel.

I must be clear tomorrow, the boys expect it of me. If we are to win, if we are to save our country, I must be clear.

At this moment he knew there was but one man who could achieve that victory, and the thought humbled him.

I must risk all now, act swiftly, firmly, and without hesitation.

The plan for movement was already in place, carefully devised, in secret, with his staff. Before dawn the steam-powered ferries of the Philadelphia, Wilmington, and Baltimore railroad, capable of hauling an entire train across the river in ten minutes, would swing into action, joined by the small flotilla of barges, canal boats, tugs, and ferries that had been quietly gathered on the north bank of the river over the last four weeks. By midafternoon he'd have a full corps across, his old glorious Third, followed then by the Fifth later in the day and the Sixth during the night. Once across, the Third would undertake a forced march on Baltimore via the main road through Abington and Gunpowder Falls, the Fifth along the road through Bel Air, the Sixth to follow as reserve. In two days they should be into Baltimore and victory. And several hours before starting the crossing, he would, as well, cut all telegraph lines to the north. Let Grant and the reporters both wait in ignorance until he could announce the victory of the Army of the Potomac.

His own ambitions were overwhelmed for the moment, and in his dreams transcended his personal desires. *We can end the war here and now.* He knew enough of Lee to realize that perhaps he was walking onto a field of Lee's design. Then so be it, for once engaged he would drive forward with a determination the likes of which the Army of Northern Virginia had never before witnessed.

And the men driving forward would be his chosen band of brothers, his comrades of the Army of the Potomac. In forty-eight hours it would be decided; he would be on the path to the presidency or he would be dead, of that he was convinced. With the Army of the Potomac by his side, he could not conceive of the latter. Victory was just ahead, a vision before him, just on the other side of the river.

Near Reamstown, Pennsylvania

August 18, 1863
6:00 A.M.

Wade Hampton reined in his mount, raising his field glasses to scan the dust swirling up from the west, several riders coming fast.

A troop of cavalry, some of his North Carolina boys, many of them on fine, sleek horses freshly requisitioned from Pennsylvania farmers, trotted past, heading northeast, pushing toward Reading. This was a wonderful country for horses. The remounts taken in the last campaign had been vastly superior to what they had been riding only two months ago, but here, in this untouched land, could be found horses of true breeding, strength, and endurance. His brigade was for once overloaded with horses, some of the troopers leading a couple of remounts as they rode.

Behind him pillars of smoke filled the morning sky. Following the tracks of the railroad that led toward Reading, the boys had been having a grand time of it, burning bridges, destroying supplies they could not bring along, knocking over water towers, and smashing switches. The evening before they had staged a grand spectacle as a parting show in Lancaster. Two trains, one hauling tank cars filled with coal oil, had been deployed a mile apart, their engines stoked up, brakes released, and throttles set to full. The amateur engineers then jumped off, and with hundreds of troopers whooping and hollering like small boys bent on devilish mischief, they watched as the trains built up speed and collided head-on, the tank cars loaded with thousands of gallons of coal oil bursting into flames. Even the civilians had watched the show with awe, children running about excitedly, laughing and clapping at this orgy of destruction.

The local farmers, many of them of the strange Amish and Mennonite

sects, had proven to be a dour lot, but so far there had been no problems. His boys had acted, as always, as proper sons of the South, respectful of women, especially the young ladies and the elderly. And more than one had actually coaxed a smile with his charming drawl and courtly manners, even as they handed out vouchers left and right for horses and food. They had noticed, as well, just how many healthy young men were standing about as if there were no war being fought but fifty miles away, or now galloping past their own farms. It was troubling. He could understand these strange Amish who had taken a vow of peace, like the Quakers, but many were not of the religious dissenters. There was barely a town in South Carolina where a healthy man between sixteen and forty-five could be found. There were enough here in just this one county to raise an entire brigade.

His men had ridden out of Lancaster in high spirits. The farms of the Amish and Mennonites had proven to be a virtual bonanza of food—slabs of hickory-smoked ham, tubs of something they called scrapple, links of fat sausages, beefsteaks, chickens, geese hung from nearly every saddle. To get fresh, roasting ears of corn or apples all one had to do was turn off the road for a moment and lean over a fence to gather in all he might desire. Loaves of fresh bread stuck out of haversacks, and a ruckus ensued when a trooper just ahead of him rode past one of his comrades and slapped the man's hat, which he had been cradling in his lap. A couple of dozen eggs were ruptured and a gooey fight broke out as broken eggs were thrown back and forth, the boys laughing.

Long before dawn, just north of Lancaster, the brigade had split up, two regiments turning to the northwest to probe toward Harrisburg, one regiment east, along the track of the Philadelphia and Columbia railroad toward Downington and West Chester, the rest of his command in the middle, moving toward Reading. The regiment going east, the Jeff Davis Regiment, was at this point nothing more than a light raid and probe with the intent of spreading panic in Philadelphia and engaging in some bridge-burning and train-wrecking.

But now, as he watched the courier's approach, he felt a tightening in his stomach. Something was up. The three of them came on fast, at the gallop, and reined in, saluting.

"Sir, we got Yankee cavalry, ten miles off."

Wade forced a smile. He had hoped they'd have another day of it before the Yankees finally reacted in their typical slow and leisurely fashion.

"Well, it's about time. We've been here a day and a half without a sight of one of them."

One of the couriers shook his head.

"Sir. It's not just a patrol. Looks to be damn near a brigade. Colonel Baker says he's going to have to pull back before them."

"How far?"

"When we were told to find you, it was about ten miles to the west of here. We were moving toward Harrisburg, as ordered. The civilians were damn closed-mouthed, wouldn't give us a word of information, though one old codger just grinned and said we were gonna wind up like rabbits in a snare, that the whole area is crawling with Yankees. The main road we were on, you could see where one hell of a lot of troopers had been marching a day or two earlier, a couple of orchards just stripped of apples, one big hay field trampled down. The farmer that owned the orchard and field was boiling mad, said that ten thousand or more Yankees had marched through two days ago from Harrisburg, then turned around and marched back, cleaning him out."

He took that in. Why? That was before he crossed the river. Drilling perhaps? Keeping the men in shape?

"Just around sunup we seen them coming," the messenger continued. "The country was open, Colonel Baker had a good vantage point, you could just make out the church spires of what we figure might be Harrisburg, and then they just came storming out on to the fields a couple miles away, filling every lane. A couple thousand at least."

Wade opened up his map case and pulled out the sketches of the region that Jed Hotchkiss had prepared for him. His forces were spread thin, and now he wondered. There had been absolutely no resistance so far. To spread out was routine at this point, cast the net wide until they hit something.

If he drew an oblong box set on one point, he was in the middle. The bottom point was their river crossing twenty-five miles away, the left point Harrisburg, the north point Reading, the east point toward West Chester.

"Any identification? Who are they?"

"Sir, we picked up a couple of deserters from the Nineteenth Corps; they were hiding in a barn not five miles from here. Said they were fed up and going home. Seems like they were the ones out on that march and these two snuck off."

"Nineteenth?"

"Yes, sir."

"Did they say where they came from?"

"Harrisburg."

Damn.

So he had one piece of the puzzle that Lee had sent him for, if the deserters were to be believed.

"Did you take them prisoner?"

"No sir, we let them go."

"Why?"

"One was so damn sick, sir, he was near dead; the other was just a scared boy, the sick man's young brother. We took their parole and left them. Colonel Baker, though, felt we should believe them."

Then the Nineteenth was in Harrisburg. And that spoke volumes.

"Anything else?"

"No sir, nothing we saw. Like I said, a few farmers said that Yankees have been marching up and down the roads the last few weeks. Carrying

306 NEWT GINGRICH AND WILLIAM R. FORSTCHEN

all equipment, the men said they were drilling. We found a farm boy wearing a Yankee cap with the corps insignia for the Thirteenth, said he found it after some troops marched by, heading back toward Harrisburg. One woman we met just before seeing the Yankees said she was born in South Carolina and she did sound like it. Married a Yankee, God save her. She said that no civilians are allowed anywhere near Harrisburg, all the roads are closed off with military guards, and you need a pass to get in or out."

That was to be expected. The Northern newspapers had openly reported that bit of information and complained bitterly about it and about the imposition of martial law on not just the city but the entire surrounding county.

"Sir, Colonel Baker says he's pulling back and he'd like some support."

Wade nodded. The Second South Carolina was less than a half hour up the road, heading toward Reading behind the First North Carolina. He'd turn the Second around now. But the First? If they could at least get to Sinking Springs and destroy some track and telegraph lines there on the main route between Harrisburg and Reading, it would be a major accomplishment. He had hoped that Baker could actually close on the outskirts of Harrisburg while he held the center here and moved on Reading. Now that was in doubt.

He hesitated. Concentrate? Suppose Baker was overreacting? Perhaps this cavalry force was nothing more than second-rate militia that would scatter when faced with a real charge?

But if not, if I let them swing behind me, cut me off from the river, and they were seasoned troopers, it could be a problem.

And yet Stuart had faced far worse numbers. He had ridden clean around the entire Army of the Potomac, raised havoc, gathered intelligence, and lost only a few score men.

No. Don't hesitate now.

"Let Baker fall back here. I'll keep Cobb's legion here and I'll stay as well. Tell Baker to fall back and lead them on. We'll give them a good drubbing here."

The couriers saluted, turned, and started back west.

Wade watched them leave and turned to look at the sun, now warm and golden in the morning sky. It would most likely be a hot day, but the weather was fair, the roads were good, the farmland was rich. He was farther north than any Confederate cavalryman had ever dreamed possible only six months ago, and he would make the most of it. Beat these men before midafternoon, then on to Reading. A fire in that rail yard would most likely be a sight to behold, outshining anything Jeb could ever hope to boast about.

In Front of Washington

August 18, 1863
7:00 A.M.

 I t had come.

General Lee found it hard to contain his excitement. For more than a year he had laid out dozens of such plans. Some had come to fruition, many had disappeared and been forgotten. For once communications were on the Confederate side. The telegraph line from the south bank of the Susquehanna clear down to his headquarters before Fort Stevens had been fully restored. Extra wire had been found in Baltimore along with some telegraphers who had volunteered to help string a line straight to his headquarters. It was a luxury he had never operated with before, to have instant communications with scouts stationed almost seventy miles away. He marveled at the new potentials he saw before him.

The first report had come in at three in the morning, Walter interrupting his sleep with the message that significant activity was going on along the north bank of the river. Steam engines were firing up their boilers. An hour before dawn the gunboats on the river had come up close to shore, and minutes later a tug pushed in a barge loaded with a regiment of troops to secure the bank. As ordered, his light screen of cavalry had traded a few shots at long range, then appeared to flee. Just before dawn the first heavy ferry had crossed, carrying nearly a thousand men.

The forward station had just closed down, the last message . . . *Dozens of ships moving on river, infantry, artillery, cavalry. Third Corps. Flags of Fifth Corps identified on heights of north bank. Must abandon station.*

As he had anticipated, the Third Corps was in the lead. That was a vanity he expected of Sickles. The man had played true to form.

There had been no movements or sightings of troops attempting to come down the Chesapeake, to reinforce either Washington or the garrison at Fort McHenry. That had been his one great concern, that Lincoln would play the card of caution and reinforce the garrison of Washington. If the Army of the Potomac had transferred here, en masse, secure behind the fortifications, it might have presented him with a strategic dilemma, a field force of maybe fifty thousand, positioned closer to Richmond than his own army, with Grant threatening from the rear. No, Sickles had played the card he wanted. He imagined Grant would be beside himself with anger.

"Walter."

As always his adjutant was waiting and was under the awning within seconds. Lee looked up at him, smiled.

Walter scanned the latest, confirming that the Army of the Potomac was beginning to ship over artillery. This was no raid or feint; it was the real thing at last.

"It's not a reconnaissance," Walter said excitedly. "They're moving. He'll have the entire army over by tomorrow morning and will be on the march."

Lee nodded.

"Send for Generals Longstreet, Hood, and Beauregard. I want this army on the march, as planned."

Walter, grinning, ran from the tent.

General Lee sat back in his chair. He felt utterly confident, a confidence that had been shaken at Fort Stevens and even by the troubling conversation with Benjamin and Rabbi Rothenberg. The game was afoot again, he was back in his element, and all doubts were put aside. The trap had been sprung as he had planned. By midday, his entire army would be on the march, streaming north through the night. By late tomorrow he would hit Sickles with everything he had, unless the man showed caution, dug in on the banks of the Gunpowder River, and held back.

But he knew this opponent, as he had known all the others. Sickles would not hesitate. He would see his chance for glory, to upstage Grant, to take Baltimore back. He would come on fast.

It would now be a footrace. Now it was a matter of weather and luck, both of which had rarely failed the Army of Northern Virginia in any of its campaigns.

Near Hinkleton, Pennsylvania
East Bank of the Conestoga River

August 18, 1863
3:00 P.M.

Wade Hampton ducked as the shell detonated only a dozen feet away, showering him with dirt. Standing back up, he saw one of his staff not moving, a glance showing that the boy was dead, a shell fragment having sliced into his temple. He looked away. There was no time for that now.

Raising his field glasses, he scanned the road they had just retreated down only minutes before. These damn Pennsylvania farmers had made the bridge spanning the river of stone, impossible to destroy. On the far side of the stream, a quarter mile away, hundreds of Yankee troopers were swarming out to either flank, riding hard, while in the center a regiment or more were dismounted, coming in on foot. Already the snap whine of their carbine fire was whisking past him, the angry, beelike buzz of .52-caliber rounds cutting the air.

Along the banks of the creek his men were spreading out as well, horse holders moving to the rear, dismounted troopers, most armed with muzzle-loading rifles, a few with the precious Sharps carbines their opponents carried. His own battery of horse artillery was up, pounding away, struggling to keep at bay the two batteries of Yankee artillery shelling the line.

The battle had been a running engagement for the last fifteen miles, opening with skirmishing just before noon, and then a full-blown run of ten miles back to this river. He had led half a dozen countercharges. In the past one such charge would have sent them reeling, half the Yankees falling off their horses in the rout.

This was different, damn different. The Yankees fell back in order as each charge advanced, and then his boys would hit a wall of fire from dismounted troopers behind a fence row, an embankment, a tree lot that would empty a dozen saddles, and he would be forced to fall back. All the time, flanking forces, at least a regiment in strength to north or south, would range out, trying to pincer in, forcing him to fall back yet again.

Focusing his field glasses on the road, he saw what appeared to be a general and his staff, directly in the middle of the road, arrogant, unmoving as a shell detonated nearby. No one he recognized. It must be that Grierson, the raider from Mississippi and Louisiana that the papers had made such a fuss over.

Behind him the last of the Jeff Davis Regiment was up, recalled from its ride toward Downington, but the horses were blown even as they arrived to join their comrades from Cobb's legion and the First and Second South Carolina. In fact, all his horses were blown after this running four-hour battle.

They had taken a few prisoners in the last skirmish before pulling back to the river. The Yankee troopers were arrogant, lean, as weather-beaten as his own. Men from an Illinois regiment boasted that Grierson had sworn an oath to entertain Hampton for dinner before shipping him to the prison camp at Elmira.

The prisoners, still under escort, were sitting nearby, now watching the battle with detached amusement, the way prisoners did when they knew they were safe. He could hear them calmly discussing the spreading fight like professionals, pointing out with glee their own regiment, advancing on foot in the center, the flanking forces even now ranging far outward, a couple of miles away, to the north and south, dust the only indicator of their movements.

He walked over toward them and they looked up. Their leader, a lieutenant, got to his feet and with just the slightest look of mocking disdain offered a salute, which Wade did not return.

"Getting hot for ya, General?" a sergeant nursing a wounded hand asked, looking up at him, shifting a chaw of tobacco in his mouth.

"Were you part of the raid with Grierson out west?" Wade asked.

The lieutenant grinned.

"Sure as hell was. Rode from one end of Mississippi to the other in three weeks. Never seen so many rebels running in my entire life. Almost as many as we seen running today."

"You damn Yankee," one of Wade's staff started to step forward, and the lieutenant eyed him coldly. Wade extended his hand, motioning for his man to stop.

The wounded sergeant chuckled and grinned.

"You ain't facing the Army of the Potomac today, General. You're getting a taste of Ulysses S. Grant and his men from the western armies," the sergeant said.

Wade nodded thoughtfully. These men were different, very different, more like his own even, the way they looked in threadbare uniforms, the sergeant with a patch on his knee, the lieutenant's hat faded, sweat soaked, his uniform jacket just a private's sack coat with shoulder bars. There was no Army of the Potomac spit and polish here. They seemed to take an easy pride in themselves.

"How does it feel to be prisoners?" one of Wade's staff snapped.

"Oh, not for long we reckon. The ball's just started, General," the lieutenant replied, and the three men sitting behind him nodded. "It's a long way back across the river for you, isn't it? Kinda figure we'll be hosting you in a day or two."

"If crossing the river is even our intent."

The lieutenant just smiled and did not reply.

"You'll be well treated. I'll have a surgeon check your sergeant. If at the end of the day there's prisoners to be exchanged, I'll see you're passed back through the lines."

"Thank you, sir," the lieutenant replied and this time the man's arrogance dropped a bit.

Wade started to turn away. He caught the eye of the sergeant, who continued to grin while staring at him, as if the man held a deep secret. The look was momentarily unnerving. These men were not beaten, not by a long stretch.

Another shell shrieked overhead, the wind of its passage buffeting Wade. Those gunners were good, damn good, ignoring the counter-battery fire for the moment, concentrating on his own knot of staff and observers, the other guns pounding the approach to the bridge.

He surveyed his line. The battle front was more than half a mile across. Troops had been detached to the flanks to cover fords, burn any bridges, and keep an eye on the flanking force. Already he could sense that their main effort was shifting southward, an obvious move to try and cut him off from running back toward the Susquehanna.

Like hell. It was time Grierson and this upstart army from the West were taught a lesson on how Confederate cavalry in the East could fight and knock some of the overbearing confidence out of them. He would dig in here, along the river, and let them come. By evening, the first North Carolina heading toward Reading should be back, hitting them in the flank. He would hold right here and let them try and take this position, then, when the timing was right, mount up and countercharge, driving them back toward Harrisburg.

Lee had sent him across the river to gather intelligence and sow panic. That mission had yet to be accomplished. By tomorrow he'd have Grierson bloodied and on the run. If this was to be the opening fight between the Army of Northern Virginia and this Grant and his so-called Army of the Susquehanna, it damn well better be a Confederate victory, no matter what the cost.

Havre de Grace, Maryland

August 18, 1863
3:30 P.M.

The army, his army, was on the march.

He had picked a spot atop the river bluff, sitting astride his charger, the road from the ferry dock weaving up from the river's edge. The river itself was swarming with activity, dozens of ships moving back and forth, the huge ferries of the railroad, each one capable of moving a thousand men, an entire battery of guns, or a hundred troopers and their mounts. Dozens of smaller boats, some of them side-wheel or stern-wheel steamers, others barges pushed by steam tugs, were pushing across as well, again loaded with troops. One of the two big railroad ferries was bringing over twenty or more supply wagons with their teams of mules.

So far it was all going without a hitch. A few horses had panicked and gone into the river; one man was reported dead drunk and falling off a boat loaded down with pack and rifle.

Engineering troops from New York were already hard at work, throwing down split logs to corduroy the road up from the docks, and a thousand contraband laborers were working beside them, many of them having worked on the riverboats and ferries repairing docks damaged by rebel raiders the month before after the mad retreat from Baltimore.

A serpentine column of men were coming up the slope, boys of his old Second Division, Humphrey's men, Brewster's brigade, New Yorkers!

He nodded to the bandmaster standing by his side. The officer was well decked out in full dress uniform, huge bearskin cap, the afternoon sun glinting off all his gold braid. The bandmaster saluted with his staff, turned, and held it aloft, announcing the song.

After the initial wave of a brigade had swept across and secured the heights, he had made certain that a band was ferried across, in fact every band from his old Third Corps, a couple of hundred men in total, along with dozens of drummers.

Morale was a precious thing and music was part of it. Commissary wagons had come over as well, loaded down with thousands of loaves of fresh-baked bread and hundreds of smoked hams, and were parked just beyond the rise.

Just before the head of the brigade reached the top of the crest, the bandmaster, timing things perfectly, held his silver staff aloft and brought it down emphatically. A ruffle from fifty massed drums sounded, a long roll that set corkscrews down the back of any soldier who heard it. The long roll continued, the beat of the charge, and it rolled on and on, joined by the steady beat of bass drums.

The head of the advancing column looked up. Massed to the fore were the flags of the brigade commander and all the regiments, officers at the fore. Brewster, arm still in a sling from Union Mills, grinned, clumsily drew his sword, and saluted Dan, who returned the salute.

Again the staff went up, drum major twirling it over his head and bringing it back down. An eerie moment of silence, and then he raised the staff yet again.

The drums sounded as one, the thrump, thrump, thrump of a marching beat, a flourish at the end. The massed brass sounded a flourish and then opened with the resounding chords one of the favorite marching

songs of the Army of the Potomac, a song that they had once sung with fervor advancing up the Peninsula. Now, after such a long and bitter year, they were hearing it again, on this bright, sunlit afternoon that promised them a dream of glory.

> *Yes, we'll rally round the flag, boys,*
> *Rally once again,*
> *Shouting the Battle Cry of Freedom!*

The effect he wished, which he knew it would create, worked its magic. The men of that column looked up, a thrill going through them. At least for this moment all was forgotten, all fear of what was to come was washed away, and in an instant, thousands of voices picked up the song, shouting it to the heavens, unmindful of all the cynicism of the past, all shattered hopes, all the sad graves and missing faces in their ranks. . . .

> *The Union forever!*
> *Hurrah boys hurrah!*
> *Down with the traitor, up with the star!*

314 NEWT GINGRICH AND WILLIAM R. FORSTCHEN

Some could not even sing the words, they shouted them out, more than one with tears in their eyes, as if the dream of a long-lost love had suddenly appeared before them, that a land of promise was still before them, and in the end, this time, yes this time, it would indeed be their day.

As the column marched past, he stood in his stirrups, caught in the moment, fully mindful of the sketch artist from *Harper's Weekly*, Winslow Homer, who stood behind him, working furiously with charcoal to capture the moment, the photographer from Brady's by his side, hidden beneath his black curtain, as he struggled to focus his camera.

The wagons laded with fresh bread were by the side of the road, quartermaster soldiers pulling out the loaves and cut slabs of smoked ham, handing them out to the passing ranks, one to each line of four, and even the most hardened cynic, who might not be roused by the song, could at least respond to this largesse of a grateful republic.

> *And we'll fill the vacant ranks*
> *Of our brothers gone before,*
> *Shouting the Battle Cry of Freedom!*

Cheer echoed onto cheer, caps were off, rifles held aloft, battle-scarred flags fluttering in the afternoon breeze.

The column pressed on, heading south, heading back into the war.

Dan Sickles turned to his staff. "My God," he gasped, "this time we will win!"

Harrisburg, Pennsylvania

August 18, 1863
5:00 P.M.

He's done what?"

Grant came to his feet, his camp chair falling over behind him. Ely Parker held the telegram and Grant snatched it, scanning the few lines, a relay of a message from a reporter with the *New York Tribune*, that Sickles's army was across the Susquehanna and moving south.

"I've already sent a query back," Ely replied. "The telegraph lines started buzzing with it just minutes ago. I'll see what more I can find."

Grant turned and slammed his fist on the table. General Ord, who had been sitting quietly with him, waiting for dispatches as to the running fight unfolding with Hampton forty miles to the southeast, shook his head.

"Always said that son of a bitch would go off half-cocked the moment he had the chance."

Grant said nothing, struggling to rein in his temper.

It had been a tense day. The raid by Hampton had severed communications down along the Susquehanna. That was to be expected; he was surprised Lee had not tried something like this before now, but the sudden dropping of the lines out of Perryville just after midnight had baffled him. He had assumed that some rebel sympathizers, working in concert with Hampton, had been the culprits, and it had been a bit unnerving. Though he assumed Lee would not try an all-out assault on Washington, nothing in war was ever assured and he had silently fretted ever since Ely had awakened him with the news just before dawn.

Now he knew. Damn it, he knew.

"I bet he cut the lines himself," Ord said, as if reading Grant's mind. "Get across and halfway to Baltimore before you can even hope to call him back. Then what are you going to do?"

General Logan came into the tent and Grant was aware that out in the headquarters compound there was a real stir, men running back and forth, shouting comments about Sickles.

Ord took the coffeepot off the small stove and poured himself a drink, looking over at Grant.

"Well, is it true, sir?"

"I'm not sure yet. Only a newspaper report. But yes, I think it's true. He knows I can't reach him, not with Hampton cutting up and the lines down."

Ely came back into the tent, holding several more telegrams, and handed them to Grant.

All were the same. Reports from the Associated Press, one from the *Philadelphia Inquirer,* complete to a brief description of bands playing and flags flying as the Third Corps set off just after dawn, the rest of the army set to follow.

It was true. *Damn it!*

He tossed the telegrams on the table for Ord and McPherson to read and stepped out of the tent. At the sight of him the dozens of officers milling about froze. The look on his face stopped all of them in their tracks.

"I think we have better things to do than run about like a bunch of old housewives chasing a headless chicken."

No one spoke, but within seconds the area around his tent was a ghost town. He struck a match on the tent post and puffed a cigar to life.

Grant had studied the maps till they were burned into his memory; he knew what would unfold. First it was dependent on Lee far more than anything Sickles did. If, as Grant assumed, the attack on Washington was nothing more than a feint to try and draw one or both of them out before they were fully ready, Lee had indeed succeeded. If Washington was still his main goal, which Grant had doubted all along, Lee would still have two days to do his worst. He would trade Baltimore for Washington; the taking and securing of that town would be too much for Sickles to resist, and that would delay his advance even longer.

But no, Lee wanted to destroy the Union armies, not to cut his own army's guts out trying to take a city. It is exactly how he would do it. It was the mistake that McClellan and all the others had never fully grasped. It was always Lee; Richmond was secondary and would fall once Lee was removed. If McClellan had gone into the Peninsula with that in mind and acted aggressively, all of this would be moot now.

Lee wanted the Army of the Potomac, and now Sickles was heading straight at him.

There was now, as well, a darker thought. Had Sickles acted alone, or did someone goad him? Surely it wasn't Lincoln. Grant found that impossible to accept. They had given each other their word and lived to it.

Stanton?

But why?

Why risk all now, when in another three weeks everything would be in place, and with a united front he could have advanced, combined with the garrison in Washington outnumbering Lee at more than two, perhaps even three to one with rifles in the field.

There was no sense in wasting thought on it now. All of that was now out the window. He would have to start afresh as of this moment.

Regardless of its leadership, Grant had no doubt that the Army of the Potomac was a hard-fighting lot. All the rivalry between East and West aside, they were men that could sustain ten, fifteen thousand casualties in a day, something that he had seen only at Shiloh, and then turn around and do it again. Approximately forty-five thousand men. If given good ground and an open fight, one that Sickles did not bungle, they just might make a damn good accounting of themselves. But only if Sickles did not bungle.

Of course he'd send the order out to recall. There was a chance he could reach Sickles before nightfall, and under pain of relieving him from command pull him back from this folly. But he knew in his heart that that would be an exercise in futility. The man was too crafty. Grant knew that no general was entirely above playing the game at times, making sure a dispatch was lost or a telegraph line cut yet again.

No, he would have to recast all on the assumption that Lee and Sickles would meet, maybe as early as tomorrow afternoon, definitely within two days.

He stepped back into the tent.

"Ely, write up a telegram of recall."

"Send it on the open wire?"

Grant hesitated.

No, he couldn't do that. It'd be in every paper in the country within two hours, revealing dissension in the ranks, confusion, and could even trigger a panic. If Stanton had directly ordered Sickles to advance, especially based upon information of which Grant was not aware, perhaps if Lee had indeed attacked and Grant sent a recall, it would bring into the open a confrontation that Lincoln would have to address on the spot. If Washington was on the verge of falling and he ordered Sickles back it, could be a disaster, even though he knew the chance was remote.

He shook his head.

"No, Ely. No telegram. A sealed dispatch. You are to take it personally. I will draw it up."

"Are you going to fire him?" Ord asked.

Grant looked over at his old friend, who should have known better than to ask. Ord said nothing and just shook his head.

"General Ord, let's get this fracas with Hampton wrapped up. I want you to see to it; I don't have time now."

Ord nodded, saluted, and left, McPherson following.

He sat down and began to draft the dispatch, knowing it was already a useless exercise. And in his mind, he began to contemplate how he, and the army gathered around him, would respond as well.

Near Claysville, Maryland

August 18, 1863
7:00 P.M.

C.S.A. General Lee looked to the west, to where the sky was beginning to shift to gold and scarlet. Already the days were turning shorter and, he realized, in another month the first touch of autumn would be in the air.

The afternoon heat was beginning to abate, the first cool breeze of twilight wafting along the road, which was packed solid with troops as far as the eye could see.

The men marched now with grim purpose. Orders had been given. They finally knew what they were doing, and he could sense that many of them were relieved. They had come down this same road only days before, for some the fourth time now that they had passed up and down it over the last month. In the march south, many had dreaded the thought that they were marching to a frontal assault on some of the heaviest fortifications in the world. He had not been able to share with them his thoughts and plans, that the march had been nothing more than a maneuver, a feint, to bring out the Army of the Potomac. Their efforts, their exhaustion, their marching under the hot sun of August had achieved for him that goal.

The wiser of them had undoubtedly figured it out long ago, and those not so wise would now boast that they had known from the start. And now they were marching again, forewarned that this pace would continue through the night. Fifty minutes of march and ten minutes of break, hour after hour, with two hours' rest just before dawn, then back on the road yet again.

He thought for a moment of Jackson. This was the type of maneuver that Jackson relished and that a year ago was a forte that only he could claim. But in the last seven weeks that spirit had moved into the rest of the ranks, even to Old Pete, who at this moment was at the fore of the column a dozen miles up the road. His corps had been farthest back from Washington, placed there in anticipation of this moment. They were to spring forward, prevent Sickles from gaining Baltimore and the potential fallback position of the harbor, where the Union navy could support him. Then they were to pin him in place, then hold him till Hood came up on his right flank and Beauregard was properly deployed to spring the trap.

He knew Longstreet would see it through, a march to add another laurel like the one gained in the march from Gettysburg to Union Mills.

The road ahead drifted down into a darkly shaded hollow cut by a shallow, meandering stream. He drifted from the side of the road, the troops pressing on, passing over a rough bridge that had been built during the agonizing mud march of the month before. The stream was again a meandering trickle, thick, high grass and weeds bordering its banks.

The air in the hollow was damp, cool. Fireflies weaved and danced above the meadow grass. He let Traveler edge into the stream, loosening his reins, his old companion drinking deeply.

Alongside him, in the shadows, the bridge rumbled with the passage of troops, the closely packed column moving at a relentless pace, few of the men recognizing him.

This river of strength flowed by him, tens of thousands of his boys, his men, this flower of the South, these victors of so many hard-fought battles. And tomorrow they would go in again; none needed to be told of that.

He watched them in silence, and suddenly there were tears in his eyes. The tears came unbidden, surprising, as if waiting in the damp cool-ness of the stream to embrace and overwhelm him.

How many will I lose tomorrow? How many more must die? He caught a glimpse of a young drummer boy, silhouetted, exhausted, slumped over, riding on the pommel of an officer's horse, the officer with his arms around the boy to keep him from falling off. A man with rifle slung over his shoulder, banjo in his hands, was trying to pick out a tune. He passed on. Several men were momentarily illuminated by the flash of a match, someone lighting a pipe, then shadows again. Boys, young men, old men, rifles on shoulders, slung inverted, held by barrels in clenched hands. All were leaning forward slightly, blanket rolls and backpacks chafing shoul-ders. As always, the steady clanging rhythm of tin cups banging on can-teens; a muffled curse as one soldier suddenly hopped about while trying to keep pace, his friends laughing when they realized he had picked up a splinter from the wooden bridge while marching barefoot.

Voices, hundreds of voices, filled the night, mingling together, over-lapping, rising and falling, snatches of conversation as they approached the bridge, then disappearing as they marched over it and beyond . . .

"Gonna be a real fight tomorrow and you'll see 'em run . . . tell you I'm worried; her last letter said the baby was due and I ain't heard a word in eight weeks. . . . Did you see his face when Jimmie threw down them three aces? . . . It's been four months since I even kissed a girl and it's driv-ing me just crazy. . . . Ma said they buried Pa next to my little sister. . . . Next war, I'm joining the navy I tell you. . . ."

And thus it continued as they passed.

He took off his hat.

"Oh, merciful God," he whispered. "Guide me with Thy infinite love and mercy. Help me to do what is right. Help me to lead these men yet again. If battle comes tomorrow, I beg Thee to let it be swift and to bring this war to an end. Please, dear God, guide all those who fall into Thy in-finite and eternal love. Comfort those who shall lose their loved ones. Guide me as well as Your humble servant to fulfill Your judgment and let the scourge of war soon pass from this land.

"Amen."

Traveler was done drinking; his head was raised, looking back at him, and Lee felt a flood of warmth for his old friend. It seemed as if the horse knew that his companion was praying, and waiting patiently for him to finish. He patted the horse lightly on the neck, whispering a few words of affection. He heard someone cough, and, a bit self-conscious, Lee looked over his shoulder and saw by the edge of the river his staff, all of them with hats off, many with heads still lowered.

He put his hat back on and crossed the stream, falling back in with the Army of Northern Virginia as it marched on through the night.

Chapter Eighteen

CSA "Tell General Lee all that you've seen here. Remember, if they start to close in, don't hesitate to destroy the dispatches. Now ride!"

Wade Hampton watched as the half-dozen couriers galloped off into the morning mist.

It had been a running battle throughout the night. Just before dusk he had been hit by three devastating pieces of news, one on top of the other. The first was that the Yankees, flanking wide, had cut across the Conestoga River a half-dozen miles above and below his line and were pincering in. The second, that a brigade of their cavalry having moved, the night before on a wide sweep, a fifty-mile ride to his north and around Reading, was falling onto his rear. The third, that his way out, the river crossing, had already been cut by cavalry now joined by a brigade of infantry, which had been moved down by rail from Harrisburg to Columbia. Additional units were blocking every other ford. He wasn't facing a lone regiment, or even a brigade of experienced troopers. He was facing an entire division of cavalry backed by infantry, and they were good, damn good, the best he had ever seen.

The morale of his men, so high and exuberant just the morning before, was beginning to crumble. Word had filtered through the ranks that their comrades with the First North Carolina had been cut off somewhere up toward Reading and wiped out. A prisoner released by Grierson just before dawn had come riding in, confirming the news, and bringing with him an offer of honorable surrender.

Like hell! If need be, he'd ride clear to the outskirts of Philadelphia, shake them off during that long ride, then turn about and sweep down to the river. All his men had been ordered to pull in remounts and to move, to keep moving. These damn Yankees from the West might ride through Mississippi, but they were facing Wade Hampton now. He would damn well give them the ride of a lifetime, drive them clear into exhaustion, then leave them in his dust.

"Let's go," he shouted.

Even as the rattle of carbine fire sounded in the west, he set off, heading east toward Christiana. It was in the exact opposite direction of where he had hoped to go, but that was finished for now. The race was on.

Washington, D.C.
The White House

August 19, 1863
7:00 A.M.

He's done what?"

Incredulous, Abraham Lincoln looked at Elihu Washburne, who was holding a sheaf of dispatches in his hand.

"Yesterday morning, just before dawn, General Sickles started to move the entire Army of the Potomac across the Susquehanna. I passed through there late yesterday, asked by General Grant to look at the situation myself and then report to you, Mr. President."

"Merciful heavens," Lincoln sighed.

"I don't know how much mercy is involved in this one, Mr. President. I will confess, it was one hell of a show, what little I saw of it; massed bands, rations being handed out like there was no tomorrow. It was a regular circus. As I was leaving on the courier boat, the Fifth Corps was embarking, with the Sixth lined up to follow."

"We've had no word from Perryville since yesterday, all courier boats stopped," the president commented in exasperation.

"General Sickles ordered a shutdown of all traffic; he claimed it was for security reasons, but I daresay it was to keep you and Grant in the dark as long as possible as well. I was able to get a boat because no one was willing to face me down on the issue, but it was a damn slow boat and took hours longer to get here."

"Shrewd move by Sickles," Lincoln sighed. "Does Grant know of this?"

"I would assume he does by now, but he didn't know about it when I left him."

"Did he order it? Perhaps after you left?"

"Absolutely not. He asked me to convey to you the usual correspondence you two have maintained over the last month. He was optimistic when I left him. Supplies are still coming in; he's still short of wagons and pontoon bridging; he's still waiting for some additional men; for example, that colored division, but things were going on schedule up until this thing with Sickles broke loose. Yes, he's aware that Lee is in front of Washington, but not overly concerned. As we discussed last month, Baltimore will force Lee to stay in Maryland, and Washington will serve as the bait for him to try an attack, most likely under pressure from Davis."

"Davis is no longer with the Army of Northern Virginia," Lincoln replied.

"Sir?"

Lincoln smiled and tossed over a copy of the *Richmond Enquirer.* Elihu scanned the front page and the report that the rebel president was back in the Confederate capital after a successful tour of the front.

"Why do you think he pulled out?" Elihu asked.

"That, my friend, is indication enough that Lee's move on Washington was a feint. Davis would never have left if an attack was pending that could have given him the glory of riding up here to the White House to take possession. No, he's back in Richmond, because Lee is not going to try to fight his way into Washington."

"But why?"

"Pressure in Tennessee, perhaps. Sherman will link up with Rosecrans within the week."

"And?"

"As you know, General Grant will put Sherman in command there. Maybe word of that leaked. Perhaps his leaving is a cagey politician's instinct not to be here if Lee should suffer a defeat. Besides, with the weakness of Confederate communications, it was most likely impossible for him to run the government from a hundred and fifty miles away. But whatever the motive, it was proof enough to me that some of our people have been overreacting to the sight of rebel banners in front of Fort Stevens.

"Besides, to confirm it all, reports are coming in now from Heintzelman. The rebels abandoned their position during the night."

"Now, that is news."

"I'm surprised you didn't hear of it on the way over from the navy yard."

"I took a carriage; my driver didn't say a word."

It struck Elihu how information was now so fragmented. Grant had no idea at this moment about the abandonment of the Washington front by Lee; Lincoln only this moment knew about Sickles's move. Damn it, most likely the only one who knew what was really going on was Lee, yet again.

"Another deserter came into the lines just after midnight," Lincoln continued. "Claimed the entire line was abandoned."

"One would think nearly all those deserters were nothing more than plants by Lee. Two days ago they were affirming the big attack was about to begin."

"I felt the same way," Lincoln replied. "Though most of those gold-encrusted popinjays over at the War Office hang on every word said by each deserter who comes in. This rebel though, I'm told, was a boy from Kentucky, sick of the war, just wants to go home. He said that at mid-morning the entire army started to move, the last of them pulling out around nine last night. So our General Heintzelman sent over a patrol around three this morning and they reported the entire line is empty except for a few detachments of cavalry busy stoking campfires. Lee has slipped off."

"And is now heading straight toward Sickles."

Lincoln sighed and nodded.

"I don't understand any of this at the moment," Lincoln said. "Yesterday there was dang near a panic in this city with the shelling, everyone, including Stanton, telling me that Lee would attack come nightfall. And now this."

"I think, sir, we've been humbugged."

"What?"

"Just that. Humbugged, sir. Lee knew his game and played it. He didn't dare attack directly. Yes, he might have taken the city, but he would have lost twenty, thirty thousand doing it. And then Grant, as we've talked about so many times, would have come sweeping down to finish him off. All along the two of you agreed that Washington and Baltimore would be the bait for the trap. Keep Lee in Maryland until Grant was ready with an overwhelming force to cross the Susquehanna and then finish him.

"It was a bold gambit on your part and you played it well. Not leaving the city, to hell with all the traitors and naysayers up north. In fact, this city being cut off was a blessing to you, and you stayed."

"But this move by Sickles?"

"The man saw his chance. In the end he is no different than McClellan, Halleck, McClernand out west, Butler, all the others. They might be loyal, though at times I had my doubts about McClellan."

"Don't speak too harshly of him," Lincoln replied. "When ordered to resign, he did so."

"And even now is maneuvering to run against you on a peace ticket next year. But as to Sickles. Look at it from his side. The Army of the Potomac, God bless them, was finished as a fighting unit after Union Mills. But those boys, after two years of bitter defeat, will not easily concede that they need Grant and his Westerners to help them now. Sickles played on that. With Hampton raiding and cutting the telegraph lines, with Lee making all appearances that he was about to make his grand assault on Washington, even though you doubted it as did Grant, Sickles saw his chance and grabbed for it. He wants a final showdown with Lee, and he thinks he can win this war on his own. Then he can run for president as the victory candidate, the man who saved the Union when you had failed."

"Damn it."

Lincoln slammed his fist on his desk, a display of temper so rare that it stunned Elihu. Lincoln looked up at him, hollow-eyed.

"Just once, just for once, can't we act together? We all have the same goal, I daresay even General Lee does, though the results he desires are different. We want this war to end. And yet we always seem to be working at cross-purposes to each other. If only Sickles had kept his horses reined in, if he had but waited one more month, he and Grant could have advanced together, working in unison to see it through."

Elihu smiled sadly.

"You are talking idealistically, sir, when we should be talking about the realities of running a republic."

Lincoln sighed and sat down. Picking up a pencil, he twirled it absently as he looked out his office window.

"We politicians are divided into two types in this war, in any war," Elihu said. "The majority, though they might proclaim that the dream of the republic motivates them at heart, are ultimately swayed by the advantage they can gain for themselves. They will proclaim to their followers that the good of the republic is the sole cause for their actions, and many will then follow.

"The second type, God save us, like you and Grant, are so rare. You two actually do wish to see this ideal, this dream, survive, and would give your lives for it without hesitation. Never confuse the two. I think it will always be thus, a hundred, a hundred and fifty years from now, if we survive; there will still be men and women who will proclaim their love of the republic, perhaps even believe it, but at heart are in it only for their own power.

"There is much of Sickles I like. He's a damn good general in his own right, but ultimately he is blinded by the light, the power, the dream that he can be the savior of this cause, and therefore he marched off yesterday morning, either to glory or disaster. But in either case, he will always say it was to save the republic."

"Stanton," Lincoln whispered.

"Sir?"

"It was Edwin who was behind this."

Elihu nodded sagely.

"He could not accept my removal of Halleck. He felt I stepped on his toes in that. Halleck as well had poisoned him about Grant. Stanton was all aflutter over Lee being in front of the city again, now reinforced by Beauregard. I think in some way he must have goaded Sickles into action."

"That's what I was thinking as well, sir."

Lincoln sighed again, rubbing his eyes after yet another sleepless night.

"Is there any hope of recalling Sickles?" Lincoln asked.

Elihu shook his head.

"All three of his corps are across the river by now, moving on Baltimore. Lee, as you just told me, is storming north to meet him. I think by late today they will meet. All I can say is, let's pray that Sickles somehow proves himself, though politically that worries me."

"How so?"

"If he wins, if he defeats Lee in an open fight, sir, his next conquest will be your office. He wants to be president."

Lincoln laughed softly and shook his head.

"By God, Elihu. If he does win, if he ends this war, I'll gladly give it to him as a prize. I'll do anything at this point to see an end to the killing as long as the Union is saved."

Near Gunpowder Falls, Maryland

August 19, 1863
10:00 A.M.

The day was hot. The sun had risen a dark-red orb, promising yet another August day of sweltering heat for Maryland. It was now more than halfway up the midmorning sky. Dan Sickles took off his hat and wiped his brow.

The men marching past, his old Third Corps veterans, had rested well during the night. He had balanced the odds of calling a halt to the march. Press on and force-march into Baltimore, but then his men would be exhausted, or let them get six hours' rest, a hot breakfast, so that if action did come they'd be fresh.

It was a hard decision, balancing one factor against another, and balancing what Lee might do or not do. For Lee to disengage from Washington, turn around and march north, would have taken all of yesterday. Moving one man, of course, was the simplest task in the world, but fifty thousand, with rations, ammunition, artillery, supply wagons, ambulances; even the best trained units would take the better part of a day to disengage, form up, and then put the head in front of the tail. If Lee was deployed for an assault on the capital, the roads for miles to the rear would be clogged with supply wagons.

Then, on the other hand, he just might fling himself north and thus exhaust himself, and if so, his men would have the edge yet again, having rested and eaten.

He had to wait for the Sixth to come up. If he advanced too quickly, with all his men and supplies funneling through the one river crossing, his army would be strung out across twenty-five miles of road. He wanted them compact, ready to go in as a single force, and thus one other reason for waiting six precious hours.

Though he had been part of the old Meade crowd, Sickles had given the Sixth to Gouverneur Warren. The man had conducted himself well in the Gettysburg campaign, was popular with his command, and had a tremendous eye for ground. Warren had reported that it would not be until midmorning before the old Sixth would be fully across the river and deployed to march. Behind them would come a thousand wagons and more, which would be infuriatingly slow in moving, as always. Though Stoneman had assured him that his small cavalry force would protect the flank, it would be just like Stuart to try and cut in and wipe out this crucial supply link, thus stalling his advance, making him dependent on the navy to move supplies into the various ports along the Chesapeake Bay. That would be a logistical nightmare when it came to cross-service cooperation, especially with everything based upon speed, speed that he planned to make the most of today.

Coming up over a low crest, riding near the head of his column, Sickles reined in, shading his eyes, scanning the land to the south. Downtown Baltimore was less than fifteen miles away. They had covered over half the distance. Several of his staff, who had climbed into a tree, were exclaiming that they thought they could see the church spires of the city.

The call went up for the advancing column to halt, the usual ten-minute break after fifty minutes of marching. Two miles an hour, if the roads were good, the center of Baltimore by late afternoon, a triumph in and of itself. And not a rebel in sight, except for the distant screen of gray cavalry that drew back a step with each step of his advance. There was the occasional pop of a carbine, skirmishers firing at long range, but Stuart did not seem intent on holding him back.

Curious. Usually there'd be a fight for each ford, each bridge, if still intact. The countryside was peaceful, civilians out lining the road, some friendly, reporting that the rebel cavalry had run like cowards, others sullen, just watching, saying nothing.

The only wrinkle—the first courier had come up an hour ago with the report that Ely Parker from Grant's headquarters had crossed the river at Perryville and even now was riding to meet him. His people would, as ordered, "lose" Ely, dragging him about in a frantic search to find the commander of the Army of the Potomac to no avail. By the time Ely found him, he'd be into the city, and there was no way in hell that Grant would then order him to retire.

It was a good day for a march and perhaps a bloodless retaking of Baltimore. Lighting a cigar, he fell back in along the road, empty for the moment of troops, and rode forward, the men raising a cheer as he passed.

Baltimore, Maryland

August 19, 1863
10:00 A.M.

C.S.A.   The endless, relentless column of Longstreet's corps flowed along the roads into the western edge of the city. The men had covered nearly thirty miles in just under twenty-four hours, and the exhaustion was showing. In the last few hours straggling had increased; old men, young boys, seasoned soldiers, pale-faced from diarrhea, a stomach complaint, or lung illness, were now falling out. Unlike Jackson, he felt some slight pity for these men, especially after their nightlong march, and he had ordered his provost guards to deal lightly with them, to give out passes and tell them to fall back in when they were able.

Longstreet reined in, watching as a regiment of boys from Georgia flowed by. Marching order had broken down during the night, the neatly formed columns of fours replaced by a surge of movement, men jumbled together, most with rifles slung over shoulders, the roadside now littered with backpacks, blanket rolls, strange booty picked up over the last month and now tossed aside. Quilts, books, surprisingly a box of cigars, a clock, newspapers most likely hoarded not as reading material but for more practical purposes, a brass candelabra, a woman's silk dress, a framed painting of a ship, cooking pots, the usual decks of cards and whiskey bottles, all of it littering the side of the road as they passed. Nearly all were stripped down now to just musket, cartridge box, canteen. They kept on coming, most exhausted beyond caring, some with a fire still in their eyes, for the Army of Northern Virginia was on the march and there was a battle ahead. Most regimental commanders had passed the order that the men could strip down in the heat, so uniform jackets were slung over shoulders, revealing white cotton shirts long since gone to dirty, sweat-soaked gray. Men who had stripped off their shoes in the countryside now grimaced as they marched over cobblestones, cursing, of course, when they hit horse and mule droppings.

A courier came up, shouting, "General Longstreet!" Venable guided the man in, a trooper with Stuart.

"What's the word?" Longstreet asked.

"Sir, General Stuart begs to report that the Yankees are advancing again. They stopped just after two in the morning."

"I know that; when did they start to move again?"

"Sir, their Third Corps has come out of Abingdon; their Fifth Corps, which stopped at around three, is now advancing out of Bel Air. They fell back in just before eight or so."

Longstreet smiled.

He had stolen a march on the Yankees, his men moving over thirty miles to Sickles's twelve to fourteen. He shook his head even as he smiled. In spite of the Yankee general's bombast in the papers, he was keeping to their usual pace, but of course that could change; there was a slightly unpredictable element to Sickles, in spite of General Lee's confidence in dealing with the man.

He looked at his men streaming by. He would prefer to give them a few hours' rest now, for the day ahead promised to be scorching hot and the few hundred he had lost so far to straggling could swell into the thousands by midafternoon, but his orders were clear, his destination clear.

He looked over at Venable.

"Get one of our boys with a fast horse to report this to General Lee. You know where to find him. Send another rider back to General Stuart and tell him that we are coming up fast and he should execute the plans that General Lee ordered. A courier to Pickett as well that he should know his orders and engage in the appropriate manner."

It was going to be an interesting day, a most interesting day.

One Half Mile South of Gunpowder Falls, Maryland

August 19, 1863
Noon

C.S.A Jeb Stuart, hat off, the heat intense, trotted over to the light horse batteries that were drawn up across the road looking down toward the Gunpowder River. On the far bank, several Union batteries were deploying. His own guns were already at work, shelling the Union guns. The skirmish line of dismounted troopers, pushing forward, was thickening as he committed his reserves from Jenkins's and Fitz Lee's old brigades. The men were confident, with casualties so far light. They knew the game they were about to play, and they would play it with relish.

Chew's, Hart's, and Griffin's Maryland batteries were hard at work shelling the opposite slope and the approach down the gentle slope to the Gunpowder River. To add additional punch, a heavy twenty-pounder battery of Parrott guns, captured and kept in reserve at Baltimore, had come up as well, their deeper, throaty roar distinctive on the battlefield. On the opposite slope regiments of Yankee infantry were deploying out into battle lines, ready to surge forward and charge the valley.

He was relishing the moment. Independent command, far ahead of Lee and the infantry, a holding action, their old enemy in front of them again. This was going to be interesting.

The first regimental volley sounded, a Yankee regiment on the far bank of the stream letting fly at long range at his own troopers in skirmish line. The men saw the puff of smoke, dived for the ground; several were hit, but the rest stood up and pushed forward to the bank looking down on the stream. The battle was beginning to unfold.

He looked back down the road toward Baltimore. Pickett was supposed to have come out just after dawn. Lee did not want to spring the trap too soon, so this would take careful timing. And yes, in the distance he could see the dust boiling up on the road; the infantry support was coming.

Gunpowder Falls, Maryland

August 19, 1863
12:30 P.M.

US **D**an Sickles raised his field glasses yet again, scanning the opposite bank of the river, the shallow valley dividing the two forces. It was beginning!

It was still dismounted rebel cavalry over there, but reinforced now by a heavy battery, most likely brought up from Baltimore. The boys from his beloved Third Corps were shaking out from marching columns to lines. With the thump of artillery, the distant rattle of musketry and carbine fire, the veterans of the old army knew that the elephant was waiting. They were to see battle again, and here, six weeks after Union Mills, was a chance to restore their pride. Some were nervous, wide-eyed, especially the new ninety-day regiments, but the old hardcore looked ready, and as they reached the crest, swinging from marching formation into battle front, they appraised it professionally, a tough advance, but against dismounted cavalry it might not be so bad, and the ground was shallower than Union Mills.

David Birney, the commander handpicked by him to run the Third Corps, rode up.

"So it's starting, is it?" Birney cried.

"Looks that way. Stuart turned about a half hour ago. He chose some good ground."

"Think there's infantry behind him?"

"Maybe. The garrison in Baltimore might come up, though I'd have assumed they would have waited in the fortifications. If it's the garrison, it just might be Pickett; word is that he was left behind." Sickles pointed to the distant dust on the road heading from Baltimore.

"I'd dearly love to thrash that arrogant bastard," Birney announced.

"Well, David, now is your chance. Force this stream; I don't want to get tangled up here. Send in the First Division."

"What about Sykes and the Fifth Corps to the north?"

"They're coming out of Bel Air now, reporting the same thing, intense cavalry skirmishing."

Dan shook his head.

"I want Baltimore by dark. Lee must be moving by now. If he gets into that city and the fortifications, it will be hard to drag him out. We've got to be in there by dark."

He did not add that sooner or later Parker would show up with the order of recall, and it was crucial to have Baltimore in his pocket or it would indeed be hard to press on to continue the action.

Birney rode off and within a couple of minutes bugles sounded, the cry going down the line of the hard-fighting First Division, Third Corps, to prepare for a frontal advance. The fight was definitely on.

Ellicott City, Maryland
Headquarters Army of Northern Virginia

August 19, 1863
1:00 P.M.

The heat was becoming staggering as General Lee allowed himself a few minutes' break under a grove of pine trees, gladly accepting a glass of lemonade offered up by an elderly woman, the pitcher cold, dripping with moisture.

He felt exhaustion coming on after a sleepless night in the saddle, broken only by a half hour nap in a shaded glen just before dawn. The men of Beauregard's corps were marching past, all chatter having long since ceased, the roadside littered with cast-off debris.

His huge train of artillery was moving at a good pace, the roads well paved, veteran batteries mingled in with newly created units manned mainly by hastily trained infantry. Gun after gun rolled by, the horses lathered in sweat as they strained at the harnesses of Napoleons, three-inch ordnance rifles, ten-pound Parrotts, limber wagons, and forge wagons. Here would be a killing punch, well over two hundred guns, stretching for miles on the road. Across fields and narrow farm lanes to either side of the main road columns of infantry pushed forward, a tidal wave of humanity on the march.

The latest dispatch from Longstreet had just come in. The action was opening up on Gunpowder River, just as he had planned. *If I had been forced to defend Baltimore, Sickles might be discouraged from attacking, and, worst of all, circle to the west, there to wait for Grant to come down, pinning the Army of Northern Virginia in the city. This fight had to be fought north of the city, while Sickles was alone.*

He had authorized his generals to spread the word to the troops, to share with them, as Napoleon did before Austerlitz, what his plan now was, and that confidence was reflected as they pushed on. He had seen stragglers, most of them humbled, apologetic, asking but a few minutes to catch their breath, more than one of them staggering back up to their feet and falling back in as they saw him ride past.

His army continued to press on.

Gunpowder River, Maryland

August 19, 1863

1:45 P.M.

C.S.A. For George Pickett, it was again the dream. His heavy division, reinforced by the two brigades that had missed Union Mills because of being used as garrison troops, swung out into battle line on the double, ignoring the long-range artillery fire bursting in the air, an occasional round plowing into the ranks.

It would be another Taneytown for him, and he gloried in it. He understood his orders, to give ground slowly, but first he would at least let his heavy division show its mettle and tear into whatever the Yankees might throw at him; there'd be time enough later to fall back. Sword raised, he shouted for his Virginians to advance.

The Battle of Gunpowder River, Maryland

August 19, 1863

2:00 P.M.

C.S.A. David Birney led the first division of his corps down into the shallow, open valley, sweeping around mill ponds, men plunging into the cool stream below mill dams and storming up the open slope. Atop the crest, the line of cavalry troopers fired a final volley, dozens of men dropping from the impact. The attacking Union division barely wavered. They had taken far worse on many another battlefield.

The charge moved up the slope on the double, artillery fire shrieking overhead as a fourth Union battery deployed on the slope behind them. Stuart's men pulled back fast before the relentless advance of the Union battle line sweeping half a mile of front.

August 19, 1863
2:10 P.M.

L o Armistead, sword raised high, led his brigade forward. His regiments held the center of the line, three of them advancing shoulder to shoulder; fifty yards behind were the other two regiments of his brigade, acting as immediate reserve, red St. Andrew's crosses held high, the dark blue flags of Virginia beside the scarlet banners. A hundred yards behind them the two reserve brigades of Pickett's division advanced in similar formation.

He turned, walking backward for a moment, the sight sending a chill down his spine. The battle front of the division covered nearly a half-mile front, the lines undulating, breaking up for a moment as the men scrambled over fences, swinging around rough ground, passing a farmhouse and barnyard, pigs and goats scattering as troops knocked down a pen. Long-range shells from the Union batteries fluttered overhead, bursting in the air, plowing up ground, one shell exploding over his own Ninth Virginia. Several men dropped.

It was hot, damnably hot. Sweat poured down his face. He caught glimpses of individuals in the rank, some of the men grinning, their eyes afire with that strange light that imbued soldiers going into a fight; others looked frightened, features pale. Rifle barrels glistened in the glare of the August sun; the air filled with the sound of tramping feet, the clatter of tin cups banging on canteens, the distant shouts of officers and file closers, yelling for the men to keep their alignment, drummers marking the beat.

He turned, looking forward again. Cavalry troopers, some mounted, some on foot, were streaming back, a few turning to fire, smoke drifting across the field; the advancing and retreating Confederate lines passed through each other. The infantry offered some taunts, good-natured in general, about the cavalry getting out of the way now that the real fighting had begun, the troopers offering in turn shouts of encouragement.

Now he could see them, a wall of blue, coming up out of a low valley a quarter mile away, their battle line spreading out, flags marking regiments, a dozen flags at least, a division-wide front. He scanned the lines. This was going to be a straight-out, head-on collision, no fancy maneuvering, a knockdown battle out in the open. The ground a couple of hundred yards ahead dropped down into a shallow ravine. It looked to be marshy ground with high pasture grass, with the Yankees now advancing on to the slope on the other side of the marsh.

Both sides closed, coming straight at each other, their combined rate of advance covering over two hundred yards a minute. What had been a wall of blue was now emerging into individuals, officers out front, flag bearers holding colors aloft. The range was now about three hundred yards. The ground ahead was sloping down. Lo looked over at Pickett, who was still mounted, in the lead. Pickett caught his eye, held his sword out sideways, signaling a halt.

"Battalions! Halt!"

The cry went down the length of the front. Kemper's Brigade to the left flank continued on for another twenty yards or so before they finally came to a stop. Across the gentle, open swale, the Yankee division was coming to a halt as well, range roughly a hundred and fifty yards.

On both sides across that open pasture, all could see what was about to happen. A loud murmuring rose up, some cursing, a few laughing, many praying. Lo, trying to maintain some dignity, moved back into the ranks, even as he shouted for the brigade to take aim.

A metallic ringing echoed, the slapping of the brass fittings on rifle slings as weapons were taken from shoulders, held high, then lowered into firing position. The clicking of thousands of hammers as the .58-caliber Springfields and Enfields were cocked.

From across the field, the Union troops were enacting the same ritual, gun barrels flashing in the sunlight.

A long, drawn-out pause, which was only a few seconds but to all seemed an eternity, some rifle barrels held stock-still, men planting their feet firmly, drawing careful aim, second rank leaning forward, poising their weapons between the left and right shoulders of the men in front of them in the first rank.

"Fire!"

The thundering, tearing volley raced across the front line, thousands of rifles igniting, a blinding sheet of smoke boiling out, thousands of one-ounce bullets shrieking downrange at nine hundred feet per second, and almost at the same instant the Union volley swept in, the air buzzing with bullets, a sharp eye able to pick out piercing eddies in the smoke, marking the passage of an invisible round.

Scores of men dropped, some collapsing soundlessly; others picked up and knocked into the second rank, some screaming, cursing as they doubled over or, dropping their rifles, grabbed at a broken arm, or a thigh now gushing blood from a slashed artery.

"Reload!"

These were veterans, they had done this ritual before; they pulled open cartridge box flaps, drew paper cartridges even as they let their rifle butts drop to the ground. Tear cartridge with teeth, pour powder, push bullet into muzzle, draw ramrod. Thousands of arms were now reaching up, pushing rounds down, some resetting ramrods in the rifle stock, others slamming them into the ground to stand now like iron stakes. Raise rifle, half cock, pull out percussion cap, set cap, bring weapon to the shoulder, signaling they were ready.

"Volley fire, present!"

Again thousands of rifles were poised, another thundering crash. The Yankees, several seconds slower, volleyed in return, more men dropping, though not as many as before, both sides masked by smoke, the flashing of pinpoint lights in the yellow battle fog the only indicator that their opponents were still there.

Yet another volley and a volley in return.

"Independent fire at will!" The cry raced up and down the line.

Within a minute it was a continual roar of musketry, the faster loading three or more times a minute, the slower at two rounds a minute, some now fumbling, forgetting to prime with a percussion cap, others pushing the bullet down before pouring in the powder.

Men dropped, the file closer's cry a continual chant—"Close on the center, close on the center!"—while officers screamed for them to keep pouring it in. The continual roar was deafening, artillery from both sides throwing in both shell and solid shot, men screaming, crying, cursing, praying, shouting incoherently as the battle frenzy seized them. Lines might surge forward a dozen feet as if a spontaneous charge was about to be unleashed, then be swept back, as if an invisible wall of death awaited any man who stepped one foot farther.

No one could see, all were now firing blindly; the experienced, those with a cold logic still in their mind, took their time, aiming low, searching for a flash of an enemy gun muzzle in the smoke, then swinging to aim at it. Here and there the smoke would part enough to show a flag on the other side of the field, and then a storm of shot would rake into it, the banner dropping, coming back up, going down again, the horror of this hitting on both sides, so that around each regimental color guard a dozen or more men would be sprawled out dead or writhing in agony.

Clips of meadow grass seemed to leap into the air as bullets cut in low, the grass leaping up as if an angry bee were slashing through the stalks at blinding speed. An artillery shell, winging in low as well, would plow up a terrifying furrow of grass and dirt, then plow into a volley line, bowling men over.

Men's eyes stung from the blinding smoke, faces streaked black from the mixture of black powder, sweat, and saliva. Uniforms were caked with dirt, powder, sweat, blood.

Lo stalked up and down behind his regiments, saying nothing, watching as the volley lines gradually contracted on the center, the fallen dropping almost in an orderly row, wounded streaming back to the rear. Twenty or more rounds per man had been fired, and still there was no slackening of fire from the other side. It was impossible to see; all was blinded by smoke, the only indicator of the enemy presence the continual buzz of bullets slashing overhead, the cries of his own men being hit, the dim pinpoints of light from the other side of the pasture.

He heard a shouted command to the rear, looked back, and saw Garnett's brigade, which had been advancing behind him, filing off to the left on the double, moving to extend the line, whether to flank or to prevent being flanked he could not tell. He caught a glimpse of Pickett galloping past.

It had been going on for at least fifteen minutes now, a stand-up, knockdown brawl. He had heard the orders, to engage after they crossed the Gunpowder River, hold briefly, then start to fall back, luring them in. Shouldn't they start?

"General Pickett!" he shouted, trying to be heard above the thunder of battle, but George rode on, standing in his stirrups, eyes afire with that strange light of battle.

The rate of fire from his own line was slackening, not through lack of will, but after such sustained fire guns were fouling, barrels so caked with the residue of black powder that men were grunting as they pushed down on their ramrods. Some had stopped shooting, were pouring precious water from canteens down the barrels, their guns so hot that steam would come bubbling out as they then hurriedly ran a swab down the bore, filthy black water cascading out of the barrel. Inverting the gun would make the gluey mess dribble out—then another swab to wipe it dry, pour in another round, and resume firing.

And still the enemy fire slashed in.

August 19, 1863
2:45 P.M.

Birney stalked the firing line, a Pennsylvania regiment in front of him standing solid, musket fire flashing up and down the line. To his right he could see another rebel brigade swinging into battle front, extending the line. Already his own Second Division was racing behind the volley line on the double, men panting and staggering in the heat, lead regiments shaking out from column into battle front, rifles held high as they formed. A roaring volley erupted: Each regiment fired as it came into place.

"Birney!"

It was Dan Sickles, riding up on his black charger, staff trailing behind, the flag of the commander of the Army of the Potomac held high. He pushed his way through the column of the Second Division, the men cheering him as they raced by, Sickles standing in his stirrups, hat off.

"Give it to 'em! Remember Union Mills and give it to 'em!" Sickles roared.

He came up to Birney, grinning.

"How is it here?" Sickles shouted.

"Damn hot, sir. That's a full division across this pasture."

"Can see that, Birney. Blue flags, looks like Virginians; it has to be Pickett. He's left Baltimore wide-open, the damn fool."

"Did you expect Pickett this far north?"

"Of course," he lied. "That madman can't miss a fight."

He stood back up, raising his field glasses, but the smoke was hanging thick in the humid, windless air, a smothering, choking blanket filled with the stench of rotten eggs, strangely, a smell Dan reveled in.

If the Virginian was going to stand and fight, why not in the fortifications, why out here, a dozen miles north of town? Even Pickett would not be so foolish as to pit his lone division against three entire corps. It could only mean that Lee was coming up. But how fast? When would he gain the field? Surely not by this afternoon, unless he had been willing to push his army forty miles in this grueling heat.

He smiled. *If so, let him; his men will be exhausted and then we'll make it a stand-up fight.*

"I'm putting the entire Third Corps in here," Sickles announced.

Birney nodded his head in agreement, instinctively dodging as a rifle ball hummed by so close that he could feel the wind of it on his cheek. Dan laughed.

"If it's got your name on it, Birney, it's got your name, no sense in dodging."

Grinning, he rode off.

Five Miles South of Gunpowder River, Maryland

August 19, 1863
3:00 P.M.

Longstreet could clearly hear the rumble of battle in the distance. Coming up over a low rise he could see the cloud of smoke on the horizon billowing up, tiny puffs of white erupting in the air from shell bursts. A courier had just come in from Stuart, who had shifted to the left, reporting that the Union Fifth Corps was pressing forward on the road from Bel Air, approaching the upper end of the Gunpowder River Valley. Stuart had committed all his reserves, and the fight was beginning to spread.

Now was the moment of choice—push his lead division, McLaws's, up to Stuart or over to Pickett. Pickett had five full brigades now, the heaviest division in the army. Capable, for a time, of standing up to a Union corps. No, McLaws would extend the fight to the left and hold the Union Fifth Corps in place till the rest of the army came up. It would be a bloody, uneven match for the next three to four hours, until first Hood and then Beauregard arrived. A courier had just come up from Baltimore; the army was moving hard, but the rate of march was slowing in this killing heat, and stragglers were now falling out by the thousands. Pickett should be giving ground now, slowly falling back onto Hood.

Grim as it was, hard as the casualties would be, it would suck Sickles in, give him more confidence, play to his arrogance.

He passed the orders for McLaws to move forward to the left and prepare for battle.

Gunpowder River, Maryland

August 19, 1863
3:15 P.M.

Though only a colonel in the presence of a major general, Ely Parker found it nearly impossible to conceal his rage. He knew without doubt that his so-called guides had been leading him on a wild goose chase throughout the morning and into the early afternoon as they weaved back and forth on the two main roads leading south from the river crossing. Over the last hour the thunder of battle had con-

tinued to swell and finally, ignoring the shouts and threats of the staff sent
to fetch him along, he had ridden off, heading for the center of the battle,
knowing that the man he sought would be there.

A mile back from the battle line he rode past dense columns of troops,
swinging out from the road, tramping cross-country on the double, heading down across a shallow ravine to ford a stream and then back up the opposite slope. Seeing one of their command flags, he recognized it as the
Second Division of Third Corps and fell in with them, riding as fast as his
exhausted mount would carry him. Coming up over the crest he reined in
for a moment. Several hundred yards to his front a long volley line was
dimly visible in the smoke, blazing away, wounded by the hundreds limping back, ambulances already up, stretcher-bearers at work, loading the
men in.

He had to admit it was a magnificent sight. The volley line seemed
solid, no faltering in their work, flags waving back and forth. Puffs of dirt
kicked up around him as spent rounds smacked into the ground and rico-
cheted off, his horse dancing nervously as one nicked its leg.

He pushed on, carefully watching the line, looking behind it, and
then he spotted the flag of the army commander. Spurring his mount for
one last effort before his quarry rode off, Ely Parker of General Grant's
staff galloped up and reined in hard. Sickles was surrounded by staff, giving orders, pointing to various details of the fight, one of his men holding
up a rough sketch map that Sickles was examining. Without observing
protocol, Ely pushed his way in.

"General Sickles, I am Colonel Parker, adjutant to General Grant."

Sickles looked over at him and actually smiled.

"In a moment, Colonel, I am busy now."

"Sir, I have been led back and forth by your staff to no avail for the last
eight hours looking for you. We need to speak now, sir."

"In a moment," Sickles barked and turned away.

"Brewster, keep extending your line to the right, push it out; I want to
get enfilade into their left. Now move!"

Brewster saluted and galloped off, and Dan turned to yet another officer.

"Get back to Warren, tell him to push his first division up at the double to reinforce Birney. Those men have fired sixty or more rounds; their
rifles are fouled; they need to be pulled back to clean weapons, reload, get
water and a few minutes' rest. I want that fresh division on the line within
the half hour!"

More staff galloped off. Dan snapped his fingers to yet another staff
officer, who pulled out a flask and handed it over. Dan briefly hesitated,

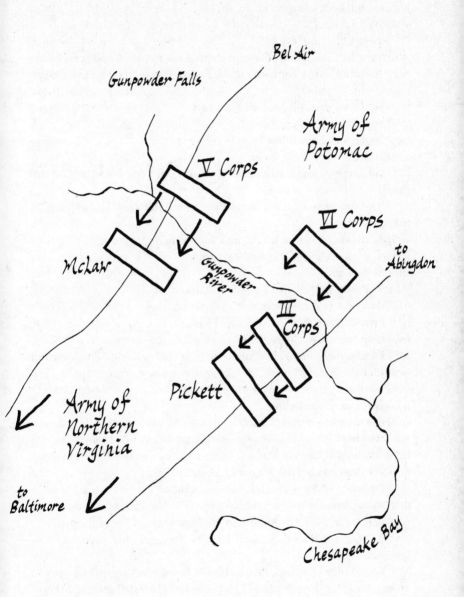

Bel Air

Gunpowder Falls

V Corps

Army of
Potomac

VI Corps

to
Abingdon

McLaw

Gunpowder
River

III Corps

Pickett

Army of
Northern
Virginia

to
Baltimore

Chesapeake Bay

then took a drink, turning slightly as he eyed Parker. He screwed the lid back on the flask and then finally spoke.

"Well, Colonel?"

Ely glared at him coldly.

"Sir, I've been sent by General Grant. I have written orders for you to withdraw back to the north side of the river and then to report to his headquarters in Harrisburg."

Dan threw back his head and laughed.

"Should I do this right now, Colonel? This very instant?"

"Those were the orders I was to convey to you."

Dan edged his horse closer.

"Goddamn it, man, do you know how stupid you sound at this moment?"

"Sir, I am carrying orders from the commander of all Union forces in the field."

"Again, do you know how stupid, how idiotic you sound?"

"Are you calling General Grant idiotic, sir?" Ely snarled, features turning dark red.

"You're an Indian, aren't you?" Dan asked.

"What the hell does that have to do with it, sir?"

"I would think that one with your blood would enjoy a good fight. Well, my brave, you got one right here," and Dan pointed to the volley line.

"I am in the middle of an all-out fight at this moment. That's Pickett over there, Stuart a couple of miles to the northwest. We are holding and we are savaging them and we will beat them. Now do you honestly expect me to order a general retreat?"

Ely said nothing. Tragically, he knew Sickles was right. The fight was on; there was no way to disengage without the threat of a rout. The long hours of delay thrown in his path had given this man enough time to get into a tangle he could not get out of, short of victory.

"General Sickles, you acted without authority; in fact you acted in direct contradiction to the plan that General Grant had laid out to you at your last conference with him. I know, sir, for I was there, if you will recall."

To his amazement, Sickles actually shrugged his shoulders and grinned.

"War changes all plans, Parker. If your Grant was here, he'd agree and order me to push in everything I had. The old plan is off and the Army of the Potomac is back in the fight and we will win this day. Now if you will excuse me, I have a battle to fight."

"General Sickles, I believe that once this affair is over, you will face an inquiry from General Grant as to the arbitrary and irresponsible nature of your actions."

"Let him. Just tell him, though, to first check with the secretary of war."

Stunned, Ely could say nothing.

"Now stay out of my way, Chief Parker. Though if you want to fight, be my guest. If you want to see how the Army of the Potomac can win battles when properly led and not held back on a leash, stay and watch."

Laughing, Dan spurred his mount and rode off. Ely remained behind, oblivious to the constant whine of bullets passing overhead. There was nothing he could do now to stop this, and considering the respective skills of Lee and Sickles, he feared what was to come.

Chapter Nineteen

C.S.A. Voice long since gone, Lo Armistead staggered up and down the line, limping slightly from the rifle ball or shell fragment that had creased his left leg just above the knee.

His brigade, his precious brigade, was bleeding out. A half hour ago he had committed his two reserve regiments, pushing them into the volley line, pulling his already committed regiments back one at a time to give the men ten minutes to clean their rifles, replenish ammunition, gulp down some water . . . and still it continued, the most sustained firefight he had seen across two years of war.

The smoke was a dark blanket hovering over the battlefield. The air was so thick from the humid heat combined with the smoke of battle that he was beginning to lose as many men from physical collapse as from enemy fire. Few were now standing; most of the men were hunkered down, kneeling, lying; some had stopped shooting and, with bayonets, were frantically digging in. The dead lay in almost orderly rows, most where the brigade had first engaged two hours ago; yet more were sprawled out now where the brigade had pulled back a hundred yards, back to a low crest and a fence row.

No one could see the Yankees in all the smoke, though they were still out there, the incoming rounds evidence enough of their presence. All was fire, smoke, screaming men, the maddening buzz of bullets sweeping past, the sickening thunk when one hit a man.

"General Armistead!"

He looked up and to his amazement saw Pickett, still mounted, though his horse was bleeding from several wounds, the general nursing an arm in a sling. Lo wearily saluted, barely able to focus.

"You must hold this center, sir," Pickett shouted, his voice breaking, carrying a hysterical edge.

"Sir! What about our orders?" Lo cried.

"What orders?"

Lo stepped closer to Pickett's side.

"We were supposed to engage then withdraw, sir; those were our orders."

"And show our backs now?" Pickett shouted. "I'd sooner burn in hell! We've bloodied an entire corps over there, Lo, an entire corps! Hood and the rest will be up soon enough, but I'm not giving away this ground now. The blood of Virginia is on it!"

"When will we be relieved?"

Pickett shook his head.

"I'll be damned if I know. McLaws went in on our left an hour ago. Hood should be up within another hour."

"An hour? If they push now, sir, I can't promise we'll hold."

"You are talking about the honor of our division, General Armistead. We will hold!"

Pickett savagely turned his mount and rode off.

Armistead watched him ride off and shook his head. They were in a brutal head-on fight; the entire division was bleeding out. They were outnumbered, exhausted; men not down from wounds were collapsing in the boiling heat, and still George was determined to hold and to make it a point of honor.

Cursing under his breath, he resumed his walking up and down the line, oblivious, if for no other reason than exhaustion, of the continual rain of bullets and shells striking his line.

4:45 P.M.

General Warren, when will you be ready to commit?" Dan shouted, eyes wide, face contorted in anger as the commander of his Sixth Corps rode up.

Maj. Gen. Gouverneur Warren rode up to Sickles and saluted.

"Sir, my First Division is already in support of Birney."

"I want the rest of your corps in now; push them right up the center. I ordered that an hour ago, General."

"Sir, we are deploying even now in the valley back there." Warren pointed to the ravine of Gunpowder River.

"I want them now. By God, Gouverneur, we are ready to bowl those rebels over."

Warren looked past Sickles, to the hundreds of wounded painfully staggering back from the front line two hundred yards away, the boiling clouds of smoke. Just behind Sickles, a battery of three-inch rifles fired a salvo, redoubling the smoke around them, and Warren shook his head.

"A word of caution, sir."

"I have no time for caution now. We're on the edge of driving them from this field. Their fire has been slacking off. The time is now."

"Sir. The Sixth Corps is your only reserve. We've only marked the location of two of their divisions, Pickett here, and McLaws to the north, facing the Fifth Corps. Where is the rest of Lee's army?"

"Undoubtedly they are coming up," Sickles cried, "but they are not here yet. If I can destroy two of their divisions before the rest arrive, we might get them rolling back and running."

"Sir, that is Lee over there," Warren replied, trying to stay calm, for it was evident that the commander of the Army of the Potomac was caught up in battle hysteria. "I think I should advise caution. You've done a masterful job, sir, but the losses to your old corps are heavy; we can both see that. Push them back tactically, sir, but do not go in with a full pursuit now. The men are exhausted, the heat is killing. Just do a local advance so they break, then stop and consolidate our forces so we can respond to whatever Lee is preparing."

He pointed back across the Gunpowder River.

"That is good ground back there; pull back, dig in, then let the rest of Lee's forces come to us, and we will defeat them from a sound defensive position at little risk to ourselves."

"Did I ask you for advice?"

"No, sir, but perhaps advice is needed," Warren replied. "Sir, I know ground. Remember, I was topographer for this army before you promoted me. You have a good position here. The good ground is right at your back. Hold on the north bank of this river. Let Lee come up, and then savage him. We have but half the numbers we did at Chancellorsville. We don't have the reserves for an aggressive pursuit."

"And Lee would have good ground on this side of the river if we give it back to him! We are driving them," Sickles replied sharply. "I listened to caution at Chancellorsville, at Gettysburg, and Union Mills. We've caught two of their divisions out in the open. We will roll them up and de-stroy these divisions and then do the same to the rest of those damn rebels tonight and tomorrow. Now put your men in!"

Warren was silent for a moment, looking straight at Sickles.

Wearily, he saluted.

"Yes, sir."

Near Christiana, Pennsylvania

August 19, 1863

5:00 P.M.

C.S.A. His horse collapsed, sighing, going down on its knees, and he felt a moment of pity as he pulled his feet from the stirrups and dismounted.

It was a beautiful animal, chestnut, well-bred, and he had driven it without mercy throughout the day. As a born horseman, he felt revulsion at having pushed this faithful animal to the point of death.

Tradition demanded that he shoot it, not let it fall into enemy hands, but he could not bring himself to do it as the stallion looked up at him wide-eyed, panting hard, lathered in sweat.

He turned to one of his few remaining adjutants.

"Get my saddle off him; find me another mount," Wade barked.

His staff wearily dismounted, one of the men gently urging the trembling beast back up to its feet so they could undo the saddle and bridle.

They were atop a low ridge. In the valley looking back toward the village of Christiana, he saw hundreds of his troopers streaming across the open fields and farm lots. The incessant crackle of carbine fire echoed in the distance and there, a mile away, the damnable Yankees, still on his tail, still pressing, still keeping pace.

How could they? he wondered, filled with mixed admiration and rage. These were not Yankee troopers, they couldn't be. Anytime in the past he would have left them a dozen miles in the rear by now, and yet doggedly they pressed on, scooping up those exhausted men of his dwindling brigade who fell behind.

He had long since abandoned his battery of guns, the artillerymen cutting the axles and spiking the touchholes. The few supply wagons loaded with ammunition had been abandoned as well, so that his men rode only with what they carried in their cartridge boxes and saddlebags.

He would still outrun them; he had to. Never had this happened across the entire war, and he would not be the first of Stuart's cavaliers to be cut off and ignobly defeated by a bunch of damn shopkeepers and mechanics on horseback.

The Battle of Gunpowder River, Maryland

August 19, 1863
5:10 P.M.

"General Longstreet, thank God!"

Pete rode up to George's side. His division commander looked on the edge of complete collapse, hat gone, arm in a sling, blood dripping down his uniform and on to his leg.

Pete took all this in with a sharp glance. For the last half hour, in his final dash up to the front, he had seen the wreckage of battle streaming to the rear, wounded by the hundreds, ambulances filled with casualties, men staggering back, dropping from heat exhaustion, dead men sprawled in the middle of the road, and always forward the incessant roar of a pitched battle.

"What is going on here?" Longstreet cried.

"Sir, as ordered, we advanced out of Baltimore shortly after dawn," Pickett gasped. "At around two I deployed into battle formation, three brigade front, and moved forward to relieve General Stuart. We ran smack into the middle of their Third Corps, one division to start. We met them head-on and gave them hell."

He sighed, trembling, swaying in the saddle, so that Pete had to lean over and brace him.

"Go on."

"Sir. They brought up a second division, deployed to my left, so I extended my line, then a third division, which forced me to withdraw several hundred yards and refuse the left. I know McLaws is to my north, but I couldn't extend enough to make a solid front and lost contact with him. Now I think their Sixth Corps is coming in. We've held them for three hours, but if their Sixth comes in, I think we'll be forced back."

His voice trailed off for a moment and he lowered his head.

"My God, Pete. My division. My boys. I think I've lost half my men in this fight. We can't hold much longer. I need support."

"You weren't supposed to do this!" Pete roared. "You were to engage, then withdraw slowly back on your support."

Pickett looked at him wide-eyed, unable to speak.

"You were to fall back, not wreck your division!"

"I'm sorry, sir," George replied, voice breaking. "I felt I could handle them, and I did until they brought up another corps."

"General Hood's been forced to move his lead division farther forward to try and support you!" Pete shouted. "His men have forced-marched over forty miles. You were to fall back, damn it!"

Longstreet looked past Pickett to the volley line, shadowy in the smoke. This was typical of George, focusing on the ground. Ground that had been insignificant a day before, now suddenly so important that a thousand should die holding it, if for no other reason than pride. Now he had bled most of his division out fighting an entire corps. Granted, he had most likely given back as good as he received, but still, the butcher bill was beyond anything he or Lee wanted to pay.

"I want you to prepare to withdraw now," Pete said.

Pickett looked at him, incredulous.

"Sir, my men have paid dearly for this ground."

"It's not the ground I want at this moment," Pete snapped. "General Lee wants Sickles, but not at the price of destroying the only army we have left on this field. Hood's old division even now is deploying behind you, a mile back. You are to fall back."

"I object, sir. Ask Hood to come forward. I think we should hold here. My boys have paid a terrible price for this ground, and to retreat now," he sighed, "it will mean defeat. I cannot see surrendering ground that gallant Southern blood has been split upon."

Longstreet looked at him, incredulous. It had been the same at Gettysburg, the first day, General Lee suddenly obsessed with ground purchased by blood, not willing to give it back, not able to see at that moment the broader nature of the fight, the battle, the entire war. Thank God, Lee had realized it in time, and then developed the plan that had created Union Mills. And now Pickett was caught in the same lust.

"Hood's men cannot move another foot. Damn it, follow my orders," Pete snapped. "Obey my orders now or surrender your command to someone who will!"

5:30 P.M.

That's it, Warren. Go, boys, go!"

Riding at the front of his Second Division, Gouverneur Warren turned, sword raised, offering a salute to Sickles.

Behind Warren a division was deployed on a front a third of a mile wide, coming up out of the swale of Gunpowder River, advancing at the walk, bayonets fixed, rifles held at the "bayonet charge." The vast, terrifying, machinelike line marched into the smoke slowly drifting back from the thundering volley line held by the shattered remnants of the forward divisions, Third Corps and his own division, which he had thrown in an hour ago.

Already some of his men were dropping from sheer exhaustion, the heat most likely hovering at a hundred degrees. Here and there distant, spent rounds were striking men with still enough force to fracture a skull or break an arm. As quickly as men fell, others closed up the ranks.

Knowing that the ritual moment had passed, Warren reined in as they went into the smoke, letting the first wave of five regiments, all of them Vermont boys, press forward. Those closest to him raised kepis in salute and pressed on into the fog of battle.

He swung in behind the first line, in the swirling smoke catching sight of the second wave, tough, hardened veterans of the old First Corps, still carrying their original corps banner though they had been incorporated into his own. He stood tall in the stirrups.

"Old First. Remember Gettysburg! Remember Reynolds. God be with you!"

His salute, a reminder of glory and tragedy past, roused them and a cheer went up.

"The First, the First, the First, remember Reynolds!"

He fell in to their front, riding with them.

The volume of fire ahead increased, deep thunder of artillery adding in, the whirl of spent canister rounds slashing overhead.

The line passed the ground where the first volleys had been fired, crossing over the prone formation of hundreds of dead and dying men, of the Third Corps, their reduced numbers a cold, frightful testament to their courage, their resilience, and discipline, to having stood under the blazing August sun, exchanging volley after volley with Pickett's legion.

Lying on the ground, a few of those wounded looked up, raising clenched fists in salute.

"Give 'em hell, boys, give it to them!" the cry echoed. More than one of the advancing line stripped off a precious canteen and tossed it to the fallen; hands touched hands, the fallen and those still to fall.

These men of the old First knew, they knew far more than perhaps any veterans of the war, what was to come. These were the men that had held Seminary Ridge at Gettysburg, losing seventy percent of their numbers. These were the men who had gone in at Fredericksburg, charged the Cornfield at Antietam, and stood in volley line against the Stonewall Division at Groveton. The humiliation of Union Mills burned in their souls, and it was time to right that, to restore pride, even if it meant dying in the act of succeeding. They were the inner heart, the steel soul of the republic.

"Here they come!"

Lo Armistead looked up, torn away from the side of a dying comrade who was whispering a final farewell, a wish to be buried alongside his wife in Stanton.

He could see nothing for a moment. His eyes stung, watered, and with a blood-soaked hand he tried to wipe them clear.

Yes, my God, he could see them, a solid, blue-black wall emerging out of the smoke.

"Oh, my God, here they come!"

The cry went up and down the line. Exhausted men coming back to their feet. With a final burst of draining energy, men struggled to ram another charge down fouled barrels. Where a thick, solid double line had stood two and a half hours ago, now there was little more than a skirmish line, here and there half a dozen feet between men, thicker clusters around shot, shredded battle flags.

Lo wept unashamedly at the sight of it, tears streaming down his blackened face. Victory or defeat, never had he known such pride as he did at this moment, his men still not giving back, still standing defiant. And yes, pride in his foe as well, who he knew had suffered as grievously as his own brigade, and yet were still coming on.

"Volley fire," his words came out as an inaudible croak.

He turned to one of the few of his staff still standing; the man, knowing what he wanted, handed over his canteen. Lo took a deep drink, then another, hawked, and spit, clearing his parched throat.

"Volley fire. Virginians! Volley fire!"

His desperate cry was echoed and picked up.

"Lo!"

It was Pickett and, to his amazement, Longstreet at his side, oblivious it seemed to the wall of Yankees coming at them.

"Fire and withdraw!" Pete shouted. "Try and keep formation; don't let your men break!"

The two galloped off before Lo could respond in outrage to the order. He would be damned if his men would ever break.

The Yankee line was closer, a hundred and fifty yards out.

"Volley fire, then withdraw fifty paces on my command!" Lo shouted.

"Virginians, take aim!"

Where once more than twenty-five hundred rifles would have been lowered in response, now barely a thousand remained.

"Take aim!"

Again the reassuring and yet frightful sound of hammers being pulled back.

"Fire!"

A wall of fire erupted. Not coordinated, starting at the center, then rippling down the line to either flank.

"Virginians. Back fifty paces!"

His men seemed to hesitate. Heartbreakingly, he saw one of his men directly to his front lean over, an elderly man, beard gray, kissing a fallen boy on the forehead, laying a Bible on his breast.

The battle line started to fall back, the few surviving officers shouting for the men to hold steady. The elderly man was by Lo's side and Lo reached out, touching his shoulder.

"I'm sorry," Lo whispered.

"My only boy," the man replied and then lowered his head.

5:45 P.M.

They're breaking!"

Warren pushed his mount to a canter, coming up behind the line of the Vermont regiments. They were across an open, marshy stretch of pasture, leaving behind the exhausted men of the Third Corps and his own first division. The sight had been horrific. Here had been a fight like Groveton, the Cornfield, a stand-up, knockdown volley fight at two hundred yards that had endured for hours, neither side willing to give back, neither side able to advance under the withering fire delivered by their opponents. In places, the dead and wounded of the Third Corps were heaped two and three deep, the survivors hunkered down behind the fallen.

The marsh was actually stained pink with blood, as hundreds of wounded from both sides had crawled down to the water, desperate for anything to drink. The formation of the Vermonters broke repeatedly and re-formed as they swung around clusters of the fallen. They pushed up the slope, and a volley hit. In the seconds before it slashed in, he saw what they were facing, a thin line, looking to be nothing more than skirmishers, which disappeared behind the smoke. But their fire was still deadly, dozens of boys from Barrington, Bennington, and Stowe dropping.

Without orders from him, the cry went up for advance on the double, drummers increasing the cadence, men now leaning forward, picking up the pace of their advance. Behind him he could hear the third brigade shouting, surging forward, crying Reynolds's name.

A second volley hit, not as effective as the first but dropping more nevertheless, and then there was a shadow across the crest, and for a second he hesitated. It looked as if a solid line was down on the ground, waiting now to stand up and deliver a scathing volley at point-blank range.

But these were men who would never stand again. The dead were piled thick, the ground behind them carpeted with wounded crawling back. The attack slowed for a second, as soldiers stepped gingerly over the enemy fallen, then pressed forward yet again, only to encounter a second line of fallen a hundred yards farther back, atop the low crest of a hill.

"Forward, keep moving! Forward!"

As they crested the hill, they began to emerge out of the valley of smoke and death.

He could see them now, a broken, pitiful-looking remnant, not a line really, just clusters of men clumped under blue flags of Virginia and the red St. Andrew's crosses of the Army of Northern Virginia, falling back on the double, men struggling to reload, groups of them turning to fire, then falling back yet again.

The Vermont regiments halted, again without his orders. He would have just pushed. But the men were too exercised now that their foe was finally in sight.

"Take aim!"

A thousand muskets were leveled.

"Fire!"

The volley swept the front; in the split second before smoke obscured everything, he saw rebels dropping by the dozens.

"Reload!"

Ramrods were drawn, charges pushed home in gun barrels that were still clean, the metallic rattle of ramrods in barrels echoing along the line.

"Hold boys, now hold!"

Rifles came up, were shouldered.

"Charge bayonets!"

With a wild shout, a thousand rifles were brought down from shoulder arms, poised now level at the waist, bayonet points gleaming in the late-afternoon sun.

"On the double, quick! Charge!"

A wild, hysterical shout rose up. The line surged forward, men screaming incoherently, the lust of battle upon them, the lust of revenge, of pent-up rage, of all that they had suffered and endured; a chance to restore the honor of the Army of the Potomac was here at last.

5:55 P.M.

C.S.A   Any hope of controlling his brigade was gone, and for the first time in his life on a battlefield, Lo Armistead ran for his life. He did not know where he could gain one more ounce of reserve to move one step farther. He weaved like a drunken man.

The old man who had lost his son was down, shot in the back of his head, his brains staining Lo's jacket, the impact of that round nearly pushing Lo into panic.

He wanted to shout for his men to hold, to rally, but he could no longer find voice for it.

Out of the smoke of the battle line he could see the survivors of Pickett's division streaming back, running across meadows, pushing through cornfields, climbing over fences, men collapsing from exhaustion and wounds. A knot of men were gathered around a barn, leaning against the building, which was beginning to burn. They fired away, then turned to run.

He caught a glimpse of Pickett, staff trailing, riding across the front of the retreat, waving his sword, crying for the men to hold fast. But after more than three hours they had been pushed beyond all endurance. Longstreet was nowhere to be seen. Beyond all caring, Armistead staggered up to an abandoned farmhouse. Wounded were sprawled on the porch. From a shattered ground-floor window, he saw several men peering out, one of them raising his rifle to fire. A man came bursting out the front door and then just collapsed, shot in the back.

Lo looked back. The Yankees were charging less than a hundred yards away, bayonets flashing, a terrifying wall, coming on remorselessly, overrunning a battery position, the gunners breaking away from their pieces and fleeing before them.

"Come on, General, let's get the hell out of here!"

An arm came under his shoulder, a burly corporal, a giant of a man at over six feet by his side, lifting him up.

"Come on, sir, time we got the hell out of here."

"I'm all right, leave me."

The corporal laughed.

"Can't say I left my brigadier behind. Just promote me to captain when this is over. Now let's get the hell out of here!"

6:05 P.M.

CSA   "Form here!" Longstreet roared. "God damn it, get into line here!"

General Robertson, leading Hood's old division, saluted and galloped off along the edge of the woodlot. A battery of guns, Rowan's North Carolina, were already into the woods, barrels of their pieces projecting out over the low split-rail fence, infantry swarming in to either side of the guns.

Behind him he could hear hundreds of men running through the woods, pouring off the main road coming up from Baltimore, shaking out from column to line, the men panting with exhaustion, officers shouting for men to load, to get ready, to keep inside the woods.

Already the first of Pickett's division were coming in, staggering out of the cornfield to their front, their passage marked by the swaying of the head-high corn. Raising his field glasses, he could see to the far side of the cornfield a quarter mile away, where the relentless advance of the Army of the Potomac was pushing forward, driving the stragglers of Pickett before them.

Pickett's boys had been routed by this last charge, but he could not blame them. They had faced off against a corps and a half for three hours under a killing sun, inflicted thousands of casualties, and had baited the trap, which was beginning to unfold. But it would only be a trap if their panic did not envelop the exhausted reinforcements now coming up.

Robertson's division was filing into position. Behind them, a mile away, Hood's entire corps was advancing and deploying out as well. It was possible, just possible, that after more than forty miles of marching with thousands—perhaps ten thousand or more stragglers dropping out on the road, the rumors sweeping back of defeat—even these hardened men might break and run. On such things, on such moments, battles often turned.

He rode along the edge of the woods, eyes blazing, watching intently as division broke into brigades, brigades into regiments, regiments into companies, falling in along the fence at the edge of the woods, men hunkering down, loading, sliding rifles over the top of fence rails, staring blindly now into a cornfield where the enemy would not be visible until he was only thirty feet away.

Robertson's division waited for the impact of the charge.

6:10 P.M.

US old them back!" Warren shouted.
The Vermonters were already into the cornfield. The men were panting from the heat, the pursuit of the last mile that had carried them across pastures, fields of winter wheat, corn, orchards, and farm lanes. They had swept up hundreds of prisoners, all Confederate resistance collapsing. But in the cornfield ahead, there was something that was triggering in him a sense of foreboding.

"Hold back!"

His cry went unanswered. He turned, riding across the front of the reserve brigade, the boys from the First Corps, shouting for them to halt, but only those directly to his front followed orders. The battle front was nearly a half mile wide, and one lone voice at such a moment could not be heard.

The charge plunged into the cornfield, trampling the crop under as it advanced.

He caught a glimpse of Sickles coming up, army commander banner held high, staff trailing behind him. Warren raced back.

Sickles was exulting, swept up in the moment of glory, of victory.

"Call it off!" Warren cried.

Sickles slowed, looked at him.

"For God's sake, we've driven them. It's enough for now."

"I know. God damn them, we're driving them. Your boys are magnificent!" Sickles cried.

"No, sir. Halt now!"

Sickles looked at him, incredulous.

Warren gasped. "We don't know what's waiting ahead. Stop this charge!"

Sickles, eyes blazing, said nothing, and then rode past, following the charge; Warren, knowing not where to go at this moment, falling in behind him.

6:15 P.M.

C.S.A. old your fire, boys, hold it!"
Longstreet rode back along the line concealed in the woods. Hundreds of Pickett's men were still passing through. He caught a glimpse of Pickett, face ashen, riding past, then Lo Armistead, limping, helped along by a huge enlisted man who pushed him up over the fence, the two collapsing on the other side.

"Steady!"

From the slight rise within the woods he could see them coming, a relentless wall, corn being knocked down by their advance, bayonet points sticking up, flags rising above the corn. To his left a volley erupted where one of Robertson's brigades, on the far side of the woods, was engaging. In the woods all was strangely quiet for a moment, officers hissing commands, a gunner screwing up the rear screw of a field piece, dropping the muzzle lower, loaders already standing ready with double canister alongside the muzzles of the guns, a few officers looking north, a man up in a tree shouting that the Yankees were only fifty yards off, then jumping down. Rifles were leveled over the fence, hammers back, here and there a man firing, foul oaths shouted at the nervous to hold fire, hold fire, hold fire!

Blue legs appeared in the cornfield, bayonets above the corn, a last few stragglers running, heaving themselves over the fence, some still in the corn seeing what was directly ahead, knowing they would not reach safety in time, flinging themselves to the ground.

The surging wall of blue appeared, shouldering the corn aside, shouts echoing, huzzahs, officers waving swords, someone on horseback shouting.

"Fire!"

He did not give the order; he did not need to. Regimental commanders did it on their own, judging the moment. In those last few seconds the advancing Yankees, so exuberant, had slowed, seeing something, seeing the fence, the dark forms hunkered behind it, the muzzles of Napoleons and ten-pounders, rifles poised as if each was aimed straight at them.

There was a moment, a second or two, of shouted and confused orders, to halt, to take aim, to charge, to keep moving.

"Fire!"

The volley burst from the wood line, a thousand or more rifles at point-blank range, bursts of double canister from six guns. Five hundred or more dropped; it was impossible to miss so dense was the Union line. The frightful canister, nearly a thousand iron balls, tore into the corn, shredding stalks high into the air in the split second it took from when the burst of canister left the barrel and traversed the twenty to thirty yards into the advancing line, mowing the corn down as if someone had worked with maniacal speed to cut every stalk off inches above the ground.

A groan cut through the cacophony of noise, the screams of hundreds of men, wounded, men who would die in a few seconds as hearts beat out a last pulse. Shattered rifles, body parts, blood literally rose into the air and tumbled back in a blizzard of destruction.

"Reload!"

The rebel infantry stood up, ramrods already drawn and stuck into the ground, cartridges laid out along fence rails; gunners leapt to their pieces, swabbing out bores, then ramming in yet another charge of double canister.

The men of Vermont, staggered by the blow, could barely respond. Here and there a desperate few leveled their rifles, men who but seconds before were pursuing a defeated foe now were out in the open being slaughtered. But some would still die game, would fire back.

"Take aim!"

Again the mechanical-like motion, a thousand rifles raised then lowered, the men behind them now standing.

"Fire!"

Another volley swept into the cornfield, hundreds more fell, and seconds later a second blast of canister tore in from the battery, some of the rounds crashing into the reserve brigade, struggling to get forward over their own dead and wounded Vermont neighbors.

Again reload, even as the reserve brigade, among them survivors of the old Iron Brigade, pushed into the confusion, men screaming, cursing, some from Vermont already falling back, comrades to their rear pushing forward.

"Take aim!

"Fire!"

Another volley.

The sheer momentum of the reserve brigade of the Second Division, Sixth Corps, actually pushed the charge forward to within ten yards of the fence. These hardened veterans, filled with rage, would not break in spite of the surprise, the terror that had met them in this cornfield. It was Antietam again, and as one of them had once said, after Antietam, nothing would frighten them ever again.

In turn, without orders, they leveled rifles, took aim impossible to miss, and fired. A hundred or more Confederates tumbled back from the fence, most of the gunners down.

"Charge!"

The reserve brigade pushed the last ten yards into the fence, even as their opponents prepared to deliver yet another volley, and what ensued was the nightmare of hell, the unleashing of all that this war had created. Boys from Indiana and Wisconsin slammed into boys from Texas, jabbing, thrusting, clubbed muskets raised.

For the first time in the war, Pete actually drew his own revolver, leveled it, and dropped a man who came over the fence, bayonet poised, racing straight at him. He lost sight of the battle as his staff pushed around

him and then forcibly drove him back from the line, Venable cursing as he took a bayonet thrust to the leg.

A sickening, mad melee unfolded, the split-rail fence collapsing under the weight of Union troops. Hood's men staggered backward, giving ground a foot at a time, thrusting, parrying, those with a few seconds reloading and firing at point-blank range.

A desperate hand-to-hand fight erupted around a flag of the old Iron Brigade, the flag bearer pushing forward, then cut off, a wild cry going up from his comrades—"Our flag, our flag!"—and by the dozens they dropped as they fought to retrieve their colors. A Texan flag bearer, a red-bearded giant, Sergeant Robinson, the same man who had stopped General Lee from his suicidal gesture to lead a charge at Taneytown, waded into the melee holding his own flag aloft, clubbing the Union flag bearer with his staff, then snatched the colors of the Nineteenth Indiana from the dying man's hands.

Longstreet, pushed fifty yards back from the fight, turned viciously on his staff, swearing at them, caught up in the madness of the moment. The heat, the terrible hours of volley fire along Gunpowder River, the memory of Union Mills, all the dreams, all the hopes, all the bitter frustrations were now played out along this nameless fence row bordering a nameless cornfield in Maryland.

Neither side would give, and both sides fought with passion, with abandon, all the causes of this insane conflict forgotten except the desire to win regardless of cost.

And then behind him, coming out of the smoke-filled gloom of the woods, Longstreet saw a wall of men advancing, colors to the fore, Jubal Early in the lead. Hood's corps was coming up.

Jubal, spying Longstreet, rode up and saluted.

"I'm coming in," Jubal announced triumphantly.

And for the moment, all the rivalry between the two was forgotten. Longstreet reached out and grasped Jubal's hand.

"You know what to do!"

Jubal grinned.

"Hell of a march and now a hell of a fight!"

Jubal reined his mount around, even as the horse whined and writhed in pain, a minié ball striking its neck, blood spraying out.

"Louisiana, charge!"

Hays's Louisiana brigade leapt forward, baying like wolves at the scent of blood. It was only fifty yards to where the Texans struggled with the Sixth Corps, and the collision of wood and steel with wood, steel, and bodies reverberated, staggering the Union line back. The Louisiana brigade charged with rifles loaded, and as they pushed past the Texans, they leveled their weapons and fired at point-blank range; hundreds of Union troops dropped from the onslaught, and within seconds, they broke, streaming back into the cornfield that was now leveled for most of its width.

Regardless of pride, of memory, of all that they fought for, in that hundred-degree heat they could no longer withstand this arrival of fresh brigades, where only minutes before they had been pursuing a beaten foe.

The Texans and the soldiers of the bayous began to swarm over the shattered fence in pursuit.

"Hold, hold your position!"

Longstreet's command was already being shouted by Early, Robertson, and brigade and regimental commanders.

"Load!"

Men feverishly drew rammers; the Texans, many driven back from where they had stuck ramrods in the ground, tossed weapons aside, picking up the Springfield rifles of the Yankees piled around them.

The retreating men were now a hundred yards back, some disappearing back into the corn that was still standing, some turning, defiant, ready to renew the exchange.

"Take aim!"

With that, as rifles were leveled, the will of the Union troops broke, some flinging themselves to the ground, others falling back, but a brave few, the tragic remnants of the Iron Brigade, still remorseful over the loss of a precious flag, were trying to regroup, and many a rifle turned in their direction.

"Fire!"

The volley cut across the field, cornstalks going down, men going down, and what was left of the élan of that confident Union charge broke as the survivors fell back into the corn and disappeared.

A defiant cheer erupted from the rebel line, men from neighboring states slapping each other on the back, yelling, laughing, even as they drew cartridges and reloaded. Some fired blindly into the smoke and tattered remnants of corn, but there was nothing left to aim at.

Longstreet dismounted and walked down to the volley line, men turning, looking at him wide-eyed, as some were beginning to emerge from the hysteria of battle, the wild cheering now replaced by panting for breath. Some men sinking to the ground, some doubling over and, from nervous exhaustion and heat stroke, beginning to vomit, some laughing with a wild, mad edge in their voices. Most were silent, shocked, taking in the carnage around them.

Longstreet caught sight of the man who had snatched the prized flag of an Iron Brigade regiment, the Texan sitting on the ground, surrounded by admirers, but his head was between his legs, the man was sobbing, hand grasping the sleeve of the Union flag bearer he had just killed. His comrades were understanding, respectful, one rubbing the back of his neck.

He saw Lo Armistead struggling to stand up, still helped by his corporal, a few Virginians gathering around him like children having just found a beloved parent. These men were silent, some taking their hats off.

Robertson, fiercely proud, this fight an exoneration for the defeat at Fort Stevens, walked the line, shouting congratulations, but few responded.

Longstreet turned, looking up at Venable, who was still mounted, blood streaming from the bayonet slash to his thigh.

"You all right, son?" Longstreet asked.

"Didn't go in, just cut me," Venable replied.

"Get a courier to General Lee. Tell him we've held the line; they won't come on again tonight and I now await his orders."

Venable saluted, turned, urged his winded horse up to a slow canter, and rode off.

Pete, unable to control the shaking of his legs, sat down against a tree, sap oozing out from where it had been torn by a dozen or more rounds. Exhausted, he simply lowered his head and closed his eyes.

Harrisburg, Pennsylvania
Headquarters Army of the Susquehanna

August 19, 1863
7:00 P.M.

Some of the more excitable around headquarters claimed that they had been able to hear artillery fire. That was absurd; the battle that was most likely unfolding was over a hundred miles away; though late the day before, he did believe that he had heard some gunfire from Grierson engaging Hampton.

Grant sat wrapped in silent gloom. The doctor from the headquarters hospital had just left his tent.

Herman Haupt was dead.

He had died two hours ago from acute dysentery. The genius who had been responsible, perhaps more than any other, for the miracle of moving an entire army nearly a thousand miles, supplying it, bringing it nearly up to fighting level, was gone and Grant raged at the loss.

Grant cursed himself. He should have ordered him relieved from duty weeks ago, and yet he had used him. Used him up as easily as he would use a division of troops to take a hill, buy time, storm a fort, watching dispassionately, knowing that a thousand would die by his command to go forward.

And yet, in the using, what had been achieved? He looked at the final manifest that Haupt had submitted to him only yesterday before staggering out of the tent and collapsing facedown on the ground. Rations to feed seventy-five thousand for a month stockpiled, three hundred rounds of rifled ball per man, three hundred and fifty artillery rounds, mixed, solid shot, shell, canister, eight hundred and fifty more wagons coming in, three thousand six hundred mules to pull them, two thousand nine hundred remounts, four hundred tons of oats, only the pontoon bridges, enough wagons, some of the replacement bridges for the railroad, and, of course, the men, still not enough men.

One more division was starting to come in; already the trains were unloading them, but he would have preferred another entire corps. Couch's militia had proven to be little more than an abysmal waste. They had signed for ninety days, and most of them were making it clear that in three more weeks they were out of the army, but for the moment he still had them.

He wasn't ready to go; his plan had been meticulous, well laid out, and now Sickles had completely destroyed it.

That Sickles would meet Lee, alone, was now a foregone conclusion. The telegraph line from Perryville, up to Philadelphia, New York, and then to Harrisburg had been fully restored and had been buzzing all day with reports from "The Army of the Potomac before Baltimore." The first reports boasted of a victorious advance; the last, dated an hour and a half ago from a correspondent with the *New York Tribune*, reported heavy fighting and casualties.

He knew what would happen; there was no doubt of it in his mind.

"Ely?"

He turned, and felt embarrassed. Ely was down there with Sickles, most likely to no avail.

His tent was empty. He thought of Elihu, wishing he was present to offer some advice, though Grant was a man who seldom if ever now sought the word of another.

He thought of a drink but that thought only lingered for a second. There was no need of it now. Maybe, just maybe, after the war was over, he would indulge himself, just one more time perhaps. But not now.

He contemplated the odds that Sickles had now given him. Even, at best, but then again maybe a bit better, or, on the other hand, somewhat worse, if Lee pinned and shattered the Army of the Potomac once and for all. The old plans were out and it was time to recast them. That in and of itself did not bother him. Sherman had once said he had ice water in his veins. Now was the time to prove it. Reaching over to his desk, he pulled out a sheet of paper, drew a pencil from his breast pocket, and began to draft his orders to the army.

Twenty Miles East of Harrisburg, Pennsylvania

August 19, 1863
7:30 P.M.

US The train rolled slowly westward, the long rays of the setting sun casting shadows across the Pennsylvania farmland. John Miller stood against the open doorway of the boxcar as it rattled along on its journey, the scent of wood smoke from the locomotive wafting past.

They had left Philadelphia an hour after dawn, the city wild with rumors that Wade Hampton would be into the town before midday. It amused him in a way. Whereas only a week before many of the citizens of that fair city had been openly disdainful of black soldiers, more than one now begged them to stay as they paraded down to the depot to take the train. That disdain, however, had not been shown by the colored of the city, who turned out in droves, proud of their sons, their brothers, and fathers, waving American flags, shouting with joy as the columns of troops marched by.

He was now a company sergeant, and absently he reached up to touch the three stripes on his sleeve. From the little time he had been in service, he knew enough to realize he and his men were not yet ready, but some emergency had called them, and now they were heading west—rumor was, to Harrisburg. It was a bit of a mystery as to why they were pulled from Philadelphia, what with rebel raiders about, but he and his comrades had quickly surmised that the threat could not have been great if an entire division of them had been taken out of the city.

As the trains passed from Philadelphia across New Jersey, then switched westward to Allentown through a mountain pass at Hamburg, and now rolled through a beautiful valley flanked by mountains, he was awed by the size of this nation, its changing nature, the people he saw.

As they passed through northern New Jersey, the land seemed to be one of factories belching smoke, not unlike Baltimore, rail sidings packed with cars loaded with artillery, limber wagons, ambulances, boxes of rations, beef and horses packed into boxcars like the one he was in, all of it seemingly guided by some invisible hand pushing its cargo by force of will to the front lines.

The people who were along the tracks had looked upon him and his comrades with amazement. Here was a colored division going to war. Where in the past he had learned to stand detached, head lowered, as if he was not really a man, now he stood looking them in the eye, and many of them waved, some shouting blessings, a woman in a village in western New Jersey passing up a basket of fresh-baked bread.

Perhaps Frederick Douglass was right; perhaps the blue uniform, the cartridge box stamped US, and the rifle in his hand had at last bestowed upon him the rights of citizenship; perhaps he could now claim this land as his as well. And that thought filled him with a swelling of pride, a sense of what he was about, of what he would now do for this land.

The memory of his dead son caught him for a moment. The land would not belong to him, it never would, but for his daughters, for his grandchildren, perhaps for them, at last the promise would be true. He looked back into the boxcar, to the regimental sergeant major and a young private asleep against the sergeant's shoulder.

They were an interesting pair, with an interesting tale. The sergeant claimed that his father worked in the White House for Abraham Lincoln and he had grown up there. Soldiers were used to tall tales, and though the man was well-spoken, could read, and wrote with a beautiful hand, no one had believed him until only this morning, when a note with THE WHITE HOUSE stamped on the envelope had arrived. The sergeant, half-asleep, still had the letter and envelope clutched in his hands.

Everyone in the boxcars aboard the entire train now knew the content by heart:

> *To Sergeant-Major Washington Madison Quincy Bartlett*
> *I take pen in hand to wish you and your comrades well. Know that your father is safe here in the White House and sends his blessings. Sergeant, the duty you and your comrades perform in service to our Republic shall write a new chapter in the history of our nation. The sacrifice in blood you lay upon the altar of our country shall be forever honored and remembered by a grateful nation.*
>
> > *Sincerely,*
> > *Abraham Lincoln*

Sergeant Miller knew that if this promise would indeed be honored, this was now a cause worth dying for.

Headquarters Army of Northern Virginia

August 19, 1863
10:00 P.M.

It had been a long day. General Lee looked up at Venable and nodded wearily.

"Was it really that bad?" Lee asked.

"Sir, it's hard to say, but I saw what was left of Pickett. The division most likely took fifty percent casualties, maybe more. I can't speak for McLaws, but I know Robertson was hit hard as well, but we stopped them cold."

Lee wearily shook his head. Pickett had been ordered to delay, to draw back slowly, not get into a head-on confrontation with an entire corps, two corps actually, from the sound of Venable's report.

Every man lost was one less man available for the real fight, the confrontation with Grant that Lee knew would come next. So far it had, more or less, gone according to plan. Sickles was in the field on his own, the garrison in Washington still immobilized, Grant still in Harrisburg. No news from Wade Hampton, but that was to be expected; in another day or two he would most likely cross the river with details regarding the dispositions of the enemy forces.

He had to defeat Sickles in detail. Not just another defeat and retreat, but to take him out of battle forever. Then turn back on Washington, harass it, and wait for Grant to emerge and come to the relief of the city. He had assumed all along that Grant would do so, but would do it in conjunction with Sickles, a combined force he could not have defeated except with extreme luck. Pickett wasting his division in a stand-up fight . . . well, he would deal with that later.

"Get some rest, son. Colonel Alexander will find you a comfortable place and a surgeon to look after that wound."

"Sir, I should report back to General Longstreet."

"An order from me, son. Get some rest, get your wound attended to. Tomorrow you'll have more than enough to do."

Venable nodded.

"Thank you, sir. And bless you."

"And God bless you, too," Lee responded.

Venable left his tent.

Lee looked back down at the map spread before him. Longstreet, with Hood overlapping his position, had things well enough in hand. Together they could parry any thrust Sickles might offer, and it was more than fair to assume Sickles would indeed attack come dawn.

He would have preferred that it was Hood or Longstreet guiding the next step in his plan, but the simple logistics of marching order had put Beauregard on his left, and thus it would be Beauregard's role to spring the trap come morning. Instinct told him that he should move to that flank. Beauregard was an unknown quantity and that was where his moral influence could have the greatest impact. He decided then and there to arise long before dawn and ride to the left of the line.

There was nothing more he could do now. Outside his tent he could hear his weary troops marching by, men who had forced-marched over forty miles, the last of the columns coming up, exhausted, staggering, the stragglers now filling the roads as well, provost marshals guiding them to where their units should be deploying.

Judah Benjamin had come up to join him and was asleep now in the next tent, stricken by the intense heat of the day. He longed to talk to him but knew he could not disturb the man. He had been dangerously ill by the time he reached headquarters, and even now a surgeon was still attending him, wrapping his body in cool, wet towels.

What I would give now for but one more corps, he thought yet again, the conversation with Rabbi Rothenberg still haunting him. *If we had acted that day, that very day when Maryland had declared for the Confederacy, even now a hundred thousand more would be mobilizing across the South.* There was many a man of color already in the ranks, those of half blood, quarter blood, servants loyal to their masters, even here and there free men who had fallen in with local friends, but the majority? The vast majority, they of course would never fight for a cause that in the end only promised them bondage.

France would be inconsequential this year, most likely always. The crisis was here and it was now. *I have but one army left; I spent a fair part of it at Gettysburg and Union Mills. I spent more of it before Washington and now again today on Gunpowder River. I can spend no more and yet still hope to win.*

But one corps more and how different it might all be, a decision that, if given the chance, I myself would proclaim and adhere to. We are saddled by this madness of slavery, this abomination that sets men against men, though of a different color, nevertheless, still created by the Creator. The rabbi was right; in Heaven would we dwell separately? What would the Savior say of this?

Too many thoughts were beginning to flood in, diverting him from the moment, the task ahead in the next day, the next week.

He leaned over and blew out the coal oil lamp. Standing up, he unbuttoned his tunic and took it off, draping it over a chair, and then knelt.

"My God. Guide me as to what Thy will shall be. May there be some purpose in Your eyes for the suffering that now afflicts our nation. Those who fell today, both friend and foe, I beg You to grant them eternal joy in Your presence, and grant peace to those who mourn. I beg this in the name of Jesus. Amen."

He lay down upon his cot and tried to go to sleep while outside his tent men continued to march through the night.

Chapter Twenty

Headquarters Army of Northern Virginia

August 20, 1863
4:00 A.M.

C.S.A. There had been precious little sleep, and with the announcement that Pete Longstreet had arrived, Walter had come in as ordered, bearing a cup of coffee, and gently shaken him awake. As Lee stood and stretched, he wiped his brow; the night was sultry, hot, promising another day of killing heat. He pitied his men having to fight in this.

Walter handed him the tin cup, and he gratefully took it, gingerly holding the handle, blowing on the rim, inhaling the rich fragrance.

He caught a glimpse of Longstreet standing outside and motioned for him to come in. Pete looked haggard, eyes dark, blood staining his uniform. Venable had told him about their nearly getting overrun by the charge, of Pete in the middle of it, pistol drawn, dropping a Yankee at nearly point-blank range.

Pete was carrying a cup of coffee as well, and Lee motioned for him to sit down on one of the folding camp chairs.

"General Longstreet, a favor this day," Lee said.

"Anything, sir."

"Stay back from the fighting."

Longstreet lowered his head.

370 NEWT GINGRICH AND WILLIAM R. FORSTCHEN

"It caught me by surprise as well, sir, that charge, the way they came in. I didn't expect it."

"Even if they didn't charge, you were within easy range of musket fire. I cannot bear to lose you, sir; you have become my right arm."

He chose that phrase deliberately and Longstreet looked up at him startled, features suddenly going red.

"Thank you, sir. I will of course follow your orders."

"Very good, General; now tell me what has transpired."

He briefly reviewed the previous day's action, Lee shaking his head as Pete described the breaking of Pickett's division and the relentless Yankee charge that followed.

"I thought all division commanders were clearly aware that we cannot afford the loss of a single man in such an action. Why did General Pickett press the attack so? Why did he not fall back as we discussed in our last staff meeting prior to the return march on Washington?"

"Sir, you know George. His enthusiasm for a fight was up; he thought he saw a chance to drive the Yankees."

"An entire corps or more?"

"I know. I should have come up earlier to supervise him, but the long march; frankly, sir, I'll confess I was on the point of collapse myself from the heat."

"Don't blame yourself. That is why we are supposed to have division commanders, men who can think independently when required, but also men who can balance that independence with an understanding of the broader scope of the plan. I am gravely disappointed in General Pickett for throwing such a fine division into a frontal battle when he should have given ground back slowly, leading Sickles into our main advance."

"I agree."

"I am not going to relieve him, but I shall indeed talk to him once this fight is over. Now, tell me, how bad was it?"

"The returns still are not in, a lot of stragglers, but I believe we lost close to five thousand men yesterday, roughly four thousand of those with Pickett. Garnett is dead, Kemper severely wounded and out of this campaign."

Lee sighed. Another division fought out. Four veteran divisions fought out since June; Heth, Pender, Anderson, and Pickett nothing more than shattered wrecks. *God, how much longer can we bear this cost?*

"There is one positive side to this," Longstreet interjected. "Pickett savaged their Third Corps. We took some prisoners when they finally fell back, and word is that their First Division is now a hollow wreck."

"Trading man for man is a game we can never win," Lee replied.

"I know that, General, sir, but as you have told me repeatedly these last few weeks, this is a battle against General Sickles. That was his old corps and he had his pride in that corps. Well, sir, I understand that pride. His men took terrible losses yesterday, but ultimately they did drive one of our best divisions from the field. Sickles will be spoiling for a new fight this morning."

Lee nodded in agreement.

"Everything is set?"

"Yes, sir. We will engage just after dawn, then retreat as you planned."

Lee smiled, blowing again on the rim of his cup. Yes, Longstreet was right. It was a chess match, and Sickles would move aggressively forward, especially if he thought he saw the queen moving off the field. His passions would be up after yesterday's losses and the momentary glimpse of what he thought was victory. Lee understood that feeling; it had almost seized him as well more than once.

"Fine then, General. It's after four in the morning. Daylight will be upon us soon. God watch over you. I am going to join Beauregard on the left and I will see you at sundown when we close on Sickles's army."

Headquarters Army of the Potomac

August 20, 1863
4:30 A.M.

G en. Dan Sickles stepped out of his tent, stretching, looking out across the plains south of Gunpowder River. The smoke from a thousand circling camps hung low in the early-morning mist, men gathered about the fires, cooking breakfasts, orders ringing in the still air, companies beginning to form up.

All of it filled him with a deep pleasure, a love for all that this had given him. The smell of fatback frying, the wood smoke, the rich heavy air of an August morning, the shadowy glimpses of companies forming lines, companies forming into regiments, and regiments into brigades, all these were sources of satisfaction.

Men were beginning to load up, rolling up blanket rolls and slinging them on, buttoning uniform jackets. A group of men from one of his New York regiments were gathered in a circle, on their knees, heads bowed as a priest offered absolution and then communion. Nearby another group,

Baptists probably, were standing with heads bowed as one of them read a Psalm.

Here and there a drum sounded, a few notes of a bugle; a flag was uncased and held up, officers rode back and forth shouting orders and encouragements. All of it sent a chill down his spine. A few years back he couldn't have dreamed that there would be such a moment in his life, and he thanked God that it had been given to him. He loved this army more than his own ambitions. His pride in it was unbounded, and today he would do his all to see them served rightly, to give unto them the victory they had thirsted for across two bitter years, a victory they so richly deserved. Once achieved, nothing could ever take that away from them, no general out of the West, no president in the White House. No one could ever steal away again the honor of the Army of the Potomac.

Yesterday, in that final charge, he had sensed the moment when Warren had swept forward, thought that perhaps here was the moment when they would see the Army of Northern Virginia break at last, flee the field, the glorious banner, the Stars and Stripes, sweeping the field of all who dared to oppose it. It had been so close, except for that final shock, the cunning trap at the edge of the cornfield. He had to admit it was masterful, a grudging nod to old foes, most likely Longstreet.

But that would not happen today.

All three corps were deploying now. His battered Third on the left, the Fifth to the right, again the Sixth in the second line. They would advance as one. If Lee wished a stand-up fight like yesterday, he would give it to him, but he doubted if Lee would stand. He knew the numbers. Lee could no longer afford such losses; he would give back, retreat, most likely falling back on the defenses of Baltimore. If they could but trigger the beginning of a rout, get Lee dislodged, just for once, and on the run, they could bowl him over and win the day, and in that winning of the day win the war.

And, thinking coldly, he knew it had to be today. Parker was still with him, still waving his orders. If he did not press the engagement at dawn, claiming he was forced into the fight, he would have to fall back as ordered. If he refused a direct order while not caught in the heat of battle, even his staunchest advocates would no longer be able to defend him. And once he pulled back, he knew Grant would replace him. He had to press it today; this was his one and only chance, and he smiled at the thought of it. This was just the kind of gambit he reveled in.

An orderly came up, leading his mount. Already, in the predawn light, the skirmish lines were coming to life after their night of informal truce. The battle had begun.

The White House

August 20, 1863
5:00 A.M.

G ood morning, Jim, how are you today?"
Lincoln walked into the kitchen, and at the sight of
him the servants began to scurry. James Bartlett, who obviously
had been asleep, head resting on a table, looked up, startled, and came to
his feet. Lincoln smiled.

"Sorry, Mr. President, must have dozed off," James said a bit nervously, and Lincoln smiled again.

"Wish I could doze off like that. It's been a long night."

"Sir, would you like some breakfast?" James asked.

"What do we have?"

"I could get you a nice slab of smoked ham, sir, a couple of eggs,
freshly ground coffee."

"That sounds good, Jim."

The servant looked over at the kitchen staff, who did not need to be
told. Within seconds the ham was being sliced, eggs cracked into a frying
pan. Lincoln sat down at the servants' kitchen table and motioned for Jim
to sit as well. The man looked at him, a bit surprised.

"I'd like some company for breakfast, Jim, join me."

"Sir?"

"You must be hungry, too, after a long night. Make that an order for
two breakfasts and join me."

"Yes, Mr. President."

The staff looked over at the two wide-eyed, saying nothing as more
eggs went into the frying pan.

"Have you heard at all from your son and grandson?" Lincoln asked.

"Not a word in nearly two weeks, sir. I know they're drilling in
Philadelphia; word is they are to become part of General Burnside's
corps."

"Not a word?"

"No, sir, the last letter was dated two weeks back. They're in good
health and they say the men of their regiments are eager to get into the
fight."

Lincoln smiled. His letter to Jim's son was a secret; word would come
back soon enough, and he could imagine the man's delight, this man who
had known every president since Jefferson. It was not in any way whatso-

ever a calculated move, though he knew that everything a president did, from where he walked to whom he smiled at, was reported and commented on remorselessly. If a letter from a president to a colored soldier should become news, then so be it. It would show his own resolve on this matter and serve notice as to his intentions once this madness was finished.

They were coming down now, in this crisis, to a question of numbers, and the men of his breakfast companion's race might very well be the final weight that tipped the scales.

After the horror of the draft riots, he had carefully and quietly rescinded the draft in most places. Besides, Grant and others reported that the draftee troops coming in were worse than useless, an actual burden on the army, the bulk of them deserting, many of them besmirching the honor of their uniforms by thievery, desertion, cowardice. The vacant ranks must be filled, but in this country the tradition still was that it had to be volunteers. After the disasters of the spring and summer, draftees and bounty men were not the answer, and in fact would hinder this final effort.

It would have to be the men of color of this nation. The offer now was plain and clear. Not just emancipation, though he knew that if he was ever to honor the promise of the Declaration of Independence, full emancipation for all was a foregone conclusion. But what after that? There was a time when he had agreed to the idea of returning these men and women of Africa back to their homeland, filled with doubt that after the bitter legacy of slavery, and the way it polluted both sides, the two races could live side by side.

He knew now that was impossible. As he looked at Jim, who sat self-consciously across the table from him, as he looked into this man's eyes, he could see the divine spark, the core of humanity that made him an equal in every sense of the word. It was the quiet, humble courage of this man on the terrible day when it looked as if Washington might fall that had stiffened his own resolve. It was the look on the faces of the men of Colonel Shaw's regiment as they charged to the front, the pride in their faces when the following week he had received a delegation of them in the White House, that made him realize that all along he had been guided toward this path and understanding.

The promise had to be full equality, full rights, a place beside all men. This was now the great experiment of this nation. For more than four score years the experiment had simply been one of freedom—could common men govern themselves wisely? Most of the world had at first watched scornfully but now stood in admiration, and, for some, yes, even fear for all that this rule of common man implied.

Now that question had evolved to the more fundamental one—could they indeed create a nation in which all men did have full and equal rights? A new America was evolving; the poet he had met sung of it, of a brawling, growing strength, of farms, factories, cities, and villages filling an entire continent. Men and women from around the world were now flooding in, drawn by the promise of the dream, of those first lines of the Declaration. The Irish with their strange Catholic ways, which many hated, but it was the Irish who had stormed the heights of Fredericksburg and Union Mills, and surely their blood had bought them a right to this land. The Germans, the Scandinavians filling the woods of Minnesota, even the Chinese coming off the boats in San Francisco to work the gold fields. Was this not now the great experiment, and were not the son and grandson of the man sitting across from him entitled to it as well?

Though Jim did not know it, at this very moment his son and grandson, dressed in Union blue, rifles in hand, were most likely in Harrisburg, and in another month would march forth, and perhaps die in battle. Like the Savior, they would shed their blood for the sins of others, and he must see that there would be some offer of hope, some light at the end for them.

A servant put a plate down in front of Lincoln and then one before Jim. Jim was looking at him, saying nothing, as Lincoln silently mused.

"May I offer a prayer, Mr. President?"

"Of course."

The two lowered their heads.

"Merciful God. Please guide this man who sits before me. Guide him as he leads our nation to a just peace, a peace where North and South, former slave and former master, can sit together and break bread together in charity and peace. And, dear Jesus, please extend Thy loving blessing to my son and grandson when they march upon the battlefield. If it is Your will that they should fall, let them die with honor in service to our country.

"We thank You for the blessing of this food. Amen."

Jim looked back up, gazing into Lincoln's eyes. Lincoln did not know what to say. Many had prayed over and for him over the years, but few prayers were as heartfelt as this one.

He knew that this morning, like so many other mornings of these last few months, the fate of the nation might be in the balance. Sickles's army might just win, but if defeated it could give Lee a free hand yet again, perhaps to turn back here or to even force the Susquehanna and march on Wilmington and Philadelphia.

But it was out of his hands now . . . and, strangely, he felt at peace.

"Thank you, Jim," he said softly. "Now let's enjoy our meal together."

Two Miles South of Gunpowder River, Maryland

August 20, 1863
6:15 A.M.

Dan Sickles reined in atop a low rise where a knot of officers were gathered. He recognized Birney, dismounted, a field telescope resting across the saddle of his mount. Dan rode up to join him.

"Damn strange," Birney announced, pointing south.

A constant rattle of musketry echoed around them, but the fire was light all along the line. It was more like an open field skirmish than a major battle fought at a divisional level. They had advanced well over a mile in the last hour across the same ground that the Sixth Corps had charged yesterday, passing the horrible wreckage and destruction of the previous day, but there had been no hard contact. The dreaded woodlot, where so many hundreds had fallen, was now in their hands after a brief, sharp skirmish, but of nowhere near the intensity of the day before.

Dan came up to Birney's side, and his corps commander offered the telescope.

"Look down that road, about three or four miles, I'd judge."

Dan took the long tube, balanced it on the saddle, adjusted the focus slightly. Yes, it was a column of troops, some wagons mingled in, and they were heading south, away from the fight.

He handed the telescope back to Birney.

"There's no fight in them this morning. We push and they give. I know we have Hood's old division to our front, some contact with Early, and McLaws to our right, but nothing else; it's damn curious. Anything from the cavalry?"

Dan shook his head.

As usual, Stoneman's troopers were almost useless. They had gone into this campaign not fully mounted; after the horrible drubbing of the last month they were timid, slow, and now easily contained by Stuart, who ranged along the left front and overlapped the left flank as well.

"Prisoners?"

"A couple of dozen. Mostly exhausted stragglers. Word is they pushed all the way up from Washington in yesterday's heat and are played out. Most of them are saying the rest of Lee's army is stuck south of Baltimore; they just couldn't keep up the pace of the march and the order is to now fall back into the city and dig in."

Dan took this in.

"Any other reports?"

"Two prisoners state the whole thing is a ruse, that all of Lee's army is out there. One of them says he's a deserter from a supply train and Hood is just waiting for us to close."

"Any civilians?"

"Very few; most lit out when the fighting started."

Dan grunted, saying nothing, pacing back and forth for a moment, digesting the information. He had expected by now that they would have been into a full-scale, head-on fight, a toe-to-toe brawl where the Army of the Potomac would prove its mettle and drive the rebels from the field. Now this.

Was it a trap, or was he retreating?

Sickles wiped the sweat from his brow. Already the temperature must be well into the mid to high eighties. He uncased his field glasses, braced them, and scanned the ground ahead.

It was a broad, open plain, gently rolling ground, scattered farmhouses, a few small villages. A half mile away, wavering lines of blue deployed in battle order moved forward, a quarter mile ahead of them a heavy line of skirmishers, puffs of smoke marking their advance. In front of his own skirmishers he could see darker forms, giving back. Firing a shot or two, running, falling in behind a fence or tree to fire another shot, then falling back again.

Their retreat was orderly, unhurried, no sense of panic, as if they were following orders given before the start of the day.

He lowered his field glasses and continued to pace.

Hold, advance, or press on aggressively?

Was it possible that yesterday's fight had broken something in Lee? Their advance had revealed the extent of casualties inflicted, five thousand, maybe seven or eight—if that many, it would be a goodly percentage of Lee's best troops.

Could he have broken Lee's will to offensive action yesterday? If so, what a fitting testament to his boys of the Third, a laurel to a crown they so richly deserved.

But what now?

A small voice of caution whispered to hold up here, let Stoneman probe forward. Let his men rest through what would be a day of frightful heat, then push on in the evening.

But if he did that, Lee would withdraw into the fortifications of Baltimore, and there was the other factor.

He looked over his shoulder. Ely Parker was still trailing along behind his staff. There was no way he could order the man off the field; he was, after all, an official representative of the field commander. *If I stop now, that man would again press me to retire as ordered, and it would be all but impossible to deny that order and keep my command.* For that matter, unless he finished this with a resounding victory, Grant would most likely remove him anyhow.

No, he had to continue the advance.

He raised his field glasses yet again, focusing on the distant road. It was hard to distinguish, but it looked as if a wagon had just broken down. A dozen men were around it, disconnecting the mules, and then they simply upended it off the road.

Curious. It wasn't like the rebels to abandon a wagon like that. Were they actually retreating, with orders to abandon anything that could not be taken along? Already his advance had captured a half dozen guns—spiked, true, but still abandoned and captured.

Was this Chancellorsville again? Were they moving? He remembered the moment with deep bitterness. If Hooker had only unleashed him, he would have plowed into Jackson on the march and finished him. The same on the second morning at Gettysburg.

No, never again.

He looked over at Birney.

"They're retreating, that's clear enough."

Birney reluctantly nodded, saying nothing, features flushed.

"I want the advance redoubled. I want our main line to go forward quickly and establish contact. If they are retreating I think we can push them off balance, and once they are off balance we must drive them, sweep them up."

"It's going to be a killer of a day," Birney offered, shading his eyes and looking at the blood-red orb of the sun.

"The same weather for both us and them."

His gaze fixed on Ely, who said nothing.

"No orders from General Grant this morning?" Sickles asked.

"You know the orders, sir."

"I have a beaten foe in retreat, Colonel. My duty this day is clear. Once I'm finished, General Grant may come down and claim what he wishes."

Ely did not rise to the bait and the scornful looks of Sickles's staff.

Sickles mounted.

"I want a general advance all along the line. Push the men on the double, if need be, until we establish contact. I want to force them off those roads and to form a rear guard. Then we will overrun them. Gentlemen, this will be a footrace, and to the fastest runner goes the victory!"

A ragged cheer erupted as he spurred his mount and headed forward. Ely reined up beside Birney, who was mounting as well.

"Do you think all of Lee's army is in retreat?" Ely asked.

"It's not my opinion that counts, Colonel," Birney replied coolly. "But I'll tell you this. This army has been misused too many times, mostly through temerity. We just might be on to Lee in retreat, his forces spread out. We could see that at Antietam, at Second Manassas, at Chancellorsville—hell, in damn near every battle we've ever been in. If General Sickles is right, we could finish it this day, before they retreat into the fortifications at Baltimore."

"And what does General Lee think at this moment?"

Birney looked at him, saying nothing.

"There is a third corps, Beauregard's. Have you marked their position?"

Birney shook his head.

"I would be concerned."

"Every battle is a concern," Birney replied, now into his saddle, bringing his mount about, facing south.

"You might not believe this, General," Ely said, "but I actually do pray that your General Sickles is right."

"So do I," Birney said with a smile. Spurring his mount, he galloped off, following his commander down into the open plains.

Six Miles to the West, in the Valley of the Gunpowder River, Maryland

August 20, 1863
7:30 A.M.

The vast columns were deployed, the twenty thousand men of Beauregard's brigades. For the men who had fought in the swamps and heat in defense of Charleston, this was nothing new, another day that promised temperatures near a hundred degrees. They had long ago grown used to it, or died. For the militia regiments, the home guards, some of them from the cool mountains of western North Carolina and eastern Tennessee, the last day had been a torture, their ranks already thinned by half from straggling, scores of their comrades dead, collapsing from heat stroke.

They had filed west and north throughout the previous day, following back tracks and farm lanes, a route that Lee and Jed Hotchkiss had ridden over the week before, while contemplating what to do if Sickles should indeed jump first.

Though Lee loathed analogies with Napoleon, especially when applied to himself and his army, he had to admit it was indeed something like Austerlitz. He had picked this ground long before the battle and analyzed it. He had conceded what Sickles would perceive to be the good ground, on the banks of the Gunpowder River down close to the Chesapeake. If he had fought him there, he would have held the good ground, to be certain, but it would have been a bloody, senseless fight, with severe casualties and little to show once Sickles was beaten and had retreated. Granted, he had lost five times the number he had wished for yesterday, but it had indeed lured Sickles across that stream.

And now Sickles was pushing south. A courier had just come in reporting that the Union commander had increased the pace of his advance, was pressing into the rear of Hood's and Longstreet's supposed retreat. In another two miles he would finally run up against what the rebel forces were already calling "the line," a hundred and thirty-five guns concealed behind a reverse slope.

Stuart was shadowing the flank, keeping any probing eyes back. All civilians, painful as it might be, had been rousted out, ordered, "for their own welfare," to abandon their homes and retreat toward Baltimore. In Virginia he would not have worried, but here in Maryland, one or two civilians bearing tidings of a rebel column having disappeared late the day before, marching to the northwest, might have been warning enough to stop Sickles.

Sickles was playing his hand as Lee thought he would. The tantalizing chance to finally catch the Army of Northern Virginia on the march would be too much for him to not grab for.

All they needed to do now was to wait for the sound of the guns.

August 20, 1863
9:00 A.M.

"Sir, I think we got a problem ahead!"

Dan looked over at the courier riding in, a cavalryman, John Buford's old division.

"What is it?"

"Sir, we're moving ahead of the Second Division of the Third Corps, and we seen a hell of a lot of guns."

"What kind of guns?"

"Artillery, sir, rows of 'em. Maybe twenty or more batteries. One of the boys climbed a church steeple to get a look around and he seen them down in the next valley. I was ordered to come back here and find you."

"Are they moving?"

"No, sir, that's just it. Their gunners are standing ready."

"I'm coming."

Following the cavalryman, his staff trailing, they rode across an open pasture. Some stragglers dotted the field, men already dropping out because of the heat and exhaustion. A few wounded in the field, an ambulance up to retrieve them, one of them a rebel officer, sitting on the ground, holding a leg up as a hospital orderly tightened a tourniquet. The man grimaced, saw Dan, and offered a salute, which Dan returned.

"Hot day, General."

"That it is, Captain."

"Gonna get a hell of a lot hotter for you soon, General."

The rebel was grinning now, and Dan rode on.

He came to a split-rail fence, rode parallel to it for fifty yards until he found a place where it had been knocked down, a few more casualties, Union and Confederate together, sitting and lying under the shade of an apple tree, the men who had fought each other only minutes before now talking, a rebel holding a canteen for a young Yankee cavalryman, the boy gut-shot.

He rode up through the orchard, its lower branches picked clean even in the middle of a running fight; soldiers of both sides would forage even if the apples were still green.

More men ahead, a ragged combination of columns and lines, white insignia of the Third Corps, Second Division, on their caps. Few if any still had on field packs or blanket rolls. Many, against usual custom, had their blue jackets off in the heat, but they still carried rifles and cartridge boxes, which was all that mattered to him at this moment.

The column was stalled as he rode past. He caught sight of a regimental commander.

"Why are you stopped?" Dan shouted.

"Sir, we just got word from the skirmish line up front that there's trouble ahead."

"What, damn it?"

"Artillery."

"Then go forward and take it!" Dan shouted.

He pushed ahead of the column. Looking to his left and right he saw where the entire division was stalled, formation ragged, some still in battle line, some in column by company front, flags hanging limp in the still, humid air.

Ahead he could see a heavy skirmish line atop a low crest, each man several feet apart from comrade to left or right, some standing, others crouching. He rode up to them, men looking back as they heard his approach.

"Keep this line moving, Goddamn it! We are going to Baltimore by tonight. Keep it moving!"

August 20, 1863
9:10 A.M.

They've slowed, sir.'

Porter Alexander, at General Longstreet's side, pointed to the low crest six hundred yards away. A Yankee skirmish line was atop the crest, having appeared only minutes ago, and the sight that greeted them had undoubtedly caused their coming to a halt.

Twenty-six batteries, a hundred and thirty-five guns, nearly all of them pieces captured at Union Mills, were deployed across a front of more than half a mile. Most of the gunners were new to their tasks, men pressed into the artillery from infantry service, each crew having but one or two veterans to try and train and direct the new hands. But the men were eager, like boys with a new toy. Their morale was good, many gladly proclaiming that if they had known how soft life was in the artillery they would have joined years ago. Then again, none of them had yet to endure a close-in fight, known the terror of mechanically loading while infantry took aim from fifty yards away, or the horror of what happened when a twelve-pound solid shot took the wheel off a gun, flying splinters tearing the crew apart.

Longstreet was silent, watching the opposite crest. If the skirmishers were this close, it was evident that the advancing army was not far behind. Even now they would most likely be pushing around the flanks of this position. The feigned retreat was almost over.

"Now, Porter, give it to 'em now. Remember, this is a signal as well!"

Porter grinned and stood up in his stirrups, clenched fist held heavenward.

"Battalions, on my command!"

The cry raced down the line.

"Fire!"

US Even as Sickles shouted the order for his army to continue the advance, a deep thunder exploded to his front. It started in the middle, several batteries firing simultaneously, and then spread like a string of firecrackers along the entire front, thunderclap building on thunderclap into a continuous roar.

He was a man of courage, and yet instinctively he hunched over when, three seconds later, the blizzard of solid shot and shrapnel swept the crest of the hill. Shells detonated; solid shot skipped and screamed; skirmishers fell flat on their faces, hugging the ground; branches were torn from apple trees, whirling into the air. One of his staff went down, his horse torn nearly in half, screaming horribly as it thrashed about, its legs tangled into its spilled intestines.

The division he had ordered forward was coming up, the men protected by the low rise, but more than one fell from airbursts, from broken branches that drove through the ranks like javelins, thousands of splinters from trees raining down on them.

What is this? he wondered. *How?* Yet the sight before him, though cloaked with heavy smoke, was clear enough. The bulk of Lee's artillery was deployed here, in the center between the two main roads they were using for their retreat. Was he turning to fight?

The division came up, columns shaking back out into battle lines, men hunching low as they reached the crest and then hesitated, not sure what to do next.

He could not leave this in his center, cutting his advance along the roads. If Lee was retreating, was this a throwaway gesture? Perhaps the guns captured at Union Mills? Or were there infantry in the woods beyond, ready to support?

His own artillery was coming up, but already he could see they would be outnumbered. It would take time to bring them forward, organize them on the reverse slope, then push them all up at once.

Could he take this directly? He calculated the odds. He would never be so foolish as to send men into a frontal assault against guns. Though he cared little for Henry Hunt, he thought of him at this moment, wished he were here to offer advice.

Birney was by his side, wide-eyed. The faster of the gunners had reloaded, and he noted that it had taken them time, a minute or more. These were not well-practiced men.

"Birney, take your men forward!" Dan shouted. "But for God's sake, don't get into canister range. Stop before then, get your men firing, and sweep those bastards. If Lee wants to give us back our guns, by God, we'll take 'em!"

The battle line swept forward into the valley.

9:15 A.M.

p, men, up!" Beauregard shouted, saber drawn, riding across the front of the columns resting under the shade of the trees.

The unmistakable volley of guns from six miles away had come as a dull continual rumble.

General Lee, who had been anxiously looking at his watch every five minutes, and was on the verge of ordering Beauregard in, signal or not, breathed a sigh of relief. The signal meant that Sickles was fully engaged six miles to the southeast. Beauregard was now to slice directly east, rolling up the valley of the Gunpowder River.

The men, eager to begin, raced forward, following narrow woodsman's trails, a country lane, breaking through woods and briars, advancing on the double, unable to be restrained, and he rode with them. Again the joy of battle was filling his soul.

9:45 A.M.

That's it! Keep feeding it in, boys, you're breaking them, you're breaking them!"

The volley line of the Second Division, Third Corps, fought like the experienced soldiers they were. They had been at it for over half an hour, advancing under terrifying fire to within two hundred and fifty yards of the rebel artillery, down nearly into the bottom of the swale, and there stopped. They had long since gone to independent fire at will, some standing, others kneeling. Orders were for them to take careful aim, to make every shot count.

And the casualties they were taking in turn were terrifying. These men were not getting hit by .58 caliber minié balls; what was coming back was solid shot and shells cut to one-second fuses to burst in front of them. Men were not just killed; they were torn to pieces by the frightful solid shot and jagged pieces of metal bursting over and around them.

Still there was no infantry support for the rebel guns; they were out there, in the open, pouring in fire, the guns having recoiled in places more than fifty yards, gunners not bothering to drag them back up. The smoke parted for a moment, and he scanned their line; scores, perhaps hundreds of rebels were down. Several pieces were silent, abandoned, surviving crews doubling up. But still they kept at it, and he would not push his men into the murderous swath of canister that would greet them if they closed to under two hundred yards. Occasionally a rebel gun lofted a charge of canister in, but it had little effect at this range; shot scattered wide, though here and there an unlucky man would be cut down. No, they were saving that deadly dose for a final charge that Sickles was not yet ready to commit.

But his men were suffering terribly, the artillery fire improving at times in accuracy, solid shot striking just in front of a file, bounding up, obliterating two men in a rank and then bounding on up the slope. It was in many ways far more unnerving than facing a volley line, and the strain was showing. His men were now cursing, down on the ground, loading, trying to take aim, firing, then rolling over on their backs to pour another measure of powder down the barrel, not daring to stand up.

He rode along the volley line, shouting encouragement. Screaming for them to pour it in. He knew he should have left this sector by now, to check on the advance to either flank, but his attention was focused here. If they could finally overrun these guns, by God, what a victory that would be. Then he could plunge straight up the center and catch the rest of Lee's army in the rear.

A constant stream of couriers came in, many hunched low, frightened by the bombardment, reporting that the Third Division of the Third, supported by the Sixth Corps, was even now pushing around the flank of the guns. Another report from the Fifth Corps, that they were continuing to drive McLaws two miles to the north, asking if a brigade should be detached to catch the guns on the other flank, a request to which he agreed.

"Pour it in!" he continued to scream. "Damn them to hell, pour it, boys!"

9:50 A.M.

Back a quarter mile behind the line, reluctantly following the orders given to him by General Lee, Longstreet watched the struggle down in the valley below. Behind him an entire division was concealed—Dole's men, rested and waiting—but he would not spring them yet. The time was not yet right.

Overhead and around him a continual rain of branches, leaves, bits of bark floated down or whirled past, tens of thousands of minié balls, fired high, plunging into the woods.

"General Longstreet!" It was Venable. "I've just come from General

Lee, sir. He wishes to inform you that the advance of Beauregard has begun. Do not engage until it is clearly evident that the Yankees are in retreat."

"Thank you, son. How are you?"

Venable grinned.

"Turning into one hell of a fight, isn't it?"

"And he's taken the bait," Longstreet replied, pointing to the battered line out in the middle of the field. "Hell, I might of taken it as well, the chance to capture so many guns unsupported by infantry. Masterful by General Lee. Now let's hope Beauregard pushes it!"

10:00 A.M.

General Sickles!"

Dan looked to his left; a courier, the Maltese Cross of the Fifth Corps on his cap, was riding down the line at a gallop. The courier, a captain, reined in.

"From General Sykes, sir!" He handed over a folded piece of paper.

To the General Commanding
9:25 AM August 20
Sir,

I've observed a large formation of Rebel infantry upon my right, coming out of the woods to my west two miles away. They are formed for battle and advancing on the double towards my rear. Sir, I must stop my advance and turn to face them. I recommend that you come yourself to observe. Flags indicate they are South Carolina, perhaps of Beauregard's corps. Please come at once.

(Signed)
Sykes
Fifth Corps

Dan crumpled the paper in his hand.

Goddamn! Was he being flanked?

He looked forward. Still no sign of their infantry. Was this the bait of a trap, so many guns that he would of course stop, engage, try to flank, commit his reserves? And now another whole corps appears on his flank and rear?

He felt a shiver of fear. *My God, am I being flanked? Did Lee just trick me, knowing I would pursue what I thought was a retreating army?*

"How long ago?" Dan shouted, looking at the captain.

"About a half hour, maybe forty minutes, sir."

"Did you see them?"

"Yes, sir. I was with General Sykes. Division front at least, thousands of them, coming on fast, cavalry skirmishers to their fore."

"Did no one look toward those woods?" Dan asked.

"No, sir, our cavalry patrols were pushed back throughout the night. And, sir, our orders said to follow down the road in pursuit."

"Goddamn you, I know what my orders said!" Dan shouted. "But your flank, man, your flank, didn't anyone look?"

The captain did not reply.

"Birney!"

"Here, sir!"

"Birney, I'm going up to the Fifth Corps. It might be Beauregard on our flank up there. Press the action here in the center. Keep pressing . . ."

His words were cut off.

The solid shot screamed in, brushing the flank of his horse and then striking his right leg just below the knee. In the split second it took to pass, the twelve-pound ball, moving at just under seven hundred feet a second, struck with frightful energy. It tore the bone of his lower leg out of the joint of his knee, severing ligaments, arteries, tearing cartilage, whipping the lower leg back at a ninety-degree angle, popping it out of the stirrup.

The angle of the shot carried the ball into the right rear quarter of his horse, shattering its hip, exploding out the back of the tortured animal in a spray of commingled blood, muscle, and bone both from horse and rider.

He gasped in surprise. There was no pain, just a terrible shock. All feeling, sound, sensation, thought were blanked out for a second. Instinct drove him to pull the reins of his mount, which was rearing back and then beginning to collapse onto its right side.

Though he did not see it, the courier from Sykes, who had actually felt the brush of the ball, was already leaning out, grabbing the horse's reins. Birney, on the other side, did the same, his shoulder getting dislocated as the horse pitched and fought.

More men came up, struggling to keep the horse upright. General Sickles, blood now draining from his face, numb, remained stock-still, frozen in part by fear, in part by the realization that his body would not re-act, that he could not control the struggling animal beneath him.

Hands reached up, grabbing him on the left side.

"Get him down, gently, get him down!"

He started to collapse, sagging. He thought he should pull his right foot from the stirrup. He actually thought he had done so. Somehow they were dragging him up over the saddle, then lowering him to the ground.

He caught a glimpse of the courier, still holding the reins of his horse with one hand, pistol in the other. The man cocked his pistol. He wanted to shout a protest. It was a good horse, a damn good horse, a gift from the governor.

The man pushed the pistol against the ear of the dying animal and fired, the poor thing collapsing in a heap.

He looked around. Men were kneeling by his side, Birney, arm hanging limp, struggling to dismount; a private was gazing down at him, wide-eyed, frightened.

The fear came into him, and like all wounded men he tried to sit up. He still wasn't sure where he was hit.

Please, God, not my stomach, not that. I'll lose an arm, a leg, but not in my gut. Seen too many die. He tried to tear at his jacket, to open it up, but hands were restraining him.

"Let me up!" he gasped, and they released him.

His body was still numb; he couldn't tell where he was hit, how bad.

He sat up and looked down at his body.

It was the leg and when he saw it was when the pain hit. Strange how that worked, he thought. His right leg was dangling off at an angle, shreds of muscle and ligaments all that was holding it to his body. A pool of blood was spreading out from the torn stump.

He took a deep breath.

"Tourniquet!"

Already a doctor from his headquarters staff was up by his side, leather bag opened, hands trembling.

"Get a tourniquet on that, damn you," he gasped.

"I am, sir."

The man wrapped the strap around his leg above the knee and started to turn the screw that would tighten it. He felt the strap bite in, dig deeper; he gasped. Damn it. It hurt almost as much as the wound. Still deeper. His fingers dug into the ground, he gritted his teeth, eyes focused on his life blood still pouring out. The pulsing stream lowered, dribbled, became a slow, oozing flow.

He looked over at the doctor.

"Sir, I've stopped it for the moment, but I've got to get you back, tie off the arteries."

"And my leg?"

The doctor looked down at the torn remnant and then back at Dan, shaking his head.

"Take it off now, damn it. There doesn't seem to be much left to it anyhow."

"Would you want me to give you ether first, sir?"

Dan looked up at the ever-growing crowd gathered around him, hearing distant shouts that "the general" was down.

No, he was Gen. Dan Sickles, commander of the Army of the Potomac. As he looked at his men, he knew that for them, there was still one more duty to perform this day, whether this day would be one of victory or defeat. He would do it with the style he had always shown.

"Anyone got a good cigar?" he gasped.

The private who was closest to him fished into his breast pocket and with a trembling hand drew out a thick Havana. A shot screamed in, bursting overhead. All ducked for a second, but no one was hit. The private pulled out a match. Dan bit off the end of the cigar, spat out the stub, and nodded. The private struck the match and Dan puffed the cigar to life.

"Who are you, Private?"

"Paul Hawkinson, sir. Seventy-third New York, been with you since the Peninsula, sir."

"Well, Private. You're Sergeant Hawkinson now, and when this is over, come and see me, and a box of good Cubans is yours."

Hawkinson grinned and reached out, patting Dan on the shoulder.

"That's the spirit, sir. The old Third is with you this day."

Dan nodded and looked back at the surgeon.

"Cut away and be quick about it."

"The ether?"

"I heard that stuff explodes around a lit cigar. Now cut away, damn you!"

Dan made it a point of not lying back, of not looking away. The surgery was over in seconds, a few quick slashes with a scalpel, a few strokes of the saw to sever a bundle of ligaments. Strangely, he didn't feel a thing. The men around him watched it, gazes shifting from the cutting to Dan's face and back again.

"Hawkinson, find a stretcher and be quick about it!"

"My ambulance!" the doctor shouted, and left with Hawkinson.

Dan sat quiet, smoking the cigar, holding his stump up in the air, bracing it with his hands.

He knew he should think, should pass orders as to what must be done next. Shock was taking hold, he had to focus, and his focus was now on but one more gesture.

Hawkinson and the doctor came back, carrying the stretcher. Eager hands reached out, lifting him off the ground, bringing him up, turning to head for the ambulance.

"No, damn it, stop!"

"I'm taking you back to the rear, General," the surgeon shouted, ducking low as yet another shot winged overhead.

"No. Now up on your shoulders, boys, on your shoulders."

"General, are you mad?"

It was Birney, dislocated arm cradled against his side.

"Eight of you, on your shoulders with the stretcher. I want the boys to see me this day!"

The surgeon started to cry out in protest, but Hawkinson shouldered him aside.

"Goddamn it, you heard the general, now who's with me!"

Men pushed in, shouting, eager for this moment, and together they hoisted Gen. Dan Sickles, commander of the Army of the Potomac, up high, struts of the stretcher resting on their shoulders, the general above them, cigar clenched between his teeth, sitting up, stump of his leg held high. At the sight of him a ragged cheer went up.

"Now down the volley line!" Dan cried. "Walk me down the volley line."

The strange procession set off, moving in behind the fighting men of his old Second Division, and at the sight of his approach the men looked up, fell silent, those on the ground coming to their feet; hats came off, men began to shout.

"Give it to 'em, boys!" he screamed hysterically. "Remember you're the Army of the Potomac! Now charge and give it to 'em! Remember you are the Army of the Potomac . . ."

"General Sickles, your orders!"

It was Birney, nursing his dislocated arm, running alongside the stretcher. Dan looked down at him but his eyes were wild, filled with battle lust, this final march of a warrior to some Valhalla, like departure from the world of mere mortals.

Birney fell back, watching as his old general was carried off, disappearing into the smoke. Around him men were on their feet, shouting madly, clenched rifles raised, and then, incredibly, they started down the slope, heading toward the enemy guns.

"For God's sake, General, who is in charge here now?"

Birney saw that it was Ely Parker by his side.

"Colonel?"

"I heard that report. You are being flanked. You must get this army out. Who is in charge here now?"

Birney drew his sword with his one good hand.

"I don't know, Colonel," he gasped. "I don't know. But I can tell you this: when it's over, tell General Grant we died game. We set the stage for what he will do after we're gone. Now, Colonel, get the hell out of here."

Birney, sword raised high, disappeared into the smoke, following his men.

On the Banks of Chesapeake Bay, near Gunpowder, Maryland

August 20, 1863
3:30 P.M.

The Chesapeake Bay, sir," Walter Taylor announced.

Lee nodded, lowering his head. Numbed by exhaustion, he struggled to get his right foot out of the stirrup. Traveler, trembling and lathered in sweat, remained still. An orderly ran over and ever so gently helped Lee to swing his leg up over the saddle and dismount.

For a moment he had no feeling in his legs, the sensation frightening. Forgetting all sense of protocol and decorum, he unbuttoned his uniform jacket and, when the first cooling breath of air hit his sweat-soaked body, he almost staggered, head light, nausea taking him. Embarrassed, he tried to turn away, the world spinning as he doubled over and vomited.

Walter was by his side, holding him by the shoulder, shouting for someone to fetch towels, something cool to drink. He tried to wave them off.

He slowly righted himself.

"War is for young men, Walter. I'm getting rather old for this."

"Sir, many a man half your age has collapsed today," Walter offered.

Lee felt weak, frighteningly weak, fearful for a moment that he might faint.

Walter and two others led him up to a wide, open porch, shaded from the glaring afternoon sun. The porch was packed with men, most of them wounded, Yankee prisoners who looked at him wide-eyed, a few coming to their feet, respectfully saluting. He was ashamed that they should see him thus, but his body no longer cared about propriety.

A woman came hurrying out of the house, bearing an earthenware pitcher, cool droplets coursing down its side, a white towel in her other hand. Her ivory-colored day dress was deeply stained with blood. It was obvious she had been tending to the wounded when he rode up.

"Madam, I thank you for the charity you've shown to these men," he gasped as they guided him to a wicker rocking chair. Walter had his coat off and they sat Lee down. The woman upended the pitcher, soaking the towel, then ever so gently wiping his face and the back of his neck. The cool water hit him like a shock, and for a second he feared he would vomit again, something that would have mortified him. He leaned over, gagged, but fought it back.

Another woman was by his side, a colored servant, kneeling down, holding an earthen mug.

"Cool water, General. Just the thing you need; now drink it slowly, sir."

She held the mug as he took it with trembling hands, slowly swallowing, the servant looking at him, an older woman, his age, perhaps older, smiling, nodding her approval, whispering as if he were an ill child taking his medicine. He drained it and she took the mug.

"Now you let that settle for a moment and if it comes back up, I don't want you to feel no shame. It'll take the heat out of your body."

"Thank you, thank you," he gasped.

She smiled, refilled the mug, and offered it to him even as the mistress of the house continued to wipe his neck and brow.

"Now you can hold your own mug, sir, but sip slowly; you'll be all right in a few minutes."

She stood up and scurried off, going back to a Yankee lying on the porch, kneeling down to wipe his brow with the hem of her dress, her face filled with the same beatific compassion she had shown him.

His staff stood around him in respectful silence. He waited a moment; another spasm of nausea hitting him, not as strong as the last. He fought it down without gagging.

He felt something cool running down his back, and looked up at the woman; she was slowly pouring a trickle of water down his back.

"Thank you, ma'am; your kindness is a blessing."

She nodded, eyes lowering.

"I am sorry, ma'am, if we have inconvenienced you this day."

She started to turn away, then hesitated.

"I have a hundred dead, dying, and wounded in my house, sir," she announced, her voice beginning to break. "Is that an inconvenience? There are two boys I don't even know dying in my daughter's bed."

He could not reply.

"For God's sake, General, when will this madness end? Is it worth it anymore?"

She stood frozen, as if horrified by her outburst. The pitcher dropped, shattering on the porch floor. All were silent, and she looked around at the Confederate staff, the Union wounded.

"Put an end to this!" she screamed, and then, gathering up her apron to cover her face, she fled back into the house. Her black servant watched her go, gazed upon Lee for a moment, then turned back to the Union soldier she was tending, lifting his head up, cradling it in her lap, and, leaning over, she began to whisper in his ear. And Lee could hear, ever so faintly, her words. . . .

"The Lord is my shepherd, I shall not want. . . ."

He lowered his head again, filled with remorse, exhaustion, even a sense of loathing for all he had seen this day, this day of yet another victory. He finally raised his head and looked down toward the Chesapeake.

Thousands of Yankee soldiers were swarming down into the bay, the docks at a small port filled with them. Along the low heights, scattered commands were coming up from his own army. He had lost sight of Beauregard long ago, within the first ten minutes after the attack had swept into the flank of their Fifth Corps, but he knew that the man had proven himself today, driving with relentless passion, as if eager to assure beyond all doubt his ability to lead, even when General Lee commanded the field.

An hour after they had struck the flank, the entire Union formation began to give way, and then just collapsed. The shock of the surprise blow had been part of it. He knew that the weather had played to him as well. The heat was killing. Chances were that when the tally was finally done, maybe one out of five of the dead would be found with no mark upon them. But in that moment, when some believed victory was near, and others faced defeat, exhaustion created by the heat would drive those filling with despair over the edge.

The Fifth had broken, but their disengagement had been masterful, their General Sykes yet again guiding his men out of the trap, pushing relentlessly back northward, back toward the shelter of Perryville and the gunboats on the Susquehanna.

As for their Third and Sixth Corps, they were into the sack now, swarming down to the broad, open bay. Many were casting aside their guns, if for no other reason than to dive into the tepid waters of the bay to seek some relief.

Someone had already ordered up a rescue force. Dozens of small boats were coming into the dock to take off the broken Army of the Potomac; a lone gunboat was visible, coming down the bay.

He sat back in the chair, saying nothing, watching the spectacle as his men, all formation gone, pushed down toward the water.

He saw General Longstreet riding up and breathed a sigh of relief. Longstreet dismounted and his face was filled with concern as he stepped on to the porch and took his hat off.

"Are you all right, sir?" Longstreet gasped.

"Just the heat, General. I'll be fine in a minute."

"Sir, you are staying put right here for the rest of the day," Walter

Taylor announced forcefully. "I know your surgeon will order it once he comes up."

Lee nodded his head in agreement. As he had ordered Longstreet to protect himself, he knew he should do the same at this moment.

"Sir, I can see to what is left," Longstreet said.

Lee nodded.

"What did it cost, Pete?" Lee whispered.

Longstreet lowered his head, looking over at the Yankee soldiers on the porch only feet away from them.

"Go on, General. They are our guests for the moment; talk freely."

Longstreet found that, as he spoke, he could not look at Lee; instead his gaze was fixed on those who had faced them this day.

"They fought us with reckless courage, sir. I've never seen anything like it before. Word is that General Sickles lost a leg. We might capture him, I'm not sure.

"I cannot speak for what you saw against the Fifth Corps, sir. But their Third and Sixth, when they knew they were trapped, fought it out to the end. I think we'll bag most of them down there," and he pointed to the bay, "but, General, it was a bloody, costly fight. We might have lost another five, maybe eight thousand more than yesterday."

Lee lowered his head, the shock of his losses a visceral blow. Why did each victory have to be so costly? Combined with yesterday, maybe ten thousand or more gone from the ranks.

He sighed, wiping his face, and then leaned back, grateful for the cooling water that had been poured down his neck and back.

He looked over at the wounded Yankees, who gazed at him, some warily, some with hatred, some with respect. A major, catching his eye, stood up and formally saluted. The man grimaced with pain, clutching his side with a bloody rag. Lee rose up and walked over to him, returning the salute.

"General Lee?" the major asked weakly.

"Yes, I am he."

The major nodded, saying nothing.

"You are sorely hurt, sir," Lee said. "Please sit down; my medical staff will see to you shortly."

"I'll be fine," the major whispered. "I want my men taken care of first. Just assure me of that, sir; it is all that I ask."

"Major, I am sorry for your injury. I will pray that you return safely to your family."

"Thank you, General. Just take care of my men. They're good soldiers."

"I know they are good soldiers; you should be proud of them." He said the words loud enough so that all on the porch could hear.

"I regret the divisions that force us to fight each other now. I hope, sir, when this is over, we can again be friends."

The major swayed slightly, then stiffened.

"Major, rest assured your men will be treated with honor. As quickly as arrangements can be made, all of the men of the Army of the Potomac, wounded or not, will be paroled and exchanged. Till then, the kind owner of this house and my medical staff will look after you."

"Thank you, sir," the major whispered. An elderly sergeant stood up and came to the major's left, protectively putting an arm around his side, and helping him to sit back down.

Lee turned away and walked back to Pete, motioning him to fall in by his side.

"We can't handle twenty thousand or more prisoners," Lee said softly. "I can't detail more men off as escorts to take them South. I'll have Walter find a printing press, we'll run off parole notes, and let those people go. The exchange can free thousands of our boys now held up in Elmira and Camp Douglas."

Pete nodded in agreement.

"Unfortunately, the men we will get back with the exchange will not be fit to fight immediately."

"I don't care about that, though I wish it were different. We must make the gesture; besides, it is the only thing we can do now."

"Yes, sir."

"Thank you for your efforts this day, General Longstreet. This time you were the anvil, and you've gained us another brilliant victory."

"The cost though," Pete sighed. "I am leaning toward relieving George of his command. He badly mishandled his division yesterday."

"General Longstreet, we walk a fine line, at times, between daring and foolhardiness. We praise when it works; we blame when it doesn't. Maybe it could be said that General Pickett's actions emboldened Sickles to press forward into the trap, maybe not. I suspect that will be yet another issue historians will argue about long after we are gone. I'll review the issue later when we have time, look at the ground, talk to Armistead and the other brigade commanders, then decide."

"Yes, sir."

"It is Grant now that we must think of."

Pete smiled.

"This will put a twist in his tail."

"Yes, but the question is, How will he jump now that his tail is twisted?"

"I think, sir, he just might hold north of the Susquehanna. He's lost maybe upward of a third of his total available field force this day. I think the assumption was fair that he planned to move in a concentrated manner: Sickles along the Chesapeake to hold our attention while he crossed over the South Mountains and sought to engage us. After this he might very well hold back till spring to build up sufficient force."

Lee looked across at the bay. A heavy line of his infantry were sweeping down toward the docks. Rifle fire snapped and rolled as last-ditch survivors from the Union side turned and continued to fight. A battery of artillery clattered past the plantation, moving at a swift canter, horses panting, lathered in sweat, deploying out into a field a hundred yards away, preparing to shell the harbor. The killing was still going on. Even in its death agony the Army of the Potomac was still kicking back; a shell winged in to detonate over the heads of the deploying battery; several gunners dropped.

Lee shook his head.

"No, General Longstreet. He will move. But it will take him time to absorb the shock of this defeat. His plans now are in disarray but Lincoln cannot afford a stalemate into next spring. For that matter, nor can we. If Grant does not move, we will eventually turn back to Washington, tighten the noose, and then try to starve it out through the winter. Lincoln and Grant both know that would be my next step now that the Army of the Potomac is gone.

"No, sir, he will move, but it will take him time to absorb what happened. I'll give him a week, two weeks, perhaps, but I do want it to come.

"We'll move up toward the Susquehanna tomorrow; there is still their old Fifth Corps to bag. Once there, we'll see what develops. If he does move, we'll try to catch him in midcrossing; if not, we turn back on Washington yet again."

The battery in the yard below opened up, solid shot arcing up, plummeting down, geysers of water soaring up around the docks swarming with men. It had to be done, but still it was sickening to him. Why couldn't they just lay down their arms? He'd take their paroles without question and then send them safely home, as long as they pledged to no longer fight. But no, this was his old rival, the valiant Army of the Potomac, so badly led on so many fields, yet its men still willing to fight to the bitter end.

He had yet to face Grant, to see a single soldier of the much heralded western armies, but he sensed now that they were of the same stern stuff as the Army of the Potomac and, for that matter, his own men. Yes, perhaps more like his own for they were not tainted by defeat; they would be eager to match wits and fire against him, general against general, regiment against regiment, man against man.

"We have been blessed with two stunning victories, General Longstreet; we must make it a third to finish this once and for all."

He turned and slowly made his way back to the porch to sit under the shade, his body trembling with exhaustion.

As he gained the porch he saw a knot of Union soldiers kneeling by the side of the major he had spoken to only minutes before. The man's face was gray, eyes closed. . . . He was dead.

The major's head was cradled in the sergeant's lap. He could sense the bond between the two. The fair young officer, the old tough regular who had nursed him along and now held him in death.

The sergeant looked up at Lee.

"How many more like this, General Lee?" the sergeant asked.

"I am sorry," Lee whispered. "I pray no more."

The sergeant shook his head.

"No, sir, there will be more."

"I know," Lee admitted sadly and turned away.

He looked back down toward the bay. His advancing infantry were almost to the docks. He could catch glimpses of Union flags still held aloft, knots of men refusing to quit gathered around them, fighting to the end. More batteries were unlimbering just below the plantation, firing down into the harbor.

If only it was Grant down there, and this was the final battle. Then he could find solace in knowing that this, indeed, was the last day.

That was what he must now seek. Lure Grant across the river in a week or two, once his men had been well rested, refitted, and reorganized after this grueling fight. Seek out Grant . . . and end it.

Chapter Twenty-one

C.S.A It was a beautiful early morning, the intense storm front of the night before having wiped the air clean of the stench of battle, dropping the temperature so low that it almost felt like the opening of an early autumn day in mid to late September.

General Lee watched as his men, filled with swagger in spite of the night march, approached the high bluffs looking out over the river.

They were a victorious army yet again. They had driven Sykes back, taking thousands of prisoners; the last huddled remnants of his force were down in the harbor at Perryville, loading aboard the ferries. Lee would bring up artillery to shell them at long range, but he would advance no farther. The gunboats, which had fought to cover the withdrawal of the survivors of the Third and Sixth Corps, had steamed through the night to cover as well these last few units still in retreat.

He had shattered, once and for all, the Army of the Potomac. Reports were that nearly fifteen thousand had fallen in the two-day fight, another twenty thousand taken prisoner. The old foe was finished forever, and yet Lee felt no joy in it this morning.

The butcher bill, as Longstreet put it, had been tragic for his own army as well. Over ten thousand dead and wounded in the two-day fight along Gunpowder River, thousands more collapsed from heat exhaustion.

Yet again a bitter price. Over twenty percent of his men under arms out of action. And this time there would be no replacements.

In his hand he held a dispatch that had come in during the night.

Wade Hampton was dead. His entire force had been cornered up in Pennsylvania and wiped out. A lone courier and one released prisoner had brought back word of the disaster.

Stuart was almost beyond consoling. When he had broken the news, his young cavalier had, at first, demanded permission for a vengeance raid, to take his entire force across the river. That would have been a mad impulse, and Lee had refused him emphatically and sternly.

They were on the banks of the Susquehanna, much farther north than he had wanted to be. The task of capturing prisoners and equipment had drawn them far beyond his desired position. Grant still awaited him. Lee's next step, the step needed to end this war, wasn't certain. It would depend on whether Grant would come down the river. His thought now was to demonstrate, to threaten a crossing en masse, for surely that would bring Grant into play. He would need Stuart here, on this side of the river, to watch for the site of Grant's attempted crossing.

"Good morning, General Lee."

Lee looked up and smiled. It was Judah Benjamin, trailed by an escort of Virginia cavalry. Lee smiled with genuine affection.

"Sir, you gave us a bit of a scare there two days ago."

Judah smiled good-naturedly.

"I heard that you said war is the sport of young men. Sir, I agree. That heat, how your boys marched and fought in it, it is beyond me."

"They did their duty, sir."

"I fear I did not do mine. Sorry I collapsed like that."

Lee smiled, feeling a bit self-conscious, remembering his own collapse, which had put him into bed for half a day.

"Perhaps it is best that secretaries of state do not go gallivanting around following armies," Lee said.

"Couldn't resist it, sir."

Judah came up by his side and looked out over the river, to the swarming river traffic taking off the last of the Fifth Corps.

"Too bad you couldn't have pinned them down there," he said.

"We could have, but to what final purpose? I'd have lost another thousand from their gunboats; we'd have harmed two, maybe three thousand, taken some prisoners. But to what avail now? They are out of the war. They're good soldiers; let them go in peace."

"You are learning to conserve men," Judah replied.

"Sir?"

"Just that. I know you, General. A year ago you would have ordered a charge down into that valley, not let one of them escape. We are running out of men, and you know it."

Lee did not reply.

"I still dwell on that conversation in Baltimore," Judah said.

"As do I."

"Imagine what a hundred thousand more men would do for our cause now. Imagine if the moral paradox was lifted. Sir, at this moment I would be very confident that we would win."

Lee did not reply.

"The president said no, and we must obey."

"I know. Damn it," Judah said, "I know, and though you've given us another victory, I wonder if it shall prove to be enough."

Lee turned and gazed at him.

"It has to be enough," he said sharply. "My men have suffered too much for this. It has to end; it has to be enough."

It was Judah now who could not reply.

"General Lee?"

It was Walter Taylor, coming up behind them. Lee turned, smiling, but Walter's face was drawn, features tight.

"What is it, Walter?"

"Sir, this message just came in. I felt I should give it to you personally."

"I don't have my glasses with me, Walter; just tell me what it is."

Walter looked over at Judah and nodded.

"A report came in to our headquarters a half hour ago, sir, from scouts reporting by telegraph out of Carlisle."

Lee felt his heart constrict.

"Go on."

"Last night General Grant put a pontoon bridge across the Susquehanna River at Harrisburg. Even now his army is crossing."

"Which direction?"

"Not toward us, sir. He is moving down the Cumberland Valley, advancing toward Virginia."

"Merciful God," Lee whispered.

Judah looked at him, wide-eyed.

"Mr. Secretary," Lee said quietly, "sir, if you will excuse me, I have orders to give. Walter, general officers' meeting in one hour; I want Longstreet, Hood, Stuart, and Beauregard. This army is to prepare to move at once."

He turned and rode off.

Judah watched him go.

"One more corps," he whispered to the back of the departing rider, "do you wish for them now, sir?"

Harrisburg, Pennsylvania

August 22, 1863
7:15 A.M.

His army was on the march. The bridge had been thrown across the river under cover of darkness. Though rebel scouts had been driven back, still there might be some spies along the opposite bank. It had taken his engineers eight hours to build it, sections having been already built up above Marysville and then floated down into place.

The first of his corps, Ord's, just about finished crossing.

Even as his Army of the Susquehanna began its march, orders had gone out to Sherman, who no later than tomorrow would be up with Rosecrans. Sherman was to assume full command of the forces in Tennessee, to drive Bragg out of that state, take Chattanooga, pull in the Twenty-third Corps to his support, and then, regardless of threat to his flanks and rear, advance on Atlanta. *Let them try and swallow that pill at the same time that I am advancing.*

He had surmised quickly what had happened with Sickles, even as the newspaper reports flashed across the wires, and now it was time to force the issue. If he was in command, then he would indeed be in command. Washington, as far as he was concerned, was cut off and there was no longer any need to seek Stanton's approval on any order now issued. He had forwarded the memo from Stanton, which gave Sickles latitude to move, straight back to the president, with the simple note on the back, "Mr. President, did you authorize this?"

A damn good army had gone down to yet another useless defeat.

But was it entirely useless? he wondered. The boys of that tragic, vanquished army had gone down fighting. All reports of that were clear. They had not mortally wounded Lee, but they had indeed savaged him. Another division, perhaps two, of the Army of Northern Virginia were no longer fit for battle, the others weary, exhausted after their mad dash in the killing heat. Out of that debacle a new plan had formed. Lee had been pulled much farther north than Grant had ever dared to hope.

Now he would make Lee dance to his tune. . . . The waiting was over, a month ahead of his plan, but it was over regardless. He would come

crashing down the Cumberland Valley. With this fair weather, in two days he could be across Pennsylvania and into Maryland, threatening Lee's rear communications. If Lee should move up across Maryland to try and cut his own lines, then he could turn to the Baltimore and Ohio. For, God bless him, Herman Haupt still did march with this army, having laid in trains, bridging material, supplies to support him from as far away as Ohio.

It was his fourth cigar of the morning, and he coughed, even as he puffed it to life.

The long pontoon bridge, snaking across the river, bobbed and swayed as the endless stream of men passed, rifles at the shoulder, the men marching out of step as ordered to avoid setting up a rhythm that might cause the bridge to break.

They were in high spirits, a jauntiness to their steps. Well rested, lean, arrogant, ready for a fight. The last of Ord's infantry and artillery passed.

Supply wagons, loaded on to trains, would snake north up above Marysville then come south, advancing as far as the track would allow, then unloading, keeping the bridge open for his faster moving infantry. Haupt's well-trained railroad men were already at the forefront of the advance, surveying the damage, a mobile telegraph station set up, sending back word for what needed to be sent forward to repair the rebel damage to the right-of-way down the valley. Hundreds of flatcars, numbered and loaded, were waiting to be sent up.

The head of Ninth Corps was now on the bridge, General Burnside in the lead, a tall man, strange, high-crown hat, muttonchop whiskers freshly brushed, a grin on his face as he rode past Grant, saluting.

"Good day for a little march, isn't it?" Burnside cried, and Grant nodded, saying nothing.

Behind him came the new Third Division of the Ninth, the men eager, moving briskly, all of their regimental banners at the fore, brand-new flags denoting the regiments of the United States Colored Troops. Though they were new soldiers, he could sense their passion, for if any men in this army now had a reason to fight, it had to be them. They were coming on with a will. They already had been warned of the custom of this army, to not cheer the general, but still their enthusiasm could not be contained, and in silent salute they took off their hats and held them high as they passed, row upon row, filling the bridge and the road clear back into Harrisburg.

Grant, unmoving, astride his horse, cigar clenched firmly, took off his hat and returned the salutes.

The Army of the Susquehanna was on the march. It was his army and it would march, he realized, until either he was dead, along with all those passing before him, or the final victory was won.